HONOUR-BOUND GROOM
BY
YVONNE LINDSAY

AND

CINDERELLA & THE CEO
BY
MAUREEN CHILD

MILLS & BOON

His lips were only millimetres from hers. Already he could feel her breath against him.

"Alex, wait!"

He drew in a shuddering breath, constraining his desire.

"Don't worry, Loren. I will make tonight one you will never forget."

"No, it's not that," she said, pulling out of his arms. "It's about us. Our marriage."

"Us?"

What was she talking about? They were married.

Tonight would see the consummation of that marriage.

"Yes, Alex, us. I love you. I've always loved you one way or another. And even knowing you don't love me, I agreed to marry you in part because of my feelings for you, but also to honour my father, and his promise to yours." Her eyes glistened in the candlelight with unshed tears. "Can you honestly tell me that you have done the same?"

Dear Reader,

When this trilogy first started to grow in my mind I really let my imagination wander. Initially this was going to be a royal trilogy, because doesn't everyone love a royal? Well, after a little gentle guidance from my editor at the time, I was persuaded away from the over-the-top fairy-tale aspects of the stories I'd initially outlined and my mind spun off on another tangent. A wealthy family bound by a three-hundred-year-old legend and a curse, and living on a totally fictional Mediterranean island called Isla Sagrado. Just goes to show that all those years of daydreaming in class (and my school reports will support this) were worthwhile after all.

So here we have it. Book No.1 of *Wed At Any Price*— Alexander and Loren's story. My working title for this was *The Spaniard's Honour Bride,* which kept me focused on the deep sense of honour Alex has in his duty to the people of his country and to his family. Of course, his bride was a girl promised to him virtually from the cradle and who has loved him her whole life. The challenge of bringing them together and *keeping* them together was great grist for this writer's mill.

I hope you enjoy *Honour-Bound Groom* and that you look forward to the next instalment in the trilogy, *Stand-In Bride's Seduction,* where Alex's brother, Reynard, meets his match and learns that love is not all about appearances.

Happy reading and very best wishes,

Yvonne Lindsay

HONOUR-BOUND GROOM

BY
YVONNE LINDSAY

Published in Great Britain 2011
by Mills & Boon, an imprint of Harlequin (UK) Limited,
Eton House, 18-24 Paradise Road, Richmond, Surrey TW9 1SR

© Dolce Vita Trust 2010

ISBN: 978 0 263 88311 4

51-0811

Harlequin (UK) policy is to use papers that are natural, renewable and
recyclable products and made from wood grown in sustainable forests. The
logging and manufacturing processes conform to the legal environmental
regulations of the country of origin.

Printed and bound in Spain
by Blackprint CPI, Barcelona

New Zealand-born to Dutch immigrant parents, Yvonne Lindsay became an avid romance reader at the age of thirteen. Now, married to her "blind date" and with two surprisingly amenable teenagers, she remains a firm believer in the power of romance. Yvonne feels privileged to be able to bring to her readers the stories of her heart. In her spare time, when not writing, she can be found with her nose firmly in a book, reliving the power of love in all walks of life. She can be contacted via her website, www.yvonnelindsay.com.

This book is dedicated to all my wonderful readers,
who make it possible for me to keep writing books.
Thank you from the bottom of my heart.

Prologue

Isla Sagrado, three months ago...

"*Abuelo* is losing his marbles. He talked again of the curse today."

Alexander del Castillo leaned back in the deep and comfortable dark leather chair and gave his brother, Reynard, a chastising look.

"Our grandfather is not going mad, he is merely growing old. And he worries—for all of us." Alex's gaze encompassed his youngest brother, Benedict, also. "We have to do something about it—something drastic—and soon. This negative publicity about the curse is not just affecting him, it's affecting business, too."

"That's true. Revenue at the winery is down this quarter. More than anticipated," Benedict agreed, reaching for his glass of del Castillo Tempranillo and taking a sip. "It certainly isn't the quality of the wine that's doing it, if I say so myself."

"Put your ego back where it belongs and focus, would you?" Alex growled. "This is serious. Reynard, you're our head of publicity, what can we do for the family as a whole that will see talk about this stupid curse laid to rest once and for all?"

Reynard cast him a look of disbelief. "You actually want to lend credence to the curse?"

"If it means we can get things on an even keel again. We owe it to *Abuelo,* if not to ourselves. If we'd been more traditional in our ways then the issue would probably not have arisen."

"The del Castillos have never been renowned for their traditional outlook, *mi hermano,*" Reynard pointed out with a deprecating grin.

"And look where that has put us," Alex argued. "Three hundred years and the governess's curse would still appear to be upon us. Whether you believe in it or not, according to the legend, we're it—the last generation. If we don't get things right, the entire nation—including our grandfather—believes it will be the end of the del Castillo family. Do you want that on your conscience?" He stared his younger brother down before flicking his gaze to Benedict. "Do you?"

Reynard shook his head slightly, as if in disbelief. He seemed stunned that his eldest brother had joined their grandfather in the crazy belief that an age-old legend could be based in truth. And more, that it could be responsible for affecting their prosperity, indeed, threatening their very lives today.

Alex understood Reynard's skepticism. But what choice did they have? As long as the locals believed in the curse, bad publicity would affect the way the del Castillo family could do business. And as long as *Abuelo* believed, the paths he and his brothers chose could make or break the happiness of the man who had raised them all.

"No, Alex." Reynard sighed. "I do not want to be responsible for our family's demise any more than you do."

"So what do we do about it?" Benedict challenged with a humorless laugh. "It's not as if we can suddenly drum up loving brides so we can marry and live happily ever after."

"That's it!" Reynard declared with a shouted laugh and pushed himself up and out of his seat.

His abrupt movement and shout unsettled the dogs sleeping in front of the fire, sending them barking around his feet. A clipped command from Alex made them slink back to their rug and assume their drowsing state.

"That's what we need to do. It'll be a publicity exercise such as Isla Sagrado has never seen before."

"And you think *Abuelo* is losing his marbles?" Benedict asked and took another sip of his wine.

"No," Alex said, excitement beginning to build in his chest. "He's right. That's exactly what we must do. Remember the curse. If the ninth generation does not live by our family motto of honor, truth and love, in life and in marriage, the del Castillo name will die out forever. If we each marry and have families, well, for a start that will show the curse for the falsehood it is. People will put their trust in our name again rather than in fear and superstition."

Reynard sat back down. "You're serious," he said flatly.

"Never more so," Alex answered.

Whether he'd been kidding around or not, Reynard had hit on the very thing that would not only settle their grandfather's concerns but would be a massive boost to the del Castillo name. Its ongoing effect on the people of Isla Sagrado would increase prosperity across the entire island nation.

While Isla Sagrado was a minor republic in the Mediterranean, the del Castillo family had long held a large amount of influence on the island's affairs, whether commercial or political. As the family had prospered so, by natural process, did the people of Isla Sagrado.

Unfortunately, the reverse was also true.

"You expect each of us to simply marry the right women and start families and then, hey, presto, all will be well?" Reynard's voice was saturated with disbelief.

"Exactly. How hard can it be?" Alex got up and patted him on the shoulder. "You're a good-looking guy. I'm sure you have plenty of candidates."

Benedict snorted. "Not the kind he'd bring home to *Abuelo,* I'd wager."

"You can talk," Reynard retorted. "You're too busy racing that new Aston Martin of yours along the cliff road to slow down long enough for a woman to catch you."

Alex walked over to the fireplace and leaned against the massive stone mantel that framed it. Carved from island rock, the hearth had seen generation after generation of his family sprawl in front of its warmth. He and his brothers would not be the last to do so. Not if he had anything to do with it.

"All joking aside, are you willing to at least try?" he asked, his eyes flicking from one brother to the next.

Of the two, Benedict looked most like him. In fact some days he felt as if he was looking into a mirror when he saw his brother's black hair and black-brown eyes. Reynard took after their French mother. Finer featured, perhaps more dramatic with his dark coloring because of it. Female attention had never been an issue for any of them, even from before they'd hit puberty. In fact, with only three years in total separating the brothers, they'd been pretty darn competitive in their playboy bachelorhood. They were all in their early thirties now and had mostly left that phase behind but the reputation still lingered, and it was that very lifestyle that had brought them to this current conundrum.

"It's all right for you, you're already engaged to your childhood sweetheart," Benedict teased him with a smirk, clearly still not prepared to take the matter seriously on any level.

"Hardly my sweetheart since she was only a baby when we were betrothed."

Twenty-five years ago their father had saved his best friend, Francois Dubois, from drowning after the latter had accepted a dare from their father to swim off Isla Sagrado's most dangerous beach below the castillo. In gratitude, Dubois had promised the hand of his infant daughter, Loren, to Raphael del Castillo's eldest son. In a modern society no one but the two men had ever really given any credence to the pledge. But the two men were old-school all the way back down their ancestral lines and they'd taken the matter very seriously indeed.

Alex had barely paid any attention at the time, despite the fact that, virtually from the day she could walk, Loren had followed him around like a faithful puppy. He'd been grateful when her parents had divorced and her mother had taken her away to New Zealand, clear on the other side of the world, when Loren had been fifteen. Twenty-three years old at the time, he'd found it unsettling to have a gangling, underdeveloped teenager telling his girlfriends that she was his fiancée.

Since then, the engagement had been a convenient excuse to avoid the state of matrimony. Until now, he hadn't even considered marriage, and certainly not in the context of Francois Dubois's promise to Raphael del Castillo. But what better way to continue to uphold his family's honor and position on Isla Sagrado than to fulfill the terms of the spoken contract between two best friends? He could see the headlines already. It would be a media coup that would not only benefit the del Castillo business empire, but the whole of Isla Sagrado, as well.

He thought briefly of the dalliance he'd begun with his personal assistant. He didn't normally choose to mix business with pleasure, especially from within his own immediate work environment. But Giselle's persistent attempts to seduce him had been entertaining and—once he'd given in—very satisfying.

A curvaceous blonde, Giselle enjoyed being escorted to the high spots of Sagradan society and entertainment. Certainly she was beautiful and talented—in more ways than one—but wife material? No. They'd both known that nothing long-term would ever have come of their relationship. No doubt she'd be philosophical and he knew she was sophisticated enough to accept his explanation that their intimacy could no longer continue. In fact, he'd put a stop to it right away. He needed to create some emotional space between now and when he brought Loren back to be his bride.

Alex made a mental note to source a particularly lovely piece of jewelry to placate Giselle and turned his mind back to the only current viable option for the position of his wife.

Loren Dubois.

She was from one of the oldest families here on Isla Sagrado, and had always taken great pride in her heritage. Even though she'd been gone for ten years, he'd wager she was still Sagradan to her marrow—and as devoted to her father's memory as she had been to the man during his lifetime. She wouldn't hesitate to honor the commitment made all those years ago. What's more, she'd understand what it meant to be a del Castillo bride, together with what that responsibility involved. And she would now be at the right age, and maturity, to marry and to help put the governess's curse to rest once and for all.

Alex smirked at his brothers. "So, that's me settled. What are you two going to do?"

"You have to be kidding us, right?" Benedict looked askance at Alex, as if he'd suddenly announced his intention to enter a monastery. "Lanky little Loren Dubois?"

"Maybe she's changed." Alex shrugged. It mattered little how she looked. Marrying her was his duty—his desires weren't relevant. With any luck she'd be pregnant with his child within the first year of their marriage and too busy thereafter with the baby to put any real demands upon him.

"But still, why would you choose her when you could have any woman alive as your wife?" Reynard entered the fray.

Alex sighed. Between them his brothers were as tenacious as a pair of wolves after a wounded beast.

"Why not? Marrying her will serve multiple purposes. Not only will it honor an agreement made between our late father and his friend, but it will also help relieve *Abuelo's* concerns. And that's not even mentioning what it will do for our public image. Let's face it. The media will lap it up, especially if you leak the original betrothal story as an appetizer. They'll make it read like a fairy tale."

"And what of *Abuelo's* concerns about the next generation?" Reynard asked, one eyebrow raised. "Do you think your bride will be so happy to ensure our longevity? For all you know she may already be married."

"She's not."

"And you know this because?"

"*Abuelo* had an investigator keep tabs on her after Francois died. Since his stroke last year, the reports have come to me."

"So you're serious about it then. You're really going to go through with a twenty-five-year-old engagement to a woman you don't even know anymore."

"I have to, unless you have any better suggestions. Rey?"

Reynard shook his head. A short sharp movement of his head that bore witness to the frustration they all felt at the position they were in.

"And you, Ben? Anything you can think of that will save our name and our fortunes, not to mention make *Abuelo's* final years with us happier ones?"

"You know there is nothing else," Benedict replied, resignation to their combined fates painting stark lines on his face.

"Then, my brothers, I'd like to propose a toast. To each of us and to the future del Castillo brides."

One

New Zealand, now...

"I have come to discuss the terms of our fathers' agreement. It is time we marry."

From the second his sleek gray Eurocopter had landed on the helipad close to the house she'd wondered what had brought Alexander del Castillo here. Now she knew. She could hardly believe it.

Loren Dubois studied the tall near stranger commanding the space of her mother's formal sitting room. Her eyes drank in the sight of him after so long. Dressed all in black, his dark hair pushed back from his forehead and his brown-black eyes fixed firmly on her face, he should have been intimidating but instead she wondered whether she'd conjured up an age-old dream.

Marry? Her heart jumped erratically in her chest and she tried to force it back to its usual slow and steady rhythm. Years ago, she'd have leaped at the opportunity, but now? With age had come caution. She wasn't a love-struck teenager anymore. She'd seen firsthand what an unhappy alliance could do to a couple, as her parents' tempestuous marriage had attested. She and Alexander del Castillo didn't even know one another anymore. Yet, for some reason, the way he'd proposed marriage—in typical autocratic del Castillo fashion—made her go weak at the knees.

She gave herself a swift reality check. Who was she kidding? He hadn't proposed. He'd flat out told her, as if there was no question that she'd accept. It didn't help that every fiber in her body wanted to do just that.

Wait, she reminded herself. *Slow down.*

It had been ten years since she'd laid eyes on him. Ten years since her fifteen-year-old heart had been broken and she'd been dragged to New Zealand by her mother after the divorce. A long time not to hear from someone by any standards, let alone from the man she had been betrothed to from the cradle.

Even so, a part of her still wanted to leap at the suggestion. Loren took a steadying breath. Although their engagement had always been the stuff of fairy tales, she was determined to stay firmly rooted in the present.

"Marry?" she responded, drawing her chin up slightly as if it could give her that extra height and lessen Alex's dominance over her. "You arrive here with no prior warning—in fact, no contact at all since I left Isla Sagrado—and the first thing you say to me is that it's time we marry? That's a little precipitate, wouldn't you say?"

"Our betrothal has stood for a quarter of a century. I would say our marriage is past due."

There it was—that delicious hint of accent in his voice, characteristic of the Spanish-Franco blend of nationalities of their home country, Isla Sagrado. It was an accent she'd long since diluted with her time in New Zealand, yet from his lips the sound was like velvet stroking bare skin. Her body responded to the timbre of it even as she fought down the wave of longing that spiraled from her core. Had she missed him that much?

Of course she had. That much and more. But she was grown-up now. A woman, not a child, nor a displaced bratty teen. Loren attempted to inject a fine thread of steel into her voice.

"A betrothal that no one seriously expected to be fulfilled, surely."

Somehow she had to show him she wouldn't be such a pushover. In all the time since she'd left Isla Sagrado he'd made no contact whatsoever. Not so much as a card at Christmas or her birthday. His indifference had hurt.

"Are you saying that your father made such a gesture lightly when he offered your hand?"

Loren laughed, the sound of it hollow even to her ears. She still missed her father with a physical ache, even though he'd been dead these past seven years. With him had gone her last link to Isla Sagrado and, she'd believed, to Alex. But now Alex was very much here and she didn't know how to react. *Stay strong,* she told herself. *Above all, stay strong. That's the only way to earn the respect of a del Castillo.*

"A hand that was little more than three months old when it was promised to you—you yourself were only eight," she said with as much bravado as she could muster.

Alex moved a step toward her. She almost felt the air part to allow him passage; he had that kind of presence. Despite her inexperience with men of Alex's caliber, it was one she responded to instinctively.

Alex had always been magnetic, but the past ten years had seen a new maturity settle on his broad shoulders, together with a stronger and more determined line to his jaw. He looked older than the thirty-three years she knew him to be. Older and harder. Certainly not a man who took "no" for an answer.

"I'm not eight anymore. And you—" he paused and ran his eyes over her body "—you are most certainly no longer a child."

Loren's skin flared hot, as if he'd touched her with more than a glance. As if his long strong fingers had stroked her face, her throat, her breasts. She felt her nipples tighten and strain against the practical cotton of her bra. And the longing within her grew harder to resist.

"Alex," she said, her voice slightly breathless, "you don't know me anymore. I don't know you. For all you know I'm already married."

"I know you are not."

He knew? What else did he know about her, she wondered. Had he somehow kept tabs on her all this time?

"It would be foolish for us to marry. We don't even know if we're compatible."

"We have the rest of our lives to learn the details of what we can do to please one another."

Alex's voice was a low murmur and his eyes dropped to her mouth. Please or pleasure? Which had he really meant, she thought, as she struggled against the urge to moisten her lips with her tongue. The longing sharpened and drew into a tight coil deep within her. Loren fought back a moan—the pure, visceral response to his mere gaze shocking her with its intensity.

Her lack of experience with men had never bothered her before this moment. All her dealings with guests and male staff here at her mother's family's sheep and cattle station had been platonic and she'd preferred it that way. It had been difficult enough to settle into the isolation of the farm without the complications of a relationship with someone directly involved with the day-to-day workings of the place. Besides, anything else would have felt like a betrayal—to her father's promise and to the lingering feelings she still bore for Alex.

Now, that lack of experience had come back to haunt her. A man like Alex del Castillo would certainly expect more than what she had to offer. Would demand it.

In her younger years, she'd adored Alex with the kind of hero worship that a child had for an attractive older person—and, oh yes, he'd been attractive from the moment he'd drawn his first breath. She'd seen the photos to prove it. She'd believed that adoration had deepened into love, love not dimmed by Alex's vague tolerance of the scrawny kid who followed him like a shadow around the castillo that had been his family home for centuries.

For as long as she could remember she'd plagued her father to repeat the story of how Alex's dad, Raphael, had saved him from drowning on the beach below the castillo after a crazy dare between friends had almost turned deadly. And she'd hung on his every word as he'd reached the part where, in deepest gratitude, he'd promised his newborn daughter in marriage to Raphael's eldest son.

But her childish dreams of happily ever after with

her fairy-tale prince were quite different from the virile, masculine reality of the man in front of her. Every move he made showed that Alex had a degree of sensual knowledge and experience she couldn't even begin to imagine, much less match. It was exciting and intimidating all at once. Was she already in over her head?

"Besides," Alex said, his voice still low, pitched only for her ears, "it is time now that I marry and who better than the woman to whom I've been affianced all her life?"

Alex's dark brown eyes bored into hers, daring her to challenge him. But, surprisingly, beneath the dare, Loren saw something else reflected in their depths.

While he'd appeared so strong and self-assured from the moment he'd alighted from the helicopter and strode toward their sprawling schist rock home nestled near the base of the Southern Alps, there was now a hint of uncertainty in his gaze. As if he expected some resistance from Loren to the idea that they fulfill the bargain struck between two best friends so long ago.

The scent of his cologne wove softly around her like an ancient spell, invading her senses and scrambling her mind. Rational thought flew out the window as he took another step closer to her, as his hand reached for her chin and tilted her face up to his.

His fingers were gentle against her skin. Her breath stopped in her chest. He bent his head, bringing his lips to hers—their pressure warm, tender, coaxing. His hand slid from her jaw to cup the back of her neck.

Loren's head spun as she parted her lips beneath his and tasted the intimacy of his tongue as it gently swept the soft tissue of her lower lip. A groan rippled from her throat and suddenly she was in his arms, her body aligned tightly against the hard planes of his chest, his abdomen. Her arms curved around him, snaking under the fine wool of his jacket and across the silk of his shirt. The heat of his skin through the finely woven fabric seared her hands. She pressed her fingertips firmly into the strong muscles of his back.

She fit into the shape of his body as though she had indeed been born to the role, and as his lips plundered hers, all she could, or wanted to, think of was how it felt to finally be in his arms. Not a single one of her frustrated teenage fantasies had lived up to the reality.

This was more, so much more than she'd ever dreamed. The strength and power of him in her arms was overwhelming and she clung to him with the longing of a lifetime finally given substance. It barely seemed real but the solid presence of him, his skillful mouth, the sensation of his fingertips massaging the base of her scalp, all combined to be very, very real indeed.

Every nerve in her body was alive, gloriously alive, and begging for more. She'd never experienced such a depth of passion with another man and was certain she never would.

She knew to her very soul that this connection, this instant magnetic pull between them, was meant to be forever, just as their fathers had preordained. And, with this one embrace, she knew she wanted it all.

In the distance she heard the front door slam, its heavy wooden thud echoing down the hardwood floor of the main hallway. Reluctantly she loosened her grip and forced herself to draw away from Alex's embrace. The instant she did so, she almost sobbed. The loss of his warmth, his touch, was indescribable. Loren fought free of the sensual fog that infused her mind as her mother swept into the sitting room, the staccato tap of her swift footfall fading into silence as she stepped onto the heirloom Aubusson carpet.

"Loren! Whose is that helicopter out on the pad? Oh!" she said, displeasure twisting her patrician features. "It's you."

It was hardly the kind of welcome Naomi Simpson generally prided herself on, Loren noted with a trace of acerbity. As her mother's gaze darted between her and Alex, Loren fought not to smooth her hair and clothing, drawing instead on every ounce of her mother's training to appear aloof and in control—at least as far as her hammering heartbeat rendered her capable.

Alex remained close at her side, one arm now casually slung about her waist, his fingers gently stroking the top of her hip through her red merino wool sweater. Tiny sizzling tendrils of electricity feathered along her skin at his lazy touch and she found it hard to focus.

Her mother had no such difficulty.

"Loren? Would you care to explain?"

There was no entreaty in Naomi's words. Even phrased as a question she demanded answers and, if the frozen look of fury on her face was any indicator, she wanted those answers right now.

"Mother, you remember Alex del Castillo, don't you?"

"I do. I can't say I ever expected to see you here. I'd hoped we were completely shot of Isla Sagrado the day we left."

With typical Gallic charm Alex nodded toward Naomi. "It is a pleasure to see you again, Madame Dubois."

"I wish I could say the same. And, just for the record,

I go by Simpson now," Naomi answered. "Why are you here?"

"Mother!" Loren protested.

"Don't worry, Loren," Alex murmured into her ear. "I will deal with your mother."

The warmth of his breath against the shell of her ear sent a tiny tremor down her spine. He exaggerated the two syllables of her name, emphasizing the last to give it an exotic resonance totally at odds with her everyday existence here on the station.

"Nobody needs to deal with anyone," she replied. She cast a stern look at Naomi. "Mother, you are forgetting your manners. That is not the way we treat guests here at the Simpson Station."

"Guests are one thing. Ghosts from the past are quite another."

Naomi threw herself into the nearest chair and glared at Alex.

"I'm sorry, Alex, she's not normally so rude," Loren apologized. "Perhaps you should go."

"I think not. There are matters that need to be discussed," Alex answered, his attention firmly on Naomi's bristling presence.

He guided Loren to one of the richly upholstered sofas before settling his long frame at her side. A shiver of awareness rippled through her as his presence imprinted along her body.

"I believe you know why I'm here. It is time for Loren and me to fulfill our fathers' promise to one another."

Naomi's snort was at total odds with her elegant appearance.

"Promise? More like the ramblings of two crazy men who should have known better. No one in the developed world would sanction such an archaic suggestion."

"Archaic or not, I feel bound to honor my father's wish. Much as I imagine Loren does, also."

Loren felt that shiver again as Alex responded to her mother's derision. Naomi wasn't the kind of woman who liked to be contradicted. She ruled the station with an iron fist and a razor-sharp mind and was both respected and feared by her staff. Despite her designer chic wardrobe and her petite frame she was every bit as capable as any one of the staff here. A fact she had proven over and over again. But she was very much accustomed to being in charge, with her decrees accepted without question. The problem was, Alex was used to that, too. This confrontation could get messy, especially once her mother realized whose side Loren was on.

"Loren." Her mother turned to her with a stiff smile on her carefully tinted lips. "Surely you're not going to take this seriously. You have a life here, a job, responsibilities. Why on earth would you even consider this outrageous plan?"

Why indeed, Loren wondered as she looked around her. Yes, she had a life here. A life she'd been dragged to, kicking and screaming and full of sullen teenage pout. She'd never wanted to live with her mother but her father hadn't contested his wife's petition for full custody of their only child. Loren had later realized that had in part been because he'd never believed Naomi would actually go through with the divorce and relocate to the opposite side of the world. But his apparent indifference had hurt at the time and she'd arrived here at the Simpson Station feeling as though her entire world had been ripped apart. With that kind of beginning, it was hardly surprising that she'd learned to accept her place at the station, but she'd never learned to love it.

And as for her work here and her responsibilities? Well, it would only be Naomi who missed her, and then only for as long as it took to browbeat some other assistant into docile submission. No. Loren had nothing to hold her here. She and Naomi had never enjoyed the kind of mother-daughter relationship that Loren knew others had and she had learned very early that it was easier to accede to her mother's wishes than fight for her own. On Isla Sagrado, Loren had been almost solely her father's child, and Loren had always believed her mother had taken her from the island more as a punishment for Francois Dubois than out of any kind of maternal instinct.

She'd missed Isla Sagrado every day of the past ten years. Of course that pain of loss, the wrench of being repatriated, had dimmed a little over time, but it was still as real now as the man seated alongside her.

Seeing him again was as if he'd brought with him the heat and splendor and lush extravagance of Isla Sagrado. Not to mention the promise of the revival of a passion for living that had lain dormant within her since she'd left the country of her birth.

Yes, her initial reaction to Alex's arrival here had been shock and disbelief. But it was clear he meant what he said. Why else would he have traveled half the world to come and see her?

Thoughts spun through her mind with lightning-fast speed. Her earlier objections, as weak as they were, had come reflexively—a direct result of surprise at the manifestation of the man who'd been a part of her dreams her entire life. She'd wanted—no, she'd *needed*—to hear him refute her doubts to her face. To tell her they belonged together as she'd always imagined, as she'd pretty much lost hope of imagining.

Now she knew what it was like to be in his arms, to feel truly alive for the first time she could remember, there was no way she was going to turn her back on her destiny with the only man she'd ever loved.

"Why would I consider marrying Alex? I would have thought that was quite straightforward," Loren responded with as much aplomb as she could muster under her mother's piercing gaze. "Inasmuch as Alex wishes to honor his father, so do I mine. I've always understood that this would be my future, Mother." She turned her face to look at Alex. "And it's what I've always wanted. I would be honored to be Alex's wife."

"How on earth could you know what you want?" Naomi demanded, pushing up out of her chair and pacing back and forth between them. "You've barely been off the station since we've lived here. You haven't experienced the world, other men, anything!"

"Is that what it really takes to make a person happy? Are *you* truly happy?" Loren held her mother's gaze as her questions unerringly hit their mark. Naomi gaped for a moment, clearly surprised to hear Loren fight back. But even Naomi couldn't deny the truth of what Loren had said.

Naomi's affairs were legend in New Zealand—her power and beauty made for a magnetically lethal combination—and yet, even though many had tried, no man had captured her heart. Loren knew she didn't want that life for herself.

"We're not talking about me. We're talking about you—your future, your life. Don't throw it away on a pledge made before you can even remember. You are worth so much more than that, Loren."

Loren felt the walls, her mother's walls, closing in around her and she pushed them back just as hard.

"Exactly, Mother." Loren sat up straighter, confidence coming from Alex's warmth against her side—confidence to speak her mind at last and say the words she'd locked down deep inside for too long. "I stayed here because I had nothing else to do. Growing up on Isla Sagrado, I believed I had a purpose, a direction. When you and Papa split up I lost that. You took me away from the only future I ever wanted."

"You were just a child—"

"Maybe then, yes. But I'm not a child any longer. We both know I've been marking time these past few years. You know my heart isn't in the station like yours is. You always felt displaced on Isla Sagrado. That's how I feel here. I want to go back.

"As you so correctly pointed out, we are talking about *my* future and *my* life—and I want that to be on Isla Sagrado, with Alex."

He could hardly believe it had been so easy. Alex savored the exhilaration that surged within him as Loren's words hung on the air between mother and daughter.

His body continued to throb in reaction to the slightly built woman at his side, remembering how it felt to be pressed against her far more intimately. Yes, kissing her had been a risk, but he'd built his formidable business reputation on taking big risks and reaping even bigger rewards. This had definitely been a risk worth taking.

Just one look at her had been enough to prove the information he'd been given about her sheltered lifestyle. She appeared as untouched and protected as she'd been the day she left Isla Sagrado. But beneath that inexperienced exterior beat a sensual heart. Wakening that side of her would be a delight and would make the whole process of providing *Abuelo* with a great-grandchild, as proof the curse did not exist and laying it to rest once and for all, an absolute pleasure.

Alex tilted his head slightly to watch Loren as her mother began a tirade of reasons why she should not return to Isla Sagrado. He wasn't worried about Naomi's arguments. If there was one thing he remembered most clearly about Loren as a child it was that despite her quiet attitude, there was no matching her tenacity once she had made up her mind. The vast number of his girlfriends she'd scared off being a case in point.

Instead of following the argument, he took the time to fully take in the woman who would be his wife. Her long black hair, scraped back in a utilitarian ponytail, showcased the delicate structure of her face. And what a face—the child's features he remembered had matured into those of a beautiful young woman's. Her brows were still strong and delicately arched but the eyes beneath them, dark brown like his own, glowed with an inner fire, and her lips were full and lush. Fuller, perhaps, because of their recent kiss, and certainly something he wanted to taste and savor again.

Where had that gawky kid who'd followed him around incessantly disappeared to? In place of the slightly older version of her that he'd expected, he'd discovered a woman who, while she had every appearance of fragility and a vulnerable air about her that aroused his protective instincts, somehow had managed to develop a backbone of pure steel.

He was reminded of Audrey Hepburn as he looked at her now. The gamine features, matured into beauty—the delicate bone structure, intensely feminine. Something else roared to life from deep inside of him. Something ancient, almost feral. She was his—betrothed to him as a matter of honor between friends, but his nonetheless. And she'd stay that way. Nothing Naomi could say would ever change that.

Two

Despite the luxurious trappings of first class, Loren had been unable to sleep during the long journey from New Zealand. After a day and a half of travel and changeovers she felt weary and more than a little disoriented as she made her way through Sagradan customs and immigration. Nothing about the airport was familiar to her anymore. Still, she supposed as she hefted her cases from the luggage carousel and onto a trolley, it was only natural that change had come to Isla Sagrado in the ten years she'd been gone.

Even so, a pang for the old place she'd left behind lodged behind her heart. Loren shook her head. She was being fanciful if she expected to be able to walk back into her old life as if she'd never left. So much had changed. Her father was gone, her mother was now half a world away and here she was—engaged and preparing to reunite with her fiancé of only a few weeks.

It didn't seem real, Loren admitted to herself—and not for the first time. Everything had moved so fast from the moment she'd told her mother she was returning to the home of her birth. Well, at least once Naomi had recognized that she could not sway her only child's stubborn insistence that she would be marrying Alexander del Castillo.

Alex had taken control once her mother had ceased her objections and washed her hands of the matter, smoothing the way toward having Loren's expired Sagradan passport renewed and booking her flights to Isla Sagrado. Loren hadn't had to lift so much as a finger. Well used to taking care of such details for both her mother and for the overseas guests who visited the massive working sheep and cattle station, it had been a pleasure to have someone else take care of her for a change.

Once he'd had everything organized to his satisfaction, Alex had departed, but not before arranging a private dinner for just the two of them, off the station. They'd choppered to Queenstown, where they'd visited a restaurant on the edge of Lake Wakatipu. The late autumn evening had been clear and beautiful and the restaurant every bit as romantic as Loren had ever dreamed.

By the time they'd returned to the station she knew she was totally and irrevocably in love with him. Not the innocent adoration of a child nor the all-absorbing puppy love of an adolescent, but the deeper knowledge that, no matter what, he was her mate in this lifetime and any other.

He'd been solicitous and attentive all night and, before walking her to her small suite of rooms in the main house at the station, he'd kissed her again. Not with the heated, overwhelming rush of emotion that consumed her the day he'd arrived, but with a gentle, sure promise of greater things to come. Her body had quivered in response, eager to discover the depths of his silent promise right there, right then. But Alex had backed off, cupped her cheek with one warm strong hand, and told her he wanted to wait until their wedding night—it would make their union more special, more intimate.

It had only made her love him more and had served to leave her fraught with nerves the entire journey to Isla Sagrado. Nerves that now left her giddy with exhaustion and made battling the broken wheel on her luggage cart all the more taxing. Fighting the way the thing wanted to veer to the left all the time, Loren paid little attention to the sudden silence in the arrival hall as she came through the security doors after clearing customs.

A silence that was suddenly and overwhelmingly broken by the flash of camera bulbs and a barrage of questions flung at her from all directions and in at least three different languages.

One voice broke over all the rest to ask in Spanish, Isla Sagrado's dominant language, "Is it true you're here to marry Alexander del Castillo and break the curse?"

Loren blinked in surprise toward the man, even as a multitude of others around him continued with their own questions.

A movement at her side distracted her from answering. A tall and stunningly beautiful woman, wearing a startling red dress, hooked an arm around her and leaned forward, her long, honey-blond hair brushing Loren's arm like a swathe of silk.

"Don't answer them. Just smile and keep walking.

I'm Giselle, Alex's personal assistant. I'm here to collect you," she murmured in a French-accented voice that was very un-assistantlike. Her emphasis on the word *personal* hinted strongly at things Loren herself had no experience of.

"Alex isn't here?" Loren blinked to fight back the sudden tears that sprang to her eyes as sharp points of disappointment cut through her.

Believing he'd be here to welcome her home at the end of her journey had been what had kept her going these past few hours. Now, she fought to keep her slender shoulders squared and her sagging spine upright. Struggled to keep placing one foot in front of the other.

Giselle put her free hand on the handle of the luggage cart and directed it, and Loren, toward the exit. Airport security had miraculously cleared a path and beckoned them toward the waiting limousine at the curbside.

"If he'd have come, the media circus would have been worse and we'd never have cleared the airport," Giselle said in her husky voice. "Besides, he's a very busy man."

Giselle's intimation that Alex had far more important things to attend to than collecting his fiancée from the airport pierced Loren's weariness, making her stumble slightly.

"Oh, dear," the other woman said, tightening her hold around Loren's waist. "You're a clumsy little thing, aren't you? You'll have to improve on that, you know, or the media are going to have a field day with you."

While Giselle's tone was light, Loren felt the invisible slap of disapproval behind her words. But there was no chance to respond right away. They were at the car at last. There, a uniformed chauffeur, who looked more like a bodyguard than a driver, hefted her cases into the voluminous trunk of the limo as if they weighed little more than matchsticks. Once that was taken care of, Loren took the opportunity to speak.

"I'm tired, that's all. It's been quite a trip," she responded as she slid over onto the broad backseat of the limousine, her voice a little sharp, earning her an equally sharp look from Giselle in return.

"Touchy, too, hmm?" Giselle narrowed her beautiful green eyes and gave Loren an assessing look. "Well, we'll see how you measure up. Since Reynard issued the press release about Alex's engagement, the whole drama of your father's near drowning and him giving you away afterwards has been front-page news. Goodness knows paparazzi will be crawling all over you to find out about you."

"I'm surprised. I thought Alex might have kept that quiet," Loren said, frowning at the thought of having to rehash the story of her and Alex's fathers' actions over and over again.

"Quiet? Hardly. With the way things are here they need all the strong publicity they can get. You must remember how the island's prosperity seems to be intrinsically linked with the del Castillos'. Whether there's any truth to the curse or not, everyone here is lapping up the story. Promises of happily ever after and all that. Honestly, they've made it all sound so sweet it's almost enough to give you cavities." Giselle finished with a high-pitched laugh that didn't quite ring true.

"So you don't believe in happily ever after?"

"Sweetie," Giselle replied with a smile stretching her generous lips into a wide curve of satisfaction, "what's more important is if Alex believes in it. And we both know he's far too pragmatic for that. Besides, it's not like you two are going to have a real marriage."

"Well, I certainly expect we'll have a real marriage. Why else would we even bother?"

"Oh, dear, you mean he hasn't said anything yet?"

Loren felt her already simmering temper begin to flare. "Said anything about what?" she asked through clenched teeth.

"About keeping up appearances, of course. Though perhaps he thought it would be clear. After all, if he'd had any interest in a *real* marriage he'd have wanted to have some say in the organization of the wedding ceremony and reception, wouldn't he? Instead, he gave me carte blanche. But don't you worry, I'll make sure you have a day to remember."

"Well, *I'd* like to go over the wedding details with you later on, when I'm more rested," Loren asserted, pausing for effect. "Then I'll more than happily take the arrangements off your hands. I'm sure you have far more important things to occupy yourself with."

Loren chose to ignore the rest of what the woman had said. She knew she and Alex had little time before their proposed wedding date only two weeks away, but surely he hadn't left everything to his assistant—his *personal* assistant, she corrected herself.

"Oh, but I have everything under control. Besides, Alex has signed off on what I've done already. To change anything now would only cause problems."

The implication that Loren would bear disapproval from Alex for those problems sat very clearly between the two women. Loren took a steadying breath. She wasn't up to this right now but she knew what Giselle was doing. She'd probably taken one look at Loren and totally underestimated her. Clearly Giselle had some kind of bond with Alex that she didn't want to let go. Maybe she'd even harbored a notion of a relationship with him.

Whatever might have happened between Alex and Giselle before she had arrived home, Loren was his fiancée, and she'd prove she was no walkover. Her battle with her mother to come here in the first place had proven to her that she was anything but that.

"Well," she said, injecting a firm note into her voice, "we'll see about that once I've checked everything over and conferred with Alex." At the other woman's sharply indrawn breath she added, "It is *my* wedding, after all."

Loren settled back against the soft leather upholstery and gazed out the window of the speeding limousine, wondering if she had gone too far in establishing where she stood with Giselle. Perhaps she'd been oversensitive, worn out as she was with travel. But underneath Giselle's self-assuredness and apparent solicitude she sensed a vague but definite threat, as if she was stepping where she wasn't fully welcome by coming back to Isla Sagrado.

She stifled a sigh. She'd expected her homecoming to be different, sure, but when push came to shove she couldn't forget what—or more importantly, *who*—had brought her here.

Alex.

Just thinking about him created a swell of longing deep inside. Without thinking, she traced the outline of her lips with her fingertips, silently reliving their last kiss. If she tried hard enough she could still feel the pressure of his mouth against hers, still experience the heady joy of knowing he'd traveled to New Zealand to fulfill their fathers' bargain—that he'd seen her and still wanted *her*.

Loren let her hand drop back into her lap and stared out the passenger window, searching for familiar signposts and buildings. The landscape had changed so much that Isla Sagrado hardly felt like home anymore, she thought sadly as the unfamiliar roads and buildings swept by them.

The soft trill of a cell phone startled Loren from her reveries. From the corner of her eye she saw Giselle lift a phone to her ear.

"Alex!" Giselle answered, her voice warm and sweet as honey.

Loren's stomach clenched in excitement and she waited for Giselle to hand the phone over to her so she could speak with him herself.

"Yes, I have your future bride here in the car. I expect we'll be at the castillo in about half an hour." She cocked her head to one side and smiled as she listened. "Fine. Yes. I'll let her know."

Giselle flipped the phone shut and gave Loren a smile. "Alex sends his apologies but he won't be able to meet with you until this evening. Business, you understand."

If Loren wasn't mistaken, there was a distinct hint of smugness in the other woman's glittering emerald gaze. She swallowed her disappointment. Not for anything would she yield so far as to display even one hint of weakness, no matter how bitter the pill that Alex couldn't spare even a few minutes to greet her on her first day here.

"Of course. I look forward to the opportunity to have a little rest and freshen up before I see him." Loren smiled in return, summoning a bravado she hoped she could pull off. "Besides, Alex and I have the rest of our lives together. What're a few more hours?"

Alex put down his office phone and stared out the window. It looked down and over the sprawling luxury waterfront resort that was his main concern in the management of the del Castillo financial empire. From his position, it looked beautiful and peaceful, but appearances could be deceiving.

A matter between two of his key management staff that he'd thought Giselle had settled weeks ago had flared up again today with no apparent warning. He sighed. There was no accounting for personalities and how people could either rub along together or end up rubbing one another entirely the wrong way. Add to that the constant harping on about the wretched governess's curse, both in the media and in the whispers among the staff—suffice it to say that the sooner this wedding was done and Loren was pregnant with his child, the better.

How a nation of well-educated and forward-thinking people could remain so superstitious defied belief. The legend of the governess and her curse on the del Castillo family when she was spurned by her lover was just that. A legend. There was no proof. Even the media interest he himself had encouraged had turned into a two-headed beast he could barely tolerate. Giselle had been an enormous help, always stepping in to deflect questions away from him so she could handle them herself.

And she had come to his aid again today. In the face of the urgency in dealing with today's debacle, her calm suggestion that she collect Loren from the airport had been welcome. Giselle was a consummate professional.

He knew she'd make Loren feel at home and get her comfortably settled at the castillo.

If he'd gone to get her, the press would never have let them leave. They'd still be there, posing for pictures, answering questions—wasting time that could be better spent letting Loren unwind after her flight and letting Alex get this administrative headache straightened out. It would be much better for Alex to spend time with her tonight, at the quiet family dinner he'd organized with his brothers and his grandfather, and no press around to badger them.

He allowed himself a small smile at the thought of his grandfather's excitement over their planned dinner. *Abuelo's* reaction when told that Loren would be returning to Isla Sagrado as his future bride had been worth the time away from the problems at the resort to visit with her.

He thought back to when he'd broken his brief liaison with Giselle. She'd pouted a little but had taken his decision, and the diamond tennis bracelet he'd bought her as a severance gift, with good grace and assured him her efficiency in her work would continue. And she'd reiterated her willingness to take up where they'd left off should he ever change his mind.

Until he'd seen Loren again, he'd given Giselle's offer some serious thought. After all, once he'd married and met *Abuelo's* concerns by ensuring the next del Castillo generation would be born, why shouldn't he have some fun? But, despite the clinical manner in which he'd imagined this alliance would go forth, from the second his lips had touched Loren's there had been something about her that had pushed Giselle's offer right out of his mind.

That Loren was unschooled in the ways of love was

clear, but how unschooled? The thought that she might be a virgin both intrigued and enticed him. To be her first lover, to unlock the sensual creature he'd tasted in that first kiss? Oh yes, there were definitely aspects of his marriage to Loren Dubois that he found himself looking forward to far more than he'd anticipated. Now, if he was going to enjoy any time with Loren later today he needed to catch up with his work here at the resort. Fortunes didn't make themselves—legend or no.

By the time Giselle returned to the office he was entrenched in his work. He lifted his head only briefly when she came in with some papers.

"I hope Loren didn't mind I couldn't be there to greet her. Is she all settled now at the castillo?" he asked, scoring his signature across the letters she leaned over to place on his desk.

"Of course she minded you weren't there. Wouldn't any woman?"

Giselle laughed, but he noticed her smile did not quite reach her eyes.

Her fragrance, as heady and sensual as the woman herself, wove around him. But rather than the usual reaction it evoked in him—an anticipation of pleasurable things to come—he was reminded instead of the contrast between his assistant's overt sexuality and Loren's more subtle blend of allure. For some perverse reason, the latter was now far more appealing.

"And yes, in answer to your question, I made sure she was completely comfortable in her suite," Giselle answered. "Although she did seem very weary from her travel."

"Too tired for the dinner with *Abuelo* tonight, do you think?"

"Well, obviously I can't speak for her but, yes, she

did look rather shattered. I wouldn't be at all surprised if she slept all the way through until morning."

Alex furrowed his brow in a frown. Until morning? That wouldn't do. *Abuelo* was looking forward to renewing his acquaintance with the daughter of the man who'd been his son's best friend for so many years. An edge of irritation slid under his skin at the thought that Loren would prefer to sleep rather than spend the evening with him. Alex had planned to present her with the del Castillo betrothal ring tonight. The official seal of their engagement. He huffed out a breath.

"Well, she's just going to have to find her strength from somewhere. The dinner is far too important to postpone."

He missed the subtle curve of Giselle's mouth as he voiced his frustration.

"She probably will benefit from a few good meals, Alex. She does look rather…frail," Giselle commented as she collected the papers off his desk and turned to go back to her desk in the outer office.

"Frail?"

Alex frowned again. Certainly Loren was very slightly built, but in his arms he'd felt the strength and suppleness of her body. Plus, he'd witnessed firsthand her mental determination.

"Appearances can be deceptive," he concluded. "She will be fine, I'm sure."

"Would you like me to make sure she's ready for the dinner tonight?"

"No, Giselle, that won't be necessary, but thank you."

"No problem." His assistant smiled in return before closing his door behind her.

Alex sat staring at the door for some time, comparing

the disparities between the two women. Aside from the obvious physical differences—Giselle's lush femininity versus Loren's more gamine appearance—they were worlds apart in other matters. While Giselle tended to be exactly what she appeared to be, and wasn't afraid to say exactly what she wanted, Loren had hidden strengths. The way she'd dealt with her mother's objections being a case in point. The phrase "still waters run deep" had been designed with someone like Loren in mind, he was sure.

Had he done the right thing? He pinched the bridge of his nose in an attempt to alleviate the throbbing headache that had begun behind his eyes. He had to have made the right choice. To have done anything else was unacceptable. Loren had all the credentials—from her bloodlines right down to her experience within the milieu where he moved socially. This marriage between them *would* work. She was everything he needed in a wife and he would do whatever he had to in order to be what she needed in a husband.

The late-afternoon sun slanted like a blush of color across the golden brick of the castillo as he approached. A wry smile tweaked at Alex's lips as he realized just how much he took for granted that the medieval stronghold, in his family for centuries, was indeed his home.

While still remaining true to the age-old architecture and the style so typical of the island, the interior had been modernized to make for very comfortable living. Several del Castillo families could, and had in the past, share the various apartments the castillo offered for private family living, if desired. Despite that, his brothers had chosen to make their own homes elsewhere on the island—Reynard in a luxurious city apartment overlooking the sparkling harbor of Isla Sagrado's main city, Puerto Seguro, and Benedict in a modern home clinging to the hillside overlooking the del Castillo vineyard and winery.

He understood why they each felt the need to carve out their own space but he still missed their presence around the castillo, for all the rare time he spent at home these days. Between himself and *Abuelo* there was a great deal of space to fill. A little more of the castillo had been filled today because Loren was inside right at that moment—waiting for him. Something about the thought of his bride-to-be newly settled in his home made it all abruptly real to Alex. After all the planning, she was finally here. In a few weeks, she would be his wife. And hopefully, in the not-too-distant future, the building would fill with the sounds of children again. *His* children. The thought made something deep inside him swell.

It would be good for *Abuelo* to be distracted from the rigors of growing old by the prospect of amusing the next generation of del Castillos. He had a wealth of family history to share. It was only right he have the opportunity to do so.

With that thought in the forefront of his mind, Alex swept his sleek black Lamborghini through the electronic gates and inside the walls, toward the stables that had been converted to a multicar garage thirty years ago. In minutes he was on the large curved stone staircase leading to the next floor, which housed the private suites of family rooms. Loren's was close to his own and he hesitated at her door, his hand poised to knock.

Something stayed his hand, and he let his fingers curl

instead around the intricately carved heavy brass handle of her door. It lifted smoothly, gaining him entrance. He would have to speak to her later about keeping her door locked. While the castillo's security was advanced, paparazzi were not above masquerading as one of the many staff, or even bribing them, in an attempt to get the latest scoop on the family.

Long silent strides on the thickly carpeted floor led him to her bedroom. There, sprawled across the covers, lay his future bride. Every nerve in his body surged to life as he observed her, arms and limbs askew, hair spread like a dark cloud around her head. There should be a childlike innocence about her, he thought, yet instead there was only the lure of her female form.

Small breasts pressed in perfect mounds against the fine cotton of the T-shirt she'd obviously chosen to sleep in. And only the T-shirt, he observed, keeping himself grimly in check even as he feasted on the sight of the faint outline of her nipples against the well-washed fabric. He tore his eyes from their gentle peaks and instead gazed upon the long slender length of her legs. Not one of his most sensible decisions, he thought as a heated pulse beat low in his groin.

One of her arms curved up and over her pillow, the other was flung out to one side, her unadorned hand curled like a delicate shell.

Alex dropped to his knees at her bedside and leaned over the mattress. He felt the warmth radiating from her, as if it were a tangible thing, as his lips hovered over the softness of her palm. Then he bent his head and pressed his lips against the fleshy mound at the base of her thumb, the tip of his tongue sweeping across its surface to taste her skin.

Loren's fingers curled to cup his cheek and he sensed

the precise moment she emerged from her slumber. Heard the sharp intake of breath through her lush pink lips. Saw the awareness flare in her eyes as her lids flashed open.

"Alex?"

Her voice was drugged with the residue of sleep yet its huskiness sent a lance of pure heat cutting through his body, provoking him to full, aching arousal. Right now he wanted nothing more than to sink onto the soft mattress with her, to envelop her in his arms and to taste all the delights her body had to offer. But he'd already promised to wait until their wedding night and they would be expected amongst company very soon. He forced his unwilling flesh to cooperate and gently pulled away from her touch.

"I know you're tired, but you must begin to ready yourself for dinner tonight."

"Dinner?"

She sounded confused. Surely Giselle had informed her of this evening's expectations.

"Yes, dinner. My grandfather looks forward to welcoming you back home."

He averted his gaze as she pushed herself upright and sat with her legs crossed beneath her. The creamy skin of her thighs and the shadowed hollow he knew lay at their apex, just beyond the hem of her shirt, were pure torment as he imagined touching her softness and delving into the hidden flesh there.

Arousal flared anew, this time even more demanding than before. But Loren's next words, delivered with an unmistakable note of challenge, doused his ardor as quickly as it had flamed into searing life.

"And you? Do you also welcome me home, Alex?"

Three

He fought back the flare of irritation that swelled inside him at her words. Was she criticizing him for not having been at the airport to welcome her? Giselle's insinuation echoed in the back of his mind. He fought for an edge of control, reminding himself she was no doubt still overtired from her journey and perhaps still wearing her disappointment he wasn't there to welcome her in person.

"Ah, I see you are still upset I was not at the airport to greet you. I thought Giselle explained why I could not be there."

"Oh yes, she explained." Loren unfolded her legs, threw them over the edge of the bed and rose to her full height.

Barefoot, the top of her head barely even reached his shoulder, and dressed as she was she gave an almost childlike impression. But there was nothing childlike in her demeanor, nor in the very female brand of dissatisfaction reflected in her eyes. He was reminded of the times he'd upset his mother. Never one to raise her voice, she'd only needed a look such as this to put him in his place.

"I would have been there if I could." Alex softened his tone. He should have made more effort to be at the arrival hall. He realized that now. He'd tried to make things easier for both of them, but instead he'd made matters worse. Still, the situation wasn't beyond salvaging and now he was determined to recover as much ground as possible.

"I have been looking forward to seeing you this evening," he said, his voice low.

He saw pleasure light her eyes and felt an inner relief as her full lips curved into a smile.

"So have I," she said shyly, dropping her gaze.

"So, you will dress for dinner and come down to share our repast?"

"Of course I will. I'm sorry I was a bit cranky. I'm never at my best when I first wake."

Alex allowed his mouth to relax into a smile. "I'll make a special note to remember that for after we're married."

She laughed, a delicious liquid sound that penetrated the last remnants of his temper and scattered them to the corners of the room.

"It might pay to." She smiled. "Now, tonight. What time and where? I'm assuming your family still dresses for dinner?"

She must have been half-asleep already when Giselle told her, he decided.

"Yes, we change for dinner. We meet for drinks in

the salon usually about eight and dine at nine. Late, I know, if you aren't used to it anymore."

"Oh, don't worry, I'll acclimate. Will you take me down?"

"You no longer remember where the salon is?" He cocked a brow at her.

"Of course, I don't imagine the castillo has changed all that much. I just…" She worried her lower lip with perfect white teeth. "No, don't worry. I'll meet you there at eight."

Alex dropped a chaste kiss on Loren's upturned face and moved away before the disappointment he sensed in her encouraged him to take more. Now that she was here and they were on the verge of achieving his goal of settling the governess's curse, there was no need to rush into anything. There would be plenty of time to kiss her the way he wanted—after they were married.

"Good girl. I'll see you there."

Loren watched her door close behind Alex's back and she fought the urge to stomp her foot in frustration. Now she was here he'd reverted to treating her like a child. Gone was the attentive lover who'd wooed her back in New Zealand. In his place was the old Alex she remembered so well. Slightly indulgent and full of the importance of his role as eldest son.

Well, she'd show him she was no infant to be coddled. Her body still hummed with her reaction to the soft kiss he'd pressed in her palm to wake her. Just one small caress and she'd shot to full wakefulness, her joy in seeing him only to be dashed by his reminder of her duty to be at some formal dinner tonight.

She knew they still adhered to the old ways, ways she'd taken for granted until moving to New Zealand with its more casual approach to lifestyle and mealtimes, but she'd hoped for a private dinner with her new fiancé. It wasn't so much to have expected, was it? Surely Alex's grandfather would have granted them this first night alone together?

There was nothing for it now, though, she reminded herself as the chime from an antique ormolu clock in her sitting room chimed the half hour. She had to fulfill Alex's expectations. At least she knew she'd have fun catching up with his brothers. As for Alex, well, maybe she'd punish him a little for not pressing to have kept her to himself tonight. She had just the perfect outfit in there. She'd bought it with Alex's reaction to her very firmly in mind.

She looked about her room for her suitcases and was surprised to see them gone. A quick look in her dressing room solved her problem as she espied her clothing already unpacked and hung neatly on hangers or folded away in the built-in drawers. She must have been totally out of it not to have heard the maid come in and see to her things.

She quickly filtered through the selection of dresses she'd bought, her hand settling on the rich red silk organza cocktail dress she wanted to wear tonight. The bodice was scattered with tiny faceted beads that caught the light and emphasized her small bust, while the layers of fabric that fell from the empire line below her breasts had a floating effect that made her feel as though she was the most elegant creature on the planet. Not a feeling she embraced often, Loren admitted silently.

She laid the dress on her bed and chose a pair of stiletto-heeled sandals in silver to wear with it.

"And if that's not dressed up enough for dinner, then nothing will do," she said out loud.

She made her way into her bathroom and took a moment to appreciate the elegant fixtures. The deep claw-foot bath beckoned to her but she knew she had little time left to get ready. She wondered briefly why Alex had acted as if she should have known all along about the dinner tonight. Perhaps Giselle had meant to tell her and had forgotten. Although Loren suspected that Giselle forgot very little indeed.

No, it must have been an oversight somewhere along the line. What with all the paparazzi at the airport, it was something that could easily have slipped Giselle's mind. She was prepared to be charitable. After all, she was finally *home*. Back on Isla Sagrado. Back with Alex.

She hummed happily to herself as she took a brief and refreshing shower. After toweling herself dry with a deliciously soft, fluffy bath sheet that virtually encased her from head to foot, she swept up her hair into a casual chignon and applied her makeup with a light hand. She studied her appearance for a moment then decided to emphasize her eyes a little more and to apply a slick of ruby-red gloss to match her dress. With the strength of color of her dress she'd disappear if she didn't vamp things up a bit, even if she normally only wore the bare minimum of cosmetics. Finally satisfied with her smoky eyes and glossy lips, she reached for a clean pair of panties and then slipped into her gown.

Loren loved the shimmer of the fabric as it brushed over her skin. The tiny shoestring straps and the low back of the dress made it impossible to wear a bra, but the beading hid any evidence that she was braless. She slid her feet into the high-heeled sandals and bent to do up the ankle straps before checking herself in the antique cheval mirror in her room.

Yes, she'd do nicely for her first meal at home with the del Castillo men, and for whoever else might be joining them. She wondered whether either Reynard or Benedict would have companions for the evening. Both of Alex's brothers' eligible bachelor status led them to be featured highly in magazines even as far away as New Zealand, and she doubted either of them would have far to look to find company.

A quick look at the clock on the bedroom mantelpiece projected her through her suite and out the main door into the corridor to the main stairs. She was grateful for the ornate carpet runner because she had no doubt her heels would have caught on the ancient flagstones beneath it as she hurried down the stairs.

For a moment the sense of longevity about the castillo seeped through her. How many del Castillo brides had traversed this very path to their betrothed over the centuries, and how many of those marriages had been as happy as she hoped hers and Alex's would be? She shook her head a little, chiding herself for being fanciful as a sudden weight of expectation settled upon her shoulders. A small chilled shudder ran down her spine, as if she was being watched—judged, even.

Loren hesitated on the stairs and looked around her, but of course there was nothing there but the gallery of portraits of successive heads of the family over the past many years. She injected a little more urgency in her step as she reached the bottom of the staircase and headed to where she remembered the salon to be.

The murmur of deep male voices, punctuated by the sound of laughter, was comforting as she approached the room where Alex had said to meet. Loren quashed the lingering effects of the sense of disquiet that had hit her earlier and focused instead on the prospect of an evening with the man she'd loved for as long as she could remember. Nothing could go wrong now, nothing. Her life was finally what she'd always dreamed it would be.

With a smile on her face, she entered the salon and was treated to the impeccable manners of four gentlemen rising from their seats to welcome her. Loren nodded in greeting to Reynard and Benedict, each easily recognizable and, she noted with some surprise, unaccompanied by female adornments.

Alex stood a little to one side. His hair, still wet from a recent shower, was slicked back off his forehead, giving him a sartorial edge that went well with the black suit and shirt he'd donned for the evening. But the serious set to his mouth and his darkened jawline made him appear unapproachable.

His dark eyes caught hers and burned beneath slightly drawn brows. She felt her smile waver a little under his gaze, but then he smiled in return and it was as if another giant weight had been lifted from her.

"You look beautiful," he said, his eyes glowing in appreciation.

A flood of pleasure coursed through her at his words, warming her all the way to her toes.

"Come, say hello to *Abuelo*. He has been impatient to see you."

She crossed the room, straight toward the silver-haired figure nearest the fireplace. Despite the fact it was May, a fire roared in the cavernous depths, throwing heat into the room and adding a cheerful ambience that chased the last of the lingering shadows from Loren's mind.

From his proximity to the fire she deduced Alex's grandfather felt the chill far more than he used to, and she couldn't help noticing the slight droop to one side of his face and the way he leaned heavily on an ebony cane. It saddened her to see he'd aged so much since she'd left, but one look at the spark in his eyes showed her that *Abuelo* was still very much the patriarch and very much in control.

Her lips curved in genuine pleasure as she placed her hands in his gnarled ones and leaned in to kiss him on the cheeks.

"*Bienvenido a casa, mi niña,*" he murmured in his gruff voice. "It is past time you were back."

"It is so good to be home, *Abuelo,*" she replied, using the moniker he'd insisted she call him back when she was a child.

"Come, sit by me and tell me what foolishness has kept you from us for so long."

The old man settled back into his easy chair and gestured to the seat opposite.

"Now, *Abuelo,* you know that Loren's mother insisted she move to New Zealand with her," Alex said, coming to stand behind Loren's chair and resting one hand upon her shoulder. "Besides, you cannot monopolize her when she is here to see everyone."

Loren felt the heat from his palm against her bare skin and leaned into his touch, relishing the sizzling contact.

"I do not see any ring upon her finger, Alexander. You cannot monopolize her while she is yet a free woman."

"Ah, but that is where you are wrong, *Abuelo,*" Alex teased in return. "Loren is most definitely mine."

A fierce pang of joy shot through her, catching her breath, at his words. If she'd had any doubts, they were now assuaged.

Loren felt Alex's hand slide down the length of her arm, to her left hand. Clasping it, he drew her upright to face him. Butterflies danced in her stomach as she saw the intensity in his dark eyes. Alex was a man who obviously thought deeply, not sharing those thoughts with many, but if the possessive fire she glimpsed burning bright in his gaze was any indicator, she had no doubt that he was about to stake his claim to her before his family.

Alex slipped his free hand into his jacket pocket and withdrew it again.

"This is a mere formality, as Loren has already consented to be my wife, but I want you, *mi familia,* to witness my pledge to marry her," Alex announced as he revealed the ring in his hand.

"That's if she hasn't taken one look at us and changed her mind," Reynard taunted his elder brother and was rewarded with a quelling glare.

"I h-haven't. I w-wouldn't," Loren stuttered slightly as she saw the exquisitely beautiful, smooth, oval ruby set in old gold.

"Then this is for you," Alex murmured, sliding the ring upon her engagement finger.

The gold felt warm against her skin and the ring fit as if it was made for her and her alone. She'd recognized it immediately when he'd drawn it from his pocket. The del Castillo betrothal ring, handed down from firstborn son to firstborn son, had been in the family for centuries. The last woman to wear it had been Alex's mother.

The gold filigree on each shoulder of the ring had been crafted into delicate heart shapes and the stone appeared to take on a new glow against her skin.

"It's beautiful, Alex. Thank you," she said, lifting her eyes to meet his. "I'm honored to accept this."

"No, Loren, you honor me by agreeing to become my wife."

"I've always loved you, Alex. It's no more than I've ever wanted."

The air between them stilled, solidified, almost becoming something corporeal before Benedict interrupted them with two glasses of champagne. He thrust one at each of them.

"This calls for a toast, yes?"

He passed another glass to their grandfather before raising one of his own.

"To Alex and Loren. May they have many happy years."

A look passed between the brothers, something unspoken that hovered in the air as they connected silently with one another, then as one lifted their glasses to drink. Whatever it was, it was soon gone as sibling rivalry and teasing took over the atmosphere, leading even *Abuelo* to laugh and admonish them gently, reminding them of the lady in their midst.

Now she really belonged, Loren thought as she smiled and sipped the vintage French champagne, letting the bubbles dance along her tongue much as happiness danced through her veins. And, as the subtle lighting in the room caught the ruby on her finger, she knew that no matter how distant Alex had been today, everything was now perfect in her world.

Four

"I see he's given you that old thing."

Loren forced her shoulders to relax and her instincts not to bristle at Giselle's throwaway remark. It was three days after her arrival at the castillo and the first time she'd been forced back into Giselle's company. Days that had been filled with dress fittings and learning her responsibilities toward the staff at the castle. At least in the matter of her wedding dress she'd been able to choose for herself. As far as the wedding ceremony and reception went, Loren had been forced, with so little time left, to refrain from making any changes.

She chewed over Giselle's comment about the ruby. Clearly the woman wanted to belittle both her and Alex's gift, but she'd chosen the wrong target. What would the other woman know, or even begin to understand, of del Castillo tradition and the importance and validation behind having received the ring Alex had given her?

"I'd have asked for something more modern myself," the other woman continued.

Giselle lifted one hand from the steering wheel of the car in which she'd just picked Loren up from the castillo. Shafts of sunlight caught on the diamond tennis bracelet she wore on one wrist.

"Something more like this."

Loren merely smiled. "Your bracelet is beautiful, but I prefer knowing that there is only one of this ring and understanding the history behind it. I feel privileged to be chosen to wear it."

And she did feel privileged. Being given the family heirloom had cemented her place at Alex's side, no matter how emotionally and even physically distant he had remained since that night. She was confident that in time their emotional distance would close and eventually disappear altogether, especially if their reaction to one another was anything to go by. She closed her eyes and momentarily relived the pressure of his mouth against hers as he'd said good-night at the door to her suite on the night he'd given her the ruby. She'd all but ignited under his masterful lips and tongue.

She'd wanted to clutch at the fabric of his shirt and pull him toward her, to feel the length of his body imprint against hers as it had when he'd kissed her back in New Zealand. But he'd stepped away slightly—only allowing their lips to fuse, their tongues to duel ever so briefly, before pulling away and wishing her a good night's rest.

What would he have done, she wondered, if she'd taken him by the hand and pulled him into her suite and closed the door firmly behind them? Would he have taken her to her bed and finally taught her the physical delights of love that she'd only read about?

Her timidity frustrated her. What kind of woman
was she, coming to marriage to a man of the world such
as Alex with no experience beyond a few unsatisfying
furtive fumblings and clumsy kisses? She was eager
to learn from Alex, but anxious at the thought of dis-
appointing him.

She cast a sideways glance at Giselle. No doubt she'd
never faced such a conundrum. The woman looked as
if she'd been born ready to take on the world and all its
challenges. She also didn't look like the kind of woman
to whom Loren could confide her insecurities.

She wondered who'd given Giselle the bracelet she
wore so proudly. No doubt some man who'd found her
particular brand of confidence and self-assurance as
sexy as her lush figure and thick, cascading blond hair.
She probably had an array of jewelry like it.

As if suddenly aware of her scrutiny, Giselle flicked
her a glance.

"Where would you like to start today? Alex said
you're to spare no expense on your trousseau. I imagine
you were limited for choices where you lived in New
Zealand."

"A little, yes, but aside from the usual imported
labels we have access to our own wonderful designers,
too. I just rarely had the necessity to dress up all that
much."

Loren shifted in her seat, a little uncomfortable with
the unspoken suggestion that her wardrobe lacked for
anything. Had Alex said as much to Giselle? Did he even
trust her to choose her own clothing? The answer was
obviously no. Why else would he have insisted Giselle
come with her today, when she'd already hinted she'd
prefer to spend her time with him, not his assistant?

Besides, everything she owned was of excellent

quality, even if the outfit she'd chosen today lacked the European flair of Giselle's tailored trousers and open-necked silk blouse.

"Well, that will all change as Alex's wife, you know. You'll need a good range of items that can take you through any occasion. We frequently entertain royalty and overseas celebrities at the resort and Alex likes us to keep a personal touch with those special guests."

Giselle's casually possessive use of the words *we* and *us* struck Loren as more than accidental. Was she hinting that she had acted at Alex's side in a role as something more than merely his employee? They'd certainly have made a striking couple—he with his dark good looks and she with her golden beauty. Loren silently chastised herself for the pang of envy she felt. Giselle was Alex's right-hand person—of course she'd have escorted him on company business.

She took a steadying breath before replying, "Yes, we pride ourselves on that level of care at the station, too. You'd be surprised at the caliber of guests we have entertained there. But that was nothing new to me. As you know, I grew up here and my father was also a prominent member of Sagradan society. I'm well used to moving among royalty and celebrity and I look forward to accompanying Alex in the same regard. Now, with the shops, I think we should start from the skin out, don't you? I love lingerie shopping."

"Good choice. I know just the right shop to start at and Alex already has an account there."

Loren stiffened. There was no avoiding it. Alex kept an account at a lingerie store, which meant he was well accustomed to purchasing women's lace and finery—from the skin out. Taking a deep breath, Loren reminded herself that there could be an innocent reason for why he kept such an account—perhaps for those special guests that Giselle had already alluded to. Luggage went missing, or was delayed, every day around the world, and things were occasionally lost or damaged in hotel laundries. It would make perfect sense for him to hold an account, Loren rationalized silently.

But in spite of the logic of that explanation, a bitter taste settled in her mouth. Yes, Alex probably used the account for business reasons—but she was a fool if she thought that was the extent of it. Of course he was a man of the world and had no doubt had multiple lovers. Even as a teenager, she'd noticed the way women flocked to him. At the time, she'd dealt with it by trying to scare them all off, but she hadn't been naive enough to believe that she'd succeeded. And now she had proof. She didn't have to like it but she was going to have to learn to live with it, one way or another.

Unconsciously she twisted the heavy ruby ring on her finger. She hadn't expected any words of love from him when he'd given it to her, even though she'd expressed them herself. How could he have learned to love the person she was now, anyway? She'd changed so much from the sometimes petulant and demanding child he remembered. But they had plenty of time for him to learn to love her. They were to be married and she was going to do everything in her power to make it a long and loving marriage.

At the lingerie store Loren was overwhelmed by the multiple arrays of delicate fabrics and colors on offer. She fingered a satin-and-lace nightgown of the sheerest oyster pink. There was a matching wrap that had an exquisitely detailed lace panel in the back. She knew she had to have it.

"Oh, that's pretty," Giselle commented over her

shoulder. "But I wouldn't waste too much money on things like that. Alex isn't keen on night wear."

Loren stiffened again. And she'd know that snippet of information how? Okay, so maybe the other woman's earlier comments could have been misconstrued but there was no doubt that Giselle had ceased to be subtle about her allusions to things about which she appeared to have a very personal knowledge.

A needle of pain worked deep into Loren's chest. So, Alex had indulged in an affair with his beautiful assistant. May indeed still be doing so, for all she knew. Did he plan for it to continue even after their marriage? Loren swallowed against the bile that rose, sudden and foully bitter, in her throat.

Giselle still hovered at her side, her green eyes narrowed slightly as if gauging the result of her comment on Loren. Loren knew she had to say something— anything to get through the next few minutes—but she also knew that she dare not show any sign of weakness. A woman like Giselle would capitalize on that weakness and run with it and there was no way Loren was about to let that happen.

"Hmm," she murmured calmly, nodding slowly. "Good to know. Thanks, but I think I'll get it anyway."

She was rewarded with a sharp look from her companion, puzzlement followed swiftly by acceptance, as if Giselle realized that she'd made her point but had failed to rattle Loren as she'd so obviously intended.

It was a hollow victory.

The rest of the day stretched ahead interminably for Loren. The mere thought of absorbing and defusing more comments from Giselle extinguished every last moment of pleasure she'd anticipated in the day.

Loren suggested they take a break with a coffee at one of the harborside cafés. Once they were settled at their table and had placed their orders she sat back and let the warmth of the late spring sunshine seep into her body. She took a deep, steadying breath. She knew what she had to do.

"Giselle, look, I appreciate that you've taken time out of your day to help me with my shopping but I think I'd like a little time to myself and see if I can't catch up with some old school friends instead. You head back to the resort, I'm sure you have plenty of work you'd rather be doing. I'll just get a cab back to the castillo later today."

"Alex specifically asked me to assist you today. I can't leave you just like that," Giselle protested.

"Come on, let's be honest here. You don't want to spend time with me any more than I do with you. You've made it clear that you and Alex have a history. I accept that. But it is now very firmly in the past."

So back off, the unsaid words hung in the air between them.

Loren's heart hammered in her chest. She wasn't used to confrontation of any kind—avoided it like the plague on most occasions, to be honest. But when shoved hard enough she always stood her ground and right now she'd drawn her demarcation line.

"So you're sending me back to be with him? A bit risky, don't you think?"

The smile on Giselle's face was predatory.

"Risky? Well, it was me he traveled half the world to visit and asked to marry, wasn't it?"

Giselle snorted inelegantly. "Nothing more than the fulfillment of his duty to allay an old man's concerns and create some strong publicity for the del Castillo business empire. You can ask Alex about that yourself if you don't believe me." She bent and collected her handbag and rose gracefully from her chair. "Well, I can see I'm no longer wanted here. Far be it from *me* to stay where I don't belong."

Loren sat and watched Giselle walk away, the clear insult about Loren's presence on Isla Sagrado, in Alex's life, echoing in her ears.

But Giselle was wrong, Loren had no doubt about that. If anything, *Giselle* was the intruder here, not Loren. Not when Loren had been born and raised here. Not when Alex had brought her back. Her hands curled into tight fists in her lap. She did belong here, Loren repeated silently in her mind. She did.

When Alex returned to the castillo that night Loren half expected him to mention something about Giselle returning to the office early, or even insist that she avail herself of the other woman's expertise. She'd prepared at least a dozen responses to him by the time she'd finally returned home herself, her arms laden with parcels after a full afternoon of shopping on her own. Her feet ached with the miles she'd walked but inside she'd reached a state she could finally call happy. No matter what Alex said to her about Giselle, she wouldn't let it bring her down.

The number of people who'd recognized her, the old friends she'd indeed bumped into who had been excited to see her—all had made her feel so thoroughly welcomed back.

As it transpired, she hadn't needed a single one of her arguments. Alex was distracted all through the evening meal, letting *Abuelo* direct most of the conversation and listening to her tell him of all she'd seen and done during the day.

After their meal, Alex walked her to her suite as he did every night. As she unlocked the door he put out a hand to cover hers.

"Would you mind if I come in with you this evening?" His voice was deep and the sound caressed her ears like a lover's touch.

"Not at all," she answered with a smile as she swung the heavy door open and stepped inside. "Please, come in."

Loren's heart fluttered in her chest. Had Alex decided not to wait for their wedding night? Nerves, plaited with a silken thread of longing, pulsed deep inside, slowly stoking a furnace of heat within her. Her skin grew sensitive. So sensitive, even the newly bought gown she'd worn to dinner felt too heavy against her.

She turned to him, aware that her cheeks were warm and no doubt bore a flush of color quite at odds with the elegance of her appearance tonight. Her eyes raked over him. Ah, she never tired of drinking in the sight of his masculine beauty. Of the breadth of his shoulders as they filled the designer suit he wore with such effortless grace and style. Of the press of his chest against the crisp white cotton of his shirt. Even the way his throat moved above the knot of his silver-and-black striped silk tie mesmerized her.

Her mind filled with the prospect of placing her lips to that very point where she could see the beat of his pulse—of pressing her lips into his skin, allowing her tongue to caress that spot and taste him, tasting so much more.

She clenched her thighs against the sudden thrum of energy that coiled there. But instead of lessening the sensation, it only intensified it, sending a small shock of pleasure through her and driving a tiny gasp past her lips.

She felt as though she was poised on the balls of her feet, ready to move into the shelter of his arms and feel once more the press of his body against hers. Her whole body was attuned to the man only a few short feet away from her.

"There is something I need to discuss with you," Alex said, the abruptly businesslike tone of his voice quelling her ardor as suddenly as if she'd been drenched by a rogue wave on the rocky bay beneath the castle.

Was he now going to take her to task for her dismissal of Giselle today? Loren felt the lingering remnants of desire slowly flicker and die. She swallowed and took a steadying breath.

"Well then, would you be more comfortable sitting down? Perhaps I can pour you a drink?"

"Yes, thank you. A cognac I think. And pour one for yourself, too."

Did he think she'd need it? Suddenly Loren wished he had simply stuck with their usual routine. Even a noncommittal kiss at the door was bound to have been better than being castigated for rejecting his assistant's company. Not that she was going to take any criticism of her choice today without putting up a decent protest of her own. But was she ready to face the truth if she asked him about his relationship with Giselle?

She crossed the sitting room of her suite to the heavily carved dark wooden sideboard against one wall. She took two crystal snifters from within and then lifted the cut-crystal stopper from one of the decanters on the edged silver tray that sat on the polished surface. Alex's warm hand closed over hers.

"Here, let me pour, hmm?"

A fine tremor ran through her as his touch sent a sizzle of electricity coursing up her arm.

She pulled away from him and forced her suddenly uncooperative legs to take her over to one of the two-seater couches. She lowered herself onto the richly upholstered fabric, yet couldn't bring herself to sit back and relax against the cushioned back, instead perching on the edge.

Alex crossed the room and handed her one of the glasses. Loren bent her nose to the rim, taking a deep breath of the aroma of the dark amber liquid before lifting it to her lips and allowing the alcohol to trickle over her tongue and down her throat. She never normally drank hard spirits, but she had the distinct feeling that tonight she was going to need it.

She swallowed, welcoming the burn the distilled liquor left in its path, and watched as Alex sat down opposite her. He unbuttoned his jacket and reached inside, drawing out a folded paper packet. He carefully placed the packet on the coffee table between them, then took a sip of his cognac.

The liquid left a slight sheen upon his lips, capturing her gaze with the inevitability of a moth to a flame. He pressed his lips together, dissipating the residue, allowing her to look away.

"Is that what you want to discuss?" Loren pressed as he made no effort to explain the papers he'd laid before them.

"Yes. It's a legal document I need you to read and sign before we are married. Someone can take you into the notary's office tomorrow for it to be witnessed."

"What kind of legal document?" Loren asked, not

even bothering to point out that she could quite capably make her own way into the city.

Alex's dark eyes bored into hers. "A prenuptial document."

"Well, that is only to be expected," Loren said matter-of-factly, even as she forced herself to quell the swell of disappointment that rose within her. Did he really find such a document necessary?

As far as she was concerned, this marriage was forever. She had no desire and no plans to ever leave Alex, nor, if such a heartbreaking event should occur, could she imagine she would ever make unreasonable financial demands against him.

"Perhaps it would be best if you read it first. If you have any questions I'm sure the notary will be able to answer them for you."

Alex put down his glass and rose from his seat. "I'd better get going. I have an early flight tomorrow."

"Flight?" Loren asked. "Where? May I come with you?"

"It is nothing but a business trip to Seville. You would be bored. Which reminds me, you will need to ask Reynard or Benedict to take you to the notary as Giselle will be accompanying me. Actually, best to call on Reynard. Benedict drives like a demented race-car driver at the best of times and I would hate for anything to happen to you before the wedding."

Loren fought back the bitter disappointment his words evoked in her. "I'll bear that in mind," she replied through stiff lips. "When will you be back?"

"In a couple of days, certainly no more than three."

Three days away with Giselle? Loren felt the news

deep in her gut, as if it was a physical blow. Perhaps her earlier fears of today were true after all.

"Good night, then." Alex walked the couple of steps that brought him to her side and bent to kiss the top of her head before leaving the room.

As she watched the heavy door of her suite close behind him she blinked against the prick of tears that had begun behind her eyes. She would not cry. She would not.

Loren reached across the table, lifted up the legal packet and slid out the folded document. Her eyes scanned the information. As unaccustomed as she was to legal jargon it all seemed to make sense until she reached a paragraph headed up with the words *legal issue*.

She read the paragraph, then read it again to be certain she understood the terminology. If she was correct, to ensure the continuation of the del Castillo bloodline she and Alex must make love at the time when her body was at its most fertile, and to ensure the correct timing, her menstrual cycle was to be monitored. Even the details of the clinic she would be monitored by were in the agreement.

Loren let the papers slide from suddenly nerveless fingers.

The legalese twirled around in her mind, sentences fragmenting before joining back together. Did this mean that she and Alex would *only* make love when she was ovulating? That was, what? A span of a few days at most in each month. And what if she got pregnant? Would he still share her bed, still make love with her as a husband did with his wife? Or would her job have been done, leaving him free to go back into Giselle's arms?

Just what kind of marriage was she entering?

Five

Loren heard the knock at the door to her suite and wondered if perhaps her maid had forgotten something. She'd only just sent her away, preferring to spend these last few moments before her wedding alone. She picked up her voluminous skirts and went to open the door.

"Giselle!" Loren stepped back, startled to see the blonde there. She let her skirts settle back down to the carpet beneath her, the ivory French taffeta giving a distinctive rustle.

"My, don't you look every inch the fairy-tale princess," Giselle remarked, coming into the sitting room.

Loren tolerated the woman's scrutiny of the dress that was the fulfillment of all her childhood dreams. Yes, she did feel like a fairy-tale princess in the strapless gown. Somehow the words from Giselle's glossy red lips made the idea more of an insult than a compliment.

"Was there something you wanted?" Loren asked coolly.

"No, Alex asked me to come up and check on you. He thought you might benefit from some female company since your mother isn't here."

Loren bit back the retort that immediately sprang to her lips. She would not fight, not with anyone, on her wedding day.

"That's lovely of him. But as you can see, I'm fine, thank you."

She waited for Giselle to leave but instead she settled herself on one of the couches. Loren had to admit, she looked beautiful. The woman certainly knew how to make the most of her features. The dress she wore would have looked vampish on anyone else, but on Giselle it was elegantly sensual.

"You know, I have to hand it to you. I thought you'd have given up by now," Giselle said.

"Given up?"

"Well, how many women would have signed that prenuptial agreement, for a start? I know I certainly wouldn't."

"Perhaps you would if you loved your fiancé enough," Loren commented quietly. "As I do."

Giselle waved her hand as if dismissing Loren's words, the very gesture making Loren's spine stiffen in irritation. She'd wanted this time alone to reflect on her coming marriage, and particularly on the terms of the prenuptial agreement that Giselle had mentioned. Clearly, the blonde knew all about it, and that fact rankled with Loren. It should have been a private matter. One between her and Alex alone.

This past week had been such a whirl of activity with a museum opening to attend along with several charity functions, all of which gave her a taste for what her duties would be like as a del Castillo bride. She and Alex, while together for much of their waking moments, had barely had a moment alone to talk. Whenever she'd tried to bring the subject of the prenuptial document up, Alex had brushed it off until later. Now, today, was about as late as it could get and Loren was still unsure of where she stood on the agreement she'd eventually signed.

"Well, whatever," Giselle continued, oblivious to Loren's obvious displeasure in her company. "You've really gone above and beyond the call of duty. It's either incredibly naive of you to stick with it or incredibly kind."

"Kind?"

"To agree to the terms just to help the company out and keep an old man happy."

"I don't know what you mean. I'm marrying Alex because I love him. Because I've always loved him," Loren stated as firmly as she was able.

"Surely you're aware that Alex is only marrying you because of the curse."

"The curse?" Surely she didn't mean the old governess's curse?

Loren knew well the story of the woman who'd been brought to Isla Sagrado from the south of France to educate the daughters of one of the original del Castillos on the island—a nobleman from Spain. The poor woman had fallen in love with her employer and entered into an affair that had lasted years.

Legend had it that she'd borne him three sons, but that in view of the fact his wife had only borne him daughters, he'd taken her boys from her and he'd raised them as his legitimate issue, paying her off with a ruby necklace from the del Castillo jewel collection. Paintings in the family gallery that predated the nobleman showed the necklace, known as *La Verdad del Corazon*—the Heart's Truth. It was a stunning piece of chased gold with a massive heart-shaped ruby at its center. Loren had always privately believed that it was more the type of gift a man gave to his one true love than as payment for services rendered.

When the nobleman's wife died, however, he'd married another woman—one from a high-ranking family. In her misery the governess was said to have interrupted the wedding, begging her beloved to take her back. When her lover—and her sons—turned their backs on her, she cursed the del Castillo family. If, in the next nine generations, the del Castillos did not learn to live by their family motto of honor, truth and love, the ninth generation would be the last. With that pronouncement, she cast both herself and the Heart's Truth from the cliffs behind the castle and into the savage ocean. Her body was later found, but the Heart's Truth had been lost ever since.

Loren had always found the story to be truly tragic and, as a child, had often imagined a happier ending for the governess and her lover.

If the curse was to be believed—not to mention previous generations' total disregard for its power—it was responsible for the steady diminishment of the family over the past nine generations. But to believe that Alex was marrying her in an attempt to break the curse, well, that was just ridiculous. What happened three hundred years ago had no bearing on life today.

"Surely you must know of it. You're from here, after all, and the papers have been full of it, especially since the announcement of your engagement. The boys are the ninth generation—the last of the line. Old Aston was starting to have concerns that they would stay that way. Alex is trying to downplay it but you know what his grandfather is like once he gets an idea into his head. He believes he's even seen the governess's ghost. Can you imagine it? Of course, Alex would move mountains to please the old man—especially if it also happened to be good for business.

"Anyway, they came up with this fabulous publicity drive where they'd all get married and have babies to prove to everyone, their grandfather especially, that the curse isn't real."

Giselle laughed but Loren was hard-pressed to quell the shiver that ran down her spine. Even more so when she weighed the truth in the other woman's words. If, as she'd said, *Abuelo* was genuinely concerned about the curse, Alex *would* do anything to alleviate those concerns. It was the kind of man he was and his loyalty and love for his family were unquestionable.

Would that loyalty and love extend to her, she wondered, or was Giselle right and was Loren merely the means to an end?

Giselle rose from her seat and brushed an imaginary fleck of dust from her dress.

"Well, I can see you don't need me. I'll go down to Alex and let him know you're ready. The cars are waiting to take everyone to the cathedral."

"Thank you."

Loren forced the words past her lips and tried not to think too hard about the ceremony ahead.

She would much rather have married in the intimate private chapel that formed a part of the castillo's family history, but her wedding to Alex was to be quite a show. Visiting dignitaries from all over Europe would be in attendance along with the cream of Sagradan society. Hundreds of guests, if the lists she'd seen were any indication.

Hundreds of strangers.

As the door closed behind Giselle's retreating figure it struck Loren how alone she truly was. The few old school friends she'd managed to touch base with since her return all viewed her differently now. Sure, they were friendly, but it was as if there was an invisible wall between them. As if she was unreachable. Untouchable.

Well, untouchable certainly fit in well with how Alex had continued to treat her. Maybe he was saving himself, making sure he was locked and loaded for when they met the terms of their prenuptial agreement, she thought cynically. Or maybe he managed to sate his appetites elsewhere, a snide voice niggled from the back of her mind. She pushed the thought from her head but couldn't quite get rid of the bitter aftertaste in her mouth at the thought.

Loren crossed the sitting room to the large window that looked out past the castle's walls and over the landscape. The sun was hot and bright today, a portent of the burgeoning summer months ahead. The sky was a sharp clear blue, broken by slender drifts of cirrus cloud here and there. It was a perfect day to be married by any standard, so why then did she suddenly feel as if it was anything but?

Alex fidgeted with his cuff links for what felt like the umpteenth time today as he stood at the altar of the cathedral.

"Do that again and they'll fall off," Benedict cautioned from his side.

"Funny guy," Alex responded, but forced himself to relax.

He looked back across the rows and rows of guests, some faces he knew well, others hardly at all. The cathedral was packed. Today's ceremony would be the beginning of the new age of del Castillos that would lay old ghosts to rest, and everyone who was anyone wanted to be there to see it. He met *Abuelo's* stare from the front pew, the one carved with the del Castillo crest. The old man gave him a slow nod of approval and Alex felt his chest swell with pride. Any doubts he might have had about whether he was doing the right thing were nothing in the face of his grandfather's happiness.

"Do you know what the delay is?" Reynard asked. "Maybe she's got cold feet and has made a run for the airport."

Alex gave his brother a glare, but he felt a short sharp pang of concern. Loren had been different since he'd given her the prenup to read and sign. A little more distant and a little less eager to please. Had the agreement bothered her that much? Surely she could see the necessity for such an agreement without it affecting their marriage. The financial considerations of providing for her, should he die unexpectedly or should their marriage fail, aside, of primary importance was ensuring the next generation. Once that was out of the way then, well, they could take whatever came next at their leisure—a prospect that, he had to admit, filled him with pleasure. It had been hell keeping his hands off Loren these past two weeks, especially when she'd obviously been eager to take their relationship to an intimate level.

But tonight his wait would be rewarded. Granted, the timing of their union meant that their liaison tonight would not be part of the agreement they'd both signed. It would instead be the consummation of the promises they would make to one another before all these witnesses today.

The importance of those promises settled in his chest like a solid lump of lead, pressing down on his heart, his very honor. It didn't settle well with him to be pledging to love another for the rest of their days when, in truth, he didn't love her.

Love. It wasn't something he and Loren had discussed. Hell, it wasn't even something Alex had considered until she'd declared her feelings for him the night he'd given her the engagement ring.

When she'd first agreed to marry him back in New Zealand, he had assumed she cared for him, perhaps admired him a little the way she had when she was a child. He'd also *known* she was attracted to him—just as he was attracted to her. And she'd wanted to honor her father's memory, in much the same way that he'd wanted to ease his grandfather's mind. So Alex had been comfortable with the arrangement—with the idea of a marriage based on mutual regard, a healthy dose of desire and shared respect for family. Love had never been part of the plan.

But something about her sweetly serious declaration when she accepted his ring and gave him her heart had moved him unexpectedly, making him feel almost shamed. Was it fair to her to accept her love when he was not yet prepared to return it? A picture of his parents flashed through his memory. He wondered what they'd think of the choice he was making today.

They had known real love. It had been considered only fitting that if their light had to be extinguished so early that they die together. The avalanche that had taken them, while on a romantic skiing holiday together without their sons, had wiped out joy as the boys had known it up until that time. Yet they'd been lucky to have had *Abuelo,* who'd put his own grief aside to continue to guide and raise the three teenage boys whose anger at their parents' fate sought many outlets.

It had been *Abuelo's* steady love and firm hand that had brought them through. Love they reciprocated. Taking another look at his grandfather's beaming face, Alex knew that while he would not be telling the truth as he made his vows to Loren today, the gift of hope it would give his grandfather was worth far too much for him to give in to second thoughts now.

"Last chance to back out," Benedict said under his breath. Before Alex could respond, a sudden hush spread through the cathedral. The centuries-old organ, which had been delivering a steady medley of music, halted. The lump of lead in Alex's chest shifted, forming a fist around his lungs as all eyes turned to the main doors. They swung slowly open and a burst of sunlight filled the doorway, bathing the vestibule with its golden glow. And then, within the glow of light, a lone figure appeared.

The fist squeezed tighter as Alex realized how difficult this must be for Loren. In the face of her mother's blank refusal to attend their nuptials, he should have insisted she be accompanied on her journey down the center aisle of the cathedral—past the many assessing eyes of the glitterati and politically powerful. But she'd refused all offers from his brothers and *Abuelo.*

"My father will be with me in spirit," she'd said, holding that determined, fine-boned chin of hers firmly in the air, daring him to challenge her wishes. "I need no one else."

He'd had to accede to her wish. After all, it was the only thing on which she had insisted in all the matters pertaining to the ceremony.

The powerful organ began again and as Loren began to glide down the aisle toward him, Alex realized he'd misjudged his bride's strength and fortitude.

Pride suffused every cell in his body as she walked toward him with effortless grace—her bare shoulders squared and her spine straight, her slender neck holding her head high. Loren's skin gleamed against the strapless ivory gown that hugged her torso and exposed the gentle swell of her breasts before spreading into a bloom of fabric around and behind her. For the first time in his memory, Alex was speechless. Beneath the gossamer-fine veil that covered her head and shoulders and drifted down to her waist he caught glimpses of light striking the diamond tiara that had once been his mother's. The matching necklace, its design the inverted image of the tiara, settled against her luminous skin at the base of her throat and spilled in a gentle V over her collarbone.

Her face was composed behind her veil, her eyes avoiding contact with his, focused instead on the altar behind him. As she drew closer he could hear the swish of the fabric of her gown as it swept across the floor, could see the fine tremors that shook the opulent bouquet of early summer blooms she carried.

"Looks like lanky little Loren Dubois has really grown up, hmm?"

Reynard's voice in his ear snapped Alex from his trance.

"For once in your life could you just shut up?" he hissed at his brother through teeth clenched so tight his jaw ached, earning a glare of disapproval from the priest in the process.

Reynard's next words, however, shocked him in a way he never expected.

"Don't hurt her, Alex. Whatever you do, don't *ever* hurt her."

"Noted," Alex replied with a swift nod.

He met his brother's eyes briefly. There was no doubting Reynard meant what he said. For some strange reason it made him feel better that Loren had a champion. That it should have been him was not wasted on him at all, but given what he'd agreed to do to save the del Castillo family and fortunes, it was only fitting it be one of his brothers. Both, if the look on Benedict's face was any indicator.

A savage rush of possession roared through his veins. They could look, certainly, they could warn him as much as they liked, but essentially, Loren was his. As she joined him on the steps in front of the altar that knowledge gave him the ultimate satisfaction.

When it came time to say their vows, Loren looked at him, truly looked at him, for the first time that day. And as she pledged to love him, he found he had to look away. Her words carried such surety, such conviction. She deserved more than empty promises in return. Her voice wobbled slightly on the last word of the formal ceremony they'd chosen. No, he corrected himself, the ceremony Giselle had chosen. Shame scored him. This was Loren's wedding day. He should have given her more say in how the day was to go.

He'd approached this all wrong. He already had her love and loyalty and he'd walked roughshod over both in the execution of *his* goals and *his* needs. Loren was more than a means to an end, she was a vital, living, breathing woman.

He would make it up to her, he promised himself

silently. As soon as they'd fulfilled the first part of the prenuptial agreement, he would definitely make it up to her.

Loren had barely spoken half a dozen words directly to him since they'd exchanged their vows. In the car from the wedding reception it was no different. Alex found the uncharacteristic silence challenging. Normally Loren found something, anything, to talk to him about—it was one of the things he found so engaging about her.

But something had changed inside her today; he could sense it in the way she held herself, the way she'd spoken to others. As if she was playing a part and was not really totally involved in what she was doing.

As their car swung through the gate of the outer wall and drew up to the entrance of the castillo it finally occurred to Alex why she was so quiet. She had to be nervous about tonight. He would make sure their first time was one she would remember forever. A special night. A memory to be treasured.

Dios, but she looked exquisitely beautiful. He could almost taste the satin softness of her skin already. Almost feel the shiver of desire ripple across her skin.

As the driver opened his door he gave a short command to the man to allow Alex himself to escort his new wife from the vehicle. He walked around to her side of the car and pulled open her door, offering her his hand.

"Come, Loren. Let me help you inside."

"Thank you," she said softly.

The voluminous skirts and sweep of the train of her dress was a confection of fabric about her, yet she handled the garment with the grace of a swan. Another definite plus in her favor—no matter the situation, she handled it with aplomb. In spite of his concerns, he knew he'd chosen well when he'd decided to marry her. She would be a marvelous asset to him in so very many ways.

"You were wonderful today, I was so proud of you," he bent to murmur in her ear as they approached the arched entrance of their home.

"It was an—" she hesitated a moment before continuing "—interesting day."

"Interesting?" Alex forced himself to laugh softly. Surely she hadn't picked up on his unease during the ceremony—or had she? Well regardless, he'd have to put her mind at ease. "It was a great success. All of Isla Sagrado knows you are now my beautiful bride and their blessings upon us will reflect back upon them. I imagine, though, it must have been difficult for you."

"Difficult?"

"Without your family to support you."

"Yes, it was difficult, but it was what my father would have expected of me."

There was a note to her voice that sounded off-key but Alex pushed the thought aside. She was obviously weary after the pomp and ceremony of the day and the obligations she'd fulfilled at the lavish reception.

Alex guided Loren up the stairs and toward the shared suite he'd ordered their effects delivered to today—the suite that had been his parents'. As they swept inside he nodded in approval at the sensual soft lighting provided by the plethora of candles he'd requested be lit before their arrival.

The heady scents of rose and sandalwood drifted on the air, feminine and masculine, yin and yang.

"Would you like to be alone while you change? Or

perhaps I should call your maid to assist with your gown?"

"No, it's all right. I can manage the lacing myself," Loren replied.

Again there was that slight discordance. Again he shrugged it away.

"I'll leave you to change then."

She merely inclined her head and moved gracefully across the room to her private chamber. Alex watched as she drew the door closed behind her then wasted no time getting to his private en suite bathroom and divesting himself of his clothing before stepping under the hot steam of a quick shower. A few swift swipes of his towel later and he was dry. Naked, he padded through to his dressing room where he reached for midnight blue, satin pajama bottoms and a matching robe.

Would her touch be as soft as the fabric that caressed his skin, he wondered. No, it would be softer, he was certain. His body coiled tight in anticipation of what lay ahead.

Before he realized it, he was at the door to her rooms, his hand twisting the handle and thrusting open the door. Candles had been lit in here, too. The large pedestal bed, swathed in cream-and-gold draperies, stood invitingly empty.

Empty?

A sound drew his attention as his bride came from her bathroom. Her satin nightgown skimmed her slender form enticingly, cascading over her gentle curves much as his hands now itched to, also. A small frown puckered her brow as she worked a brush through her hair.

"Here, let me," Alex said as she crossed the room. He took the brush from her fingers. "Sit down on the bed."

Loren did as he requested and Alex stood a little behind her and forced himself to focus on her hair and only her hair as he reached to stroke the brush through her tresses, easing out the knots and occasional forgotten hairpin.

"Ah." She sighed. "That feels wonderful."

Liquid fire pooled in his groin at her words. He planned to make her feel so much more wonderful very soon. Now that the brush flowed more smoothly through her hair he allowed himself to focus on the deliciously smooth, bare shoulders she presented to him.

Palest pink straps of satin were all that held her nightgown up. Straps that with the slightest breath could slide down those shoulders and farther, down her slender arms, exposing her back. He'd never found the prospect of observing a woman's back so enticing before. But then again, with Loren everything was different. Everything felt new.

He couldn't help himself, he had to taste her. He gathered her hair in one fist and gently drew it away from the nape of her neck then bent to kiss her, allowing his tongue to stroke across her skin in a private caress.

He felt her response ripple down her spine. Smiling to himself, he kissed her again—this time sucking gently—and was rewarded with the soft sound of her gasp. Alex let the hairbrush drop to the floor and placed both his hands upon her shoulders, coaxing her upright to turn and face him.

Her face, clean of the makeup she'd worn today, appeared flushed in the candlelight—her eyes luminous, their pupils dilated so far they almost appeared to consume the dark velvet brown of her irises. Her lips were moist and remained slightly parted. His gaze dropped to her breasts, to the clearly delineated pinpoints of her nipples as they thrust against the satin with her each and every rapid breath.

Something knotted tight and low in Alex's belly. Something possessive. Something wild. Every instinct within him roared that he plunder her lips, that he drag the delicate fabric of her nightgown from her body and expose her to him, allowing him to feast on her feminine glory. To rush her to dizzying heights she had no experience of.

To mark her as his own.

She is inexperienced, he reminded himself sternly, forcing himself to hold back, to slow down.

He let his hands skim across her shoulders and gently cup the back of her neck, tilting her head to him. He lowered his face, his eyes locked upon hers. His entire body rigid with the need to take this as gently as humanly possible.

His lips were only millimeters from hers. Already he could feel her breath against him, smell the sweetness of her breath.

"Alex, wait!"

Through the cloud of passion that controlled him he heard the plea in her voice. He closed his eyes for a moment and drew in a shuddering breath, constraining his desire.

"You are frightened. I'm rushing you. Do not worry, Loren. I will make tonight one you will never forget."

"No, it's not that," she said, pulling out of his arms, creating a short distance between them.

Already his body cried out for her. Craving her slender frame against his, aching for her warmth to envelop him.

"Then what is it?" he asked, fighting back the edge

of frustration that threatened to spill over into his voice. He didn't want to frighten her more with his hunger.

"It's about us. Our marriage."

"Us?"

A cold finger of caution traced a chilly path down his spine. What was she speaking of? They were married. Tonight would see the consummation of that marriage.

"Yes, Alex, us. I love you. I've always loved you one way or another. I accept that you don't return my feelings in the same way."

"You know I care for you, Loren," he asserted, determined to salve her concerns as quickly as possible.

"I know you do, but more as a brother would a sister."

"Believe me, my feelings toward you are most definitely not brotherly."

"Be that as it may." She waved her hand to disregard his words. "Even knowing you don't love me, I agreed to marry you in part because of my feelings for you, but also to honor my father and his promise to yours." She lifted her eyes to him. Eyes that glistened in the candlelight with unshed tears. "Can you honestly tell me that you have done the same?"

Tell her he'd married her to fulfill their fathers' vow to one another? No, not even he could lie about that. Not after the lies he'd already told before his grandfather in the church today. Lies that still coated his tongue with a tang of unpleasantness. The old promise was the reason he'd chosen to seek her out rather than find a bride on Isla Sagrado, but it was not the sole reason he'd decided to marry.

"No," he responded, his voice flat and tinged now

with the anger he bore toward himself more than to her. "But you have asked me to be honest. If you do not like my truth then you have only yourself to blame."

"But you have married me with the intention of producing an heir, is that true?"

She stood upright before him, holding her chin high, her shoulders straight, demanding his response.

"Of course."

"To dispel the governess's curse?"

Words failed him momentarily.

"The curse is nothing but an overstated legend. It has no bearing on us or on our marriage."

"So you didn't suddenly decide to travel all the way to New Zealand and then to marry me to put *Abuelo's* mind to rest? To prove that the curse wasn't real? Can you truly say that if it hadn't been for the curse you would *ever* have followed through with our fathers' wishes?"

He couldn't answer, to answer truthfully would damn him forever in her eyes—to tell a lie was impossible on top of the abomination of falsehoods he'd committed already.

"I see," Loren continued. "Well, then. It appears that we are at an impasse. I could have accepted almost anything from you, Alex, but I will not accept deception. You brought me here under false pretences."

"You say you love me, and you did sign the prenuptial agreement," Alex reminded her, the words like gravel on his tongue. "You cannot back out now."

"I will meet the expectations of that agreement. You will have your heir, Alexander del Castillo, but I see no reason why we should enter into a physical marriage." A sharp note of bitterness crept into her voice. "In this day and age of technology why would you even want to consider the hassle and inconvenience, or indeed even the inconsistency, of making *love?*

"After all, if the act is to be as clinical and bereft of mutual affection as I imagine it will be, surely a petri dish will do, as well."

Loren's words hung like icicles in the air between them. Anger welled and rolled within him, much like the violent surf they could hear from the beach below through her open casement windows.

"You are refusing me your bed?" he finally managed through a jaw clenched so tight he thought his teeth might shatter.

"No. I am refusing you my body."

Six

Loren barely dared draw breath.

Alex stood before her, magnificent in his anger. Were she less determined about her decision she would have quailed in the face of his fury. To be honest, were she less determined she would have given in to the rush of longing that had drawn through her body like a fine silken thread as he'd touched her.

All her life she'd waited for the day that Alex would turn to her and welcome her into his life, and into his arms. Too bad that when that day had finally come she'd been forced to spurn him. She had never believed it would matter so much to her that he had hidden from her his true reasons for entering into their marriage.

In the lead-up to the wedding it had been enough for her to believe, however misguidedly, that they stood a chance of making their marriage work. But in the stark face of what she'd learned today, it was clear that Alex hadn't been above using her to get what he wanted. That it was for his family didn't assuage the hurt deep inside her. Nor the anger she bore at herself for having been such a blind and love-struck fool where Alex was concerned.

That she loved Alex with a passion that went soul deep was undeniable. But now she realized it most definitely wasn't enough. In her naïveté she'd thought she could change his perception of her as a child to that of a woman. A woman capable of great passion and unswerving loyalty.

Clearly she was still that naive child to have thought she could make a difference—make him begin to love her. He'd taken advantage of the promise made between her father and his and, shamefully, she'd let him. She was no innocent in this. She should have known and understood what was at stake. She should have asked questions, demanded answers.

But, no. She'd been focused on fulfilling a childhood dream. Of returning to the land of her birth and of being his bride. She'd allowed herself to be duped—heck, allowed? She'd been a fully willing participant into a marriage that stood no chance of being real right from the beginning.

Well, now he had his bride. He had his baby-making machine. That didn't mean she needed to debase herself any further by pandering to his machinations. Whatever the scheme he'd hatched with his brothers, she would do no more than her duty. She would give him the baby he required, but she'd find a way to live through this with what was left of her dignity intact.

"I think you'd better leave," she said, her voice breaking on the last words as she struggled to hold back the tremors that threatened to turn her into a quivering wreck.

Alex's eyes narrowed as he continued to stare at her in silence.

"P-please, Alex. Go."

"This is not over, Loren. I am not a man who likes to be thwarted."

Loren didn't answer, instead turning her back even as her chest throbbed with the pain of rejecting him and her eyes burned with the tears she refused to shed in his presence. She had what was left of her pride and she would not let that go. Not for anything. Not for anyone. Not even the man she loved with every heart-wrenchingly pain-filled breath in her body.

Behind her, Loren heard her chamber door close with a gentle sound. The fact he hadn't slammed the door behind him spoke volumes to the measure of his control. Control he would no doubt have been exerting over her behind the filmy curtains of her pedestal bed right now, had she let him.

Something twisted deep inside her, something sharp and raw, and her inner muscles clenched on the emptiness. She looked at the bed now and knew she would not sleep there tonight. She could not.

Loren crossed to the deep-set casement window that had been flung open to the velvet night. Despite the warm night air that coursed past her to fill the room, Loren was suddenly beset by a chill that went to her very bones.

Without a doubt spurning Alex tonight was the hardest thing she'd ever had to do in her life—the hardest decision she'd ever had to make.

Her fingers gripped the age-old stone of the window

ledge so tight they became numb, and she stared out at the night sky wishing things could have been so very different.

The sound of gentle knocking at her bedroom door woke Loren from the fitful slumber she'd finally fallen into around dawn. She straightened from the chaise longue she'd eventually sought rest upon and quickly threw her pillows and the comforter back onto the bed. Everyone knew how servants gossiped and, despite their loyalty to the del Castillo family, the staff here were no different.

She crossed the room to unlock the door and took a rapid step back when she saw it was not her maid, but Alex standing on the other side.

"*Buenos días,* Loren. I trust you slept well?"

He was absolutely the last person she expected to see this morning. She'd anticipated being totally left to her own devices after her rejection of him last night. Instead, here he was, looking and smelling divine. As if what had transpired between them had never happened. As if she'd never rejected him.

"As charming as your nightgown is, you will need to change for our excursion today."

"Change?"

"Of course, unless you want to be seen out and about Isla Sagrado in your night wear."

"We…we're going out? I thought—"

"Yes, I'm sure you thought that after last night I would not want to be near you. You underestimate me, Loren. We are newly married. We are expected to be seen together. Do you honestly believe that after everything I've put in place to make our marriage happen that I would just dissolve into the castle walls because you have decided we are not to sleep together?"

There was a dangerous edge to his voice. A hint of a reined-in temper simmering just beneath the surface of his urbane exterior.

"Of course not. I don't know what I thought, to be honest." Loren dragged in a breath, her senses instantly on alert as his fragrance infiltrated her confused mind and sent her pulse hammering in her veins. "When do you want me to be ready?"

"Our first appointment is in about half an hour, near Puerto Seguro, so about five minutes ago would be ideal."

"Appointment?"

"Yes, a tradition in my family when someone marries."

Thinking it was to be with the family lawyer, Loren spun away and yanked open her wardrobe, choosing a slim-fitting ice-blue suit. Her arm was stayed by Alex's hand upon her. She couldn't help it, she flinched, and didn't miss the frown that descended over Alex's features. He pointedly withdrew his hand from her bare skin before speaking.

"That's too formal. Wear something comfortable but smart."

Without any further information he spun on his heel and left her room. For a moment she just watched him. Her eyes drinking in the beauty of his movement, the breadth of his shoulders beneath the lightweight cream shirt he wore teamed with dark caramel-colored trousers. The way those trousers skimmed the cheeks of his buttocks.

She forced herself to blink, to break the spell he'd unwittingly woven about her, enticing her. She shoved the suit back into the wardrobe and flicked through her hangers, finally settling upon a black sundress with an abstract white print patterned upon it, relieving the starkness of the background. A mid-heeled pair of strappy sandals would hopefully give the outfit just the right balance Alex had specified.

Gathering her dress and a fistful of clean underwear, Loren swept into her bathroom. She wanted nothing more than to wash her hair but she doubted time would allow it. She swept its length into a shower cap and stepped beneath the stinging spray of the shower before the water had even reached temperature, gasping slightly against the cold.

She reached for the shower gel and liberally lathered it over her body. Had things been different, she wondered, would it be Alex's hands sliding over her skin now? Her nipples beaded into tight buds at the thought. Shaking her head at herself, Loren quickly rinsed off and stepped out of the shower cubicle and reached for a towel to dry off.

It only took a moment to dress and spritz a light spray of perfume on her pulse points. Her hair she brushed into a fiercely controlled ponytail, which she then braided and pinned in a spiral against the back of her head, all the while trying to forget how it had felt last night as Alex had brushed her hair. He'd shown her a tenderness she knew he'd have brought to his lovemaking—had she let things get that far.

Her reflection, however, definitely gave her pause. The sleepless night had left dark shadows beneath her eyes. It would take everything she had in her cosmetic arsenal to restore some semblance of the dewy bride Isla Sagrado had seen yesterday.

It took her a further ten minutes but by the time

Loren met Alex in their communal sitting room she was satisfied that she could cope with anything the day brought.

"Where are we going?" she asked as she checked her handbag for her sunglasses.

"You'll see when we get there," Alex responded enigmatically.

"What about breakfast?"

"Breakfast was a couple of hours ago but there will be a morning tea where we are going. Can you wait until then?"

Loren hazarded a look at her husband from under her lashes as she pretended to search in her bag for something else. *Her husband!* The solid truth of those two words rammed into her chest and clutched at her heart with a sudden twist. At her sharply indrawn breath, Alex gave her a look.

"Is everything all right?" he asked.

"Fine, I'm fine," Loren hastened to assure him. "And yes, I can wait for something to eat."

"Then we should be on our way."

He held the door to their suite open and escorted her along the wide corridor and down the sweeping stairs to the front entrance of the castillo. There, in the massive entrance hall, the staff had all assembled in a line, some bearing small gifts, others with nothing to give but the warmth in their hearts and the smiles on their faces.

How could she have forgotten the age-old Sagradan custom? It was tradition that the staff celebrate the master's marriage with offerings. On that occasion, the master and mistress of the property would also give the staff a small monetary gift.

"Have you—" she started to ask in a whisper.

"I have it under control," Alex assured her as one

by one they greeted the people who worked tirelessly behind the scenes in the castillo.

As she went forward to accept each small gift— some traditional in the old ways, such as the symbol of fertility that was pressed into her hand by the cook, and some modern—Alex in turn gave each staff member an envelope.

By the time they reached his waiting Lamborghini outside, Loren's arms were full of the tokens bestowed upon them. She made it into the car without dropping a one, and once settled she allowed them to tumble gently into her lap. Alex reached behind her seat to extricate a box and passed it to her before turning the key in the ignition and easing the car into gear and out through the castle gates.

Loren gently placed each token into the box, her fingers lingering on the Sagradan symbol of fertility, an intricately carved egg, before placing it inside and closing the lid.

"That was lovely," she commented, her hands firmly holding the box on her lap as they drove along the coastal road toward Puerto Seguro.

"You think so?" Alex asked, raising one dark brow. "I wouldn't have thought you'd have cared."

"Of course I care. Why would you think I wouldn't?" Surprise brought a defensive tone to her voice.

Alex merely shrugged and Loren felt herself bristle at his nonchalance.

"Don't judge me by your other women," she said quietly, but with a strong hint of steel.

"Don't worry, I wouldn't dream of it," Alex replied. "You are nothing like them."

Unable to come up with a suitable response, Loren lapsed into silence. She watched the road ahead of them through burning eyes and wished things could have been different. Of course she was nothing like his other women. If the tabloids had carried even an ounce of truth, those women had been confident, sophisticated and unerringly beautiful. Women like Giselle, for example.

For what felt like the umpteenth time, Loren castigated herself for having hoped for anything else from Alex other than what she'd ended up with. She knew better than most that life was no bed of roses. The only child of parents who'd loved passionately and fought bitterly, she'd seen what a push-me-pull-you state marriage could be. And she'd experienced firsthand the pain that ensued when such a marriage irrevocably broke down.

But at least her parents had enjoyed many years together before the cracks had started to show. It was more than what her immediate future held, unless she was fortunate enough for a fertilization procedure to work on the first attempt. If she could fill her life with a child then she could quite possibly manage to be happy.

Loren was unfamiliar with the building they now approached. A cluster of paparazzi was waiting at the entrance. Of fairly recent style, it was a large sprawling construction set in lush gardens and toward the back she caught a glimpse of what looked like playing fields. Was this some kind of school? She wondered what del Castillo family tradition called for a bride and groom to visit a school the morning after their wedding.

She recognized the family coat of arms carved into the lintel above the door but aside from that one claim of ownership there was nothing about the building to tell her of its purpose. At least not until they set foot inside. Muffled giggles and shushing sounds came from behind closed doors.

Children? At school on a weekend?

Alex laced his fingers through hers and Loren closed her eyes briefly in an attempt to quell the sudden surge of electricity that flared across her skin at his touch. The double doors ahead of them opened and, as they walked into what appeared to be a small auditorium followed closely by the media contingent, the air filled with the sound of children's voices in song.

Loren couldn't hold back a smile as the pure notes swirled joyfully around them.

"Who are they?" she whispered to Alex.

"Orphans, for the most part. Some are from families who cannot afford to feed and clothe them. They are the lucky ones for at least they have someone."

As the song drew to a close, one little girl separated from the bunch. In her hands she clutched a colorful bouquet of flowers. The caregiver behind her gave an encouraging little push in Loren's direction, but as the child drew closer a barrage of camera flashes filled the air and she tripped and started to fall forward. Loren reached out and caught the little girl before she could face-plant on the hard wooden floor. Some of the flowers, however, did not fare as well and when the child saw their snapped-off heads her lower lip began to wobble.

"Are these for me?" Loren asked, setting the child on her feet and kneeling down in front of her, ignoring the rapid-fire clicks and whirs of the shutters of the cameras trained on them.

The girl nodded shyly, one tear spilling from her lower lid and tracking slowly down a chubby cheek.

"Thank you, they're beautiful." Loren bent forward

and kissed her on the forehead. "And look, here's a flower just for you."

Placing the bouquet gently on the floor beside her, Loren pinched off one of the damaged blooms and tucked it behind the little girl's ear, securing it there with one of the pins from her own hair.

With both disaster, and further tears, averted, the little girl happily scampered back to her group.

"Nicely done," Alex murmured in her ear as he helped Loren rise to her feet.

She hoped he didn't see how his praise affected her, and that he missed the fine tremor that shook the bouquet she now held in her hands as if it was her most precious possession.

The rest of the morning passed uneventfully as she and Alex shared tea with the children and sat through a delightful series of performances. They were then led on a tour of the orphanage and Loren felt her heart break as she was shown the nurseries and the babies there. Under Alex's silent gaze, she took the time to cuddle each one and spent several minutes discussing their welfare with the nurses charged with their care.

By the time they took their leave and got back into his car Loren was shattered. Her arms still ached to hold the parentless children, as if by doing so she could somehow alleviate the harsh blow life had dealt them.

"You did well," Alex commented as they pulled away.

"It was nothing. I adore children, I always have."

"Especially the very young ones."

"Yes, especially them. They've had little opportunity to know love and of anyone they probably deserve it the most." Loren sighed and gently stroked the petals on the now rather tired-looking bouquet she'd been given. "What happens to them?"

"The babies or all the children?"

"All of them."

"Those that can be, are fostered with families on the island. We try and keep extended family involved wherever possible. Sometimes that's not an option, however. Others, like the babies and the toddlers, are usually adopted within months of their arrival at the orphanage. For the ones who remain, they are provided with schooling and, given their aptitude, they have the opportunity to earn scholarships to train in their chosen fields. Of the nurses and teachers there, at least half are returning children."

Loren nodded. She could understand why. The atmosphere there had been one of a strong sense of community and home, as far as they could manage on such a scale.

"Does the orphanage have a patron?"

"Not officially, not since my mother died. It has always traditionally been a del Castillo bride who becomes the orphanage's patroness. Between *Abuelo* and myself we have done what we can but some things definitely require a woman's touch."

"I'd like to take that on."

"You don't have to."

"No, I know that. But I want to, if that's okay."

Loren turned to look at Alex and saw him nod slowly.

"Then it looks as if tradition will live on, hmm?"

"Yes," she said emphatically. "It will."

Loren noticed they were now driving away from the city but not toward the castillo.

"Are we expected somewhere else today?"

"Yes," Alex responded, his eyes on the road ahead.

"Well, are you going to tell me where?" Loren demanded, suddenly feeling decidedly snippy.

The emotional toll of the orphanage visit, on top of the demands of their wedding day only yesterday and the distress of last night were all making themselves felt. She wanted nothing more right now than some peace and quiet.

"Look, I'm not up to any more of your cloak-and-dagger stuff. If you won't say where we're going you may as well let me out of the car right now and I'll find my own way home."

Alex still didn't respond.

"Stop the car," Loren demanded.

"We're almost there."

"Almost where?"

Loren looked around her but all she could see were fields and trees. Then, just in the distance, she caught sight of a series of domed buildings and a fluorescent wind sock on a tall pole.

"An airfield?" she asked. "Why are we going to an airfield?"

"Because our plane leaves in a short while."

"Our plane?" Loren felt as if all she could do was dumbly question everything that came from Alex's mouth.

"Yes, our plane."

She clenched her fists in frustration. Getting information from him was like getting blood from a stone.

"And where would this plane be taking us?" she inquired acerbically, fighting the urge to shout.

"On our honeymoon, of course."

Seven

"Honeymoon?"

Loren's voice reached a pitch that should have made Alex's ears ring. He turned to his new wife and smiled.

"It is usual for a newly married couple, and it is expected of us."

"But my things?"

"Await you on the plane."

"But what about…"

As Loren's voice trailed off he allowed himself a moment of satisfaction. She may have won the first round but this one was definitely his. Until her refusal of his attentions he would have been happy to remain at home on Isla Sagrado with her for their honeymoon as he'd originally planned. But she'd laid down a gauntlet when she'd spurned him last night. He was unaccustomed to anyone saying no to him—least of all the woman who had become his wife. He had serious ground to recover if this marriage was to work.

Her words had plagued him until dawn this morning, when he'd realized what he would have to do. It would be too easy for Loren to avoid him if they stayed at the castillo, or even if they'd gone to avail themselves of one of the luxury holiday homes on the other side of the island. No, he had to take her away, get her wholly to himself.

During their trip to the orphanage it was a simple matter to have her maid pack her things and have them delivered to the private airfield. Her passport and other papers were already in his possession, having been necessary for the legal paperwork of their marriage. A short call to a friend who owned a private holiday villa in Dubrovnik, a mere two-hour flight away on the Croatian coast of the Adriatic Sea, and his plan was in action. Only five minutes out of Dubrovnik old town, the two-bedroom stone cottage was a fifteenth-century delight. Private, fully modernized and the perfect setting for the seduction of his wife.

"Loren, you have nothing to worry about. Trust me."

"Trust you?" She snorted inelegantly. "That's rich, coming from the man who lied to marry me. The man who played on my own sense of values to get what he wanted."

A burr of irritation settled under Alex's skin, aimed more at himself than at her. He couldn't deny that she was painfully right.

"And what did you want, *mi querida?*" he asked, not bothering to hold back the cynicism that laced his endearment. "Don't tell me that you, for your own part, didn't use me a little, also?"

"I never lied to you," she answered quietly, her eyes impossibly somber as they met his.

For a few seconds the air between them thickened with the pain of the emotions he saw reflected in her gaze, and for a brief moment he tasted the bitterness of shame on his tongue. But he could not afford to dwell on his wrongdoing. They were now married and that was final. How successful would their marriage be? Well, that would no doubt depend on the next two weeks.

According to Loren's doctor at the clinic, based on her normal cycle, she would be entering her most fertile time soon. If his plans remained on track there would be no need for the detached methods she'd insisted were the only way she'd get pregnant with his child.

"Come," Alex said, getting out the car and going around to the passenger side to open her door. "The pilot is waiting."

"Where are we going?"

Sensing she'd had enough of secrets, Alex didn't beat around the bush. "Dubrovnik. We can be alone there."

He felt her shrink away from him as the words sank in.

"I hope they have a good selection of reading material," she commented tartly.

Alex laughed out loud, the humor in it startling even himself. If he knew his friend, any reading material would be eclectic and with a heavy emphasis on both cooking and eroticism. Suddenly he couldn't wait to get there.

The flight in the chartered jet was smooth and over within two hours, and it took very little time to clear customs and immigration. The midafternoon sun was bright and hot as they made their way to the waiting car outside the terminal building. Through it all, Loren maintained an icy silence. A silence that Alex looked forward to thawing, one icicle at a time.

The water in the little bay, fifty yards below where the cottage perched on the hillside, was a clear crystal blue. So clear you could even see the rocks and pebbles on the seafloor. Steps had been hewn from the rocky face leading down to the private beach. The cottage itself was a delight. Despite its aged appearance from the outside, Alex had been reassured to discover the interior was comfortably appointed and supplied with everything they would need for the duration of their stay.

He'd asked that the refrigerator-freezer and pantries all be fully stocked, and had stipulated that the cleaners were only to come when he could ensure they were away from the property. He wanted no interruptions to this idyll.

Loren was outside now, on the rear terrace, gazing out at the calm seas, a light breeze tugging at the severe hairdo she'd worn since this morning. Alex's fingers itched to take her hair down and to see her relax. As tense as she was now it would take days for her to unwind. He left the narrow kitchen area and walked across the tiled open-plan living area to where she stood.

"How about a swim before we have an early dinner?" he asked, coming out onto the terrace.

"An early dinner and bed sounds good to me."

"What, not game to tackle the steps?" Alex teased, reaching out a hand to caress her bare shoulder.

She stepped out of reach and sighed. "No, Alex, I'm not game to tackle the steps. In fact I'm not game for anything right now but something to eat and a decent night's sleep."

He gave her a thorough look. She did indeed look washed-out, with the pale strain of tiredness about her eyes more visible now than earlier. He gave a small nod.

"Okay," he said softly. "It's been a busy couple of days. Why don't you shower and change into something comfortable and I'll prepare something for us to eat."

"What? You? Cook?"

Ah, so she was not so tired that she couldn't insult him. That at least was mildly promising.

"I cook very well, as you'll soon discover. Now, you'll find the bedrooms downstairs. If you don't like the one where your cases are, we can swap."

Her eyes widened. "We have separate rooms?"

"Of course. Separate rooms, separate bathrooms. Unless, of course, you'd rather share?"

"No! I mean, no, that's fine. I thought…"

Alex knew exactly what she thought, but he was prepared to bide his time.

"Go on. Freshen up. Take your time, hmm? I want to shower and change myself before starting our meal."

He watched as she walked back inside the cottage and made for the stairs that led to the two bedrooms on the lower level. Yes, he was prepared to bide his time—for now. But he would not wait forever for his recalcitrant bride to accept the very real attraction that lay between them, nor the pleasure he was certain they would find together when she did.

"Loren, wake up. Dinner is ready."

Alex's voice pierced the uneasy slumber Loren had fallen into after taking her shower. The wide expanse of bed, with its pale blue coverlet and fresh cotton pillow slips, had proven too much of an enticement. She stretched as she stirred, forcing her eyes open.

The sun was much lower in the sky now, its light sparkling across the water visible through the floor-length windows like a thousand diamonds skipping across the waves.

Loren pushed herself upright, then snatched at her robe as she felt it slide away from her, exposing her nakedness beneath.

"If you'll give me five minutes, I'll be with you," she said as coolly as she could, hyperconscious of the hot flare of interest in Alex's dark eyes as she gathered the fine silk about her.

His lips had parted, as if he was about to say something but the words had frozen on his tongue. His stare intensified, dropping to the pinpoints of her nipples where they peaked against the soft blush-colored fabric. Her breath caught in her throat, she could almost feel his gaze as if it was a touch against her skin.

She shifted on the bed, untangling her legs and pushing them over the side of the mattress, the movement making her robe slide across her nakedness like a caress. Heat built everywhere—her cheeks, her chest and deeper darker places she didn't want to acknowledge with Alex standing there, staring hungrily at her as if she was to be his appetizer before the evening meal.

"Alex?" Loren asked, finally getting to her feet and welcoming the feel of her robe settling like a cloak about her, hiding her.

"Okay, five minutes. Come out onto the terrace."

He pushed one hand through his hair, the vulnerability of that action striking her square in the chest, before turning for the staircase leading back up to the main floor. Loren took a steadying breath. She hadn't meant to fall asleep but weariness had dragged at every inch of her body. To be woken by him had reminded her starkly of the day she'd arrived at the castillo. Of how he'd kissed the palm of her hand, of how she'd believed their marriage to be so full of promise at that moment.

Even now, her body still thrummed in reaction to Alex's presence, and he hadn't so much as touched her this time. It had only been a look, but it had set her senses on fire despite how angry she was with both him and herself for the debacle they now found themselves in.

Coming here had been a terrible idea. She should have resisted. Should have demanded he take her back to the castillo. She could have avoided him there for most of the time at least. Thrown herself into her duties as patroness of the orphanage. Something. Anything but time in this isolated beauty alone together.

Loren spun on her bare foot and skittered across the floor to where she'd found her suitcase. She hadn't bothered to check its contents before her shower, only grabbing at the first thing she could find at the time, her robe. But now she wondered just what she had to wear. She certainly hoped her maid had covered all possibilities.

She flipped open the lid of the case and rummaged through the layers of swimwear with matching wraps and night wear Bella had packed for her, tossing it all to one side. Finally, thankfully, her fingers closed around some basic cotton T-shirts. Loren lifted them out and put them on the bed behind her before searching through her case again. A small gasp of relief escaped her as she found a batik wraparound skirt her mother had brought back for her from Indonesia a couple of years ago.

All she needed now was clean underwear. Loren pulled open a drawer of the dresser in her room and swiftly put away the things she'd already taken from the case, then methodically unpacked the rest—her frustration rising by degrees until the case was completely empty.

What on earth had her maid been thinking? No underwear? Not even a pair of cotton panties? She prayed that Bella had perhaps run out of room in her case and had packed her underthings with Alex's, but a rapid check of his room showed no sign of anything of hers.

The chime of a clock upstairs reminded her that she'd told Alex she'd only be five minutes. Sliding her robe off, Loren picked up the underwear she'd worn all day. The idea of wearing them again, against clean skin, just felt wrong. She'd have to make sure she rinsed them out before bed tonight and bought some more lingerie tomorrow.

Loren chose the thickest of her T-shirts and pulled it on, then swiftly wrapped the skirt about her waist and slid her feet into flat leather mules.

The cotton of the batik skirt was soft against her buttocks and she was acutely conscious of the brush of fabric caressing her bare skin as she walked up the stairs. Maybe going commando hadn't been such a clever idea after all.

Out on the terrace Alex had set a small round table with a clutch of flowers and had lit a large squat candle that flickered in the gentle evening breeze. Knives, forks and two colorful serviettes completed the setting.

"I'll have to buy you a watch, I think," Alex said as

he walked toward her holding a flute of champagne in each hand.

Loren took one and smiled in return. Not for anything would she admit what had delayed her.

"I thought it was a woman's prerogative to be late."

"When she is as lovely as you, then she's always worth waiting for."

"Even ten years?"

Loren couldn't help it. The words had popped into her mind and past her lips before she could think. Alex tipped the rim of his glass against hers.

"Especially then," he said, a tone to his voice she couldn't quite put her finger on. "To a better beginning, hmm?"

"If you say so," she replied, and took a long delicious sip of the bubbling golden liquid.

She was certain the alcohol bypassed her stomach and went straight to her legs, because all of a sudden they felt tingly, the muscles weak.

"I think I'd better have something to eat. That feels as if it'll have me on my ear if I keep it up."

"Here, try the antipasto."

Alex crossed the few short steps to a stone bench next to the outdoor grill. He picked up a platter and offered it to her, watching again with those velvet black eyes as she selected a sliver of artichoke heart and popped it into her mouth.

"How is that?" he asked as she chewed and swallowed.

"Good. Here, try some."

Without thinking, Loren picked up another piece and proffered it to him. He paused a moment before opening his lips. She held the morsel, startled as his lips closed around the tips of her fingers, their moist warmth and softness sending a jolt of need rocketing down her arm.

"You're right," Alex said after he'd swallowed and taken another sip of wine. "That was very good. Give me something else."

Her hand shook slightly as she chose a stuffed olive and held it before him. He bent his head and slowly took the fruit into his mouth, his tongue hotly sweeping between the pads of her forefinger and thumb as he did so. If she'd thought the wine had made her legs weak, the caress of his tongue made them doubly so.

"Don't!" she cried.

"Don't do what?"

"That. What you just did. Just…don't."

"It disturbs you, my touch?"

Oh, far more than he could ever imagine, but she certainly wasn't going to let him know that painful truth.

"No, I just don't like it. That's all. Here, let me put the platter on the table, then we can help ourselves."

Loren relieved him of the platter and set it on the table next to the candle then settled herself on one of the wrought iron chairs before her legs gave way completely.

The warmth of the sun-heated metal seeped through the thin cotton of her skirt—heating other, more sensitive places. Loren shifted slightly but the motion only enhanced the sensation.

"Uncomfortable out here? Perhaps you'd rather sit indoors," Alex suggested as he topped off their glasses before sitting down opposite her.

"No, it's okay. I'm fine," Loren assured him, all the while forcing her body to relax.

Maybe it was the wine, or perhaps it was merely the

exquisitely beautiful setting, but Loren felt herself begin to relax by degrees. By the time Alex rose to bake fillets of fish, garnished with herbs and lemon and wrapped in foil, on the outdoor grill she was feeling decidedly mellow. She rose from the table and took the near-empty antipasto platter through to the kitchen indoors.

The kitchen was very compact and narrow—a long row of cupboards down one side and the bench top and stove running parallel, with little more than a few feet between them. Loren searched the cupboards for a small dish to put the leftover antipasto into, and then the drawers for some cling wrap to cover it. She'd found a space for the dish in the heavily stocked fridge and was just about to rinse off the platter when Alex came through from the terrace.

He squeezed behind her, far more closely than necessary, she decided with a ripple of irritation.

"The fish is just about done. Can you grab the salad from the fridge? I'll get our plates."

He was so close his breath stirred the hair against the nape of her neck. She could feel the solid heat of his body as he pressed up against her buttocks and reached past her to grab the jug of vinaigrette dressing from the bench top.

She would not react to him; she would not. Loren clenched her hands into fists on the countertop, fighting against the urge to allow her body to lean back into the strength of his. It was almost a physical impossibility in the close confines of the kitchen.

Thankfully, Alex appeared to be oblivious to the racing emotions that swirled inside her. He propped the jug on top of the two dinner plates he'd taken from the crockery pantry behind her and was already on his way back outside.

She took a deep steadying breath before opening the fridge again and lifting out the bowl of salad he'd obviously prepared while she slept. The crisp salad greens, interspersed with feta, olives and succulent freshly cut tomatoes looked mouthwateringly tempting, but nowhere near as appetizing as the man who was currently walking away from her.

No matter how idyllic this setting, the next two weeks would be absolute hell on earth.

Eight

To her surprise, over the next few days, Loren began to relax in a way she hadn't managed in some time. Yet beneath the surface a simmering tension lay between her and Alex.

As yet, he'd made no overtures to force their relationship onto a physical level. By day she was eternally grateful for that, but every night as she lay tangled in her sheets aching for the man who slept only a corridor width away from her room, she wondered whether she had indeed made the right decision in denying him her body.

He lied to you, she reminded herself. *He appealed to you on an emotional level he knew you could not refuse. He manipulated you for his own ends.*

But he hadn't done so for personal gain, she argued back silently as the moon traversed the sky and she wriggled against her mattress and stared out through the glass doors that led onto a small balcony off her room. He'd done it for his grandfather, to assuage the old man's sudden and irrational fears about the family's longevity.

It doesn't matter, she argued back again, thumping her pillow in frustration as she tried to get comfortable. He should have told her the truth from the start. How on earth did he expect to embark upon a marriage without even honesty between them? Without truth, they had nothing, because they certainly didn't have love. At least, not a love that was reciprocated.

Giving up on sleep, Loren rose from her bed and walked over to the French doors. She pushed them open and stepped out onto the balcony. The night air was balmy and still, enveloping her in a myriad of scents and sounds. She looked up at the clear night sky, observing the constellations so different to how they appeared back in New Zealand, and suddenly she was struck with a sense of loneliness that brought sudden tears to her eyes.

A tiny sob pushed up from her chest and ejected into the darkness. She gripped the iron balcony railing tight beneath her hands, but no matter how hard she squeezed she could not stop the flow of tears down her cheeks.

This wasn't how she imagined her life would be. She'd expected happiness. A mutual respect between herself and Alex. Respect that would hopefully grow to become more. Loren dragged a shaking breath into her aching lungs and blinked against the moisture that continued to well in her eyes. It seemed that now she'd started to cry, she was incapable of stopping.

The air beside her shifted and she turned her head to see Alex standing on the balcony beside her. Wearing only a pair of silken pajama pants, he looked like some god risen from the sea in the moonlight. Silver beams caressed the muscled width of his chest and shoulders, throwing the lean, defined strength into shadowed relief.

"What's wrong?"

"I..." Loren shook her head, averting her eyes, both unwilling and unable to verbalize what ailed her.

Warm, strong arms closed around her in comfort, drawing her against the smooth plane of his chest.

At first she resisted—she didn't trust him, she couldn't—but his arms tightened around her and for just that moment she wanted to forget all her dashed hopes and give in to his silent support. She let her cheek settle against his chest, her gulped sobs calming as her breathing adjusted to his, her heartbeat slowing to his strong steady rhythm.

She felt Alex's chin drop to the top of her head, felt the slight tug of the bristles of his beard in her hair. She nestled in closer, relishing the feel of his body against hers. His masculine form felt unfamiliar to her and yet instantly recognizable—as if this was where she had belonged all her life, safe within the circle of his arms.

Fresh tears sprang to her eyes at the foolishly irrational thought. She may have thought she belonged with him, but the truth couldn't be more converse.

"Hush, Loren," he whispered against her hair. "We will work this out."

"I don't think we can, Alex."

"One way or another, we will work it out."

With a powerful sweep of muscle, Alex lifted her into his arms and took her back into her room. Still holding her to him he settled onto the mattress and leaned back against the padded headrest. Loren's head rested against his shoulder, her legs across his lap. She struggled to sit up and tried to push him away. With her defenses as weak as they were right now she couldn't afford to give him any leeway.

"Relax, I'm not going to try and force you into anything. You're upset. Let me comfort you."

She hesitated a moment before allowing the slow circular motion of his hand across her back to soothe her. Eventually her eyes slid closed and she allowed her senses to be filled with the gentleness of his touch, the steadiness of his breathing and the delicious warmth and scent of his bare skin.

Alex felt Loren relax by degrees until she finally drifted back off into sleep. Inside, his thoughts were in turmoil. Each day that passed saw them spending practically every waking moment together, yet each day she seemed to withdraw from him more and more. So much so that tonight she hadn't even felt as if she could accept his comfort.

Ironically, that had hurt more than the days they'd spent together so far, where he'd fought to keep his libido firmly under control, and far more than the nights where he'd lain on his bed, wondering if a quick dip in the Adriatic Sea would help diminish the fire raging under his skin.

He remembered back to a time when she'd been just a toddler. Her parents had been visiting his and for one reason or another she'd taken a tumble. Rather than seek consolation from either her father or mother, she'd tottered toward him, past them both, and offered her grazed palms for his inspection and reassurance that she was okay.

His brothers had teased him mercilessly. He'd been all

of ten or eleven years old and they'd thought it hilarious that Loren had come to him. But now, in the moonlit night, with her slumbering in his arms, he remembered how it had secretly made him feel. Remembered the sense of responsibility and duty he had to protect her and keep her safe from all harm.

And here he was now, having harmed her in the worst way possible. He'd betrayed her trust and brought her back to a world that was no longer familiar to her, to people whose only memories of her were as a child and not as a woman with hopes and dreams of her own.

Anger curled a tight fist deep in his gut. He should never have interrupted her life. Never have brought her back. She'd had a new world in New Zealand yet she'd eschewed all of that to return to the old one she'd left behind. For him. He owed it to her to somehow make up for that wrong.

He knew that he still had to fulfill his duty to his grandfather and the people of Isla Sagrado. But for the first time, he admitted to himself that duty to family extended beyond his brothers and *Abuelo*. He was a married man now. His wife came first.

Bright bursts of morning light stabbed at Loren's eyes, dragging her to full consciousness. Beneath her, her bed had grown increasingly lumpy as she stretched and squirmed awake.

Lumpy? Realization and remembrance dawned with a rush. That lump was her husband; in fact, it was one particular part of her husband. Sometime during the night Alex had slid them both down onto the mattress and, as unaccustomed as she was to sharing a bed with anyone—let alone her husband—Loren had remained sprawled halfway across his body.

Even now the delicious scent of his skin, that blend of spice and citrus tang combined with the heat of his own special smell, teased at her nostrils and warmed her in places that made her squirm again.

"Loren, you will have to stop doing that or I cannot be answerable for my actions."

"Oh!" she exclaimed, springing away from him as if he'd delivered a high-voltage current directly to her.

She jumped up off the bed and kept her eyes averted from his prone form, from the irrefutable evidence that her actions had not left him unaffected.

"I'm sorry, I didn't mean to."

Alex sighed. She heard him stretch on the sheets and fought the urge to turn her eyes to him, to drink in the sight of his male beauty.

"Yes, I am sure you didn't mean to."

He sounded so tired and a pang of remorse plucked at her conscience. He'd come to her in the night when she was at her most vulnerable and he'd offered solace. No questions asked.

"I'm sorry, Alex. Truly. And I…" She pressed her lips together, looking for the right words. "Thank you for last night."

"*De nada*. It is what couples do, after all, is it not? Offer one another ease?"

Her eyes flew to his. She hadn't misunderstood the double entendre in his remark if the look on his face was anything to go by.

"Yes, well, I appreciate it." She shifted her weight from one foot to the other, unsure of what else to say or do.

"Go and have your shower, Loren. You are perfectly safe walking past me. As I said last night, I am not going to force you into anything."

"Anything else, you mean."

Alex sat up and swung his legs over the side of the bed. He stood and Loren's gaze was inexorably drawn to his torso, to his taut stomach and the fine scattering of dark hair that arrowed down from his belly button to the waistband of his pajama pants.

There was a thread of steel in his voice when he spoke, a thread that warned he was barely holding on to his temper.

"Remarks like that are unbecoming to a woman of your intelligence. Whatever my sins, I did not force you into marrying me."

Loren dropped her head in shame. He was right. She had to stop treating him as if he was solely to blame for their position. He made a sound of disgust and she heard him walk past her and leave the room, his own bedroom door slamming shut behind him.

She should apologize. Before she could change her mind, Loren followed him and knocked tentatively on his door. At his response she slowly opened it and stepped inside.

"I shouldn't have said what I did. I'm sorry."

Alex gave her a hard look but the small frown lines that bracketed his mouth eased a little. He gave her a small nod.

"Apology accepted."

"Thank you." Unsure of what to do next, Loren started to close the door again. "I'll leave you to get dressed."

"Loren?"

"Yes?"

"I am not such an ogre, you know. I am merely a man. A man with responsibilities and needs."

There was something in the tone of his voice that

spoke of a deep-seated longing that struck straight to her core. She felt the inexorable pull of it even as she started to move across the room.

He stood still and watched her as she came toward him, his stance proud. There was a frankness in his eyes that spoke straight to Loren's heart. In all of this she hadn't stopped to consider what this marriage had cost him. He hadn't married her for his own gain but for that of the people of Isla Sagrado and for the sake of his grandfather's fears. Whether Alex himself believed in the curse was irrelevant. He'd married her out of his respect and love for *Abuelo* and in determination to do whatever it took to lift the spirits of the people who looked to the del Castillo family for so much.

Loren lifted one hand and raised it to Alex's cheek, her fingers gently cupping his whisker-rough skin. She slowly rose on her tiptoes and pressed her lips to his. Softly, shyly, she kissed him. To her chagrin, his lips remained unresponsive beneath hers. Uncertain, she started to pull her hand away, but Alex's hand shot up to hold it there and to press it against his face, his long fingers covering hers.

"Don't play with me, Loren. Even I have limits."

"I…I'm not playing, Alex."

She reached up to kiss him again, this time feeling a zing of power as she felt his lips tremble beneath hers. She traced the seam of his mouth with the tip of his tongue, feeling suddenly bolder than she'd ever felt before. He was a man who had everything and wanted for nothing. This was all she could give him. Her love.

Alex's arms wrapped around her, pulling her against his hard male form, showing her in no uncertain terms that he was more than prepared to accept what she offered. Loren stroked her hands across his shoulders, loving the feel of his leashed strength beneath her fingertips. His body burned into hers, making the light summer tank top and cotton shorts she'd worn to bed feel as if they were too much against her skin.

She strained against him, wanting more, yet not quite fully understanding what it was she needed. Alex's strong hands skimmed down her back and over the mounds of her buttocks, cupping them and pulling her up higher against him. Angling the part of her body that ached with a demanding throb against his arousal. A shock of pleasure radiated through her at the pressure of his sex against her. She felt herself grow damp and hot.

He pulled her to him again and flexed his hips against her, starting a rhythm that made her whole body pulse with need. Loren slid her hands up the cords of his neck and knotted her fingers in his short dark hair, pulling his face down to hers, wanting to absorb every part of him any way she could.

"Lift your legs and put them around my waist," Alex commanded, his voice vibrating with desire.

Through the haze of passion that focused her senses only on the touch and taste of the man in her arms, she managed to comply. Alex walked them to the bed and laid her down on the sheets, still rumpled from last night. Without losing physical contact, he lay down with her, their bodies aligning perfectly, his legs cradled between hers.

Loren's breasts ached and swelled against the soft cotton of her top, her nipples pressing like twin points against Alex's chest. At this moment she hated the barrier that stood between them. As if he read her mind, Alex shifted his weight slightly, then his hands were at the hem of her top, pushing it up and over her head and exposing her small round breasts with their blush-colored peaks.

"So perfect," he murmured as he traced the outline of first one dusky pink nipple, then the other, with the tip of his finger.

She watched, unable to speak, unable to move, as he moistened his finger with his tongue then retraced the shape of her again. A shudder rippled through her, bringing a small smile of intent to Alex's face. Then he brought his lips to a tight bud, his tongue flicking out to mimic what his finger had been doing only seconds before.

Another shudder spread through her body, this one bringing a swell of pleasure with it, a swell that ballooned as Alex's lips closed over her nipple and sucked hard. She nearly leapt off the bed, her body arching into him, wanting all he could give her. His hips held her pinned against the mattress and she hooked her legs around his, running her feet over his calves, the slippery fabric of his pajamas soft and sensual against her soles.

His body felt so different from her own. Stronger, firmer and with an energy vibrating from deep inside of him that excited her both mentally and physically. She knew what was yet to come, knew that there would be discomfort, possibly even pain, but she also knew to the depths of her soul that this was totally right. That out of anyone, Alex was the only man she could ever be this intimate with.

She gasped aloud as he scraped his teeth over her nipple before lavishing more of the same attention to its twin. She thought she would go mad with the sensations he wrung from her body. He was trailing his tongue along the curve of her breast, sending a rash of goose bumps to pepper her skin as, one by one, he traced each rib, lower and lower.

Despite the warm air she felt a shiver flow across her skin. His hands were at the drawstring tie of her shorts, she felt the bow loosen, the fabric begin to give way. Alex pulled himself up onto his knees and tugged her shorts away from her, exposing her body's deepest intimacy to his scorching gaze.

She felt wanton under the power of his stare and she squirmed against the sheets, relishing the feel of high-thread-count cotton softness against the bare skin of her buttocks. Her movement caused a flush to deepen high on Alex's cheekbones, made his eyes darken even more. He reached for her, his broad hands holding her hips firmly, his fingers splayed across her skin as he lowered his face to the V at the apex of her thighs.

Loren tensed, unsure of what to expect. All tension flowed from her as he pressed his lips with unerring accuracy at the central spot that was the heart of the sensations pouring through her. She felt his tongue gently glide over her sensitized nerves and lost all sense of reality. Again and again his tongue swept over her, gentle at first then firmer until, when she thought she could bear it no longer, he closed his mouth over that spot and suckled as he had done with her nipples only moments ago.

Sensation splintered through her body, at first sharp and then in increasing undulating waves of sheer pleasure reaching a crescendo of feeling she'd never dreamed herself capable of. Her entire body tensed, taut like a bow, before she collapsed back against the bed, weak, spent. Sated.

She sensed Alex's movement, heard the slither of

fabric as he shucked off his pajama bottoms. She opened her eyes as he knelt between her splayed legs, watched as he stroked his hand from base to tip of his erection. He positioned himself at her entrance and she felt the hot, blunt probe of his flesh.

A sudden shaft of fear shot through her. "I haven't… I mean, I've never…"

"Shh," Alex said soothingly. "I know. I will take care of you, Loren. Trust me."

She locked her gaze with his, searching for any hint that he could be untrue to her, even now as they lay together with nothing but their past between them.

"I do. I trust you, Alex," she whispered.

"That's my girl," he replied.

He leaned down and kissed her, his tongue sweeping inside her mouth to tangle with hers. She welcomed his invasion, letting her senses focus on the thrust and parry of his kiss, and the blend of her essence and the flavor that was all his.

She felt his hips slowly push against hers, felt him slide within her body. She stiffened involuntarily, unsure how she would accommodate him, but then he withdrew and did the same thing again, this time probing a little farther, waiting a little longer. Her body stretched and molded around him, at first uncomfortable and then not. Tremors racked his frame as he held himself partially within her. The next time he moved, she pressed back, taking him inside her a little farther.

A new sensation began to build inside her, one that demanded more, demanded him, so much so that when he thrust all the way inside her on his next stroke she ignored the sharp tear of pain and clutched at his hips, urging him to continue. With no barrier impeding him, Alex deepened his strokes, propelling her once more toward the growing pleasure whose epicenter lay hidden within her.

He gathered momentum and Loren found her body meeting him stroke for stroke, both of them reaching for the shadowy pinnacle of their desire. And then it burst upon her. Wave after wave. Bigger than before, deeper than before. A cry of sheer delight broke on her lips as Alex shuddered in release against her, before collapsing, spent, against her body.

In the aftermath of their lovemaking Loren gave herself over to the delicious lassitude that spread through her body. She knew of physical pleasure, but she'd never dreamed it could be like this. She trailed her fingers up and down the length of Alex's sweat-dampened spine and in that moment she loved him more than she ever had before.

Alex watched his wife as she slept naked in his arms. His heart still hammered in his chest. Coming down from the high of their first physical union had taken its time. Even now he still felt twinges of pleasure, aftershocks of satisfaction that seemed endless in their reach.

It had never been like this before, with anyone. Somehow the knowledge that he was Loren's husband and her first lover had lent a different note to the act itself. He'd always prided himself on being a considerate lover but it had become even more important to him to ensure that her first time be special than he'd believed possible.

And in giving he'd also received. The climax that had wrung his body dry had been spectacular. He rested one hand on her smooth, flat belly. Perhaps even now he'd managed to achieve his goal.

He had scarcely been able to believe his luck when she'd followed him to his room. After last night he'd hoped they'd gained a new high ground together, but her reaction to him this morning had dashed that hope. Until he'd heard that gentle knock at his bedroom door.

Alex dropped his head back against the pillow. He'd made that first time special for her. No matter what came after, she would always have that. Somehow that truth didn't help assuage the kernel of guilt that had nestled somewhere in his chest. She deserved to have her first time with someone who loved her. But whatever she deserved, Alex was what she had—what she *would* have for the rest of her life, since he had no intention of ever letting her go.

She stirred against him, her slender body curling around his as naturally as if they'd always slept together. He'd had enough of thinking, enough of trying to justify his decisions. Action came more naturally.

Pushing aside thoughts that could only plague him, Alex gathered Loren closer to him and began to stroke her with long sweeps of his hand. He was already hard for her again. Mindful that she might be tender, he decided this time to take things even slower.

She woke as he dragged his fingertips along the inner curve of her hip. A tremulous smile pulled at her lips, soon to be lost in a moan that tore from her throat as he slid one hand between her legs to gently stroke her soft folds.

"Too much? Too soon?" he asked, watching her face carefully, hoping against hope that she would say no to his inquiry.

"Oh!" she cried as he brushed over her clitoris. "No, not too much. Not too soon."

"Good." He smiled in return and focused on the task at hand.

She had so much still to learn about the pleasure they could give one another, and he thanked his lucky stars she was such an eager pupil.

Her legs began to quake in what he recognized as the precursor to her climax and he slowed his touch, drawing out the pleasure for her as far as he was able. When he himself could hold on no longer he pulled her beneath him and sank inside her, the action sending her skyrocketing over the edge. Just like that he was with her, his body pulsing, spilling his seed, his mind filled with nothing more than wave after wave of ecstasy and the overwhelming sense of rightness that consumed him with Loren in his arms.

Nine

While Loren loved living at the castillo she adored the compactness of this stone cottage perched on the hillside. The small kitchen that had so tormented her with its closeness when she and Alex had first arrived was now a teasing adventure. And, even though they had neighbors in abundance, with the mature trees and the staggered terrace style of building around them, she felt as if she and Alex were totally isolated. There was a delightful sense of freedom in knowing that she could do whatever she wished.

It had been one glorious week since the morning they'd first made love. A week filled with discovery as she'd learned to bring the strong man she'd married exquisite physical delight and receive the same in return. Her one regret was that while they grew closer physically with each encounter, Alex continued to maintain an emotional distance between them she couldn't seem to break through.

They'd done all the tourist things available in the area, enjoying the food and the countryside almost as much as they enjoyed one another in the close confines of the cottage. Going back to the castillo would be difficult but she had very definite plans for her and Alex to plan more time alone together.

A smile pulled at her lips as she heard Alex come up the stairs from the pebble beach below where they'd been swimming together. Only the knowledge that they'd been visible to some of their neighbors while in the water had held them back from making love as they'd floated together. But now, her smile deepened, now they were in their own cocoon of privacy again and she could do what she wished.

Alex lowered his body onto one of the sun loungers on the terrace, the white-and-navy striped cushion beneath him accenting the depth of his tan. Black swim trunks clung to him, outlining his hips and the tops of his thighs. Loren's mouth watered at the prospect of what lay hidden beneath the dark fabric.

Her hands gripped the edges of the tray she'd brought through from the kitchen and she put it down on the terrace table, none too gently, and grabbed at one of the highball glasses before it toppled over. Even after all they'd shared he continued to have the power to rattle her senses. Just thinking about him had her heart racing, her lower body flushed and eager for his touch.

She forced her hands to still so she could grab the pitcher of iced tea and pour two glasses. She took one over to Alex, aware of his eyes watching every step she took toward him.

"Cool drink?" she said, offering him a glass.

"After that swim I think I need more than a cool drink."

He took the proffered drink and drained the glass with a series of long, slow pulls. Loren watched, mesmerized by the play of muscles working in his throat. Alex put his glass down on the terrace beside him, the unmelted blocks of ice tinkling in the bottom, and gestured to Loren to join him on the lounger.

"Here, come and sit with me."

"There's no room," Loren half protested.

"So use your imagination." Alex smiled in return.

Loren lifted the folds of the emerald green sarong that matched her bikini and straddled the lounger, settling on Alex's strong thighs.

"Like this?" she said, her voice a husky rasp as she felt the hairs on his legs tickle the already sensitive flesh of her inner thighs.

"Oh yes, exactly like that."

Alex pushed the flimsy sarong aside, baring her legs completely and exposing the shadowed area of her body at the apex of her thighs. He traced the outside edge of her bikini bottoms, from the tie at her hip to her inner thigh and back again.

Heat and moisture flooded to her lower regions and she drew in a sharp breath as one finger slipped inside the edge of her bikini pants to brush lightly over her inner folds. Back and forth he stroked, until finally he slid one finger inside her. She clenched her inner muscles against him, tilting her pelvis forward and rocking slightly against his palm.

"You like that?" he asked, his voice deep and low.

"You know I do," she whispered back and gasped anew as he slid another finger inside her.

With his free hand, Alex tugged at the bows that held

her bikini bottoms together and pulled the fabric away, dropping it beside the lounger, exposing her and what he was doing to her.

Loren looked down and felt another sharp jolt of pleasure rock through her body as she watched him. She ached for release, wanted to rush toward the starburst of pleasure she knew was just around the corner, yet conversely wanted to make it last as long as she could. When Alex's thumb settled against the hooded bud of nerve endings at her core she nearly lost it, but she clenched against him, harder, tighter, determined to remain in control.

"Come for me," Alex commanded, his voice guttural now, his eyes molten with desire.

He started a gentle circular motion with his thumb, slowly increasing and releasing pressure with each stroke. She was near mindless when she felt the first flutters of her orgasm begin to wash over her. Finally, she could hold back no more. She tilted her hips some more, leaning into his hand, and let his magical touch send her flying over the edge.

Loren slowly returned to her surroundings, to the man who lay beneath her. A beautiful sensual smile pulled at his lips and she felt herself smile back in return.

"You're beautiful when you climax, did you know that?" he said.

Loren felt the heat of a blush stain her cheeks. Even after what they'd just done she still felt embarrassed when he spoke to her like that. In lieu of a response she leaned forward and captured his lips with hers. He tasted of a delicious combination of sunshine, tea and a hint of mint.

She broke off the kiss and pulled free from his arms.

"It seems to me that things are a little unbalanced here," she said.

"Unbalanced?"

Loren traced the prominent outline of his erection through his swim trunks with her fingernails.

"You heard me."

"Hmm, you could be right," Alex said, his speech thickening as she continued to tease his length. "It's always important for things to be balanced, of course."

"I was thinking the exact same thing," Loren said and rose from the lounger in a fluid movement.

She undid the knot of her sarong and let it drop to the terrace floor, and then undid her bikini top, allowing it to fall on top of the puddle of emerald green fabric. Her nipples tightened in anticipation in spite of the warm air as she bent toward her husband.

"Lift your hips," she said.

As he did, she eased his trunks down, exposing him to her hungry gaze and her eager hands. She tossed the shorts behind her, uncaring of where they fell.

"Now, spread your legs," she requested. She knelt between them on the striped cushion as he silently obeyed.

Loren leaned forward and took his erection in her hand, curling her fingers around the velvet hard length and stroking firmly from base to tip and back again. Bending down, she swirled her tongue around the tip of him. Again and again, before gently rasping her teeth over the smooth head. She smiled as a harsh groan tore from Alex's lips.

"Too much? Do you want me to stop?" she teased. She knew what his answer would be before he could even verbalize it.

"Stop now and I may have to punish you severely," Alex said through gritted teeth.

Loren laughed softly and took him in her mouth. She loved that she could do this to him, for him. Just a few months ago, she would never have dreamed she could be so bold, so forward, but he'd taught her much in this past week. Most importantly, he'd taught her how to give him pleasure and how to draw that pleasure out until he finally let go of the iron control with which he held himself.

She looked up at his face. His head was thrown back against the chair cushion, his eyes squeezed closed. He'd flung his arms back and his hands gripped the back of the lounger. Loren took him deeper into her mouth, suckled more firmly at his tip, relished the hot salty taste of him as he fought to hold back.

Then she stopped, releasing him to the warm air around them. Alex tilted his head back up, his eyes narrowed as he watched her rise and spread her legs before lowering herself back down. She guided his shaft to her with unerring accuracy.

His hands let go of the lounger, finding a new home cupping her breasts as she took his length inside her body. She leaned against the strength of his arms as she started a rhythm guaranteed to bring them both to completion. Beneath her she could feel Alex's body tremble with the sheer force of his indomitable will. She knew he would not allow himself the freedom of his climax unless he knew she too was near.

But this time she wanted to drive him over the edge. This time she wanted to show him that love was not all about control or always about giving. Sometimes it was about taking what you needed, when it was offered.

And she was offering herself. Everything. Her heart, her body, her soul.

She knew the second she'd overcome his resistance. Felt the moment his body began to let go. Intense joy flooded her mind. Hard on the heels of that sense of elation, her own orgasm shuddered through her.

Loren collapsed against Alex's body, both of them slicked with sweat, and lay against his chest, listening to the rapid thud of his heartbeat.

"I love you, Alexander del Castillo," she whispered.

In answer he wrapped his arms around her and pulled her even closer—but the words she wished to hear, more than any other from his mouth, remained unsaid.

They'd been back from Dubrovnik for nearly a week. Already their time together seemed as if it was a distant memory. Alex had disappeared back into his work as if nothing else existed. Apparently bookings at the resort were on the increase. The publicity surrounding their marriage had seemed to have done the trick as far as lifting the profile of Isla Sagrado in the media. Once again the island nation was becoming a popular holiday destination for the moneyed and famous.

Loren was pleased for Alex that things were improving so steadily although she sometimes wished the demands of his work were less so they could recapture some of the wonder of their honeymoon again. It was rare that Alex arrived home before she went to bed anymore, and he hadn't been to her room or in her bed since their first night back.

She'd believed they'd built a foundation for their future together in those exquisite days and nights at the cottage, yet now she was no longer so certain. This morning a courier had delivered her a copy of their prenuptial agreement for her records. It served as a sobering reminder of the parameters under which she and Alex had married.

Had he encouraged their intimacy, their discovery of one another, purely to make the child he was so determined to produce? Before the wedding, he'd gone with her to the doctor where she'd had a physical check and the doctor had discussed her cycle. Alex had known when she should have been most fertile. That that time had coincided so soon after their wedding was fortuitous, he'd said, as they'd driven back from the clinic.

Was that why he'd been so patient with her? So passionate? Had making a baby been the sole object of their lovemaking?

Her period had been due a few days ago but as yet hadn't made its appearance. She placed a hand on her stomach, wondering if Alex would have his wish after all. As much as she desired to bear his child, she wanted more from their marriage before she felt ready to bring a child into it. Especially now she knew just what it would be like to share a life with him.

Unless, of course, their honeymoon had been a farce—nothing but a means to an end for Alex.

"Señora?"

Loren turned from the flowers she'd been arranging for the dining table tonight and greeted the maid who'd brought a cordless phone on a silver tray.

"A call for me?" she said, picking up the handset.

"Sí, it is *Señor* del Castillo."

Loren felt an instant rush of elation and hit the hold button, saying "hello" before the maid had even left the room.

"Loren, I left some papers in my office at home and I can't spare Giselle to come to the castillo to collect them. Would you be able to bring them to the resort?"

Hard on the heels of disappointment that he didn't so much as ask how she was feeling, she found herself agreeing to do so.

"Sure, I can do that. I'm expected at the orphanage at lunchtime for a concert with the children. I can stop in to your office on my way through."

"Thanks, I appreciate it. You'll find them in the blue folder on my desk."

Without waiting for her to say goodbye, Alex disconnected the call. He'd treated her as no more than one of his staff. Loren felt a bubble of anger rise in her throat. Anger mixed with another emotion she didn't want to examine too closely for fear it would bring her to tears.

She swallowed hard against the obstruction in her throat and squared her shoulders. She would tell him what she thought of his manner when she saw him. If he thought he could treat her like that and get away with it, well, he had another think coming.

Half an hour later Loren drove her new Alfa Romeo Spider—a belated wedding gift surprise from Alex when they'd arrived home—toward the resort's main offices and pulled into the visitor parking lot outside. She looked around for Alex's Lamborghini but it was nowhere to be seen. Strange, but then perhaps he'd used a driver today.

She collected the blue folder he'd requested from the passenger seat and walked with clipped, sure steps toward the office door. Inside, with a wave to the receptionist, Loren made her way directly to Alex's office.

Even as hurt and angry as she was, her heart lifted at the prospect of seeing him like this in the middle of the day. Perhaps she'd even be able to persuade him to come with her to the lunchtime concert.

Her hopes were dashed, however, as she was greeted by Giselle at Alex's office door.

"Oh, thanks. You finally brought them, did you?" Giselle said, unfolding her elegant long legs from behind her desk and coming to relieve Loren of the folder.

"I'd like to give this directly to Alex myself, if you don't mind," Loren stated, holding firmly on to the cardboard packet.

"Oh, he's not here."

"He's not? Where—"

"Didn't he tell you? Of course, obviously not. He had a meeting in Puerto Seguro with some potential investors for the resort expansion. I'll take these with me as I'm headed that way now."

Loren let go of the documents. As she did so she was assailed with a sense of dizziness. Giselle was quick to react, putting a hand under Loren's elbow and guiding her to sit on a large sofa against one wall.

"Are you okay?" Giselle asked. "You've gone awfully pale."

"It's nothing. I skipped breakfast this morning and I shouldn't have."

"Are you sure that's all it is? After all, Alex is a very—" Giselle paused for a moment, her face suddenly reflective "—virile man. And you've just had a couple of weeks at the cottage in Dubrovnik, yes? It's so beautiful there. So deliciously private and romantic, don't you think?"

Giselle spoke so knowingly—indeed, with such familiarity—that nausea pitched through Loren's body.

Oblivious to Loren's discomfort, the other woman continued.

"Alex will be pleased if you've fallen pregnant so soon." She patted Loren's hand. "That would mean he'd be able to go back to normal so much sooner than he'd planned."

What exactly was Giselle referring to? It wasn't as if subtlety was the woman's strong point. She had to be referring to Alex and her resuming their relationship.

"Back to normal?" Loren asked, hoping against hope that her suspicions were ridiculous.

"I'm sure you know exactly what I mean." Giselle smiled in return but there was little humor in the cold glitter of her eyes. Instead, the proprietary nature of the curve of her lips said it all.

"Oh, dear, look at the time. I'd better get these to Alex before he comes bellowing on the phone, demanding to know where I am. I'll let you see yourself out. You look as though you could do with a few minutes to yourself."

Within seconds Loren was left alone with nothing but the slightly cloying scent of Giselle's perfume in the air around her.

She shook her head slowly. No. What Giselle had said couldn't be true. Go back to his old life and ways? Alex wasn't that kind of man, surely. Not the Alex she thought she knew, anyway. Before their marriage his playboy lifestyle had been well represented in the media, but months before he'd come to New Zealand he'd all but dropped out of circulation. She'd noted it at the time, long before she'd had any reason to believe his new and uncharacteristic circumspection might have anything to do with her.

Loren leaned against the big square cushion of the

couch. Had it all been part of his carefully orchestrated plan to prove to everyone that he could break the curse? Even *Abuelo* would have had a hard time believing that Alex would have gone directly from playboy bachelorhood to married. But what would happen now? Once their PR campaign of a marriage had served its purpose and they'd fulfilled the terms of the prenuptial agreement, would Alex revert back to his old social life, leaving her to sit at home with the children?

Children? Oh, Lord. What if she *was* pregnant? There was no way she'd raise a child here with him if he was going to have affairs behind her back—or even in front of her, if it came to that.

One thing was certain, Loren thought. If she was pregnant, Alex would be the last person she'd be telling until she knew exactly what kind of father he planned to be.

Ten

Loren had a pounding headache by the time she left the orphanage after the children's concert. As had become her habit, she had spent an extra couple of hours in the babies' nursery. Two had already been fostered, with a view to full adoption once all the paperwork had been processed, but a newborn had been admitted, sadly undernourished and displaying all the signs of fetal alcohol syndrome.

It broke her heart to think that a child could be abused so poorly, even before birth, and she spent extra time with the wee mite.

She drove back to the castillo slowly, her mind on the children she'd just been with and the prospect of a child of her own. That it would satisfy Alex was a given, but what of the child? Would Alex even be able to spend any time with the baby? He already worked excessively long hours. So much so that since their return they'd barely seen one another, let alone shared a bed.

Was that to be the tenor of their marriage? Passionate couplings to bring forth an heir and nothing in between?

It wasn't what she'd expected of marriage. As difficult as her parents' relationship had been, they had truly loved each other at the beginning. And even when it started to fall apart and the arguments began, they'd been together until her mother—in a fit of pique at her husband—had taken things a step too far with a mutual friend and had betrayed her marriage vows.

Naomi had admitted to Loren, when she'd been about twenty, that she'd regretted forcing Loren's father's hand to divorce her that way, but she hadn't seen any other way out. He'd insisted he still loved her, a fact Loren truly believed, but for Naomi that love had sputtered and died like a guttered candle in the face of the arguments that had become habitual between them.

Loren felt a sharp ache in her chest at the memories, still vivid, of frozen silences between her parents. Silences that would be periodically broken by vicious arguments late into the night when she was supposed to be sleeping.

She'd been about ten years old the first time she became aware of how contentious her parents' marriage had become. Back then she'd hidden under her bedcovers until things had grown silent. By the time she was in her teens she'd sit at the top of the stairs and listen as they threw accusations back and forth.

She could still hear every venomous word of the final exchange that had led to the divorce—of her mother's admission of infidelity, of her father's sobs later after her mother had withdrawn to bed.

Loren swallowed against the sudden lump in her throat and blinked back burning tears. She didn't want that for her child or children. In all conscience she could not bring a child into an unhappy and unstable relationship right from the very start.

But she'd agreed to give Alex the heir he'd stipulated in the prenup. She was honor bound to do so. It was a difficult predicament she found herself in—especially when she wanted so much more.

Only a week ago she'd almost begun to believe her husband might even be beginning to share her feelings for him. That he might be starting to fall a little in love with her, too. But the cold distance he'd maintained since their return had dashed her hopes.

Suddenly the prospect of returning to the castillo held no appeal. She pulled over to the shoulder of the road, then executed a U-turn and headed back in the direction of Puerto Seguro. She needed to be around other people, people who didn't have an agenda as far as she was concerned.

Alex looked up from his seat at the head of the boardroom table in Rey's offices, where he'd arranged to meet with potential investors today. As Giselle approached, he was relieved to see the folder he'd requested from Loren in his PA's hand. A burst of gratitude toward his wife filled him, accompanied by a deep sense of regret that he hadn't been able to spend more time with her lately. He missed her and their nights together with a physical ache, but the negotiations he was in the process of finalizing were vitally important and required all of his attention. Besides, he'd decided it would be selfish to wake her when he arrived home every night after midnight. Alex silently resolved to make it up to Loren once the deal was signed.

Giselle sidled up next to him, one breast brushing not so subtly against his shoulder as she leaned across and put the folder in front of him. There was a time when her actions might have been welcome. That time was well past. He drew away from her touch and noted the tiny crease on her forehead as her brows pulled together in a silent query.

"That will be all, thank you, Giselle."

"All?" She smiled, giving him the sloe-eyed look he'd once found so attractive. "Well, if you're quite sure…"

"Absolutely certain. I am a married man. I shouldn't have to remind you of that."

A married man who'd been neglecting his duties to his wife shamefully. His conscience pricked again.

"Loren looked a little peaked today," Giselle remarked nonchalantly as she finally moved away from his side.

A sudden swell of concern surged through him. "Peaked?" he asked. "What makes you say that?"

"She had a bit of a turn when she brought the papers in from the castillo. Perhaps you've been keeping her up a little too late at night. After all, as we both know, a man of your appetites—"

"That's quite enough," Alex interrupted before she could finish her sentence.

"I was only saying. Anyway, she told me she hadn't eaten breakfast this morning but I couldn't help but wonder if a little del Castillo isn't already making his presence felt. You did want her pregnant, didn't you?"

Pregnant? It was most definitely what he wanted.

The possibility that Giselle spoke the truth bloomed

in his mind, overtaking rational thought. Loren, pregnant with his child? All legalities and legends aside, he hadn't given enough credence to how he'd feel when such an event became a reality. The prospect that his son or daughter could even now be growing in Loren's womb caused an unexpected tightness to coil around his heart. A tightness intermingled with an overwhelming urge to discard his responsibilities to his business and race to Loren's side. To cherish her and share the wonder that they could already be on the way to being parents.

Alex gathered his thoughts together. Despite what his heart wanted, he had duties to fulfill, no matter how inconvenient to him. He looked up and found Giselle watching him carefully, as if waiting for him to confirm or deny her suspicions.

"That would be a matter between my wife and myself. You can head back to the office now, Giselle," he said with finality and looked pointedly at the door.

Giselle made her way out of the boardroom, but her words had left their mark upon him. Try as he might, Alex couldn't ignore his resentment toward the matters of business that had kept him from home so late each night, and that were now an unwelcome barrier between him and the answers he so desperately wanted from his wife.

Loren couldn't say what had drawn her to the graveyard afterward. She'd gone to the city with the determination to lose herself in some shopping, perhaps a meal out, and then to return to the castillo much later. But somehow she'd found herself driving toward the old church on the coast, with its eclectic mix of centuries-old headstones blended with those of more modern times in the burial grounds.

Locking her car in the car park, she pushed through the old wooden gate and picked her way through the headstones until she reached the Dubois family plot. It wasn't difficult to find her father's grave. The stone was the newest and brightest marble amongst the others. Loren knelt down in the grass surrounding the grave and cleared a few of the weeds that had pushed through around the base of his headstone.

"Oh, Papa, did you ever imagine what would come from the pact you and Raphael made all those years ago?" she said, a sudden gust of wind snatching her words and casting them away.

She still missed him so much. By the time her mother had imparted the news that Francois had died of complications after a bout of pneumonia, he'd already been buried. Loren had never had a chance to say goodbye.

The last time she'd spoken to him, though, on one of his frequent phone calls, he'd made her reiterate the one promise he'd asked of her when she'd left Isla Sagrado. Even now she could hear the deep baritone of his voice as he'd spoken across the long-distance telephone lines.

"Loren, mi hija, you must always follow the truth of your heart. Always. Promise me."

"Yes, Papa, I promise." Loren now spoke the words out loud. "But it's not so easy when the man of my heart does not feel the same way toward me."

She closed her eyes and bent her head, willing some of her father's wisdom and love to help her with her decision. Did she accept that she had to fulfill the conditions of the prenup, or did she tell Alex she refused to give him the child he had asked for?

Follow the truth of her heart. What was that truth

anymore? All her life she'd believed in one thing, that she was Alex's mate for life. She now accepted how naive that had been. The problem was that truth—her love for Alex—had not diminished. Yes, it had changed. It had grown from childish adoration and infatuation to something she knew was as intrinsic to her being as air was necessary for her to breathe.

So what now, she wondered. Did she accept a marriage as hollow and barren as her parents' marriage had become, or did she fight for what she wanted—what she was due as Alex's wife?

Loren kissed her fingertips and touched them to her father's headstone.

"I love you, Papa. I always will."

Never stop. His automatic response to her words echoed in her heart.

Never stop. Never give up.

And suddenly it was clear what she had to do. If she wanted her husband to *be* her husband, she had to fight for him. Had to fight for what was her right as his partner and as the potential mother of his children. Surely it would not be too much to expect of him that he remain faithful to her, especially not when they were already so obviously compatible. If she could only persuade him to give them a chance, she knew they could make their marriage work.

She straightened up onto her feet and squared her shoulders before resolutely walking back to the car. She would lay her demands on the table to her husband tonight. One way or another, she would have her answer.

And if that answer is no, a small voice in the back of her mind questioned, *what then?*

Loren shook her head as if she could dislodge the

thought before it took hold. She couldn't afford to fail in this. Not when her heart's truth was on the line.

Back at the castillo, Loren was pleased to hear from the housekeeper that Alex would be dining with her and *Abuelo* that evening; in fact, both his brothers would also be there. Knowing that time with his brothers was bound to put Alex in a good mood put a spring in her step as she ascended the stairs to their suite.

And she would make an extra effort with her appearance tonight. Somehow she knew she'd need all the additional armor she could gather around her. She looked at her wristwatch. Yes, she had plenty of time to prepare for the night's success.

In her room, she searched out the candles that had so romantically lit the atmosphere on her disastrous wedding night. She wanted to recreate that golden glow of hope when she and Alex retired to their rooms after dinner. Then she'd show her husband, with her words and with her body, what she expected of him and their marriage.

Satisfied with the placement of the candles, Loren spent a good half hour choosing what to wear for the evening. She didn't want to be too obviously seductive, after all she had a dinner to attend with the four del Castillo men before she would even have so much as an opportunity to have her husband alone. Eventually, she decided upon a simple strapless white gown that skimmed to her knees with flirtatious layers of organza. The bodice was slightly gathered, the scalloped top edge giving a soft and feminine line, while the boned built-in corset meant she could get away with the bare minimum of underwear.

She smiled, remembering her lack of underwear on their honeymoon. It was ironic that even though she'd bought replacement garments on the first day after their arrival, once she and Alex had consummated their marriage she'd had very little need, or opportunity, to wear any.

The fact that the physical side of their marriage had stopped upon their return meant that the memory left a bittersweet taste in her mouth. She pushed the niggle of doubt about her success for tonight to the very back of her mind.

She decided to team the dress with an elegant pair of gold high-heeled pumps and chose a pair of ruby drop earrings that *Abuelo* had given her on their return from their honeymoon. Given the style and shape of the stones, she believed they were probably equally as old as the heirloom engagement ring she wore on her ring finger. They'd be the perfect complement to the gown. A light cobwebby gold shawl to cover her shoulders was the perfect finishing touch.

Her spirits bolstered, she ran herself a deliciously deep bubble bath and set about her preparations.

As she had been the first time she'd descended the stairs alone at the castillo, Loren was aware of the murmur of male voices from the salon off the main entrance hall. And uncannily, as she had that very first time, she felt the weight of generations of del Castillo brides settle upon her shoulders. She knew, historically, that most marriages in the del Castillo family in the past had been structured to gain both political and financial advantage. Even Alex's parents' marriage had brought with it the alliance between his mother's family's vineyards and winery that formed part of the del Castillo brand today. They had, by the time of their marriage, been very truly in love, but they had also been not unaware of the advantages of their union. A union that in all likelihood would not have taken place if the financial gains had not been there in the first place.

That her marriage had been predestined was a fact of life in a family such as this. But a marriage based solely on duty and honor would not be enough to satisfy her. Tonight would establish whether she would finally be able to achieve the kind of marriage she wanted.

A frisson of something cold trickled down her spine and she increased her pace to get to the salon, suddenly eager to see her husband.

She slowed her steps as she drew nearer the salon. Unseemly haste would spoil the image of sensual elegance she'd worked so hard to create tonight. She paused in front of a massive gilt-edged mirror just outside the salon and checked that the somewhat austere hairdo she'd finally settled on, knowing how much Alex loved to tug it loose, remained intact.

Her hand stilled in the air as she heard her husband's voice raised with a thread of anger in it.

"Don't be a fool, Reynard. Marriage is a serious business. I know we all agreed to do our part but I can tell you up front that I regret having done what I have. In fact, I think I may have made the biggest mistake of my life."

Cold shock settled like ice in the pit of Loren's stomach.

"We all know Reynard won't go ahead with actually marrying this girl. The engagement is merely a front to keep *Abuelo* happy as we all agreed." Benedict's voice filtered through the air. "But you needn't worry that I plan on doing anything so stupid as marrying someone I don't love."

"No, we all know you'd marry your car if you

could," Reynard jeered. "I pity the poor woman you do eventually settle down with."

"Well, I pity Loren," Benedict continued. "She didn't ask for any of this."

Loren felt her knees grow weak, her legs unstable beneath her. She had to move, had to get out of there before one of them realized she'd overheard their discussion.

She forced her feet to carry her to immediate refuge in a downstairs guest bathroom and locked the door firmly behind her. Not daring to let go of the breath she was holding in so tight she thought her lungs might burst, she gripped the scallop-shaped marble pedestal basin. Right now it was the only thing keeping her vertical. She was afraid if she let go that she'd sink to the ground and never want to get up again.

The biggest mistake of my life.

Alex's words echoed, over and over, in her mind. Was that how he saw her? Saw their marriage? On the heels of the hope and determination she'd returned home with today, his words were like a death knell to her dreams.

Black spots danced before her eyes and a roaring sound rushed through her head. She forced herself to let go of the breath she'd been holding and dragged in a new breath. The spots began to recede but the pain in her heart only grew with her every inhalation.

Biggest mistake. Biggest mistake.

That she had his brothers' pity was no salve to her wounded soul. She couldn't bear to be the object of any man's pity. Not when all she wanted was Alex's love.

Somehow she had to gather the courage to go in there and face him.

Loren twisted the cold tap on and let the cool water

run over her wrists. As she did so an all-too-familiar ache started in the pit of her belly. An ache that always functioned as a precursor to her period.

Hot tears sprang to her eyes as she realized her fears that she might have been pregnant, and her concerns about Alex's presence as a father, were far outweighed by her desire to have had a part of Alex that would be her own.

She dried off her hands quickly. As she did so, the overhead light caught the bloodred of her ruby engagement ring, the color uncannily symbolic of the end of her expectations.

Alex looked up as Loren joined them in the salon. He allowed a small frown to crease his forehead. He'd expected her much earlier. Mind you, given the slant of the conversation he and his brothers had indulged in, it was just as well she was a little tardy. Reynard's announcement that he'd asked some stranger to be his wife had momentarily knocked his judgment for a loop. It was lucky that Loren had not interrupted their discussion of Rey's news.

She looked beautiful tonight, almost bridal, and for the umpteenth time this week he rued that work had kept him away from her. He'd become quite addicted to his wife in their time in Dubrovnik. Addicted in ways he'd never imagined.

Leaving her to sleep alone in her bed each night after he'd crawled in from working late had been hell, but he was conscious of the need to ensure she remained well. Replenishing the rest she'd missed during their sojourn was one way of doing that.

A flood of heat hit his groin as he remembered the highlights of that sojourn. Right now he wanted to do nothing more than lead her from the salon and take her back upstairs to their suite and into bed. It seemed it was about the only place they could be honest with one another.

Honest? He cringed internally. Their marriage hadn't started with much honesty. But that was something he was now very keen to put right. While it was true he still wanted the heir he'd demanded of her, he wanted so much more besides. And he wanted to give more, too.

He had not only made the biggest mistake of his life in marrying Loren the way he had, he'd done her a major disservice. She deserved to be cherished, to be loved.

The taste of what their marriage could be had made him hungry for more. More of what made a union real and binding.

A union based on love.

His fingers curled tight around the base of his glass as he finally acknowledged his feelings toward his wife. He loved her. Now all he had to do was convince her of the fact. He crossed the room toward her and dropped a kiss to her cool lips. Instantly he was enveloped in the subtle fragrance she used as her signature perfume. Inhaling her scent made him rock hard in seconds.

"I've missed you this week," he said.

"You've been busy. I understand."

Her response wasn't what he'd hoped for. Where was the passionate, teasing lover he'd come to enjoy so much while they were away?

"You're more understanding than most wives, I'll wager."

"But then I'm not *most wives,* am I?"

Her cryptic answer made him study her face more

carefully. She was pale beneath her makeup and there were fine lines of tension about her eyes.

Since their return home, the hope that they'd made a child together during their honeymoon had burned inside of him. That Loren looked somewhat frail this evening gave a hint of truth to the bombshell Giselle had dropped on him this afternoon and made him want to ask Loren outright if she was expecting his baby.

He'd played Giselle's words over in his mind again and again ever since she'd told him about Loren's dizzy spell at the office earlier today. Through all the meetings this afternoon and the interminable legal jargon he'd been forced to wade through, he'd had to fight to keep his focus on the business at hand.

Now that focus was very firmly on the woman before him. His wife. The woman he loved. The woman who now, hopefully, carried their child.

"Are you feeling all right?" he asked, searching her eyes for any hint of a lie.

He raised a hand to her chin and was surprised when she subtly moved clear of his touch.

"I'm fine."

She dismissed his concern with a brittle smile that didn't fool him for a second. Every instinct in him urged him to gather her up in his arms and take her back upstairs. To tie her to the bed, if necessary, until he knew the truth of what lay behind the fragile exterior she exhibited.

"Loren," Reynard interrupted them, bringing Loren a glass of champagne.

Alex was about to intercept it, to tell his brother she wouldn't be drinking tonight or any night for the next several months, but Loren forestalled him by accepting the drink.

Reynard tipped his glass to hers. "You should congratulate me. I'm engaged."

"Engaged? Really? And who is the lucky lady? I had no idea you were even seeing anyone on a regular basis."

There was a slightly wistful note to her voice that pulled at something in Alex's chest.

"Her name is Sara Woodville. She's a Kiwi girl, actually. You might have heard of her. She was here riding for New Zealand in the equestrian trials we sponsored recently."

"And she'd only been on Isla Sagrado for about five minutes before being snapped up by Reynard," Benedict commented drolly. "You've got to hand it to him, he can sure spot an opportunity."

"Well, at least he didn't wait twenty-five years," Loren said, raising her glass to Reynard. "Congratulations, Rey, I hope the two of you will be very happy."

Alex laughed at her comment along with his brothers, but he sensed the thread of bitterness behind her words even if they didn't.

"Well, we can certainly recommend a lovely spot for a honeymoon, can't we?" Alex said, hooking his arm around Loren's slender waist and drawing her against his side.

She stiffened but didn't immediately pull away.

"Oh, yes, I understand that cottage comes very highly recommended."

Again, that hint of double entendre slid like a stiletto through the air. Loren looked across to where *Abuelo* usually sat.

"Is your grandfather not joining us?" she asked.

"No," Alex responded. "His valet sent down a note to say that he wasn't feeling a hundred percent."

"That's not like him. Should I go and check to make sure he's okay?" Loren offered.

If he hadn't thought she would use the opportunity as an excuse to get away from him he would have encouraged her to go. Instead, given how distant she'd been since her arrival this evening, he feared she'd use the visit to his grandfather's rooms as a reason to stay with the old man and not to return—and right now he wanted her here, by his side.

"That won't be necessary. Javier is quite capable of seeing to his needs. Besides, you know how much *Abuelo* hates to be fussed over."

"By you perhaps, but he's never turned away a pretty face—especially Loren's," Benedict noted.

"Be that as it may, Loren can grace us with her company tonight instead. After all, it's the first evening I've had home with her all week."

"Well, don't think you won't have to share her with us. Surely the honeymoon is over by now," Reynard said with a smile designed to needle his older brother even as he hooked an arm in Loren's and drew her away to one side. "Please tell me you are tired of my brother's attentions and we can have our old Loren back again."

Loren laughed, a genuine sound that sent a thrill of longing through Alex. Something untamed knotted deep inside. Logically he knew that his brother was only teasing him, doing what brothers do best when it comes to yanking one another's chain, but he suddenly wished they lived in older times. Times where he could realistically secure Loren away in the castillo's tower rooms and force her to remain only unto him.

He had no doubt that if he answered his instincts and lay claim to her here and now by dragging her from Reynard's clasp that she would find nothing about the action appealing. Besides, forcing her into anything wasn't what he really desired. Truth be told, he simply wanted to hear her laugh—and, more importantly, to be the one who caused her such joy.

Envy didn't sit comfortably on Alex's shoulders. If anything he was the one whose life was coveted by others. That said, he would find some way to remind Reynard of his place.

"Tell us about your new fiancée, Sara, and why you didn't bring her along to meet us this evening," he said pointedly. "Worried she might take one look and decide she's chosen the wrong brother?"

And so the evening rolled on. By the time they took to the massive dining table, with each of the chairs ornately carved with the del Castillo family crest, Alex had firmly reasserted his dominance over his younger siblings. His dominance over his new wife, however, was another matter entirely. She wouldn't so much as meet his eyes and the knowledge definitely set his teeth on edge.

They had just finished their desserts and Reynard was discussing a new publicity drive for the vineyard with Benedict when the castillo's majordomo all but ran into the room. Alex was up and out of his chair before the man came to a halt.

"Qué pasa?" Alex demanded.

"It is Señor Aston, he is very ill. Javier, he asks for your help."

"Call for the doctor and an ambulance at once!" Alex barked.

"Already done, señor."

An elevator had been installed for Abuelo after his stroke when he'd refused to relocate to a suite downstairs, but Alex eschewed it in favor of the stairs that led to the old man's suite. His grandfather's words, insisting he'd die in the rooms he'd always lived in before anyone could convince him to move, rang loud and clear in Alex's ears. Suddenly the prospect that the elderly head of their family could possibly fulfill that prophecy was frighteningly real.

When Alex arrived in his grandfather's room he was shocked to find the old man lying on the floor, propped up by his manservant and covered with the coverlet from his bed. There was a gray tinge to his features and the muscles on the already weakened side of his face sagged more than usual.

"What happened?" he asked as he knelt to take his grandfather's hand. To feel for himself that the old man's lifeblood still flowed through his body.

"He said he had a headache and preferred to take his evening meal here in his rooms. When I came to take his tray away I found him here, on the floor. I called the doctor straight away and asked Armando to let you know."

Alex heard his brothers enter the room behind him.

"Should we move him onto the bed?" Reynard asked, kneeling down next to Alex.

"No, he is comfortable for now. We'll wait for the doctor and see what he recommends."

Alex felt his grandfather's fingers curl in his, the gnarled digits nowhere near as strong as they should have been. He leaned forward and murmured in Spanish.

"Relax, *Abuelo,* the doctor is coming."

But the old man struggled against him, tugging on Alex's hand as much as he was able. Alex bent closer, trying to make sense of the garbled words coming from his grandfather's mouth. His skin prickled with an icy chill as he finally understood what the old man was saying.

"It is the governess. She was here. It is the curse."

Eleven

"What's he saying?" Benedict asked.

"Nothing," Alex replied, his answer clipped. "He's rambling."

It was always the damn curse. Even now his grandfather wouldn't let go of it. Anger and frustration warred with concern for the old man. He'd done everything he could to put *Abuelo's* mind at ease. He'd married Loren. He believed she was now carrying his baby. But without conclusive proof she was pregnant he couldn't divulge that information to his grandfather.

Or could he? It might be the difference between the old man fighting what appeared to be another stroke or giving up entirely.

Alex gripped his grandfather's hand more tightly. Willing his strength into the old man's failing body.

"It is too late," Aston said, his voice growing weaker. "She has won, hasn't she, the governess?"

"No, *Abuelo,* she hasn't won. The curse, it is broken." Alex forced the words from his lips, prepared to do anything to hold his grandfather to the world around them for as long as he could.

"Broken? Are you certain?" Aston del Castillo's voice grew ever so slightly stronger.

"*Sí,* I am certain."

Just then the doctor arrived at the door, followed closely behind by an emergency paramedic team. In the subsequent bustle of activity as Aston was checked and deemed safe to move to the waiting ambulance downstairs, Alex noticed Loren hovering just inside the doorway.

How long had she been there? Had she heard the exchange between him and his grandfather? No, probably not, he consoled himself. Even Reynard and Benedict who had been at his side could barely hear his grandfather's words.

He looked at her again, studied her drawn features, the concern painted so starkly in her eyes and he knew that she would give him the answer he sought tonight.

"*Señor* del Castillo?"

Alex and his brothers all turned toward the doctor.

"I believe your grandfather has suffered another stroke. I will admit him to hospital immediately. We will need to do a CT scan and possibly an MRI as soon as possible."

"Whatever it takes, Doctor," Alex said, his voice suddenly thick with emotion. "Just make sure he can come back home again."

"We will do everything in our power. I will travel in the ambulance with your grandfather. Perhaps one of you could follow in my car?"

"We will all come to the hospital," Reynard said.

Alex cast Loren a glance. In response she gave a small nod.

"Fine," he said. "Loren and I will bring one of the estate cars and you and Benedict can travel in the doctor's vehicle. That way we all have transport back home."

He could see that Loren wanted to protest, perhaps even to suggest that she'd travel with Reynard or Benedict, but thankfully she merely acceded to his suggestion.

They completed the drive to the hospital, on the outskirts of Puerto Seguro, in silence. Alex had no need for casual conversation when all he wanted right now was to see his grandfather safely settled in the hospital and to hear a promising prognosis for his future from the neurological specialist on call.

They were pulling up outside the hospital when he placed a hand on Loren's arm and squeezed lightly.

"Thank you," he said.

"What for? I've done nothing tonight."

"For coming with me."

He meant it, too. It would reassure his grandfather to see Loren with him. Would help underline his promise that the curse was well and truly broken. That there was a power of hope ahead for the del Castillo family.

"Alex, you know I would do anything for your grandfather."

Anything for his grandfather but not for him? Alex bit back the question before he could give it voice.

"I am grateful for that," he finally managed through a throat that had suddenly grown thick with emotion.

"He's strong, Alex. He'll be okay."

Loren placed her free hand over his and pressed

firmly, as if trying to underline her words and make them a reality.

He could only nod. Drawing in a deep breath, he pulled away from her, missing the contact instantly.

"Come, let's go into the emergency department."

He helped her from the car and was relieved when she didn't pull away from him as he draped one arm around her shoulders and pulled her close against his side. Where she belonged, he reminded himself. No matter what this strange distant game she had played tonight, she was his wife and she belonged with him. Always.

It was nearly two in the morning when they made it back to the castillo. Alex's grandfather was comfortably settled in a private room at the hospital, his neurologist hopeful that because of Javier's quick call for help that they had been successful in halting any additional damage as a result of the ischemic stroke he'd suffered. They'd been able to medicate as soon as the scan results had confirmed their suspicions, falling just within the window of time vital to ensure a strong chance of survival and recovery.

Alex had taken a moment to thank Javier as they'd arrived home. The manservant had been awaiting their arrival and broke into unashamed sobs of relief when given the news that his master would in all likelihood pull through with minimal permanent damage.

Reynard and Benedict had chosen to take taxis to their homes directly from the hospital, rather than return to the castillo for their vehicles or stay over at their old family home. The next day would be soon enough to work out the logistics of recovering their vehicles. Besides, they would undoubtedly cross over with one another at the hospital as each planned to be there with their grandfather for as much time as their work commitments permitted.

Loren left Alex with Javier and went up the stairs to their rooms, feeling more than twice her age as she let herself into her bedroom and kicked off her shoes.

She looked around the room, feeling as if it had been days since she'd been here, rather than the hours it had actually been. Her eyes fell on the fragrant candles she'd set around the room in an effort to create the right atmosphere in which to seduce her husband. A seduction she'd planned before she'd heard what she suspected was the first excruciating shred of complete honesty from him in all her time back here.

In the drama surrounding *Abuelo's* stroke, the earlier events of the evening had been pushed aside, but now every word she'd overhead came rushing back in a painful remembrance.

She quickly gathered the candles up and dropped them into the wastebasket near her escritoire. She stood there, shaking with anger. How dare he have played with her life like that and then call it a mistake?

"Loren?" Alex spoke from the entrance to her bedroom. "Are you all right?"

A short sharp sound burst from her throat. It should have been a laugh but there was far too much bitterness behind it to even mimic humor. Alex covered the distance toward her and tried to take her in his arms, but she pulled free and took two steps back from him.

"Don't! Don't touch me."

She had to keep some distance between them; it was the only way she could keep her anger in the forefront of her mind when all her body wanted to do was meld with his and find again the ecstasy they'd shared for all too brief a time. She knew it took more than a physical connection to keep a marriage alive.

"Don't touch you? What is wrong? I've barely seen you all week and we've had a very distressing evening. I need to touch you. I need *you*."

"No." She shook her head.

The bleak weariness that had been on Alex's face earlier was now replaced by sharp intellect and a satisfied nod of understanding. "You are emotional. It is only to be expected. Giselle told me today you might be pregnant."

Loren couldn't believe her ears. "Giselle *what?*"

Alex continued, "Don't you think that you should perhaps have given me the news yourself?"

"And when would I have had the opportunity? You've been away from the castillo all week—not even home at night until very late and then gone early in the morning. Even today, on the telephone, you treated me as no more than a private messenger service." She cut the air between them with a sweep of her hand. "Whatever, as it happens, your assistant's conjecture is premature. My cycle was obviously out of sync. Whether it was from the travel or the stress of the wedding, it matters little. Tomorrow I will have my period."

"And you know this for sure because?" he growled.

"Because I know my own body, and I know I'm not pregnant."

Alex blew out a breath and closed his eyes, his features suddenly contorted with disappointment. When he opened his eyes she was struck by the raw regret mirrored there. She decided to ignore it. She was no doubt as wrong about his feelings on this as she'd been about so many things to do with Alexander del Castillo.

If he had any regrets it would only be that he had to continue with this total charade of a marriage to get the heir he so desperately wanted.

"I've given the matter of our prenuptial agreement further thought," she continued. "I believe it would be best for us to go back to my original request for an assisted pregnancy. In fact, I'd prefer it."

"Prefer it?" Alex echoed.

"Yes. Intercourse between us is clearly going to be a hit-and-miss affair. After all, it's not as if we didn't try hard enough before. To be honest with you, I'm not keen to resume that side of our marriage."

"Not keen." His voice was flat, his jaw rock hard.

She clenched her hands into fists at her sides, her fingernails digging small crescents.

"That's right. Plus, I believe you also wish to get on with things yourself."

"Things? Would you care to define exactly what those things are?"

Loren chewed her lower lip for a second. Did she dare acknowledge that she knew of his affair with Giselle, that she was aware he'd been biding his time to pick up again where they'd left off? She lifted her chin and met his gaze squarely.

"I think you know what I'm referring to. We both know this marriage between us was a mistake. In fact I heard you say the very thing yourself tonight."

"You heard me say that?" His voice was deadpan, as was the expression in his eyes.

Alex stepped in closer, filling her senses with his presence. Loren stood her ground. He knew very well what he'd said and now he knew she'd overheard him.

"Alex, as I said before, I will fulfill my duties to you under our legal agreement. That means I must deliver you a child. There was nothing in there about how I am to achieve that goal so I elect to use the clinical facility here on the island. Now, if that is all, it has been an extremely long and demanding day and I would like to get some sleep."

"There was also nothing in there about you being the one to elect how you should fall pregnant," Alex said.

Loren felt her heart stutter in her chest before resuming a rapid rhythm. "Are you suggesting you would force me?"

"Force? No, I doubt that would be necessary. Not when I know I can do this and have you willing in my arms."

He snaked one arm around her waist and drew her against his body, molding her hips to his lower body, widening his stance to cradle her there. Instantly Loren felt the answering call of her body to his, the intensity of awareness, the heated flow of blood through her veins.

When Alex bent his head to hers and caught her lips in a possessive kiss she found herself answering in kind. Allowing her anger an outlet, showing him he may be able to dominate her physically but he would never dominate her will.

They were both panting, their breathing discordant and harsh in the air between them, when Alex broke away.

"Out of respect for your oncoming *condition*," he said, his fingers splaying across her hip and lower belly, "I will not continue, but I believe my point has been made. You cannot refuse me, Loren. Your own body makes a lie of that."

As she watched him leave the bedroom and pull her door closed behind him she forced herself to acknowledge he was painfully right. She'd adored him as a child, been infatuated with him as a teen. Now she loved him with every cell in her body as a woman. Even knowing he would still choose another did not assuage the loss she felt as he'd walked away.

Was this how her father had felt when he'd learned of her mother's infidelity? This frantic sense of hurt and betrayal, the urgent desire to turn back the clock and start over—to get things right next time?

Her mother had once, and only once, alluded to the fact that she'd chosen to do something totally against her nature to force her husband to finally let her go. That the passionate highs and desperate lows of their rocky marriage had been as destructive as they'd been exhilarating and that she'd been incapable of bearing them any longer.

The fact that Naomi had been unfaithful to Francois Dubois to break free of her marriage had been a cop-out as far as Loren was concerned. She'd always believed that if they had loved one another enough they could have made things work. Not all marriages were always sailed on an even keel. Some people, some relationships, were just not cut out to be like that. That didn't mean they had to fall apart.

But the one thing Loren did know for certain was that when one partner loved less, or not at all, that marriage was doomed to failure.

When Loren woke the next morning with her period she was torn between relief that she wasn't yet forced to bring a baby into a loveless marriage and sorrow that the intimacy they'd shared in so much happier times, no matter how orchestrated, had not resulted in a child to love. After taking care of her needs she carried on through into the sitting room of their suite. Her maid usually ensured a tray was sent up for Loren each morning with her preference of cereal and yogurt for breakfast together with freshly squeezed orange juice. Loren usually took this quiet time in the morning to review the papers and plan her day.

She was surprised, however, to see Alex pacing the carpet when she pushed open her chamber door.

"*Abuelo?*" she asked, one hand to her throat. "Is everything all right?"

"*Sí,* he is resting comfortably. That is not why I'm here."

"Oh? What is it, then?" Loren went instantly on the defensive. "Ready to go for round two in the baby debate?"

"There is no debate," Alex responded, his voice harsh.

"Well, there certainly is no debate today. I have my period. You can go and carry on with whatever it is you're supposed to be doing today."

"Are you certain?"

Loren just stared at him. She knew she looked anything but her usual self this morning. The cramps had started in earnest shortly after she'd gone to bed and had kept her awake for the rest of the night. Her reflection in the mirror had shown her cheeks were pale, her eyes dark and shadowed.

"I will contact the doctor today and find out what is necessary to instigate the procedure."

Alex rubbed one hand across his eyes and sighed.

"Loren, it doesn't have to be like this."

"Yes, Alex, it does. We wouldn't want there to be any further *mistakes,* now would we?"

"You have taken my words out of context," he argued back.

"Just how out of context?"

Alex felt a swirl of helplessness eddy within him in the growing whirlpool of frustration he'd been feeling since the previous night. If only he could convince her to listen to what he'd really meant. Caution warned him that today was probably not the best time to broach the subject of his innermost thoughts. She was unlikely to believe him if he declared his love for her right now, and given how he'd dissembled to her already he could hardly blame her.

Just seeing her like this, looking bruised and fragile, made him want to sweep her into his arms and tuck her back into her bed. To force her to relax and regain her strength. To be the vibrant young woman he'd reintroduced himself to in New Zealand.

"I do not wish to banter with you about something as important as this when you are clearly not at your best. Perhaps when you are feeling better and more amenable to discussion—"

"This is not just some passing mood, Alex! I'm serious. As far as I am concerned, until we are discussing the creation of our child, we have nothing else to say to one another."

"Fine," he said in clipped tones, not wanting to acknowledge the hurt her words had inflicted upon his hopes. "You contact the clinic. Let me know when and where I'm needed or if you happen to change your mind from this ridiculous insistence of yours."

Alex drove to his office in a fury, barely even noticing the summer glory of the countryside that led to the resort's location.

The fact Loren was totally unwilling to resume

the physical side of their marriage completely baffled him. They had been perfect together. So she'd overhead him saying he'd made a mistake. He had. He was man enough to admit that. But her adamant refusal to enter into discussions with him unless they were discussing their child caused a pain inside him that was physical as much as it was emotional. A pain he was totally unaccustomed to feeling. If this was love, no wonder his ancestors had primarily chosen to marry for any other reason but that. Anything was better than giving someone else the power to make you hurt inside the way he hurt right now.

He thought fleetingly of the situation that had brought about his marriage to Loren. The governess's curse may not be real, but it had certainly made an impact on his life, and not one he was happy to accede to.

The three supposed edicts of the governess as she'd cursed his ancestor played back in his head—honor, truth and love. Well, he had both honored and continued to love his grandfather, and he'd tried to love his wife. Tried, and failed. It was a failure he wanted to put behind him as quickly and effectively as he could.

As he pressed the accelerator down a little harder, sending his car flying along the resort road, he vowed Loren would come back into his arms, and into his bed, on his terms or no terms at all.

Twelve

It had been two weeks since their last civil conversation beyond the frozen politeness they displayed to everyone at mealtimes at the castillo. At least those mealtimes when Alex deigned to come home.

His grandfather had been moved from the hospital, protestingly, into convalescent care. That he would be allowed back home when he met the rehabilitation markers set by his doctors was of no consolation to him. Loren had spent most of her days divided between keeping him company, preventing him from being cheerfully murdered by the staff at the facility where he was staying and performing her duties at the orphanage.

Each time she held the babies, she ached a little more for the child she did not carry. But, she told herself, that need would soon be assuaged by the procedures she would soon commence. Her doctor had agreed to begin the necessary treatments once both she and Alex were fully apprised of the information relating to them.

Now she finally had all that information to hand and she was determined to start whatever was necessary as soon as possible—which meant ensuring Alex was equally informed.

The prospect of undergoing injections to ensure she produced multiple viable eggs was something she didn't look forward to, but she was prepared to endure whatever she had to. She'd promised, legally and personally, to carry out her end of the agreement. She was her father's daughter. She did not renege on anything.

Loren checked her reflection before grabbing the file of papers the doctor and his nurse had given her. She smoothed her straight dark hair with one hand before straightening her shoulders and giving herself a small nod of approval. She was ready to go to Alex's office.

The dark blue shift she wore tapered to her slender form perfectly, and her matching sling-back shoes confirmed her businesslike appearance. And that's all this was. A business transaction. The execution of a plan.

At the resort, the receptionist waved Loren through to Alex's offices. At his door she paused, her hand curled, knuckles ready to rap on the smooth wooden surface. But then she decided against it. She was his wife, after all. There had to be some advantages to it.

She reached for the polished steel handle, pushed open the door and stepped inside only to come to a rapid halt at the sight before her.

Giselle was all but straddling Alex's lap—her hair a golden tumble down her back, her hand covering his own as it pushed up the hem of her skirt, her other arm draped around his neck and his head bent into the curve of hers.

Loren gave a startled gasp and spun on her heel before stopping and forcing herself to face the couple who were now apart. Giselle quickly stood beside Alex's chair and slowly rearranged her clothing. Her face wore a distinct look of sly satisfaction—Alex's, however, wore one of dark fury.

Loren looked from one to the other, suddenly overwhelmed with a determination that would brook no denial. She would not tolerate this. If Alex wanted a child in this marriage then he'd have to play by her rules and her rules demanded no infidelity.

It was time she grew a spine and fought back. Adrenaline coursed through her body. Suddenly she could begin to understand why people took scary risks. The sense of exhilaration was both terrifying and electrifying at the same time.

She pointed one finger at Giselle. "You. Get out."

"I beg to differ," Giselle drawled. "I believe you're the one out of place here."

"You can beg all you like, but you will be doing it elsewhere from now on. Get out, now, and stay the hell away from my husband."

"Alex!" The other woman appealed to the silent male figure at her side. "You can't let her talk to me like that. You have to tell her about us."

"What's it to be, Alex?" Loren challenged.

"Leave us," he said, his voice calm and level.

"Surely you don't expect me—" Giselle protested.

Loren smiled at her, although it was more a baring of teeth than a signal of pleasure. "I believe my husband asked you to leave."

With a sniff of disdain Giselle collected her bag,

then with a hand trailing the side of Alex's face she said, "Should you change your mind, you know where to reach me."

Loren watched as Giselle sashayed out of the office and went to close the door firmly behind her. Then she crossed back over to Alex's desk and dropped the clinic folder onto his desk in front of him.

"If you want to go ahead and have a baby with me then there have to be some boundaries. The most important is that you keep your hands off other women or you can consider our marriage over."

He gave a short laugh. "Marriage? You think what we have is a marriage?"

"We have what approximates a marriage, but we'll have what is most definitely a divorce if you so much as touch another woman again."

Alex leaned back in his leather executive chair and steepled his fingers. Giselle's move on him had taken him by surprise. He'd made it more than clear, both before he'd traveled to New Zealand and since his return and subsequent marriage to Loren, that anything he and Giselle had shared was well and truly over.

At first she'd been subtle—well, subtle for Giselle anyway. In recent weeks, her overtures had been more blatant, but nothing like today's blitzkrieg. He'd been on the verge of pushing her away—off his lap and out of his employ—when Loren had entered his office. He'd half expected Loren to simply leave again, but even then his little wife had surprised him.

Despite keeping her distance from him it was patently clear she was not prepared to share her toys, either. The knowledge gave him a surge of satisfaction. Perhaps now she would listen to reason.

He reached forward and flicked open the file she'd

dropped on his desk with one finger. His eyes skimmed the first page of details and everything inside him rebelled. No way would he accede to this barbaric coercion of nature when for them, in all likelihood, it was not even necessary.

"No other women, you say?" he asked, arching one brow and allowing his lips to relax into a smile.

"You heard me."

His wife stood opposite him, standing her ground like a sentinel.

"Hmm." Alex pursed his lips in consideration. "Yet you do not plan to share your bed with me like a dutiful wife ought?"

"We've been over this, Alex. You don't love me, yet you want a baby with me. Some people might be able to separate emotion from their physical behavior but I am not one of them. I won't share my bed with you if your only purpose in coming to me is to conceive a child."

There was a tiny break in her voice. A break that gave him the leverage he was looking for. She had not stopped loving him, he was sure of it. And if she hadn't, then he could press home his advantage and use this as an opportunity to win her back. To make their marriage the genuine article.

"I see. Well, then there is nothing for it but for me to agree to your condition that I not touch another woman."

"Thank you," she said, her breath escaping in a rush.

He raised a hand. "I haven't finished. I do agree to your condition, on a condition of my own. I refuse to allow you to submit to this process, Loren. We will conceive our child the old-fashioned way."

"No."

"Then I'm sorry. Because on this I refuse to negotiate."

"And I refuse to take another woman's leavings. Our marriage is over."

Before he could stop her Loren had turned and left his office. Over? Surely she didn't mean it. Shock reverberated through his body. Shock followed rapidly by a determination to stop her in her tracks. To somehow make her retract her statement, to admit her love for him, to allow him to admit his for her. He would not let her go, not like this, not ever. Galvanized by a combination of fear and resolve, he shot from his chair and out of his office.

By the time he reached the reception area he was just in time to see his wife's sleek convertible spin out of the parking lot and up the driveway leading to the main road. He felt his jacket pocket for his keys and cursed that he'd left them in his briefcase instead. There was no time to waste. Alex turned and zeroed in on his receptionist.

"Your car keys, give them to me now."

Flustered, the woman withdrew her handbag from a file drawer and extracted her keys.

"It's the Fiat, at the end of the staff car park," she said with wide eyes.

"*Gracias,* you'll find my keys in the case beside my desk. Take my car tonight."

"The Lamborghini?"

But Alex barely heard her. He had to reach Loren before she did something stupid, like leave him for good.

She could barely see through the tears that spilled from her eyes and down her cheeks as she grabbed clothes indiscriminately from her wardrobe and drawers and jammed them into her suitcase.

Was it so unreasonable to expect him not to have affairs?

Perhaps it was if *she* wasn't prepared to give him the surcease his male body obviously demanded. But what of her needs? What of the pleasures he'd taught her to receive and, in turn, to give? If she didn't have him, she didn't want anybody else and she most definitely wasn't prepared to share him.

Besides, he didn't want *her*. Not really. He only wanted her to create the heir he so desperately needed to provide to prove to *Abuelo* that the curse was nothing but hearsay on the tail of a three-hundred-year-old legend. She certainly had to admire the lengths he was prepared to go to set his grandfather's mind at rest, but the cost wasn't something she was prepared to pay. Not anymore. Not when beneath it all he still thought marrying her had been a mistake.

Loren bit back a sob as she shoved the swimwear and the sarongs she'd taken to Dubrovnik into the case and dashed the tears from her cheeks. A sound behind her made her pause. Before she could return to her task, she was spun around. The articles of clothing she still held were plucked from her hands and cast to the floor at her feet.

Alex stood before her, his strong hands holding her upper arms firmly so she couldn't pull away.

"I am no woman's leavings," he ground out in a harsh breath. "Unless, of course, you really are planning to leave me?"

"Of course I'm leaving you. I can't do this anymore, Alex. I can't."

"Why? Tell me." His fingers curled into her arms, pulling her closer to him.

"I can't share you. I refuse to share you. You know I love you, I always have—stupidly, now more than ever. I accepted when I married you that you didn't love me. I could live with that. But I cannot live with you taking your pleasure from other women. I lived through that with my parents. My mother's infidelity drove them both insane. I will not fall victim to that kind of desperate dependence. Not even for you."

"But you have no need to share me. I have never been unfaithful to you, Loren. Please, believe me."

She yanked herself free from his grasp and a choked laugh erupted from her throat.

"Don't treat me like a fool. From the second I arrived here Giselle has made it perfectly clear that you were only biding time with me until I provided you with an heir. Even you yourself did nothing to disabuse me of that belief."

"And our honeymoon? Did that mean nothing to you?"

"Mean nothing? It meant *everything* to me when we could finally be a couple. Yet the second we returned everything went back to how it was before. Including your relationship with your assistant."

"My relationship with Giselle has been nothing but professional for several months."

"How can you expect me to believe that? All those late nights and early mornings? I never saw you, you never spoke to me. And what about what I interrupted today?"

"I admit, I was involved with Giselle for a short period before I came to New Zealand, but once I'd decided to marry you I broke things off with her. Today was Giselle's desperate attempt to reignite a flame that never went beyond a distant flicker. What we shared was well and truly over before I asked you into my life, Loren. It's only ever been you since then."

Loren just shook her head. She wished she could accept his words as the truth but she hurt too much.

"Why should I believe you, Alex? Why should I believe my husband when he thinks our whole marriage is a mistake?"

"Because I love you!"

"Don't lie to me about that, Alex. Not now, not ever!"

She spun away from him and clutched her arms around her body as if she could somehow assuage the empty pain that filled her chest in the place of her heart and the death of her dreams.

He turned her back to face him and cupped his hands around her face, tilting it up so her eyes would meet his.

"Loren, I love *you*. I didn't plan to. To be totally honest, I didn't even want to. I thought we could marry, and that our feelings for each other would never go beyond companionship at best. How wrong I was!" He shook his head at his own foolishness. "I didn't count on falling in love with you, but from the moment you stood up to your mother, you started to inveigle your way into my heart. Day by day, week by week, I've learned to respect you and to love you.

"That's what I meant when I told my brothers I had made a mistake marrying you the way I had. It was wrong to rush into marriage merely to disprove some stupid curse that has no bearing on our lives today no matter what my grandfather believes. It was wrong to use you that way. But I do not regret marrying you, Loren.

I will never regret that. If I had this time over again I would still have brought you back to Isla Sagrado, back home, but I would have taken the time to woo you, to learn about the woman you are now, to acknowledge that love is not something to be spurned or used to a man's advantage." He pressed a kiss to her forehead. "Loren, please, give me another chance. Give *us* another chance."

Confusion swirled inside her. Half of her wanted to believe him, to have faith in his words and hold them to her forever. But the other half still hurt, deeply and most painfully. Her trust in him had been broken, her pride dashed. Deep down, she didn't want to lay herself open for any more hurt.

"I don't know if I can," she whispered. "I don't know if I even want to try again."

His dark eyes deepened to darkest black as she saw her own pain reflected in their depths.

"Then go. Return to New Zealand. I will not hold you to a marriage that you no longer can commit to. I will see to our dissolution, to your freedom. I'm sorry, Loren. I never thought things would come to this. As much as it breaks my heart, I would rather see you free to go than be trapped here with me, even as much as I need you by my side."

"You would do that? You'd let me just leave? What about the curse? What about *Abuelo?*"

"Don't you understand? Without your love, without you, I will forever be cursed. If you cannot love me then who am I to hold you here? I can only beg your forgiveness for being such a fool and for using you the way I did.

"Losing you has taught me a valuable life lesson. There is more to honoring a parent's wish and a family's expectations than just going through the motions. Without love, it means nothing."

He let her go and Loren rocked slightly on her feet as he did so. The confusion that had so clouded her mind only moments ago began to solidify into one clear thought.

Alexander del Castillo loved her.

Finally, this tall, proud man was hers.

Relief coursed through her veins followed by a bubbling rush of exhilaration. She drew in a deep breath.

"Alex," she said, in as level a tone as she could manage, "would you do one final thing for me?"

"Anything."

"Would you bring my suitcase?"

She saw his features settle into a frozen mask, but to his credit he said nothing. Merely zipped up the case and hefted it off the bed with one hand.

"Thank you," she said, and started walking through their suite and into his bed chamber.

"What are you doing?" he asked, his voice thick as if his throat was constricted.

"I don't want to be apart from you anymore—not even in separate rooms."

"Then you're staying?"

"You couldn't get rid of me now for anything."

Loren looked at him now, face-to-face, surprised to see the sheen of tears reflected in his eyes. That this powerful man was reduced to tears by the fact that she'd chosen to remain with him said it all.

"Love me, Alex."

"Forever, *mi querida*."

His arms closed around her, making her feel as if she'd finally come home. After their clothing had been torn from their bodies and they came together on his massive pedestal bed Loren knew she was home forever.

Past hurts dissolved into distant memories as his hands caressed her body with a new reverence. Fears about the future disappeared as she welcomed him inside her, not only physically but, finally, wholly and emotionally, as well.

It was late and the castillo silent and brooding in the darkness as Alex led Loren down the stairs.

"Where are you taking me?" Loren asked in a whisper.

"There is one more thing we need to do. Trust me."

He felt his heart swell as her slender fingers tightened in his. That small silent communication meant so much. To finally have her trust and to know he honestly returned it was one of the greatest gifts he'd ever received.

Their slippered feet made no sound as they crossed the great hall toward the small private chapel that formed part of the castillo's ancient history. The well-tended chapel door swung open silently beneath his touch.

"Wait here a moment," he instructed before moving swiftly down the center aisle of the centuries-old place of worship.

Moonlight gave eerie illumination to the stained-glass windows that had been fitted by successive generations of del Castillos. At the altar Alex lit the thick candles in their squat candelabra, letting their golden glow chase the shadows of the past to the corners of the chapel.

He turned back to Loren, covering the short distance

back to the door, to his bride, in seconds. Taking her hand again, he led her to the altar.

"I should have done this right the first time. I owed you that," he said, stroking the side of her face softly before letting his hands reach down to take both of hers in his own.

"It's all right, Alex. We survived anyway."

Her smile was bittersweet and Alex made a silent vow to ensure that the last of their ghosts were banished from this moment.

"We may have survived but you deserve more than that. This time I don't want there to be any doubt.

"Loren, I love you for your strength in the face of adversity, for your pride and incredible sense of honor and for the gift of your love to me, even when I didn't deserve it. From this day forward, you will never again be lonely for I will always be at your side to give you comfort and to support you in whatever you do for all of our lives together.

"I promise you, I will always be your rock, I will always honor you, remain true only to you and I will always love you—today and forever."

He lifted her hand and placed a kiss on her ring finger, sealing a brand upon her skin where his rings already claimed her as his by law. He rested their clasped hands against his chest as Loren took a deep breath and started to speak, her voice low and clear in the air between them.

"Alex, I have always loved you for your principles, for your direction and your love for your family. I am honored to be your wife, to be your partner for life and to be the one to support you and love you through whatever comes our way in the future. I treasure your love for me and will always do everything in my power to protect and nurture that love.

"Together I know we can weather any storm and be safe in the knowledge that it will only bring us closer and will only serve to help me love you more. I can't wait to have children with you, to watch them grow with your guidance and strength behind them and I promise that I will always be there for you and always love you."

She reached up and kissed him, sealing their vows to one another with a hunger and a pledge that promised a happier future.

As one, they bent to blow out the candles, then left the chapel to return to their chamber, oblivious to the fading apparition in the far reaches of the shadows—a woman in eighteenth-century dress—smiling.

* * * * *

"You make me want to throw the rules away," Tanner murmured, and dipped his head to brush his lips to her forehead.

Ivy sucked in a breath. "Rules?"

"Doesn't matter," he said, shaking his head. "You've been making me a little nuts the last few days."

"I have?"

He smiled and the curve of his mouth sent tiny electrical shocks blasting through her system.

"Yeah. And you know it," he said softly. "Every woman knows when she's driving a man crazy with want."

"Want."

Yes, she thought. Want was good. Want was very good.

Dear Reader,

I always loved the idea of actually owning a Christmas-tree farm. The idea of being surrounded by the spirit and magic of Christmas all year long really appealed to me.

Sadly, I'm not very talented when it comes to growing things. So instead, I indulged my dream by creating a heroine who lives on Angel Christmas Tree farm. Ivy Holloway is a very upbeat, positive-attitude kind of girl and she's determined to make her tree farm a thriving, year-round business.

The only problem is her new neighbor, Tanner King. He designs computer games and works at home, so he needs quiet. He bought the property next to the tree farm, thinking that he would only be bothered by noise and crowds for two months out of every year. He's not happy to discover that Angel Christmas Tree farm has expanded their business into weddings, birthday parties and events.

Ivy has to find a way to make the inveterate Scrooge come to love Christmas—before his complaints to the sheriff cause her to lose the business she loves.

I really hope you have as much fun reading *Cinderella & the CEO* as much as I did writing it. You can write to me at maureenchildbooks@gmail.com or at PO Box 1883, Westminster, CA 92684-1883, USA.

Best,

Maureen

CINDERELLA
& THE CEO

BY
MAUREEN CHILD

Published in Great Britain 2011
by Mills & Boon, an imprint of Harlequin (UK) Limited,
Eton House, 18-24 Paradise Road, Richmond, Surrey TW9 1SR

© Maureen Child 2010

ISBN: 978 0 263 88311 4

51-0811

Harlequin (UK) policy is to use papers that are natural, renewable and
recyclable products and made from wood grown in sustainable forests. The
logging and manufacturing processes conform to the legal environmental
regulations of the country of origin.

Printed and bound in Spain
by Blackprint CPI, Barcelona

Maureen Child is a California native who loves to travel. Every chance they get, she and her husband are taking off on another research trip. The author of more than sixty books, Maureen loves a happy ending and still swears that she has the best job in the world. She lives in Southern California with her husband, two children and a golden retriever with delusions of grandeur. Visit Maureen's website at www.maureenchild.com.

To Kate Carlisle and Jennifer Lyon.
Thanks for all the e-mails and phone calls and laughs.
You guys are the best.

One

"Hi, I'm your new housekeeper."

Tanner King looked the woman up and down, then once more, taking in her lush curves, heart shaped face and full lips. Late twenties, he guessed, she had long, blond hair tumbling around the shoulders of her yellow T-shirt and her faded jeans hugged her short, shapely legs like plastic wrap on a new CD. Her pale blue eyes sparkled and when she smiled, a dimple winked in her left cheek.

His body stirred and he shook his head, both at her and at the completely physical response the woman engendered. "No, you're not."

"What?" She laughed and the sound of it rolled up and over him, sending blasts of heat through his body so fast, Tanner thought it had been way too long since he'd been with a woman.

He shook his head and said, "You're no house-keeper."

One of her blond eyebrows lifted. "And you know this because…"

"You're not old enough, for one."

"Well," she said, "as nice as that is, I can assure you I am old enough to clean a house. So who were you expecting? Mrs. Doubtfire?"

He instantly thought of that old comedy with the man dressed up like a fat old woman and nodded. "Yeah."

"Sorry to disappoint." She grinned at him and that single dimple of hers made another appearance.

Oh, she hadn't disappointed. That was the problem. There was nothing about this woman that was dis-appointing. Except for the fact that there was no way he was going to be able to hire her. He really didn't need the kind of distraction this woman so obviously was.

"Let's start over," she said, holding out her right hand. "My name's Ivy Holloway and you're Tanner King."

It was a long second or two before he shook her hand and quickly let her go again. He didn't much care for the buzz of something hot and sinful that had zipped up the length of his arm the moment he touched her. Which was proof enough to him that this was a bad idea.

Nothing had gone right since he had moved into what should have been a perfect house two months before. Why he was surprised at this latest setback, he couldn't say.

Sunset was spilling over the valley, twilight shifting slowly to night and the woman's soft, blond hair lifted with the cool breeze sliding off the mountain. She was watching him as if he were from Mars or something. And he supposed he couldn't blame her.

This is what happened when a man with a penchant for privacy moved to a tiny town where everyone knew everything about everybody. He had no doubt that the town of Cabot Valley was curious about him. But he was in no hurry to satisfy that curiosity. He'd come here hoping to find some peace and quiet where he could work and be left the hell alone.

Of course, the peace and quiet thing had already disintegrated. He lifted his gaze to the borders of his property where acres of Christmas trees spread out as far as a man could see. It looked placid. Serene. And was anything but. Frustration simmered inside him briefly before he deliberately tamped it down again.

"Look," he said, moving to block the doorway by slapping one palm on the doorjamb, "I'm sorry you had to come out here, but you're not exactly what I was looking for. I'm happy to pay you for your time."

In Tanner's experience people—especially women— were always willing to be paid off. Former girlfriends received tasteful diamond bracelets and housekeepers who would clearly not work out could get a nice check. No harm. No foul.

"Why would you pay me when I haven't worked yet?"

"Because this is not a good idea."

"You don't need a housekeeper?" she asked, folding her arms beneath her breasts and at the same time lifting them high enough that he couldn't ignore them—not that he had been. Her breasts were round and full and the tops of them were just visible over the neckline of that T-shirt. Oh, he'd noticed.

"Of course I do."

"And your lawyer hired me for the job. What's the problem?"

The problem, he told himself, was that he hadn't been specific enough when his best friend and lawyer, Mitchell Tyler had offered to hire him a housekeeper. It was Tanner's own damn fault that he hadn't told the man to make sure the woman he hired was old and quiet and well past tempting.

Tanner was already behind on work thanks to all the disruptions around here. He didn't need yet another distraction right under his nose all the time.

And Ivy Holloway would definitely be a distraction.

While he was lost in his own thoughts, the woman ducked beneath his arm and scooted into the house before he could stop her. There was no way to get her out again without just picking her up and carrying her. It wouldn't have been difficult. She was small enough that he could toss her over one shoulder and have her across the porch, down the steps and onto the lawn in a few seconds. But as if she knew just what he was considering, she walked further into the main room. Then she stopped and turned a slow circle, taking it all in.

"This place is amazing," she whispered and he followed her gaze.

Dark wood and glass made up most of the house, affording him a glorious view of the very Christmas tree lot that had become the bane of his existence in the last two months. The main room of the house was massive, dotted with oversized couches and chairs, grouped together in conversation knots that were never used. The hearth was river stone and was tall enough for

Tanner to stand up in. Three-foot high bookcases ringed the room like a chair rail and gleaming tables sat atop warm, honey-colored oak floors. It was everything he'd wanted his house to be. Would have been perfect if not for—

"People have been dying to get a look at this house," she mused. "Ever since you bought the place and started your renovations, the town's been fascinated."

"I'm sure, but—"

"It's understandable," she added, throwing him a quick look. "After all, this place was empty for years before you bought it and it didn't look anything like *this*."

Oh, he knew that. Hadn't he paid a fortune to the King construction crews to spend ten months doing what should have taken two years? He'd known exactly what he wanted, and had one of his cousins, an architect, draw up the plans. Tanner had been meticulous. He'd built this place to be his sanctuary. His corner of the world, safe and inviolate.

He snorted derisively at how quickly his plans had fallen apart.

"Where's the kitchen?" she asked, interrupting his thoughts again.

He pointed. "Through there, but—"

Too late, she was already gone, her boot heels clacking merrily against the wood floor. Forced to follow her, Tanner did just that, managing to tear his gaze away from the curve of her butt only through sheer determination.

"Oh my God," she whispered as if she'd stepped into a cathedral.

The kitchen was huge, too. Bright, with its cream-colored walls and golden oak cabinets. Miles of granite countertop the color of honey topped dozens of cupboards and the big farmhouse sink overlooked a wide window with a view of the backyard. Even in twilight the yard was impressive, with sculpted trees and bushes and late summer flowers splashing the place with color.

"Cooking in here will feel like a vacation," she murmured, tossing him a quick smile. "You should see my kitchen. No counter space and a refrigerator that's older than I am."

She walked to the Subzero fridge and opened the door, cooing a little at all the space she found inside. Then she frowned and looked at him again. "Beer and salami? That's all you have in here?"

"There's some ham, too," he said a little defensively. "And eggs."

"Two."

"The freezer's full," he pointed out, though why he felt as though he had to explain himself to her was beyond him. "I'm not completely helpless."

She gave him a look usually reserved for particularly slow children. "This amazing kitchen and all you use is the microwave for frozen dinners?"

Tanner scowled. He'd been busy. Besides, he was planning on cooking, or hiring someone to do it. Someday.

"Never mind." Shaking her head, she shut the refrigerator and said, "Okay, I'll pick up some groceries for you—"

"I can buy my own food."

"Oh," she assured him, "you're going to. But I'll do

the ordering since that talent seems to have escaped you."

"Ms. Holloway." The two words sounded long-suffering, even to him.

"Oh," she waved a hand at him. "Call me Ivy. Everyone does."

"Ms. Holloway," he repeated deliberately and watched that one eyebrow lift again, "I already told you, your being here is not going to work."

"How do you know?" she asked, running the palm of one hand across the honey granite as if she were petting it. "I could be great. I might be the best housekeeper in the world. You could at least give me a try before you make up your mind."

Oh, he'd like to give her a try, Tanner thought. But not the way she meant. Her scent drifted to him from across the cooking island. She smelled of lemons and he caught himself before he could take a much deeper breath just to taste more of it.

If he had Mitchell here in front of him, Tanner thought he might just slug his old college roommate dead in the face. For years, Mitchell and his wife Karen had been trying to get Tanner settled down with a 'nice' woman. They'd done the dinner party with a surprise guest thing. They'd thrown parties where they could parade a stream of women past him. All in an attempt to bring him out of his shell.

The problem was, he didn't think of his life as a shell. He'd spent plenty of years constructing the defenses around him and he didn't have the slightest interest in letting anyone else in. He had friends. He had his cousins and half brothers. He didn't need anyone else. But try telling that to your married friends. It was as if as soon as a man got married, he wanted every guy he knew in that boat with him. Mitchell was doomed to disappointment in Tanner's case. But damned if he didn't keep trying.

And Ivy Holloway was proof of that. Mitchell had probably taken one look at her and decided that the town beauty was one sure way to get Tanner involved in what was going on around him. It wasn't going to work.

"The thing is," he said before his body could talk his mind out of what he knew needed to be done, "I work at home during the night. I sleep during the day—or try to—" he muttered. With all the noise erupting around his bucolic retreat, sleep was getting tougher and tougher to manage. "So I can't have you making all kinds of noise while I'm working and—"

"What do you do?"

"What?"

"You said you work at home." She leaned her elbows on the countertop, propped her chin in her hands and asked, "What do you do?"

Her blue eyes were sharp and focused on him. "I design computer games."

"Really? Have you done any I would recognize?"

"I doubt it," he said, knowing full well that King games catered to young men more than women. "I don't design fashion or exercise games."

"Wow," she said softly. "That was patronizing."

Yeah, it had been. He hadn't expected her to call him on it, though. "It's just—"

"Try me," she said with a grin that had her dimple appearing again.

"Fine," he said, challenge in his voice. "The last game I designed was 'Dark Druids.'"

"Seriously?" Her eyes went wide. "That's great. I love that game. And, just so you know, I'm a ninth level Master Sage," she told him with a proud lift of her chin.

Instantly intrigued in spite of himself, Tanner gave her a considering look. He knew exactly how difficult his "Druid" game was and to reach the ninth level was impressive. "Really. How long did it take you?"

She shrugged and admitted, "Six months, but in my defense, I only played at night. So what are you working on now? Is it okay to ask, or is it a big secret?"

Six months? She'd scored that high in six months? He got e-mail letters from players complaining that he'd obviously made the game too hard as they'd only reached third level in more than a year of trying. He almost forgot that he was supposed to be getting rid of her. So she was more than beautiful. Smart, too. A deadly combination.

Still, Tanner had to stop himself from discussing his current game and the roadblock he'd hit the night before. If she was that good, maybe he could bounce a couple of ideas off her. He cut that thought off fast. He wasn't looking for a collaborator. In fact, she was keeping him from working. He was standing here talking to her when he should be upstairs buried in medieval magic—which proved his point that she was too much of a distraction.

"Secret, I guess," she said, clearly reading his expression. "Okay then, never mind. Why don't you go on and get to work and I'll take care of things around here?"

"I don't think—"

"You need a housekeeper," she told him flatly "and

God knows, you desperately need someone to cook for you. And I need the extra money. I'll be so quiet, you'll never know I'm here. Promise. So why not just give me a chance?"

Clearly, she wouldn't leave without an argument and he didn't have time for one. It seemed easier at the moment to agree. "Fine. I'll be upstairs in the office. Third door on the left."

"Have fun!" She turned away and started opening cupboards, muttering to herself.

Tanner intended to talk to Mitchell and get him to fire the woman. Soon. She'd already forgotten he was there as she made notes on a tablet she'd found in a drawer. She was humming and the sound of it pushed him into moving. This wasn't going to work out. He'd give her tonight, but tomorrow, she'd have to go.

When he left the kitchen, she didn't even glance at him.

The minute she was alone, Ivy slumped against the beautiful kitchen countertop.

"That went well," she murmured to the empty room. She'd made him angry right off the bat. Though to be fair, she thought, he had already been angry when he opened the door to her. If she hadn't been so quick on her feet, she might not have gotten into the house.

And she'd had to get in. *Had* to have this job as housekeeper. Yes, the extra money would come in handy, what with everything she was trying to do at home right now, but that wasn't the real reason she was here—in enemy territory. That sounded odd, even to her. She had never actually had an enemy before. But she did now. A very rich, very powerful one.

But she wished she'd known ahead of time that her enemy was so gorgeous. One look at him and she'd actually had to lock her knees to keep them from buckling.

Tanner King should have a warning label slapped against his forehead. More than six feet of leanly packed muscle and long legs, the man was a walking hormone celebration. She knew because her own were still doing a happy dance that had her palms damp and her stomach doing twists and turns. From the moment he opened his front door, Ivy had felt as though she was trying to keep her feet during an earthquake.

His dark blue eyes, his thick black hair, shaggy and touching the collar of his shirt. His wide shoulders, narrow waist and his long legs all combined to make her insides quiver.

And that was something she hadn't counted on. How was she supposed to work for the man, subtly win him over, if her body was in a constant state of excitement?

"Maybe Pop was right," she muttered, remembering how her grandfather had tried to talk her out of this plan. Too late now though, she thought, stalking to the floor to ceiling cupboard on the far end of the room. As she'd hoped, it was a butler's pantry and one look inside at the mostly empty shelves told her that Tanner King was lucky he hadn't starved to death in the two months he had been living here.

Bur then it seemed that all he did was work on his computer games and make complaining phone calls to the sheriff.

About *her.*

She closed her eyes and took a deep breath before

letting all the air slide from her lungs again. That's why she was here, of course. One too many visits from Sheriff Cooper who had told her only two days before that he didn't know how much longer he could placate Tanner King.

Closing the pantry doors, she leaned back against them and looked at the expansive room. Beautiful but empty. Sort of like its owner, she mused. What kind of man was it who could build a house this beautiful and leave it so bare?

"Well, that's what you're here to find out, isn't it, Ivy?" she told herself firmly.

She not only wanted to understand him, she wanted to make *him* understand her and this place he'd moved to. Before he ruined everything.

It wouldn't be easy, but Ivy didn't come from a family of quitters. Once her mind was made up, her grandfather often observed, it would take an act of God to change it. She was here and she wasn't going to leave until she'd helped Tanner King to see the light, so to speak.

A little nervous about this whole thing, she knew pretending to be nothing more than a part-time housekeeper was going to be hard. After all, she was a terrible liar. But then she didn't actually have to flat out *lie* either, did she? Ivy smiled to herself. It was more of a lie of omission and that wasn't really so bad, was it? If it was for the greater good?

"Man, I wonder how many people have consoled themselves with that particular thought."

She sighed a little, wishing things were different. But wishing didn't change a thing as she knew all too well. Besides, the game was in motion, she'd already made her first move, so there was nothing to do now but go forward. She was here. She'd do the job she came to do.

And one way or another, Tanner King would find out he'd met his match.

Two

"All I'm saying," Tanner King muttered darkly into the phone, "is that a man shouldn't have to be bothered by Christmas in the middle of August."

"Uh-huh." The voice on the other end of the line sounded amused. "Now you sound like those idiots who buy a house next door to an airport and then complain about the noise."

Tanner scowled out the window at the tree farm that bordered his one acre plot of land. At night, it looked deceptively peaceful. The scent of pine drifted to him on a soft breeze slipping beneath the partially opened window and he scowled. Looking at the place now, you'd never guess what a crowded, noisy place it was during the day.

"What's your point?"

"My point," his cousin said on a chuckle, "is that you knew that Christmas tree farm was there when you bought your place a year ago. No point whining about it now."

"A," Tanner told the other man, "I don't whine. And B, what kind of Christmas tree farm is open all year round? Nobody mentioned that when I bought this place."

Of course, he hadn't asked, either. But, Tanner thought in his own defense, who would? He'd bought his house more than a year ago and hadn't given his next-door neighbors much thought, beyond the fact that the trees made for a nice view from his windows. Christmas tree farms, by definition, were Christmas-based operations, right? At least that was how it was supposed to be. Shaking his head while his cousin's voice rang in his ear, Tanner again stared out the window of his office at the property next door.

He had moved in only two months ago—since the construction crew he'd hired right after buying the place had spent nearly ten months remodeling. When he'd finally settled in, he'd looked forward to some quiet. Who wouldn't have, with a tree farm as their closest neighbor? Instead though, he had spent the last two months watching a veritable parade of visitors to the Angel Christmas Tree farm.

Except for his neighbors, the house was everything he'd wanted. Glass and wood and surrounded by nearly an acre of land, he had all the privacy he required. Or so he'd thought. From the second story window, Tanner had quite a view. Acres of trees sprawled across the landscape, stretching out for what looked like miles. But then, it wasn't the trees themselves he was having a problem with. It was the farm owner's entrepreneurial spirit. Apparently the Angel family who owned the farm, had come up with the idea of expanding their holiday business into a year-round concern.

There were event weddings taking place nearly every weekend, hayrides, picnic sites and, God help him, even kids' birthday parties. All of which had resulted in a never ending stream of cars roaring up and down the narrow road in front of his property. The Angel tree farm was turning into a pain in his ass.

But that wasn't the worst part. No, the worst part was the music, piped out of speakers attached to telephone poles. Holiday music. In August. Blistering heat outside and Tanner was forced to listen to "White Christmas" on a daily basis.

While he was trying to sleep.

"You could consider giving up the whole 'live like a vampire' thing and sleep at night like most people," his cousin Nathan suggested.

"I tried that when I first got here," Tanner muttered, turning away from the view to stare at the flat screen computer monitor on his desk across the room. "You try working on a medieval war game while listening to the sound of 'Jingle Bells' in a never ending loop."

No, working at night had been the only reasonable solution, he thought, remembering the sexy woman roaming his house. How was he supposed to concentrate on work when he knew she was here? Right downstairs?

"Okay, forget I said that," Nathan told him. "I'd rather have you crabby as hell and that computer game you're working on finished by deadline. How's it coming, anyway?"

This was why his cousin had called in the first place. Tanner's company, King Games had entered into a partnership with Nathan's company, King Computers. The new computer game Tanner was designing would be included in the software of every new King PC. It was going to be huge. If Tanner finished the thing on time.

Which, thanks to the Angel tree farm—and now, Ivy Holloway—was looking less likely by the minute.

Of course, the game was actually near completion. He'd done most of the art work months ago and the programmers had coded the damn thing. Now he was working out a few of the details in the graphics and story line itself and he was behind schedule. He could have handed the project off to any number of the designers who worked for him. But designing games was what Tanner enjoyed most—and this particular game was far too important to trust anyone else to do it the way he wanted it done.

Besides, a King game was damn well going to be designed by a King.

"I hit a snag last night," Tanner grumbled, scrubbing one hand across his eyes.

"We've got production set to roll in another month."

"Thanks, I've got a calendar. Don't need the reminder."

"I'm just saying, if we want the first of these games to be ready for the Christmas rush then you've got to bring it in on time." Nathan blew out a breath. "As it is, we'll be scrambling in production. We can't take a delay on this, Tanner."

"It'll be ready. Just don't talk to me about Christmas, okay?" Or about beautiful, clever blondes. He kept his mouth shut about Ivy. He didn't need to hear any teasing from his cousin on that score, too. Nathan was a legendary player. Had more women in his life than he could keep track of. If he got wind of what Mitchell had set Tanner up for this time, he'd never hear the end of it. Besides, she wouldn't be here long.

"Right. Look, I've got a meeting in fifteen minutes with the distributors. I'm going to be talking up this game and the new King PC so let's just stay on track here, okay?"

"Relax, Nathan. I know how important this is. To both of us."

His video/computer gaming company was already more successful than even he could have dreamed. Tanner had built his enterprise into a worldwide success—and this partnership with his cousin was going to put King Games into the stratosphere. Just where he wanted it.

All he had to do was focus.

And somehow, keep his mind off the woman downstairs.

Two hours later, groceries had been delivered from town and most of them were already stashed in the amazingly numerous cupboards.

Ivy was completely in love with Tanner King's house. *Especially,* she thought, *the kitchen.*

Oh, she loved her own place too, of course. The old Victorian where she'd grown up had plenty of character—lots of that character was grumpy, but still she loved it. There were memories etched into every square inch of the battered old house and she wouldn't trade it for anything. But if she were going to trade, she'd take Tanner King's house in a heartbeat.

"Honestly, the man has a kitchen to die for and he keeps it stocked with beer and pretzels. No wonder he needed help." She was talking to herself, which was understandable because the house was so quiet if she didn't, she might start feeling a little creeped out at the silence.

How he worked in such a barren atmosphere, she didn't know. And how he invented such intricate games that were filled with wit and magic while he was working in a black hole of solitude she'd never understand.

Ivy liked people. She thrived on the energy of being in the midst of things. Being a part of life. She was awake at dawn and resented having to close her eyes to sleep every night. There was just so much to do. So much to plan. So much to dream. She felt as though she never had enough time to accomplish everything she wanted to do.

Which made it even harder to understand a man like Tanner King choosing to shut himself away. Hard to imagine why anyone would want to live like that.

Two months Tanner King had been living in Cabot Valley and not a soul there knew him at all. Not even Merry Campbell who had been known to uncover a person's life story over a short cup of coffee. Of course, the man would have had to actually go into town and step into Merry's store for that to happen.

And he hadn't.

As far as Ivy knew, he hadn't been into town once since moving into this flawless, spectacular wood and glass palace. He had his few groceries delivered and avoided all other contact.

"Well," she corrected herself, "not all." He'd certainly been spending time talking to the sheriff of Cabot

Valley. He'd lodged at least a dozen complaints about the Angel Christmas Tree Farm in the last couple of months. The crowds. The noise. The music. The traffic.

You'd think he'd have better things to do, she told herself firmly. But no, he'd moved into the valley and immediately tried to remake everything just the way he wanted it. Well, it wasn't going to work. They weren't going to change to suit Tanner King and the sooner she could make him see that, the better for all of them. But first, she had to make him like her. Become his friend. Introduce him around, maybe. Let him see that the Angel Christmas Tree Farm was a big part of the community.

And feeding him seemed like a good place to start.

Shaking her head, she opened the oven door, pulled out the fresh loaf of bread and set it on a cooling rack. While delectable scents filled the air, she turned to the stove and stirred the pot of soup. It smelled good despite being the ninety-minute quick start variety. Better than canned, but not as good as homemade. But at least he'd have fresh bread to go with it and she was fairly sure that this meal would be better than anything he'd made for himself in the last couple of months.

Her mom used to say that any man could be won over by a good meal and a warm smile.

She sure hoped Mom was right.

Because otherwise, Ivy would never be able to protect her Christmas tree farm from a rich man who wanted to shut it down.

Tanner couldn't work. He'd tried, but every time he entered the changes he wanted on the programming form, his mind drifted to the woman in his house. Blond hair. Blue eyes. Dimple. The sound of her breathy voice and the faint, lemony scent that clung to her. Damn it, it didn't seem to matter how many times he pushed thoughts of her from his head, she came right back a moment later.

And it was more than just mental images of her. How was a man supposed to keep his mind on work when he knew someone else was in the house? He hadn't heard a vacuum or anything, but she was no doubt wandering around with dust cloths or whatever. Poking into things. Looking around. Breathing his air.

"Damn it."

Tanner sat back in his desk chair and shoved both hands through his hair. Frustration tugged at the corners of his mind. He had thirty days to get the kinks worked out of this game. And he was wasting time sitting there thinking about Ivy Holloway.

"This is just not going to work," he muttered and reached for the phone.

After three rings, his lawyer picked up. "Hello?"

"Mitchell, you've got to fire that housekeeper."

The other man laughed shortly. "Hi, Tanner. Good to hear from you. Yeah, Karen's fine. Thanks for asking."

Tanner scrubbed one hand across his face. "Very funny. This isn't a social call."

"Yes, I picked up on that." Mitchell sighed. "The housekeeper hasn't even been there one full night and already you want her fired?"

Pushing up and out of his chair, Tanner stalked to the window and stared out at his nemesis, the tree farm. "I didn't want her in the first place, remember?"

A part-time housekeeper had sounded like a good

idea in theory, two weeks ago when Mitchell had first suggested it. God knew he was tired of frozen or packaged dinners and doing his own damn laundry. But with the crunch to get the game done and his lack of sleep, now wasn't a good time.

"Forget it, Tanner. You need someone in there to cook and clean."

"Because more distraction is exactly what's required."

"You know," his old college roommate mused, "there's a fine line between brilliant recluse and nutcase hermit."

He frowned at the phone. "I'm not a hermit."

"Not yet." Sighing, his friend asked, "Would you rather she come in during the day while you're sleeping?"

"No." That would be all he needed, he told himself. Not only the noise from the tree farm, but someone inside his house making noise, too. Besides, he thought, remembering his sexy new housekeeper, if she were around when he was in bed, he'd be way too tempted to have her join him. No, better that she come in while he was working. At least then, he could tell her to stay away from wherever he happened to be and to clean around him.

"Then it's settled. Don't scare her off."

"I don't scare women," Tanner said, insulted at the suggestion. And Ivy Holloway hadn't seemed the slightest bit intimidated by him. He wasn't sure if that was a good thing or a bad thing.

"My old friend, you scare everybody but me," Mitchell told him.

Scowling, Tanner thought about that for a second or two. He didn't like people much. Preferred his own company. Did that really make him a damn hermit? A scary one at that? When had that happened? When had he gone from being a private person to a solitary one?

Sighing heavily in resignation, he changed the subject.

"Mitchell, at least tell me there's something we can do about the damn tree farm."

He'd turned his lawyer onto the problem since Tanner's last conversation with the local Sheriff hadn't resolved a damn thing. Of course, that wasn't surprising. Naturally Sheriff Cooper would side with the local against a newcomer. Still though, something had to change.

His old friend said, "I've checked into it, and I can file an injunction, but it won't get you anywhere. That farm's been in the Angel family for three generations. The town's happy with it. Brings in plenty of tourist dollars and no local judge is going to side with you on this. You'll only stir things up and probably make them worse."

"How could it get worse?"

"Piss them off and maybe you'll have Christmas music playing all night, too," Mitchell grumbled. "Tanner, you've just got to find a way to work with them."

"Perfect," Tanner muttered, sitting down behind his desk. He had the house he'd always wanted and it was sitting next to a torture factory. "You know, it's not just the traffic and the damn noise, Mitchell. I've got kids wandering over here from that farm and climbing my trees. That's a liability nightmare waiting to happen. Not to mention the fact that I don't own a dog, yet I *do* now own a pooper scooper of all damn things."

He wasn't sure, but he thought he heard Mitchell laugh.

"It's not funny. Do you know there's an event wedding over there nearly every weekend? And last weekend, there were at least thirty little kids running and screaming all over the place."

"Yeah see, that's the problem," Mitchell told him. "You go into court complaining about children making happy noises at a Christmas tree farm and you look like the ultimate Scrooge. And that's not going to make you real popular around there. It's a small town, Tanner. You knew that when you moved there. Cabot Valley is nothing like L.A."

"No kidding." Actually, the size of the tiny town was one of the things that had drawn Tanner to this part of Northern California. Cabot Valley was only a couple of hours by car away from Sacramento on one side and Lake Tahoe on the other. He could have city when he needed it, but he could be left the hell alone otherwise.

He hadn't even been into town since he moved in. He ordered groceries from the store and had them delivered. When he did leave the house, he didn't bother buying gas in Cabot Valley because he didn't want the locals getting used to seeing him around. He didn't want to be drawn into conversations that could lead to people dropping by his house just to be neighborly. He wasn't looking to make friends. He just wanted to be left alone to do his work in peace.

At least, that had been the plan.

So far, that wasn't happening.

"All I'm saying is give it a while," Mitchell told him.

"Settle in. See if you can't find a way to work around this problem before you start making enemies."

Scowling, Tanner silently admitted he didn't want enemies any more than he wanted to make friends. He just wanted some damn peace and quiet.

"Fine," he snapped. "But tell me this. You won't get rid of the housekeeper and you can't do anything about the damn tree farm. Why is it haven't I fired you?"

"Because I'm the only person you know who'll tell you the truth whether you want to hear it or not."

"Good point. I'm hanging up now."

"So am I. And Tanner…be nice."

He hit the off button and frowned. Even irritated, Tanner could admit that Mitchell was right. He did appreciate the truth. Heaven knew he'd been lied to enough as a kid to last him a lifetime. His mother always had a ready story handy to explain why she couldn't be at his school for a meeting or why she had to leave him with the housekeeper for a month or two while she flew off to Gstaad or Florence or wherever her latest lover had lived.

Instantly, he pushed those old memories away. He wasn't a kid anymore and his childhood had nothing to do with the here and now. The point was, Mitchell was right. And outside of his family—innumerable cousins and half brothers—there were very few people Tanner trusted. Mitchell was one of them.

As he set the phone down, he leaned back, closed his eyes and just for a moment, reveled in the quiet. No Christmas songs. No cars racing along the road. No kids shrieking in his front yard.

No sound from downstairs, either. *What was she doing down there? What kind of housekeeper was that quiet?* Quietly, he went downstairs, and stopped just outside the kitchen door. Something smelled incredible and his stomach grumbled in anticipation. Tanner was so used to just nuking a frozen dinner in the microwave—it had been a long time since he'd actually been *hungry.* Hard to find appreciation for flash frozen pot pies or Salisbury steaks.

He pushed the door open and stood silently in the doorway. There were mixing bowls in the sink, water gushing into them and flour was scattered across the counter making it look as if it had snowed in there. A cupboard door was hanging open, and a bowl full of fruit was on the counter. His gaze shifted to where his new housekeeper was dancing over to the table and setting two places while humming—off-key—and he sighed when he recognized "The Little Drummer Boy." *Another Christmas song. Was this whole town nuts for Christmas?* Shaking his head, he walked to the sink and shut the water off.

Instantly, she spun around, hand clapped to her chest. In the next second, Ivy shot him a near blinding smile.

"Wow. You move quietly. Scared me. Next time ring a bell or something, okay?"

"If you'd remember to turn off the water, you would have heard me."

One of her eyebrows lifted. "I would have shut it off. I'm soaking the bowls."

He ignored that, reached over and closed the cupboard door. "I thought you were here to clean. The kitchen looks like a bomb went off in here."

She just looked at him. "Has anyone ever told you that you're wound a little tight?"

"Just recently, actually."

"Not surprised," she said, then shrugged. "But that's okay."

"Thanks so much."

"No problem. We've all got our quirks." She turned away, grabbed a dishcloth and swiped up the spilled flour. "And as to the mess in here, I was busy. Besides, you have to actually make something dirty before you can clean it."

"Mission accomplished," he said wryly, then sniffed the air. "Though whatever you've been doing smells good."

She smiled slowly and the curve of her mouth tickled that dimple into life in her cheek. A buzz quickened inside Tanner and he had to battle it into submission.

"I guess it would, after living on frozen dinners for two months," she said. Walking to the stove, she swept a spoon through a pot of something that smelled delicious. His stomach rumbled in appreciation.

"What is that?"

"Soup."

The soup he made never smelled that good, he thought and told himself that maybe this hadn't been such a bad idea after all. She seemed to be good at the job and in her defense, he really hadn't heard her down here at all. Still, he hadn't been able to concentrate just knowing she was in the house.

Then his stomach made its opinion clear again and he wondered if there wasn't some way they could make this work. "We really haven't talked about this job," he said.

"Except for the fact that you don't want me here, no," she agreed, smiling.

Did she smile over everything? he wondered, then shook that thought away as irrelevant. "I admit, having someone in the house while I'm working is problematic. I like it quiet."

"Yeah, I guessed that much." She turned to a cupboard, got down two bowls and set them on the counter. "Personally, I don't know how you can stand it. Too much quiet can make you crazy."

"I wouldn't know," he said dryly, thinking of all the interruptions he'd put up with since moving to the supposedly quiet countryside.

She glanced at him and grinned. "Was that sarcasm?"

"I believe so," he admitted, leaning one shoulder against the doorjamb.

"I like it," she said moving to the cooking island to pop a fresh loaf of bread out of its pan and onto a rack. "Proves you do have a sense of humor. So what do you want to talk about?"

"Expectations," he said. "I need quiet to work. But I suppose I do need a housekeeper, too. What we need to do is work out a timetable that's acceptable to both of us."

"Seems reasonable," she mused and walked to the cooking island.

His gaze followed her. "You made bread?"

"Yeah." She shrugged. "It's nothing special. Just quick bread. I mean, I didn't have time to let yeast rise and everything, but this is good, trust me."

He studied her as she moved comfortably around the big room. She'd baked bread and if he wasn't mistaken that was homemade soup on the stove. She'd been in the house for two hours and somehow she'd already taken over. How was it possible? And was it that important, his mind taunted as he savored the scents filling the brightly lit kitchen.

Wouldn't hurt, he told himself, *to eat what she'd prepared.* Then they'd talk about this and find a way for her to be here while not bothering him. He wasn't a damn hermit, he told himself. He was a busy man with no time for interruptions. There was a difference. He preferred order to chaos, that was all.

There were rules that Tanner lived by. Simple. Uncomplicated. He kept to himself. He trusted his brothers and cousins. And most importantly, he avoided relationships that lasted more than a week or two. When he wanted a woman, he went out and found someone looking for nothing more than he was—a couple of weeks of pleasure and a quick goodbye.

Ivy Holloway was definitely not that kind of woman.

So there was no reason for him to allow her to stay, was there?

Three

"Well," she asked. "You hungry?"

"Yeah," he said, tearing his gaze from her pale blue eyes. "I am."

"I'll join you if that's okay," she said, motioning for him to take a seat at the pedestal table set into the curve of the bay window. "I didn't have a chance to eat before I left home."

"Where is home?"

There was a long pause before she said, "Um, here. Cabot Valley." She filled the bowls at the stove, then carried them to the table.

The scent of the soup wafted up to him and Tanner breathed deep, reaching for his napkin and soupspoon. "I guessed that much," he said dryly. "I meant, do you live close by?"

"Sure." She slipped a bread knife from a drawer and cut two thick slices of fresh bread. Lightly buttering them, she carried them to the table and offered him one. Then she sat down opposite him and added, "You know what they say. In a small town, nothing's far from anything."

He frowned at her evasion, but let it go. Frankly, his stomach was demanding more attention at the moment, so he gave in and sampled her soup. Good. Very good. He'd eaten half the bowl before he knew what was happening and then glanced up to see her smiling at him.

"What's so funny?"

"Not funny," she told him. "Is it so wrong for a cook to enjoy watching someone appreciate what she made?"

"No," he said with a shrug. "I suppose not. And the bread's good, too, but you do know you can buy this stuff now. Packaged and sliced."

She frowned at him. "And is it as good as this bread?"

"No, but it's easier."

"Easier isn't always better."

"Actually, I agree with you on that," he admitted, looking into her eyes. *She was more,* he reminded himself, *than just a gorgeous woman with a body to make a grown man weep.* Which, as he'd already warned himself, wasn't necessarily a good thing. Smart, sexy women could bring an unwary man down faster than anything else.

"Look at that," she told him. "We're practically friends already!"

"I wouldn't go that far," he said, finishing his soup. Before he could get up to refill his bowl, she was already standing and walking to the stove.

"You don't have to wait on me," he said.

"Trust me," she answered. "If I *had* to, I probably wouldn't. But consider it part of my job, okay? Housekeepers generally take care of more than the house, don't they? I mean," she continued as she carried the bowl back and set it down in front of him. "I've never been a housekeeper before, but seems to me that the job also includes taking care of the house owner."

He shook his head. "I don't need taking care of, thanks. Been doing just fine on my own most of my life."

"No family then?"

"Why would you say that?"

She pulled off a piece of her bread and popped it into her mouth. "Just that, if you've got family, you're not really on your own, are you?"

"That would depend on the family, wouldn't it?"

"Good point." She sat back in her chair and studied him until Tanner frowned.

"What?"

"Nothing, just wondering about why you don't like your family."

"I didn't say that."

"Sure you did."

"Are you always this direct?" He set his spoon down and leaned back in his chair. Folding his arms across his chest, he assumed an instinctive defensive posture.

"I try to be," she said. "No point in playing games, is there? Then you never get to know people because everyone's too busy pretending to be something they're not. Easier all the way around to be up front and…"

Her voice trailed off and Tanner said, "Well don't stop now, you're on a roll."

Ivy shook her head. "Never mind."

Uncomfortable now, because she *was* playing a game that she wished she weren't, Ivy changed the subject. Leaning her forearms on the table she said, "Why don't we talk about the job instead. What you want. What you don't want. Then we'll work from there."

"Okay." He nodded, thought for a moment and said, "What I want is quiet. Something that seems to be damned hard to come by around here."

She stiffened a little, stung and unable to show it. "I don't know," she said offhandedly, "Cabot Valley's really a very quiet place."

"Maybe the town is, but Christmas central here is a different story."

"You have something against Christmas?"

"In August, yeah."

She bit her tongue to keep the sharp retort she wanted to give him locked inside. Instead, she only said, "A year-round Christmas spirit seems like a good idea to me. People are always friendlier during the season. Kinder, somehow."

He laughed shortly, a harsh sound with no humor in it. "Oh yeah, retailers are notoriously kinder at Christmas."

"I'm talking about people. In general."

"The ones who spend themselves into bankruptcy and then have nervous breakdowns because nothing turned out the way they thought it would? Or how about the kids waiting for a Santa that never shows up? Or the drunks killing people on the road?" He snorted again. "Yeah, that's the kind of thing we should see all year."

"Isn't Christmas huge for your business?"

"I just build the games. I don't force people to buy them."

"Wow." Ivy looked at the dark, fierce expression on his face and knew that this was going to be much harder than she'd thought. Not only did Tanner King want to be isolated and alone, he actually *hated* Christmas. She'd never met anyone who hated the holiday before and she wasn't sure what to say to him now. How did you argue with someone who was determined to see only the negative in a situation?

And why, she couldn't help wondering, *did he feel that way?*

As if reading her expression clearly, he muttered, "Sorry. Didn't mean to go off like that."

"It's okay," she said, watching as the shutters over his eyes closed again, sealing him in and her out. He'd taken a mental step back and did it so neatly she knew it was a way of life for him. "But I have to ask, if you hate Christmas so much, why'd you buy a house right next door to a Christmas tree farm?"

He shot a glance out the window at the darkness, and as if he could see the farm, shook his head. "Because I thought it would be quiet. I thought that Christmas would be the only time I would be bothered by it." He shifted his gaze back to hers. "Turns out, the owner of the farm feels the same way you do. Year-round Christmas is the theme."

"Is it really so bad?"

"Yeah." He picked up his bowl and spoon, then carried them to the sink. Setting them down in the mixing bowl full of water, he turned. Bracing his hands on the counter behind him, he said, "I've got kids running in and out of my yard, a dog I've never seen leaving messes for me to clean up and holiday music blaring all day long. It's that bad."

"Have you tried talking to the owners?" she asked, knowing damn well he hadn't. If he had once come to her, she might have tried to accommodate him. She wasn't sure how, but she'd have tried. Instead, he'd gone to the sheriff, setting himself up as her enemy and leaving her no other choice but to fight this stealth war.

"No. I spoke to the sheriff. Several times. But haven't had any luck with it yet."

"You know, Angel trees has been in this valley—"

"—for more than a hundred years," he finished for her. "Yes, I've heard. That doesn't mean they have the right to make their neighbors miserable. I'm guessing the Christmas carols they assault me with every damn day aren't heard wherever you live."

She winced, but hid it as best she could. Who hated Christmas carols?

"I don't think it's ever been a problem before. I mean," she said, "the person who used to own this property, Mrs. Mansfield, she loved Christmas. She used to work at the farm during the season, selling jams and jellies and the wreaths she made."

And she'd been like a surrogate grandmother to Ivy. Just remembering the old woman made Ivy's heart ache at her loss. If she'd known when Mrs. Mansfield died that a modern day Scrooge would be buying her property, Ivy would have mourned her loss even harder. But the deed was done and Tanner King was the new owner and she somehow had to get through to him. Although that task was looking more and more difficult every second.

"Maybe if you found a way to work with them…"

"The only thing people understand is money and power," he told her flatly, crossing his arms over his broad chest again.

"That's not true of everyone."

He smirked at that, but didn't argue the point. Instead, he said, "We were going to talk about the job."

"Right. Okay then, what is it you want from me?" The instant the words came out of her mouth, Ivy wanted to call them back. She'd sounded a little more seductive than she'd intended.

His eyes narrowed briefly, then, as if he were deliberately mentally moving on, he said, "How long will it take you to clean and make a meal for me every day?"

She had to think about it. Big house. Lots of rooms. Still, it wasn't as if he were a partier. Everything she'd seen so far had been organized to the point that the beautiful house was more like a model home than a real one. She half expected to see a realtor pop out of a closet, talking about staging.

"A couple of hours a day, probably," she said, knowing that would be stretching it. She could probably clean the whole house in a half hour considering how barren it was. The cooking was different of course, but still doable.

"All right then." He nodded. "Then we'll try it for a week. See how it goes."

A week wasn't very long, she thought. But she would be *here*. On his turf. She could wear him down inside a week, she told herself. Wasn't her grandfather always saying that nobody could take a stand against Ivy Holloway and come out the winner?

Well, she was going to put that theory to the test this week.

And she couldn't afford to lose.

"I still say this is a bad idea." Mike Angel's voice sounded like sandpaper on stone and his deeply tanned, weathered face folded into lines of disapproval.

Ivy sighed, knowing her grandfather was not going to stop trying to argue her out of her plan. From the moment she got home from Tanner's house an hour ago, Mike had been muttering and grumbling. "Pop, we've already talked about this."

"I talked," he countered. "You're not listening."

"I did, too," she told him. "And I made my own decision. Just like you taught me to do. Remember?"

His scowl only deepened. "Hardly fair play throwing my own words back at me."

Ivy smiled at him. Her grandfather had always been there for her. He'd been a constant in her life since the first week she and her mother had moved in with him following Ivy's father's death. She was ten that year and the older man had stepped into the void left by Tony Holloway and had become both father and grandfather to Ivy. She had spent countless hours walking the acreage of the tree farm at his side. She'd learned early where to plant, when to plant and when to cut. She'd worked alongside him and his employees to trim the pines into Christmas tree shape and along the way she'd become as much a part of the land as Mike was.

Which was exactly why he'd felt comfortable retiring to Florida to join his daughter while leaving the tree farm in Ivy's hands.

The only problem was, Mike was having a bit of

trouble letting go. Especially with the problem of Tanner King hanging over their heads.

"The man's been trying to shut us down for the last two months, Ivy." Mike settled deeper into his worn, brown leather chair. "I don't see how you going to work for him is going to make the situation any better."

Ivy grinned at the older man. "To quote my grandfather... 'Am I not destroying my enemies when I make friends of them?'"

Mike snorted and shook his head until his flyaway gray hair nearly did fly away. "That's Abraham Lincoln, not me."

"Yes, but you're the one who always said it to me."

"So I'm supposed to feel better that at some point you actually *did* listen to me?"

"Exactly!" Ivy crossed the room, sat down on the brown leather ottoman in front of him and placed her hands on his knees. "You said you trusted me to take care of the farm. To protect the Angel family legacy. Did you mean it?"

His mouth worked furiously as he sucked in a gulp of air. "Course I meant it, but that doesn't—"

"So that means you trust me to make the right decisions for us, right?"

"Yeah, but—"

"Pop...either you trust me or you don't. So which is it?"

"You know all the right words to use when it suits you, don't you Ivy?" He reached out, patted her cheek and sighed. "Just like your mother, God help me. Never could win an argument with her, either."

While Mike went on to complain a bit more, Ivy took a minute to simply enjoy the sound of his voice. In a few days, he'd be on a flight headed for Florida. Even if she had to tie him into his seat.

"I don't feel right about leaving here," Mike said, his voice a low grumble. "Seems to me until this gets straightened out, I ought to be here. Backing you up. In case you need help."

Though she loved him to pieces for wanting to stay, Ivy was just as set on his leaving. Oh, she was going to miss him desperately, she knew. But sometimes change was a good thing. And it would be for the beloved grandfather whose arthritis was bothered more every winter on the mountain. Besides, Ivy's mom really needed him.

Her mom had moved to Florida two years before and now she wanted her father—Mike, to move out there with her. He had been excited about the move, too. Until Tanner King had started making trouble for them. Her grandfather was too much of a mother hen to want to leave.

"Pop, you know as well as I do that Mom needs you. She's started that nursery and you're the plant guy in the family."

He rubbed his cheek with a work worn hand. "You need me, too, Ivy. Going up against a King isn't going to be easy. That family's practically royalty in California. If he goes to a judge, he might shut you down. Then where will you be?"

"Fighting him in court, if I have to," Ivy said, wincing at the very thought of it. She couldn't afford a court case. Heck, she probably couldn't afford to hire a lawyer at this point. She had every spare dime invested in the tree farm. Not to mention the loan she'd taken out to finance her dreams.

She had such plans for the place. And some of them were already working out. For the last few months, they'd been hosting weddings at the farm and had made such a name for themselves that they were getting couples from as far away as Los Angeles and Seattle. With the acres of trees, a wildflower strewn meadow boasting a fast-moving stream, Angel Weddings was fast becoming one of the hottest spots for a romantic setting in the state.

Then there were the birthday parties.

She cringed a little, remembering Tanner's grumbling about the kids running from her property to his. But in her defense, it wasn't always easy corralling fifteen or twenty kids. A few of them might have strayed onto his yard, but mostly, they were content to play in the bounce house. Or to help feed the animals Angel Farm kept in a small petting zoo. Hmm. She was willing to bet that Tanner didn't know about the pygmy goats or he'd have been complaining about them as well.

But the thing she was most proud of was her new Adopt-a-Tree program.

People could choose their Christmas tree months in advance and then come whenever they wanted to, to help care for the tree, water it, shearing. Kids learned how trees grew and how important the environment was to everyone and their parents enjoyed spending time with their kids.

Adopting a tree stretched out the Christmas season and to Ivy's way of thinking, kept families wrapped in that lovely spirit all year. And, while the people were at Angel Christmas Tree Farm, they usually had lunch at the newly established café and bought decorative items and crafts made by the ladies in town at the gift store.

She was turning their family business around *and* helping the local economy. She was so close to making Angel Christmas Tree Farm a year-round financial success. At least, she would be, if she had the chance. But if Tanner King did end up hiring a lawyer, all of her plans would drain away. She might even end up losing the home she loved so much to pay for lawyers she couldn't afford.

"It'd be different if only David hadn't—"

Her grandfather's words ended abruptly, but it wasn't soon enough to keep an old familiar ache from settling around Ivy's heart. David. The man she had been about to marry four years ago. Until the car accident that had killed him instantly.

"I didn't mean to bring it up," Mike said quickly. "But damn it, if David were here, it'd be different. I could leave knowing you were safe."

She forced a laugh she knew he needed to hear. "Pop, I'm perfectly safe here and you know it. I'm not some fragile flower in a hothouse. I'm a tree farmer and most of the people who work here helped to raise me."

"It's not the same."

"No," she said wistfully. "it's not. But David's gone."

She'd mourned his loss for a long time, but as her grandfather reminded her, you couldn't bury yourself along with your heart. You had to move on and keep going.

Besides, it wasn't as if she would be really alone when Mike moved, anyway.

Not with ten part-time employees, people constantly running in and out of her house and an entire small town far too interested in her life. Still, she thought as she watched her grandfather worry, it was going to be hard, not having her family with her every day.

All too soon, she'd come home to an empty house, with only the memories of laughter and arguments and conversations to keep her company. Her gaze swept the familiar front room, lightly touching on the books haphazardly stacked in bookshelves and piled on tables. The handmade quilt her late grandmother had fashioned draped across the back of the sofa. The stone fireplace Mike had built when he and Grandma had first taken over the Angel family home. Scarred wooden floors, pale peach walls and the scent, as always, of evergreens.

Ivy's heart was in this old house. In this farm. In every tree on her acreage. And she would do whatever she had to do to protect every last seedling out there.

"At least tell me how you think working for this guy is going to help the situation any," Mike said, catching her attention.

"It was actually Mr. King's lawyer's idea," she said and continued despite Mike's snort of derision. Everyone in the county knew how Mike Angel felt about lawyers. "Mitchell Tyler is his name and he was very nice when he called last week. You know, right after Sheriff Cooper came out to see us about the latest complaint?"

"I remember."

And judging by the look in his eye, the memory only fueled the flames of his anger. Being told by the local sheriff that the new guy in town was out to get you was not something anyone wanted to hear.

"Anyway," she said, trying to distract her grandfather from his anger, "Mitchell explained that he needed to hire Tanner a housekeeper and that he thought it would be a great way for me to convince Tanner that I'm not his enemy. He thinks that if we just get to know each other that Tanner might be more willing to listen to reason."

"*Tanner.*" Mike snorted. "What kind of name is that, anyway? And Mitchell. Who names these people?"

"I like the name Tanner," she said. "It's masculine and strong and—" She broke off when she caught her grandfather's raised eyebrows.

She sighed. "The point is, Mitchell's trying to talk Tanner into relaxing and to stop making the complaints. But he says if I can worm my way into his good graces that could help the situation."

"And how did he hear about you? This Mitchell, I mean."

"Remember, I met him several months ago when he was up here delivering building permits and things for the crew that redid Mrs. Mansfield's house for Tanner."

"Harriet Mansfield. Now that was a good neighbor."

"Yes, but she's gone and Tanner's there now. We have to make him like it here, Pop, or he's going to make trouble for us."

"Like to see him try it," her grandfather muttered.

"Well I *don't* want to see him try it," Ivy said, leaning forward until she could meet her grandfather's steely blue eyes with her own. "He's rich and powerful and crabby. Not a good combination to have in an enemy."

"And you're gonna turn him around, are you?"

"I'm going to try," Ivy told him.

"If you fail?"

"I won't," she insisted. "Tanner's not a bad guy, Pop.

He's just too…closed up. I'm going to open up his world for him."

Her grandfather's eyes narrowed on her thoughtfully. "You're not thinking of maybe…"

"Maybe what?"

"*You* know. You're young and pretty. He's young and rich."

"*POP!*"

"Wouldn't be the first time a woman's head was turned by a rich, powerful man."

"I don't care about his money. And I'm not looking for romance." She shook her head. "I already had my shot at true love."

Her grandfather chuckled. "You really are young, Ivy, if that's what you think. You loved David, I know. But it won't be the last time you love, I sincerely hope. There'll be someone else for you along the road. Just don't look for it where you'll only find disappointment."

She flushed a little, remembering that swamping sensation of heat she'd felt at first sight of Tanner King. How just looking into his eyes made her stomach swim and her knees go weak. How the sound of his voice had seemed to shiver along her nerve endings.

But Mike was right, she told herself. Being Tanner's friend, introducing him to life in a small town and with any luck getting him to be less of a Scrooge was one thing. Romance was something else entirely. Men like him didn't go for women like her. And if they did, it wasn't a long-term commitment they were thinking about.

"I promise," she said softly. "I'm not looking for anything from Tanner except a cease-fire."

Mike studied her for a long minute, then patted her

cheek again. "Well then, I say Tanner King doesn't stand a chance. Once Ivy Angel Holloway gets going, there's not a power on earth to stop her."

Four

The next morning, Ivy and Mike were in Cabot Valley Bank to talk about the balloon payment due on the loan she had taken out. She was as nervous as a child at the dentist waiting to get a cavity filled.

While she and her grandfather sat quietly, the bank manager, Steve Johnson, looked over their loan papers with a slow shake of his head. Finally, he looked up and met her gaze.

"Thanks for coming in, Ivy," he said. "I just wanted the three of us to have a sit-down to talk about the due date on this loan."

"Trust me when I say that I know the payment is almost due," she told him and was grateful when Mike reached over and gave her hand a pat. "It's not going to be a problem."

She sincerely hoped.

Ivy had taken out a big loan to improve and expand

the farm, and she'd gotten a terrific interest rate—because she'd agreed to a huge balloon payment that would come due all too soon. If she didn't pay up, she could lose everything. The moment that thought entered her mind, she shoved it away and buried it. No room for bad karmic thoughts, she told herself.

Besides, as long as the big wedding they had scheduled came off without a hitch, there wouldn't be a problem.

"Steve," Mike said softly, "I've known you since you were a kid sneaking onto the farm at night to play hide-and-seek with your pals."

Steve squirmed uneasily in his chair. "That's—

"My point is," Mike said, "you know the Angel family well enough to know we never fail to pay our debts."

"Of course I know that," Steve answered.

"Good." Ivy interrupted before either man could speak again. She appreciated her grandfather's support, but she was the one who'd taken out the loan It was her responsibility to pay it off. "I'll see you in a couple of weeks to make that payment, Steve. You can count on it."

When she stood up, so did the bank manager. He held out one hand across his desk and Ivy took it in hers. Mike nodded at him, and as they left, Steve said, "You know I only wish you the best, Ivy."

"I know that," she assured him and didn't speak again until she and Mike were in the main room of the bank.

The old building shone like a well cared for jewel. Wood walls were polished and the windows and floor gleamed from careful cleaning. Three or four people were lined up waiting for the tellers. Even a whisper carried in the room, since the high ceilings acted like an echo chamber or something. So Ivy was very quiet as she told her grandfather, "Don't worry, I know what I'm doing."

He slung one arm around her shoulder and steered her toward the front door. "I know you do, Ivy girl. I just want it all to go well, is all."

"It will. I promise."

As they stepped outside, Ivy took a deep breath and made a solemn, silent vow. She would make the balloon payment, then finish paying off the loan. She'd keep her farm, her family's legacy and once this loan was paid off, she'd never again take such a high-risk gamble.

Three days later, Tanner was no closer to solving the problems with the game. He blamed it on Ivy, of course. The woman was everywhere. And even when she wasn't actually *in* the house, her scent lingered, the thoughtful touches she'd left in her wake remained.

The fresh flowers she brought in and arranged in vases and pitchers to leave all over the house. The sandwiches she made and left wrapped for him in the refrigerator. The fresh fruit that he'd become accustomed to snacking on when he wandered through the empty rooms searching for inspiration.

Everywhere he looked, Ivy was there.

He should be trying to find a way to get rid of her, he knew. Instead, he'd spent most of his time wondering when she would be back. A dangerous situation but one he didn't seem to be able to avoid. Thoughts of her stayed with him long after she was gone.

Even the Christmas tree farm seemed different lately.

He'd noticed that the volume on the damn carols had been cut way back—a fact for which he was grateful. Now the incessant music was no more than a background hum of irritation rather than the overpowering aggravation he was used to. Though he was curious as to why they were suddenly being so accommodating.

He looked out the window at the tree farm and the late afternoon sun speared into his eyes. That was another thing. He'd been waking up earlier since Ivy had been coming around. The only explanation he could come up with for the switch in his sleeping pattern was that his dreams were so full of her, his subconscious was waking him early so that he had more time with her.

Not that he was making use of that extra time. No, he was determined to keep his distance from the woman. She was clever and funny and sexy enough to make him want to grab hold of her every time she entered a room. But the fact was, he wasn't going to risk a brief fling with a woman who had *permanent* practically stenciled on her forehead.

Ivy was white picket fences and children at her knee.

Tanner was a solitary man and he liked it that way.

Never the twain would meet.

"Great. Now you're getting poetic." He turned from the window, walked to his desk and sat down. Glaring at the computer screen where his muscle-bound warrior knight stood glaring back at him, Tanner muttered, "Work. Damn it, keep your mind on the damn game and get it done."

This was the solution that had seen him through his life. As soon as he was old enough, Tanner had laid out a pattern for how he wanted his life to be. Orderly. Might seem boring to others, but for him, there was peace in rules. His childhood had been barely restrained chaos with a mother who drifted from one adventure to the next, always dragging her reluctant son behind her.

He'd long ago decided that his life would be different. It would be steady. Controlled. Organized. There was no room for chaos when structure ruled the situation. And his main rule was that when it was time for work, nothing else intruded.

Tanner had never had trouble with that self-imposed imperative until Ivy Holloway had come into his life. Now, he was forced to struggle to keep his mind on what used to be the most important thing in his life. His company. His designs. His future.

Shaking his head, he picked up a pen and tapped it against the sketch pad in front of him. He focused on the image of the knight on his computer screen, standing in a barren field of rocks and dead grass, the body of an evil troll at his feet.

"If the knight uses the enchanted sword against the troll, then there has to be a consequence," Tanner muttered, glaring at the knight as if this problem were all the character's fault.

When the truth was, Tanner's focus was still shattered. It seemed thoughts of Ivy were never far away no matter how much he fought them. Hell, how could he keep his mind on the problems faced by his game's hero when he knew Ivy Holloway was just downstairs?

He shoved one hand through his hair. One woman shouldn't have this kind of effect on a man. For God's sake, less than a week ago, he hadn't even known she existed.

Gritting his teeth, Tanner told himself that he might

finally end up firing Mitchell over this all too alluring housekeeper.

"Troll," he muttered. "Keep your mind on the damn dead troll."

"I'm guessing there aren't many people in the world who get to say that during an ordinary work day."

He spun around to face the bane of his recent existence. She stood in the open doorway to his office, one hand resting lightly atop a vacuum cleaner. Her jeans were faded and her dark red T-shirt clung to her breasts and narrow waist in a way that made a man want to define those curves with his own hands. She was a temptation, pure and simple. And he was losing the battle to stay indifferent.

"I didn't hear you come up."

She grinned and that dimple he so looked forward to seeing appeared in her cheek. "That was the deal, remember? Quiet as a mouse. Not disturbing you."

"Right. Yeah, I know." He frowned at the vacuum. "Judging by that, you're about to disturb me though, right?"

She patted the upright, pale blue appliance. "I sure am. So I thought I'd warn you first. Tell you to close your door against the noise."

"Fine," he acknowledged. "Not like I'm making any progress here anyway."

"Bad day at the joust?" she quipped.

"You could say that," Tanner admitted. "My knight has vanquished his foe far too easily."

She straightened up and curiosity flared in her eyes. "So what do you do about it?"

"That's the question. If the game's too easy, people complain. If it's too hard, people complain. So I walk a fine line. Right now, the game's leaning toward easy. Gotta come up with a fix." He stared into her eyes, caught up in the excitement he saw gleaming there. How long had it been since he'd been really *excited* about anything? "The question is," he said, "should it be a magical consequence or something a little more human?"

He shouldn't be asking her opinion, he told himself sternly. The games were his domain and he rarely listened to anyone else's input. The fact that she was standing there in the doorway, intruding on his work time was his own damn fault though, for leaving the door open in the first place. But then again, maybe he'd been hoping for an interruption.

Hard as it was to admit, Tanner thought, in the last few days that Ivy had been coming to his house every afternoon, he'd become accustomed to her. More than that, he'd actually begun looking forward to seeing her. So much so that he was shifting slowly out of his vampire work schedule.

So what did that say?

"What do you think?" he asked, not really expecting her to solve his problem, but not ready to stop talking to her or looking at her, either.

She abandoned the vacuum, stepped into the room and glanced at the walls where framed posters of his more popular games were hung. Silently admiring them with a smile, she walked toward him, glanced at the warrior knight still awaiting a command and said, "I think it should be something more human."

Interesting. He would have thought she'd play into the magical fantasy. "Like what?"

"Does he have a love interest?" She moved up beside him.

Tanner took a deep breath of that warm, citrusy scent and forced his gaze to the screen. "Of course. The Lady Gwen."

"Oooh, I like that."

"Ten-year-old boys won't, but hopefully everyone else will," he told her wryly.

She laughed and the sound was musical, soft, as enchanting as the magical game he was working on.

"So then," she said, leaning down, bracing her hands on the edge of his desk, "if the knight kills the troll with the enchanted sword, then Lady Gwen is swept into a dimensional prison."

Tanner blinked at her. He hadn't been expecting that. *"What?"*

She laughed again. "It makes sense, doesn't it? He does something he *knows* is wrong—I'm guessing the use of the magical element—and so his punishment is to lose what he loves most."

Intrigued, he said, "Hardly fair to Lady Gwen, though."

"Ah, she knew what she was getting into the minute she met Sir Whatever-His-Name-Is."

"Hawk," Tanner told her, thinking about her suggestion. He had to admit, he never would have gone in that direction. But now he was considering it…

"Of course his name is Hawk," she said, grinning. "Very heroic. So, Gwen disappears into a dimensional prison. Or she's sucked into a portal—"

He caught the glint of excitement in her eye and shared it. Funny. Tanner had been designing games for more than ten years. He'd always considered it the perfect profession for him. An isolated one. A career where he didn't require other people around—where he could shut himself up in his own world and create the images that had always been a part of him.

He'd never had a collaborator. Never even considered having one. Now with a quick conversation, Ivy had sparked new ideas in his mind and he knew in his gut, they were good ones.

Having Ivy in the house the last couple of days had surprised him in more ways than he would have expected. Yes, she'd been a distraction. But he'd allowed that distraction to get out of hand, too. He hadn't kept his distance from her. Instead, he'd sought her out. Talking to her as she cooked, helping her move furniture when she had decided that his living room was too sterile-looking.

But the most surprising part of all of this was just how insightful she was about the game he was currently tweaking. She'd had other suggestions for elevating the skill level while maintaining an accessibility that all game makers strive for. And now, she just might have found a way for him to change the ending into something amazing.

"She's trapped despite her powers," he mused aloud, shifting his gaze to the warrior knight before starting a new sketch on the paper in front of him. He picked up a pen and quickly roughed out an image of the Lady Gwen being dragged into a shining doorway that pulsed with energy.

"That's amazing," Ivy whispered and he realized she'd come closer, her hair now brushing his cheek.

He gritted his teeth and kept his gaze locked on his

drawing. Was it his fault that Lady Gwen suddenly bore a remarkable resemblance to Ivy?

"God, you're a terrific artist," she said, reaching past him to stroke the tip of one finger along the line of Lady Gwen's flowing gown.

"It's just a rough draft," he told her, noticing just how tight his voice sounded. His pen sketched in a deeply cut bodice on Lady Gwen's dress, displaying the tops of round, high breasts and he couldn't help wondering what Ivy's breasts would look like and feel like in his hands. His mouth.

Tanner's entire body went still. His mind blanked out and all he could see was the mental image of Ivy, stretched across his bed, naked. Blowing out a breath, he swallowed hard and fought his way back to the conversation. "This is just to give the programmers direction."

"It's still amazing," she argued, "I can't draw a crooked line and you'd think that would be easy. So, how will Lady Gwen get out of the portal?"

Tanner shrugged. "Her knight has to save her."

"Why can't she save herself?"

He sighed and risked a quick glance up at her. But turning his head to hers brought their mouths within a breath of each other. His gaze dropped to her lips and he felt a quick, sharp stab of desire slam into him. His body was hard, instantly. He felt the rush of heat filling his veins and told himself to get a grip.

The problem was, he wanted to get a grip on *her*.

Shaking his head to get rid of those thoughts, Tanner muttered, "This is a video game, not a lesson in equal opportunity."

"But it could be," she said, arguing her point. "Oh,

don't get me wrong, I suppose every woman wants her white knight, whether she'll admit it or not. But what happens when the brave menfolk aren't around? Shouldn't we be strong enough to save ourselves?"

His eyes locked onto hers as he tried to see past her interest in the game to what lay behind her words. Her eyes were soft, but with a shadow in them that looked a lot like old pain. Concern awakened inside him, pushing past the desire still choking him and he heard himself ask, "Speaking from experience? Has your own white knight let you down lately?"

Her smile faded abruptly and those shadows in her eyes darkened before sliding into the background. "I don't have one. A knight, that is. Not anymore."

Pain flickered on her expression and then disappeared again so quickly Tanner wasn't entirely sure he'd seen it at all. But whether he had or not, she clearly didn't want to discuss it and he knew better than anyone how it felt to want to keep your private life private. So he let it go.

For now.

But he knew that sooner or later, he would want to know what—or who—had hurt her. What he didn't know was *why* he needed to know.

"Okay then," he looked back to the sketch in front of him and asked, "So how do you see Lady Gwen escaping on her own?"

"It has to be impressive…"

"Oh," he said, "naturally."

If she heard the sarcasm in his tone, she ignored it.

"What if Lady Gwen is a sorceress? What if she breaks through the portal by wielding a spell that draws on her knight's love for her?"

Tanner thought about that for a moment, then turned back to his sketch pad, his mind alive with ideas. Quick strokes became a drawing rich in detail in no time at all and before he knew it, he and Ivy were brainstorming solutions that were nothing short of brilliant.

He was so caught up in what they were creating together that when she leaned in close again, he almost avoided getting lost in her scent again.

Almost.

"We're nearly finished with the shearing, Ivy." Dan Collins swung one arm out and indicated the back half of the acreage. "We've got a couple teams back there right now."

Ivy frowned a little and squinted out at the trees. It was hard to concentrate on what Dan was saying because she was so exhausted it felt as though there was a fog hanging over her brain. Hadn't gotten much sleep the night before. Mainly because after she'd left Tanner's house, her mind had been so full of him, she hadn't been able to close her eyes without seeing his image.

She'd had a good time with him, darn it. She hadn't counted on actually *liking* the man. And now she was feeling guilty. He was being...nice. And she was lying to him. Tricking him.

"Ivy?" Dan laid one big hand on her shoulder and asked, "You okay?"

"Yeah," she said, forcing a smile, "I'm fine. Just tired."

"Not surprising since you're running back and forth between the farm and the rich guy's place. You sure working for him is a good idea?" In his fifties, Dan looked at her as one of his own kids. He'd been working at the tree farm since before Ivy was born and he knew the place—and her—very well. "You're burning your candle at both ends and in the middle. Girl, you can't run the farm and the gift shop during the day and work for King at night without wearing yourself out."

"I'm fine," she insisted, tipping her head back to let the sunshine beat against her closed eyes. "Really, Dan. You know why I'm working for him."

"I do, but that doesn't mean I like it."

"Now you sound like Mike."

"Smart man."

She tipped her head to one side, opened her eyes and grinned up at Dan. "You two are peas in a pod. I swear I don't know why Pop's worried about leaving me as long as you're around."

But he didn't smile as she'd hoped. Instead, worry lines dug themselves more deeply into the furrow between his eyes.

"We got a right to be worried. All of us. That King fella could make us some serious trouble." His mouth worked as if his words tasted bitter. "All the complaining that man's done about the farm, it's only a matter of time before he does something bigger. Like a lawsuit or something."

Just what Ivy had been worrying about before she'd actually met Tanner. Now, she wasn't so sure.

"I don't think he will," she said, wondering if that was merely wishful thinking. "But turning down the volume on the music can't hurt."

He scowled and shook his head. "Who doesn't like Christmas music? I want to know."

Ivy laughed and tucked her arm through his as she started leading him off in the direction of the shearing crew. "It'll all work out, Dan. Once we pull off the big wedding, we can take care of the more immediate payment. And with the extra money I'm making now, the two weddings we just booked and the birthday parties we have scheduled, I can pay off the bank loan that much sooner and we can continue the expansion."

"I just don't like seeing you work yourself into the ground is all," he muttered.

"I'm fine. Honestly. Now," she said firmly, shifting the subject back to business, "I know we should have had the last of the trees shaped by the first of July, but with things as busy as they are…"

Dan slid into the new conversation gratefully. "Doesn't matter, really. We've got time. The ones we're working on now won't be up for purchase until next year anyway."

Ivy listened, and inspected the trees they passed along the way. The annual shearing was a big job, but it had to be done and at the right time, too. The idea was to cut off new growth as soon as it was developed—before it had a chance to get tough and woody. Shearing controlled the shape and density of the trees themselves.

Took a lot of work to get that perfect, proportional Christmas tree shape. And some of the guys who worked for Angel tree farm were downright territorial over the shearing process. Some preferred working with the Scotch pines and a couple thought the Douglas fir, that didn't really require shearing, was the better tree anyway.

But, Ivy thought, *that's why Angel trees offered a choice.* Everyone had their own idea of the perfect Christmas tree. To her though, they were *all* perfect.

Dan was still talking and she came up out of her own

thoughts to pay attention. "Got a good healthy crop up there and the latest batch of Fraser fir seedlings are coming along. The balsam firs are in even better shape. Should be fine over the winter."

"That's good news," she said, letting her gaze slide across the pines and firs they passed along the way. Most of the bigger trees she saw wore brightly colored tags, with the name of their adopted family painted on in script.

Her Adopt-A-Tree program was really starting to catch on.

Scotch pines bristled against her bare arms as she walked past and Ivy noticed the pristine shaping her crews had managed. The scent of evergreen filled her head and wrapped her in a familiar sense of comfort.

She loved all of her trees, of course, but her favorite by far was the Fraser fir. It was the tree her own family always had in the house and she thought personally that no other Christmas tree reached the same stage of perfection. The color, the scent, the height and width. It was as if God Himself had designed the perfect tree. All the Angel family had to do was grow them.

Her sneakers kicked up dirt in the rows between the trees and she idly noticed that it was time to get the crews out to thin the weeds. From a distance, she heard the sound of kids laughing. That was the main reason she loved what she did so much. They weren't just growing and selling trees here. They were making memories for families. Making Christmas as special to everyone else as it was to her.

"Maude says to tell you she sold the Wedding Ring quilt to that young couple from Fresno."

"Oh, that's great," Ivy said, remembering the couple

who had wandered the farm area for hours before coming in and booking their wedding. Satisfaction rolled through her but not just for her own operation's success, but the town's, as well. Every piece of handcrafted beauty the shop sold, helped a craftsman in town. And with every job saved, they made Cabot Valley a little more secure.

As they approached the shearing crew, Dan walked on ahead, but Ivy stopped in her tracks. She turned her head and glanced over at Tanner's house. She could just see the roof and chimney from this perspective, and she wondered what he was doing. If he was lonely in his self made prison.

But mostly, she wondered what he would say if he could see her here.

Where she really belonged.

Five

Ivy's nervous bride was taking a lot of her energy.

Patsy Harrington had lots of ideas, but most of the major decisions had already been made and changing them now was only going to create chaos. In dealing with the brides, Ivy had learned that being firm but supportive was the only real way to survive.

"We talked about this last time, remember?" Ivy pointed to the creek where a new bridge was being constructed. "You wanted to be able to pose for photos at the bridge, with the trees in the background."

"Yes," Patsy said, hitching her designer handbag higher on her shoulder, "but I was thinking that maybe it would be better to be in the middle of the trees instead. That way, we're surrounded by the greenery and our wedding clothes will really pop in the photos."

Ivy gave a small, inward sigh. She had her crew building the very bridge that Patsy had insisted on. And, she didn't really want an entire wedding party troop-ing through the tree lines. "But, your dress could get ruined that way, too, with the dirt and fertilizer…" She purposely stopped, letting her words trail off so that Patsy would come to the right decision as she considered things.

"True…" The woman chewed at her bottom lip and looked back at the creek and the graceful arch of the soon to be finished bridge. "And it is very pretty down by the stream."

"It is," Ivy agreed. "Plus, as we discussed, we'll have pine boughs attached to the railings with white ribbon and the flowers you selected. "It's a gorgeous spot for pictures, Patsy. Couldn't ask for better."

"I suppose," she said, nodding. Her expertly cut hair swung out from her chin in a graceful arc as she turned back to Ivy. "Okay then, never mind. Honestly, I don't know how you put up with me, Ivy. I'm driving my own mother insane and my fiancé keeps threatening to kidnap me and elope!"

"Oh, can't have that!" Ivy had one brief, hideous vision of the wedding being canceled and her loan com-ing due. No, no. "The wedding's going to be beautiful, Patsy. You'll see. You've made all the tough decisions, now all you have to do is trust us to pull it together."

"You're right," the woman said, checking her slender wristwatch. "And I should get going. I've got an appointment in town to talk to the florist."

Carol Sands owned the only flower shop in town and hardly ever got he opportunity to show off her artistic abilities. The Harrington wedding was giving the whole town a chance to shine and they were all eager to prove themselves.

"Carol's very excited about doing the flowers for your wedding," Ivy said. "And we all appreciate the fact that you're using the local suppliers this way."

"Only makes sense," Patsy told her as they started walking across the farm toward the front gate. Laughing, she added, "I know I don't seem like it lately, but I'm actually pretty level-headed."

"All brides get a little weirded out at times," Ivy reassured her.

Patsy let her gaze slide across the rows of trees and what looked like endless miles of bright blue sky. "I just loved this place the moment I came across your Web site. And when Tom and I came to look around, I knew this was where I wanted to hold my wedding."

"I'm glad to hear it. I think it's beautiful here, too."

"Oh, it really is," Patsy agreed. "And, since I live in Sacramento, it would be crazy to try and use city florists and musicians when I can get everything I need right here in Cabot Valley."

"Exactly what we love to hear," Ivy told her. This is what she'd been hoping for by expanding her farm. Her friends and neighbors would be part of the enterprise and the entire town would eventually benefit.

The two women continued to talk over plans as they wandered across the farm.

Maybe, Tanner told himself, Mitchell and Ivy were right. Maybe he had been too closed off since he moved to Cabot Valley. Maybe the mistake he'd made when angry about the Christmas tree farm was in going to the sheriff instead of dealing with the owners directly.

He stared out his office window at the swarms of people wandering the farm's long neat rows of trees.

From his vantage point, he could see one corner of the parking lot where dozens of cars were clustered behind a partial screen of bushes. It was definitely a booming business that he'd already learned was important to the locals.

So perhaps what he should do, he thought, was talk to the owners. See if they could find a way to work together in this. Not that he was looking to make friends. He still wasn't interested in that, but there was no reason to have an enemy either.

It was early afternoon and he hadn't even begun work yet. What better time to take a walk and meet the neighbors? Before he could talk himself out of it, he headed downstairs.

A few minutes later he was a part of the scene he'd been complaining about for two months. Here, the Christmas carols were impossible to ignore. With the summer sun slamming down onto him, he lost himself in the crowds and caught snatches of conversations as he went.

Kids whining, fathers grumbling, mothers soothing. He smiled in satisfaction that he wasn't one of their number, until it hit him that *he* was the outsider here. Everyone else had a mission. They were there to enjoy each other and their day among the trees. He was alone. As always. The solitary man in an ocean of families and couples.

And for the first time in his life, Tanner didn't care for it.

His smile faded as his gaze swept the area, taking in the tiny café with outdoor seating—not much more than a snack bar, really. The menu was simple. Hot dogs, hamburgers, chips and drinks. But there were plenty of people in line. Just as the gift shop bustled with customers. He shook his head as women left carrying huge bags filled with who knew what. At least that much in life was a certainty, he told himself. Give a woman the chance to shop and she was off and running. Though the women he was accustomed to preferred to shop where items came in pale blue boxes.

Looking around, Tanner could admit to himself that he was really out of his element here. Not only didn't he normally do crowds, but the very idea of being in the thick of Christmas central was absolutely not him. Yet, here he stood and he had to admit that it wasn't as bad as he'd thought it would be. The rise and fall of the voices around him, blending with the inevitable Christmas music wasn't hard to take.

He'd never been to a Christmas tree farm and seeing all the different types of trees spread out in front of him was…pretty. The scent of the pines filled every breath and even in the heat of summer, he got the draw. The appeal. Kids ran up and down the rows, playing in safety in the man-made forest, their squeals of laughter echoing in the air. Parents wandered, keeping an eye on the kids, while clearly enjoying themselves. Tanner wandered, too, wanting to take his time and make up his own mind about this operation before introducing himself to whoever was in charge.

He didn't know a pine from a fir, but he could see that the place was well cared for. There were few weeds growing in the separating rows and a glance at the old farmhouse told him that upkeep was important to the Angel family. The Victorian had to be at least a hundred years old, but its sky blue paint and white trim was tidy. Flower pots sat on the porch railings and hung from hooks attached to the ceiling. Window panes gleamed in the sunlight and the door stood open as if welcoming visitors. He shook his head in wonder that the owners weren't worried about someone walking into the house and stealing them blind. But apparently, small town life was a far cry from life in L.A.

"Can I help you with anything?"

Tanner turned to the younger man smiling at him. "No thanks. Just looking around."

"And you're welcome to. But if you do need something or if you find a tree you want to adopt, you just give a yell, someone will find you."

"Right, thanks." Adopt a tree? What kind of person was it who came up with something like that, anyway? He kept walking and didn't stop again until a little girl of about six stepped out in front of him.

"Mister, can you lift me up?"

He glanced around, looking for the girl's parents, but there were no other adults nearby. Wasn't anyone watching the kid? He stared down into a pair of big brown eyes and asked, "Why?"

"So I can reach Lisa."

Even more confusing. "Who's Lisa?"

She laughed. "My tree, silly. Her name is Lisa. I got to name her cause Mommy said I could and Daddy said everything should have a name and she's too pretty to just be 'tree'."

"You named your tree?" Tanner could hardy believe he was even having this conversation. But now, like it not, he was sucked in. The tiny girl was all shining innocence, with her pigtails, cuffed Levi's and bright red sneakers.

"Yes, and now Lisa's tag is all turned around," she

said, pointing at a wooden disk inside a plastic sleeve, hanging from one of the top branches of the nearest tree. "I don't want somebody else to buy her because she's my tree. My daddy said."

The girl spoke so fast, her words tumbled into each other, but Tanner had gotten the gist of the problem. "I can fix the tag for you," he offered, reaching for it.

"No!" She stopped him with that single word and when he looked again, she was shaking her head hard enough to send her twin pigtails flying. "I have to do it because she's my tree and it's my job. So can you lift me up?"

Tanner frowned when she held up her arms, clearly expecting him to do just as she had asked. He hadn't been around kids since he *was* one, yet he didn't see a way out of helping the girl without looking like a complete jerk. So sighing, he bent down, lifted the child and held her as carefully as he would have a ticking time bomb while she reached out with both hands to turn the plastic-covered tag around.

"See?" she asked, "that's my tree's name right there on the bottom. My name's Ellie and I didn't have room to put me on there, too. So just Lisa's name is on it, but that's okay, don't you think?"

Sure enough, in uneven letters was the word *Lisa* painted in a sunshine yellow. There was also an uneven candy cane done in red and white and a lopsided star in blue. At the top of the tag, an adult had printed the words, *Callendar family.*

"Very nice," Tanner said, looking at the girl in his arms. "Are you finished?"

"Almost," she assured him, and straightened the tag again, turning it so that the artwork was facing out. Then she patted the pine needles and smoothed her little hand right up to the top. "That's where our angel will go at Christmas time. Mommy says it will be a perfect fit, too. Lisa's gonna look so pretty in our house."

"I'm sure she will," he said, shooting a worried glance at the surrounding area, positive that the girl's parents would show up any second and he'd be accused of trying to kidnap the girl or something.

"Do you have your tree picked out yet?"

"What? No," he told her, staring into those brown eyes again. "I don't get a Christmas tree."

Her brow furrowed. "Why not?"

Why? Because Christmas had never been anything but a misery to Tanner. He didn't have lovely childhood memories like this little girl was busily making. He didn't have fond recollections of a happy family gathering. When he thought of Christmas, he thought of empty hotel rooms, a room service menu and a holiday movie on the television. Not exactly something he longed to repeat. But this child didn't need to know any of that— nor would she understand it. Their childhoods were not just years apart—but worlds apart as well.

"I just…don't."

She patted his cheek. "That's why you look sad. I could help you find a good one if you want and then you could be happy again. I always find our trees and Daddy says that I'm best at it."

He didn't know whether to be touched or appalled that a little girl was feeling sorry for him.

"Thanks, but—"

"Ellie?"

Thank God, Tanner thought, turning at the sound of

the woman's voice. He was still holding the little girl, still standing stiffly, as if half afraid to move.

"Hi, Mommy! This man helped me fix Lisa's tag so no one else can buy her!"

A pretty woman with light brown hair and eyes just like her daughter's stepped up beside them. She gave him a measuring stare and then must have decided he wasn't a danger because she relaxed and smiled. "That was nice of him, sweetie. But we've got to go now. Daddy's waiting for us with hot dogs and cookies."

"Oh, boy! You can put me down now, mister."

Almost surprised to find he was still holding the girl, Tanner reacted immediately and set her on her feet.

"Thanks a lot," Ellie told him as she slipped her hand into her mother's.

"Yes, thank you," her mom said. "I hope she wasn't a bother."

"No," he told her, realizing it was only the truth. "Not at all."

Both mother and daughter gave him brilliant smiles, then they walked off, hand in hand, toward the snack bar and the lucky man waiting for them.

Lucky man, Tanner mused. Funny, not so long ago, he would have thought a married man with kids was more to be pitied than envied. But now, he thought having a child like the precocious Ellie might not be a terrible thing.

Stunned at the stray thought, he told himself it was probably Ivy's influence. The woman was relentlessly cheerful and optimistic. Clearly some of that was wearing off on him. And he wasn't entirely sure how he felt about that.

Continuing on through the forest of trees, he nodded

at people he passed and even began humming along to one of those insidious carols. When he realized what he was doing he stopped, but the fact that he'd hummed along to it at all surprised him. *Was it some sort of brainwashing?* he wondered. Play Christmas music all day every day until it gets to even the most hardened of hearts?

Well, he'd never thought of himself as having a hard heart. Still, in comparison to those who thought Angel Christmas Tree Farm was a paradise, he probably sensed the Scrooge Mitchell had named him. Uncomfortable with that particular label, he shrugged it off. He wasn't *that* bad, he assured himself.

As he stepped out into a patch of sunlight Tanner saw that the full grown trees were now behind him. Ahead of him, were shorter versions and beyond them, were rows and rows of seedlings, barely a foot high. The farm was laid out well, he thought, recognizing the planning and the care that had gone into the Angel Christmas Tree Farm.

While he swept the area with a cool gaze, he stopped when he spotted a familiar blond head walking with a pretty brunette. Ivy and the other woman couldn't have looked more different from each other. Ivy wore jeans, a T-shirt and boots while the brunette wore a short-sleeved silk blouse with gray slacks and a pair of heels that were completely inappropriate for walking through trees.

What was Ivy doing here?

As they came nearer, she looked up and spotted him. His heart did a hard roll and crash in his chest that disturbed him a little. And if he was any judge, she didn't look real happy to see him, a fact that irritated him more than a little. Still, too late now to back out, so he walked to join them.

"Tanner," Ivy said, pleasure in her voice, "I didn't expect to see you over here."

"I could say the same thing to you," he admitted, then shifted his gaze to the brunette. "Am I interrupting something?"

"No," Ivy told him, then said, "Patsy Harrington, this is our neighbor, Tanner King. Tanner, Patsy is here to talk about her upcoming wedding."

"Lovely to meet you," Patsy said, then quickly added, "but I'm afraid I have to run. The florist awaits. Ivy, thanks again for talking me off the ledge."

"No problem," Ivy told her, and Tanner was struck by the warm smile on her face. "Happy to help. Any time."

"You may regret that," Patsy told her with a laugh, then gave Tanner a sly look before grinning at Ivy. "You don't have to walk me out. You two go ahead."

"What was that about?" he asked.

"Oh, nothing." Ivy smiled at him. "She's just nervous about her wedding and wanting to change everything around at the last minute."

"Well, that's irrational," he said.

"No, that's a bride," Ivy told him. "But I talked her out of it. Really, all she wants is reassurance that everything's going to come off beautifully."

"And is it?" he asked, looking into her eyes.

"It will even if I have to do it all by myself," she said firmly. She paused as if considering something, then admitted, "Angel Christmas Tree Farm took a big loan out for the expansion. There's a big payment due soon.

The Harrington wedding is going to take care of that. If anything goes wrong…"

He frowned, both at the proprietary way she was talking about the farm and at the worry in her voice. "What?"

She looked around at the all the trees and sighed. "We could lose the farm."

Interesting, Tanner thought. So the farm was in danger of going under if it couldn't pay back a loan. Then what she'd said hit him and he asked, *"We?"*

Ivy looked at him. "I mean, we as in, we who work here."

"So…what? Housekeeper, Christmas tree farm worker and bridal consultant?"

She shrugged. "Keeps me busy."

"Yeah." He wasn't sure what it was, but something was definitely off here.

"You know, small town. Take work where you can get it."

She looked more uncomfortable than he'd ever seen her and Tanner couldn't help but wonder why. Was she embarrassed that he'd discovered she worked more than one job? She shouldn't be. He had nothing but respect for hardworking people. "What do you do here?"

"Oh, a little bit of everything, I guess," she said, a little vaguely. "Whatever needs doing. Shearing the trees, watering, weed removal when they get bad." She kicked the toe of her boot at one of the offending weeds. "You know, farm stuff."

"Right. And wedding planning." He studied her and noticed that her gaze hadn't met his squarely since the first moment she'd spotted him. Strange behavior for the most upfront, unafraid of confrontation woman he'd ever known.

"But what are you doing over here?" she countered. "I thought you pretty much considered this place enemy territory."

Yeah, he had. Now though, standing in this forest of neatly tended trees with the sound of children's laughter ringing out around him, he couldn't really remember why.

"Well, I started thinking and realized that you might have been right about something."

"I like it already," she said.

"I'm sure," he said wryly. He'd never known a woman yet who didn't love hearing that she was right about something. "Anyway, you said I should have talked to the farm owner and I realized that you had a point. Thought that before I try to find the owner though, I should look around. Get a feel for the place."

"And, what do you think of it?"

He nodded, letting his gaze slide across the area as he said, "It's…nice. I met a little girl, helped her fix the name tag on her tree."

Ivy smiled at him. "That's part of the Adopt-a-Tree program." She started walking back toward the front of the farm and Tanner fell into step beside her, listening as she continued.

"The wooden ornaments are just used for identifying tags now. That's why they're in plastic sleeves, to protect them from the weather. But when the families come to cut down the tree, the tags go home with them as a keepsake ornament."

"Ellie did seem proud of the job she did on it," he mused.

Ivy laughed. "All of the kids are. And you wouldn't believe the different artwork they come up with. I've seen everything from daisies to space aliens on those tags."

"Well sure," Tanner said, "Merry Christmas Aliens."

"You got it," she agreed, laughing. "Anyway, we've got a craft table set up in the gift shop. The kids decorate the tags, then go out with their families to choose their tree. They get to hang the first symbolic ornament on it to stake their claim."

He'd picked up on one word in that description. "*We* have a craft table?"

She shrugged. "Well, I just meant *we* as in Angel Christmas Tree Farm. Anyway, most families tend to make a day of it when they're here to choose their trees. They come and have lunch, let the kids paint and then head into the farm to look for the perfect Christmas tree."

He lifted his gaze to the trees they passed. "They all look pretty perfect to me."

"Isn't that a nice thing to say. And here I thought you hated Christmas."

"Hard to hate a tree," he said.

"There might be hope for you yet," Ivy said, turning her face up to his. He stared into her blue eyes and felt something in his chest tighten. When a slow smile curved her mouth, that tightness became almost unbearable.

All he could think about was grabbing her and kissing her until the deep, raw hunger inside him was eased. But he couldn't do that here and now. So the only safe bet was to keep moving.

"Since you work here," he asked, "can you take a break and show me around?"

"I'd love to."

"You won't get in trouble with the boss?"

Her mouth quirked. "I think the boss will understand." She tucked her arm through his and he felt the heat of her body pressed against him. "What do you want to see first?"

Her naked, but that probably wasn't what she meant. So he dialed back on the desire pumping through him and decided to assuage a different kind of hunger for the moment.

"Honestly," he admitted, "how about the snack bar? Ever since I got here, I've been smelling those hot dogs."

"No wonder you're hungry. You're awake early today. I'm not even due at your place for another three hours."

"Yeah," he said, his gaze caught on the way the sunlight played on her hair. "I seem to be doing that more and more lately."

Her smile widened. "I'm glad. You should see the sun occasionally, Tanner. Don't want to turn into a mole."

He didn't say anything, but privately, he knew the reason for his switch in hours had nothing to do with sunlight. It was all about seeing her. Spending more time with her when she was at the house. Listening to her and laughing with her.

And as he followed after her on the way to the snack stand, his gaze dropped to the curve of her behind and he told himself that getting up earlier certainly had its perks.

Six

Ivy was finally starting to relax enough to enjoy having Tanner on her farm. When she had first spotted him standing in the sunshine, Ivy's heart had nearly stopped. In a flash, dozens of thoughts had rushed through her mind, most of them revolving around how to keep him from finding out *she* owned the farm. But she needn't have worried after all. Her employees all knew that she was working part time for Tanner. And they knew why.

She glanced up at him as they walked slowly down a row of Scotch pines. His gaze was sharp and constantly moving. He was taking it all in and she couldn't help wondering what he thought of her home. Of her family's pride and joy.

But she couldn't ask. Couldn't even hint at her real identity—which went against the grain for her. She hated lying. And for the first time since she'd met him,

Ivy had actually *lied* to Tanner. Before, it had all been omissions, just keeping quiet about the truth. Now, she'd been forced to actively lie and she wasn't very comfortable with that.

Still, she couldn't see that she had any choice, so she was trying to make the best of the situation. Now that she had him on her turf, she was going to take full advantage of it. They shared hot dogs and sodas, then she took him on a tour of the gift shop. One of the girls working the shop had taken one look at Tanner and practically melted on the spot. But then, Ivy couldn't blame Kathy for that, she supposed, since she felt the same way. Every time she got anywhere close to Tanner, her body lit up like a summer fireworks show.

As that thought settled in her mind, Ivy felt the slightest twinge of guilt ping inside her before she shut it down. She wasn't exactly in charge of her own body's chemical reaction to the man, after all. It wasn't as if she could turn it on and off at will. Still, she told herself to ignore the buzz of sensation his nearness caused. She wasn't looking for love—or even a fling, for that matter. What she needed from Tanner was far more important. She needed him to stop threatening everything she loved.

They wandered the gift store and she pointed out the kids' craft table where little Ellie had made her ornament tag. There were a couple of geniuses busily at work, but they ignored all the adults in the room. He seemed amazed by the crafts made by the women in town, and asked enough questions that Ivy knew he was paying attention. There were hand-poured candles and scented soaps wrapped in ribbon and stacked in baskets. There were rugs and placemats and afghans, blown glass vases and wine glasses.

"And the women in town made all of this?" he asked.

"Mostly," she said. "But Dave Benoit made the glassware. He's got a glass house behind his place. He designs and makes everything himself."

"Impressive," he said, turning to look around the shop, his gaze moving over both merchandise and customers. "And the store's open all year, too?"

"We are now."

One of his eyebrows lifted.

Immediately, she winced and corrected herself. "I mean, the Angel family figured if the shop was open all year, it would give their customers more reason to come and help out the local craftspeople at the same time."

He looked at her, his dark blue eyes locking with hers and Ivy felt that stir of something deliciously primal rise up inside her again. The guilt she was half expecting didn't show and she was grateful. She hadn't set out to entice Tanner and certainly hadn't been looking for a lover, but there was something about this one man that made her feel...

"So!" She swallowed hard and forced a smile she knew wasn't a convincing one. Oh, she didn't want to think about what Tanner made her feel. That was a one-way trip to crazytown and she just didn't have the time for it.

Or the heart. She wasn't the kind of girl for one night stands and easy, see-you-later sex. She was the girl next door. Literally.

"Am I making you nervous?" he asked.

Ivy laughed shortly and shook her head. "What a silly question, of course you don't."

"Uh-huh. Then why are you backing away from me?"

Damn it. She was. She'd instinctively taken two or three steps away from him and wouldn't you know that he'd notice.

"I was just…" She huffed out a breath. "Never mind. Come on, I'll show you the rest."

His lips curved a little and Ivy glowered. As he walked past her toward the door, she shot a look at Kathy and her mother, Anne, working the counter. Anne gave her two thumbs up and a wink which only made Ivy feel worse. Now not only was she lying to Tanner, but her friends were co-conspirators. Oh, this was getting tangled up fast.

And it wasn't helping that her body felt both loose and tightly wound all at once.

Determined to get past her own body's reaction to the man, Ivy kept a smile plastered to her face as she continued their tour. Proudly, she showed him the brides' dressing room, outfitted with three way mirrors and a lovely bathroom where a woman could get dressed for her wedding in comfort. Then she took him to the meadow and the fast moving creek to show him their most popular wedding scenes.

Finally, she stopped at the area set aside for kids' birthday parties. There, the inflated, castle-shaped bounce house stood, waiting only for children to step inside and play. The freshly painted white picket fence around the huge red and yellow bouncing palace was closed though, keeping unsupervised kids out.

They were far enough away from the main area of

the farm that they were pretty much alone. Christmas music continued sighing from the overhead speakers, but the sounds of voices were muted and at a distance. Now that they were away from other distractions, Ivy felt a little nervous and her body once again started clamoring for his touch. She took a breath and reached out to grab hold of the fence as if holding onto it would keep her from reaching for him.

God, what was going on with her?

Tanner moved in close to her. Laying one hand on the fence top, he said, "I'm surprised kids want to escape from here to climb my trees."

"You know little boys. They always want to do what they're not supposed to."

"I guess." He looked around. "Why don't they have this open for the kids all the time?"

"It wouldn't be special then, would it?" Ivy asked and flipped the latch on the gate. She swung it wide and stepped onto the neatly tended lawn surrounding the bounce house. Tanner followed in after her and she closed the gate firmly after them.

"They open it up for kids on Saturdays, and then of course, it's the star attraction of the birthday parties."

He tipped his head back to look up at the red, yellow and orange inflated structure, noting the flags attached to the topmost towers fluttering in the warm breeze. "I suppose this thing's a huge hit with the party crowd."

"Oh yeah." She walked toward the castle and gave it a pat. "Have you ever been in one?"

He laughed shortly and gave her a look that said she was clearly out of her mind. "No."

"You want to?"

"What?"

Ivy laughed at the astonishment on his face. Here, she'd been making herself insane over the physical attraction she felt for him. But now, she realized it went deeper than that. She was drawn to more than his sexy appeal. There was something in his eyes that pulled at her, too. It was that careful vulnerability, she thought, looking up at him. There was something about him that told her he'd spent his life being serious. Controlled. And there was a huge part of her that wanted to break through the walls he'd erected so carefully around himself.

Maybe she really was crazy, but if ever a man needed to learn how to have fun, it was Tanner King. He was too alone. Too somber. Too cut off from everything that made life worth living.

And in the last few days, she'd begun to care about him, she realized. More than the sexual heat she felt around him, she actually enjoyed spending time with him and she hated thinking of him all alone in that big, beautiful house. She hated knowing that when she left him, there was nothing to keep him company but the echo of his own voice.

She'd started this whole thing for her own sake. To save her family's legacy and to help her hometown grow and prosper. Now, it was more than that. Sure, she still wanted to protect Angel Christmas Tree Farm and Cabot Valley. But she also wanted to—what? *Save* Tanner King? That thought rattled her a little.

Was she picking up the mantle of Lady Gwen trying to help her knight?

"You can't be serious," he said, looking from her to the bounce house and back again.

"Why not?" she asked, liking the idea more by the minute. Anything that would shake this so stolid man up was a good thing, right? And the fact that it would be just the two of them inside that inflated fun house had nothing to do with it.

She looked around, saw that there was no one nearby and then shifted her gaze back to Tanner. "Come on. Give it a try."

"It's for kids."

"It's for *fun*," she corrected. "I've been in it lots of times."

Alternately hopping on first one foot then the other, she tugged off her boots, then tossed them to the grass. Fisting her hands at her hips, she tossed her hair out of her eyes and challenged, "Well?"

He shook his head and muttered, "You're crazy."

"That's been said before."

She turned her back on him and crawled into the bounce house. She was betting that he wouldn't be able to resist the challenge of joining her. Once inside, she looked at him through the orange mesh wall and laughed aloud. "Come on, Tanner. Live a little. Or are you scared?"

He snorted. "Are you seriously *daring* me? What are you, twelve?"

Oh, she didn't feel like a twelve-year-old, Ivy admitted silently as she watched him. Those long legs of his looked amazing in his jeans and the breadth of his shoulders made her want to strip off his dark blue T-shirt and run her hands over what she guessed was a hard, sculpted chest.

Her mouth went dry.

Nope.

No twelve-year-olds here.

"Are you turning down the dare?" she countered. "What are you...chicken?"

His eyes went wide and he laughed shortly. "You're like nobody I've ever met before."

She swayed in place unsteadily and wasn't sure if it was the inflated floor making her knees wobble—or if it was the gleam in his eyes. "Thank you."

"Not sure it was a compliment."

"I am." She walked backward, her socks sliding a little on the puffy rubber. It wasn't easy keeping her balance in the bounce house at the best of times. Now, with Tanner's influence, it was turning into quite the chore.

She watched him, holding her breath as she waited to see what he would decide. And then she blew out an expectant breath as he shook his head and toed off his black tennis shoes.

"This is crazy," he muttered, bending low to climb into the structure.

"And you don't do crazy?" she taunted, bouncing a little to unsteady him.

"Not generally," he agreed, standing up and bracing his legs wide apart. He glanced around then looked at her. "Okay, now what?"

"Now we bounce." Ivy jumped as high as she could, then landed and watched the resulting wave knock Tanner off balance.

He caught himself, staggered a little and narrowed his eyes on her. "Want to play rough, do you?"

"Whatever it takes," she said and jumped again.

"Challenge accepted." He took a flying leap, landed on his backside and the bounce knocked Ivy right off her feet.

In a hot second, Tanner was beside her. She looked up into his dark blue eyes and shivered at the hard glitter shining in those depths. He braced his hands on either side of her head and his knees on either side of her hips.

God, he was so close. His mouth just a breath from hers. His big, warm body so tantalizingly near.

Then he smiled and sent a flurry of butterfly wings erupting in the pit of her stomach.

"Lose your balance, Ivy?"

She was really afraid she had. Only it wasn't the kind of balance he was talking about. No, this balance was the delicate art of stabilizing her emotions that she'd been practicing for four years. Ever since David had died. She'd been going through the motions, living her life, doing her chores, laughing, talking and never once actually *living*. Now, thanks to Tanner King, her body and heart were waking up and it was nearly painful.

So she ignored that rush of feelings, determined to blank them out and keep them at bay. She'd think about all of that later, when there was time to examine what she was feeling and decide how she felt about it. For now, she gave herself up to the moment.

"Not for long," she answered and shoved him hard enough that he fell backward and rolled to one side.

She scrambled to her feet and ran across the wobbling floor to the opposite corner. Her hair slipped free of its ponytail and hung about her shoulders. She whipped it back and out of her way as she watched Tanner stealthily approach, that same desire-filled glint shining in his eyes.

Jumping up and down in place, she made sure his pace was inelegant and difficult. He fought to keep his balance and still kept coming, his gaze never leaving hers. *This might not have been such a good idea,* she told herself as her stomach did somersaults and her blood pressure skyrocketed. Her heartbeat raced and every square inch of her body blossomed with heat as if in anticipation.

"You know," he said, his voice a low rumble of sound that seemed to scramble her nerve endings, "I'm beginning to like this place."

"Good," she said, forcing cheerful innocence into her voice. "I'm glad you're having fun."

"Oh, I intend to have even more fun in a second or two," he promised and his eyes swept her up and down before finally locking onto hers.

"Um, Tanner, maybe we should…"

He jumped, landed about a foot in front of her and the resulting wave pelted her off her feet and tossed her at him. Instantly, Tanner's arms came around her.

Ivy's breath left her in a rush and she had to struggle to draw in more air. Her body was pinned along his and his strong arms held her in place so that even if she'd wanted to escape—which she really didn't—she would have had a hard time of it.

Her breasts were crushed against his chest and her nipples went hard and sensitive. Instinctively, she rubbed against him and when she heard him hiss in a breath, she knew he was feeling exactly what she was. Her core went hot and damp, and everything in her…yearned.

He lifted one hand, brushed her hair back from her face and then smoothed his palm down the line of her jaw, her throat. Everywhere he touched her, licks of flame erupted. Ivy had never experienced anything like it. She'd never known this kind of frenzied need that was clawing at her, demanding more.

"You make me want to throw the rules away," he murmured and dipped his head to brush his lips to her forehead.

She sucked in a breath. "Rules?"

"Doesn't matter," he said, shaking his head. "You've been making me a little nuts the last few days."

"I have?"

He smiled and the curve of his mouth sent tiny electrical shocks blasting through her system.

"Yeah. And you know it," he said softly. "Every woman knows when she's driving a man crazy with want."

"Want?"

Oh God yes, she thought. Want was good. Want was very good.

"I like your hair down," he told her, running his fingers through the heavy mass, scraping his short nails across her scalp.

Ivy sighed and closed her eyes.

"I like how you feel in my arms," he admitted.

"I like it, too."

"Good," he said, voice a low throb of need, "because I want more of it. I want more of *you.*"

Her eyes flew open in time to see him lower his head and slant his lips over hers.

The kiss staggered Ivy. All of her preconceptions, all of her idle daydreaming splintered under the reality of his mouth on hers. His lips were soft yet firm and unyielding. He parted her lips with his tongue and claimed her more intimately, more deeply.

While he explored her mouth, his hands went on a

searching mission of their own. He ran his palms up and down her spine and then to the curve of her rear where he held on tightly and pulled her closer against him. She moaned when she felt the hardness of his body pressing into hers and she squirmed as if trying to get even closer. She clung to his shoulders as if holding on for dear life and when her feet shifted on the inflated floor, she felt him move with her.

Her tongue tangled with his in a dance of desperate hunger that shattered her resolve, disintegrated her good intentions. Here was the heat that had drawn her to him from the beginning. Here was the need that had kept her awake nights, wondering what it would be like to touch him and be touched.

Tanner groaned and dropped them both to the floor. He held her cradled against him and when they landed on the cool rubber floor, they rolled, still locked together. Over and under him, she felt her body springing into life as it hadn't for more than four years.

His kiss demanded everything she had to give and she offered it to him gladly. His hands moved as he brought them to a stop, pinned against the inflatable wall. He slid one hand beneath the hem of her T-shirt and she gasped at the exquisite feel of his skin on hers.

His fingertips traced their way up her body until he reached the edge of her bra, then he pushed it up and out of the way and covered her breast with his palm.

"Tanner…" She arched into him, sighing his name.

"Oh yeah," he whispered, his thumb and forefinger twisting and teasing her sensitive nipple. "This is what I've wanted since the day I saw you, Ivy."

"Me, too. Oh, me, too," she admitted, opening her

eyes to look up into his. "Taste me, Tanner. I want to feel your mouth on me."

His eyes flared with raw hunger. He didn't say a word, only dipped his head to her breast and took her nipple into his mouth. Lips and teeth and tongue tortured her gently with sensations that coursed through her with rocketlike speed.

She twisted beneath him, unable to hold still. She lifted one hand to the back of his head and held him there, as if afraid he might stop. And oh, she didn't want him to stop.

The world fell away. All that mattered was this moment. Tanner's mouth on her body. His hot breath brushing her skin.

She wanted more and she wanted it now. Ivy forgot all about where they were. Forgot about the tree farm. Forgot that Tanner King was the one man who had the power to shut down her family's business. Forgot everything, in fact, in favor of concentrating solely on what his touch could do to her.

As if he heard her thoughts, he skimmed his hand down her belly and beneath the waistband of her jeans.

Sunlight beat against Ivy's closed eyelids and she took a breath and held it as Tanner's fingers moved beneath the elastic band of her panties and continued down, to the heart of her torment.

He touched her once and she shattered, body trembling, breath exploding from her lungs. But it wasn't enough for him, he wanted to take her higher.

"Again, Ivy," he whispered, lifting his head from her breast to look down at her. "Break for me again."

She slid her hands up his muscular arms to his

shoulders and then dug her fingertips in and held on as her legs parted for him, making room, welcoming his touch.

He dipped one finger inside her and she shivered. Then he withdrew that finger and entered her again in a slow, gliding rhythm that tore at already sensitized nerves. Her hips rocked into him as he gave and demanded all at once. She felt tension building within and embraced it.

Her gaze locked with his as she felt another climax approaching. She stared into his eyes as the first ripples of pleasure rocked her.

"Tanner!" Her voice was strained and quiet.

"Let go, Ivy," he ordered. "Let go and feel me."

She did.

She had no choice.

Maybe, she thought wildly as she trembled and shook in the safety of his arms, she hadn't had a choice from the first moment she'd walked into his house. Maybe every step they'd taken together had brought them here, to this moment.

Then he kissed her, swallowing her wrenching moans and she stopped thinking entirely.

When the last of her climax faded away, she felt both weak and energized. Her body was alive in a way she'd never experienced before and though she acknowledged another twinge of guilt at the thought, she couldn't deny it.

Tanner pulled his hand free, then tugged her T-shirt down over her breasts. Still looking into her eyes, he said, "This is just the beginning. You know that, right?"

She swallowed hard and fought down a rising tide of desire. Already, her body wanted more.

"Yes, I know," she agreed softly.

"Good." He sat up and drew her with him.

Late afternoon sunshine played through the mesh walls and lay tiny checkerboard patterns over his face. A soft wind sighed through the trees and lifted her hair from her neck. But the breeze didn't do a thing toward damping the fires he'd stirred inside her. She was burning up, aching for his touch and she could see in his eyes that he was feeling the same way.

"Tonight, Ivy," he said, lifting one of her hands to his mouth. He trailed the tip of his tongue across her knuckles and smiled when she shivered in response. "Tonight, I want it all. I want you in my bed, naked."

Her stomach spun and her throat closed up tight. It was a wonder she could breathe, let alone speak. But somehow, she managed. "Tonight, Tanner. I want you inside me."

His eyes flared. "Glad to know we're on the same page."

"Oh yeah." She leaned toward him to give him a kiss to seal their deal, when a too-familiar, outraged voice stopped her cold.

"Ivy! What the hell are you doing?"

Seven

"Mike!" Ivy sounded both shocked and horrified.

Tanner sent a quick look toward the speaker and spotted an older man, gray hair bristling, pale blue eyes narrowed, standing on the outside of the bounce house, glaring in at them.

"What the hell's going on, Ivy?" the older man demanded again.

She hurried to her feet, tossed one anxious glance at Tanner and then scuttled wobbly across the floor. "I didn't know you were here," she said.

"Yeah, well I could say the same." The old guy looked past Ivy to glare at Tanner. "I heard a ruckus. Thought I should check it out. So you want to tell me what's happening?"

"Not really," she said, half turning as Tanner walked up behind her. "Um, Mike Angel, this is Tanner King. Tanner, this is Mike."

Well hell.

The owner of the tree farm, Tanner thought. No wonder Ivy was acting so weird. She'd just been caught by her boss and she was probably embarrassed. Plus, he thought, the old man looked mad enough to fire her and Tanner couldn't let that happen.

See, his brain taunted, *this* is what happens when you relax your rules. When you forget to keep your distance from people. But even though he knew his brain was absolutely right, he couldn't really regret what had just happened between them. In fact, he was looking forward very much to more rule-breaking as soon as he could get her to his house.

For the moment however, they had to get out of this situation.

"Good to meet you, sir," he said and would have extended his hand, but for the mesh wall separating them.

"I'll bet," Mike Angel told him, then shifted his gaze back to Ivy. "You come on out of there now."

"Right." She gave Tanner a quick look that said she wasn't going to argue with the man and hoped he wouldn't either.

Tanner wasn't going to argue, he assured himself. But he also wasn't going to be treated like a ten-year-old caught throwing a baseball through a window, either.

Ivy dropped to her hands and knees and slipped out the doorway of the bounce house to sit on the grass so she could tug her boots back on. Tanner was right behind her.

"So you gonna tell me why you're rolling around in the kid's play palace?"

Ivy flushed and Tanner was struck by it. He couldn't

remember the last time he'd seen a woman blush with embarrassment. Hell, he hadn't been sure they were capable of it anymore. But Ivy, he'd already discovered, was like no other woman he'd ever known.

"I was giving Tanner a tour of the farm and—"

"Just what kind of tour was this?" Mike asked.

Tanner wasn't the kind of man to stand by and have a woman defend him—even when he needed defending, which he didn't. They hadn't done anything wrong. Although, Ivy's boss might not be too happy with her. And that worried Tanner a bit. He wouldn't want to see her lose her job over this.

He felt more himself once he had his shoes on and was standing on ground that didn't ripple and shift beneath him. The fact that he towered over the older man didn't hurt either. Still, this was Ivy's employer and the owner of the farm he'd been complaining about for two months. Maybe, he thought, that was part of why the older man looked less than welcoming. After several visits from the sheriff, who could blame him?

"Tanner King," he said, holding out one hand to the man.

Mike Angel looked at his extended hand but instead of taking it, turned his gaze on Ivy. "Anything you want to tell me, Ivy girl?"

"Not a thing, Mike," she said honestly. Pushing her hair back behind her ears. "I just thought you'd want me to see that Tanner here got a good look at the farm."

"Uh-huh."

Tanner let his hand drop and accepted that the older man wasn't happy about his being there. Still, he wasn't used to being ignored and found he didn't care for it much. "I asked Ivy to show me around, Mr. Angel. She gave me a tour of the farm and when we ended up here, I suggested we try out the bounce house."

Ivy shot him a grateful, if surprised look, as he took responsibility for slipping into the inflated palace.

He ignored it and focused instead on the older man watching him through shrewd eyes. "She's shown me your whole operation here and I've got to say it's impressive."

"Is that right?" Mike's gaze measured him and Tanner felt like a kid standing in front of the principal's desk.

"It is," he said, refusing to be cowed by the steely look in his adversary's eyes. But at the same time, he wanted to smooth things over so that Ivy wouldn't be in any kind of trouble. "Look," he said, "I realize you and I got off to a bad start."

"Didn't get off to any kind of start at all, Mr. King," Mike countered. "Since you decided to go to the police with your complaints instead of coming directly to me. Seems to me a man might come and talk to another man face-to-face if he has a problem. Rather than going to the sheriff over and over again."

Mitchell had been right about that, Tanner told himself with an inner grumble. He hadn't done himself any good at all by complaining to the local police instead of simply talking to his neighbor. But in his own defense, Tanner *never* met his neighbors. Hell, he'd lived in his condo in L.A. for five years and wouldn't have been able to recognize his neighbors in a lineup.

"Mike…" Ivy sounded worried and the tone in her voice had Tanner nodding.

"No, Ivy, he's right." He met the older man's eyes and thought he spotted a flash of admiration there. Why that made him feel better, he couldn't have said. "Mr.

Angel, I should have come to you from the start. That was my mistake. Maybe we could have worked things out between us without getting the police involved."

"Well now," the older man mused thoughtfully, "call me Mike. I got respect for a man who can admit he's done wrong." He held out his right hand and waited to see if Tanner would take it.

He did. The old man had a hard, firm grip that spoke of years of physical labor as he squeezed Tanner's hand briefly. And the look in his eyes clearly said he was short of patience and damn curious about just what had been going on before he showed up.

Thinking about that rekindled fires inside Tanner that would be better off left to smolder at the moment. There'd be time enough later to pick up where he and Ivy had left off.

"Anyway," Tanner said abruptly, shattering the strained silence, "I wanted to thank you for letting Ivy show me around. I wouldn't want her to get into trouble for taking time from her work."

"Is that right?" Mike murmured, shifting his gaze to Ivy.

She squirmed a little, obviously uncomfortable with the conversation. She and Mike stared at each other for a long minute before the older man looked back to Tanner.

"It's no trouble," he said. "Glad she took you around. But now, it's time we both got back to work."

"Of course." Tanner nodded and said, "I should get back myself. Ivy, thanks for the tour. Mike, good to meet you."

"You, too. Now, you have any other problems with the farm, you let us know."

"I will," he assured him. "And I appreciate your turning the music down."

"That was Ivy's idea," he said.

Tanner's gaze shifted to her. She'd gone out of her way to try to make things better for him and hadn't said anything about it. Ivy was, he told himself, an intriguing woman. As he stared into her eyes, he let her know, without a word spoken, that he was leaving now, but would be waiting for her later. He wanted her now more than he had before and if he had to wait much longer, it was going to drive him over the edge.

Her eyes flashed in acceptance of his silent message and he knew they were at least on the same page about some things.

"Then I guess I owe you my thanks for making things quieter around here," he finally told her.

"Guess you do," she said, her eyes gleaming with the knowledge of what they'd shared and what was to come.

"I'll have to find a way to show you my appreciation, then won't I?"

"I look forward to it," she said softly.

Tanner left it at that. Giving Mike a brisk nod, he walked off toward the front of the farm and the road that would take him to his place.

He hadn't gone far when Mike grabbed his granddaughter's arm and tugged her further off. "What in the hell are you up to, Ivy?"

"Oh, Pop," she said with a sigh, "this is getting more confusing every day."

"You're playing with fire, Ivy."

"What?" She whipped her head up to look at him. "What do you mean?"

He laughed. "You know damn well what I mean. You're getting in over your head with that man and you know it."

Her grandfather always had been able to see into her heart and mind. It had always made keeping secrets from him nearly impossible and apparently, nothing had changed.

"I didn't start out to," she said.

"Yeah, well you remember what the road to hell is paved with…"

"…good intentions, yes, I know," she said, walking beside her grandfather as he headed off toward the seedling rows. "I was going to tell him who I am, Pop. Really. At least, I've been thinking about telling him. But now, it's complicated."

"Always is when you start lying. By the time you get around to the truth, the lies are so big you can't see a way around them."

"You're not exactly being comforting, you know."

He laughed again and threw one arm over her shoulders. "I'm not trying to be. You don't need comfort, Ivy. You need to straighten this mess out, that's all."

"That's all." She sighed again and let her gaze slide across the familiar scenes around her. "When he finds out the truth, he'll be furious. And he's warming up to the tree farm, but he's not exactly a fan yet, so there's still the chance that he'll sic his lawyer on us and we'll still be up the proverbial creek."

"Seems to not be as angry as he once was," Mike said softly as he slid her a sidelong look. "You wouldn't know the reason for that, would you?"

Ivy groaned. "Just how much did you see?"

"Not much, thank you God for not striking me blind."

Mike held up one hand when she opened her mouth to talk. "It's none of my business anyway, honey. You're all grown up. You can make your own decisions. I just want to know that you know what you're doing. That you've got your eyes open wide."

"I'd like to know that, too," she admitted.

The trouble was, she told herself as she tipped her head back and stared up at the white clouds scuttling across a bright blue sky, she just wasn't sure. When she'd started all of this, it had been with the idea of getting to know Tanner, easing him into small town life and hoping that once she'd accomplished the task, he'd stop giving the tree farm so much grief.

But it had stopped being solely about that days ago. She hadn't admitted it to herself, but that was the honest truth. Sunlight speared out from behind a cloud and looked like golden fingers reaching down from the sky. She sighed and the wind carried the sound away.

"I don't have to leave tomorrow," Mike said softly, as if sensing the turmoil within her. "I can stay awhile yet."

She smiled and lowered her gaze to meet his. God, that was tempting. Keep her grandfather here as moral support while she stumbled head first into an affair that probably shouldn't happen. Because she knew that even if Pop stayed, it wouldn't make a difference. She would still go to Tanner. She would still share his bed because her body wouldn't allow it any other way. She wanted him so much that her skin was practically humming with anticipation of his touch.

So there was no reason to have her grandfather remain, just so he could watch her make a fool of herself. Besides, she wouldn't let him put his life on hold.

"No thanks, Pop," she said, threading her arm through his and giving it a squeeze. "I appreciate the offer, but there's a brand-new nursery waiting for you in Florida. Mom needs your help."

"And you don't?"

"I'll always need you, Pop," she said and tipped her head to rest it on his shoulder. "But I've got to stand on my own. This is my mess and I'll either straighten it out or sink. One or the other."

"My money's on you, kid," he told her and patted her hand. "Now, why don't we go and take another look at the new plantings. Want to make sure everything's in good shape before Tom Howard takes me to the airport tomorrow afternoon."

"I can take you, you know. You don't have to get one of your friends to make the drive."

"We've been over that, too," Mike told her with a shake of his head. "Tom's going into Sacramento to visit his son. There's no reason for you to make the trip. Especially," he added slyly, "when there's plenty going on right here."

He was right, Ivy thought, walking with him through the rows of trees, headed for the back half of the farm. There was plenty going on. And a lot of it was *inside* her. Ivy wasn't at all sure she was doing the right thing by getting even more involved with a man she was lying to. She only knew she couldn't seem to help herself.

It had been too long since she'd been touched. Wanted. Desired. And it felt good to have a man's hands on her again.

But that wasn't entirely true either, she told herself firmly. It wasn't just any man's hands she wanted on her. It was Tanner's. Her heart was falling for him and she couldn't seem to stop that, either. Even knowing as she fell that eventually, her heart would break, as it had once before. Only this time, she thought, the pain was going to be even more deeply felt. How could it not be, when everything else about her time with Tanner was richer, deeper, more profound than anything she'd ever known before?

She glanced over her shoulder at the roofline of Tanner's house. She imagined him in that glass and wood mansion, waiting for her.

And her body burned.

Three hours later, the burning had only intensified.

As if the entire world was collaborating against her, Ivy hadn't been able to get away from the farm any earlier. Was it a karmic warning system? she wondered. Was someone, somewhere trying to tell her something? Trying to get her to step away from Tanner before it was too late?

Because if they were, she wasn't listening. She shivered a little as she climbed the front steps to his porch. In fact, she was actively shutting down her own early warning systems. She didn't want to think. Didn't want to wonder or worry. What she wanted was sex. Mind-blowing, soul-searing sex. And she wasn't leaving here without it.

Her conscience screamed at her that she should tell Tanner the truth. Tell him that she'd been lying to him. She should confess that *she* owned Angel Tree Christmas Farm and tell him all about her plan to soften him up so he'd stop causing trouble.

But, she argued with herself, if the did that, confessed all, then instead of an amazing night filled with what

she hoped would be great sex and multiple orgasms…
what she'd get would be an argument. Lots of shouting
and hurt feelings and—no. She'd tell him the truth
eventually. But she wanted this night with him first.

Adjusting the collar of her white cotton blouse, she
flipped her hair back out of her face and then wiped her
damp palms on the thighs of her best jeans. Not exactly
seductive outerwear, she supposed, but she was who she
was. And Tanner hadn't seemed put off by her jeans and
T-shirt earlier.

Her blood pumped a little faster at the memory of
those two quick stolen orgasms. She wanted more.
Wanted to feel him touch her all over. Wanted the
warm slide of his skin against hers. She squirmed
uncomfortably as liquid heat pooled at her center. Even
the fabric of her jeans pressing against her was nearly
torture.

She looked over her shoulder at the sunset staining
the sky, and the roof of her home. If she had any sense at
all, she'd turn around now, go back to her own bedroom
and lock the door behind her.

Ivy took a breath, held it, then let it slowly sift from
her lungs. She was hoping for control. Hoping for calm.
What she got was a whiff of his scent as he quietly
opened the front door.

Her head whipped around and her mouth went dry.

His black hair was thick and damp from a shower.
His eyes smoldered with the promise of exactly what she
needed so desperately. His broad—as she'd guessed—
muscular chest was bare and a sprinkling of dark hair
dusted his skin, then trailed down across his abdomen
to disappear beneath his jeans. The top button of those

jeans was unbuttoned, giving her a peek of paler skin and his bare feet were braced wide apart.

He looked her up and down quickly and Ivy was pretty sure she could actually *feel* flames licking at her skin under the intensity of his gaze.

"What took you so long?" he growled in a voice that was low and barely restrained.

She took another short breath and whispered, "Does it matter, now?"

"Nope." He grabbed her hand, tugged her into the house and slammed the door behind her. In seconds, his fingers were undoing the buttons on her shirt. He threw the garment to the floor as she swayed into him.

Ivy lifted her hands and slid them over his chest, loving the feel of his warm, smooth skin beneath her palms. Her thumbs flicked across his flat nipples and he hissed in a breath as he made quick work of the front clasp of her bra. When he slid the straps down her arms to let the damn thing fall on the floor, he filled his hands with her breasts and Ivy groaned aloud.

"I've been wanting you to do that all day," she admitted, beyond pride, beyond anything but the overwhelming need for him.

"Baby, I'm just getting started," he said, then shifted his hands to the waistband of her jeans.

Ivy was way ahead of him. She toed off her sandals and then wriggled in place to get rid of the denim that was separating her from him. Now only her pale pink panties stood between her and Tanner—when he tore them from her, she could only be grateful.

"Oh yeah, this is how I've wanted you for days," he murmured, dipping his head to kiss her, once, twice. His teeth and lips tugged at her mouth and delicious sensations spiraled through her in response. Her entire body was sizzling. She wouldn't have been surprised to glance down and see that she was actually giving off sparks.

"Well, you've got me now," she said and linked her arms around his neck, going up on her toes so that she could kiss him back more forcefully.

"Damn straight," he said, undoing the buttons of his jeans to allow his really impressive erection to spring forth.

Ivy's stomach did a slow dip and roll and the dampness at her core increased. He was bigger there than David had been. She wasn't a virgin, but she wasn't exactly the most experienced woman on the planet, either. She'd only had one lover and that had been the man she had planned to marry.

Well, there was no marriage in sight here, she told herself as she looked from Tanner's hard, all-too-eager flesh up to his eyes again. But she wasn't looking for that anymore, either. What she needed from him was more basic. More primal.

She was here and she wasn't going to second-guess herself. She and Tanner had been heading toward this moment since the first day she'd stepped inside this house. She knew that without a doubt. There was an attraction between them. A fundamental link that pulled them toward each other even when reason should have kept them apart.

And she wouldn't argue with it. Not today.

Reaching for him, she closed her hand around the thickness of him and watched as he closed his eyes and drew in one long, deep breath. She was more than ready for this. More than impatient to feel him inside her. When she stroked him and slid her fingertips across the sensitive tip of him, he stopped her, and shook his head. "Just a minute."

He reached into his pocket, grabbed a condom and tore it open. She smiled. In her hunger and hurry, she'd tossed caution out the window along with good sense. Thank heaven Tanner was still conscious enough to do the right thing.

When he'd sheathed himself, he looked into her eyes, gave her a slow grin and then set both hands at her waist. Lifting her off her feet, he ordered, "Hook your legs behind my back."

She locked her gaze with his and did just as he'd ordered.

His big hands cupped her bottom and kneaded her soft flesh with an urgent tenderness that sent ripples of expectation rolling through her. "Tanner..."

"Right there with you, baby," he murmured, his eyes staring directly into hers.

She read the same wild, raw desire in his eyes that she knew was written in her own. She struggled for air as an invisible iron band tightened around her chest. She held on to his shoulders and gasped as he pushed himself into her body in one sure thrust. She gasped at the intimate invasion. It had been a long time for her and her body had to adjust to his presence. She settled herself more firmly over him and quickly felt tingles of appreciation light up inside her.

Ivy moved on him then, and her eyes slid shut on a groan as she twisted her hips, reveling in the thick fullness within her. Impaled on his body, she opened her eyes again to meet his. As he moved her up and down on his length, their gazes remained fixed, as if neither of them could bear to break the intimate connections binding them together.

She felt him shudder and watched a muscle in his jaw twitch as he fought for control. She smiled to herself as she silently admitted that she didn't want him controlled. She wanted him wild, abandoned. So she took his mouth with hers, tangling her tongue with his, giving him her breath and greedily taking his for her own. She lowered one hand to stroke his flat nipple with the edge of her thumb and when he groaned into her mouth, she knew she'd won.

He spun around abruptly, braced her back against the door and with his mouth still fused to hers, took her in just the way she wanted. Over and over again, he plunged in and out of her body with a soul shaking rhythm. Each thrust was harder, deeper, than the one before, until all that mattered was the next one and the next. Her mind splintered of thoughts beyond the all-consuming need to reach the pinnacle she was racing toward.

She cupped his face in her hands and kissed him hungrily as his body lay siege to hers. Tension coiled and tightened inside her as she strained for the release she knew was just out of reach. At last, when she thought she might die from the pleasure, a blinding orgasm crashed down on top of her.

Ivy tore her mouth from his and shouted his name as a flood of incredible sensations raced through her with the force of an explosion. And moments later, as the last of the ripples wound through her, Tanner buried his face in the curve of her neck, groaned her name aloud and emptied himself, shuddering in her arms until they were both trembling and clinging to each other for support.

Seconds, then minutes ticked past and still they stood there, braced against a door, each of them too shaken by what had happened to try to move.

Heart hammering in her chest, Ivy absently listened to the mingled sounds of their harsh breathing. When she thought she could speak without her voice breaking, she whispered on a strained chuckle, "Tanner King, you're a man of many talents."

"Ivy Holloway," he managed to say before he lifted his head to meet her eyes, "you ain't seen nothin' yet."

Eight

He carried her upstairs to the bedroom.

Ivy smiled up at him and Tanner felt like a damn superhero for carrying her. The truth was, he didn't want to let go of her long enough for her to climb the stairs on her own.

He'd had her once, hard and fast and it had only fed the quickening fires inside him. Now he wanted to see his fantasy in the flesh, so to speak. He wanted to stretch her out, naked, across his bed. Then he wanted to take his time and lick his way up and down her amazing body.

Instantly, he was hard again and wishing he'd just peeled his jeans off downstairs. The walk down the long, dimly lit hallways seemed to take forever. But soon enough, he was kicking his bedroom door open and stalking across the room.

The heavy, bloodred quilt was pulled back already,

displaying fresh white sheets. A dozen pillows were mounded against the headboard and the last glow of the sunset painted the sky outside the window a deep orange. One bedside lamp was turned on, creating a golden puddle of light and when Tanner laid her down on the bed, her bare skin seemed to glow in its radiance.

She stretched her arms up over her head and sighed as she wriggled against the mattress. "I feel wonderful," she told him.

"You're about to feel even better," he said.

"Promises, promises," she teased and held her arms out for him.

Tanner shook his head slowly, tore off his jeans and grabbed a fresh condom from the bedside table. He sheathed himself again and noticed that her gaze was locked on the motion. Instantly, he went even harder and he wouldn't have thought that possible. It seemed though, that where Ivy was concerned, his body couldn't get enough.

"Tanner, come to me," she coaxed.

"In time," he said and went down on his knees beside the bed. Grabbing hold of her, he pulled her to the edge of the mattress and draped her legs over his shoulders.

"Oh, Tanner…" She pushed up on her elbows to look at him and she was still watching him when he first tasted her. She gasped aloud and moved against his mouth.

He ran his tongue along her slick folds and tasted her as if she were running with honey. Her scent flooded him and Tanner gave himself up to the fantasy of having her at his mercy, naked and writhing.

Again and again, his lips, tongue and teeth worked her most sensitive flesh. The only sounds in the room were the sighs of her breathing and the slapping of her hands against the mattress as she fought for something to hold on to.

He relished her and when he felt her coiling for release, her body tightening, he stopped, pulled back and grinned at her outraged squeak of "Don't stop now!"

She was shaking with unanswered need and Tanner skimmed the tips of his fingers across her center. She jolted and then settled down again, waiting breathlessly for him to finish what he'd started. And when he couldn't wait another moment, he did just that. He flicked his tongue across the one spot that held so many sensations and then he suckled her as she splintered in his grasp, crying his name.

When her climax at last ended, he rose up, joined her on the bed and rolled her over onto her stomach. She sighed blissfully as his hands rubbed up and down the length of her spine, tracing every curve, every line of her body. His mouth went next and he licked and kissed his way across her skin until he knew her body as well as he did his own.

She squirmed against him, rubbing her bottom into him and the fires inside him roared.

"Again," he muttered thickly. "I need you again. Now."

"Now," she agreed and when he pulled her up to her knees, she threw her hair out of her face and looked back over her shoulder at him. "Be in me, Tanner. Be with me."

"Grab hold of the headboard," he said and moved to cover her body with his. When she had a grip on the intricately carved oak wood, Tanner held her hips still and entered her to the hilt. He buried himself as deeply as he could and knew it would never be deep enough.

He loved the feel of her hot, slick flesh surrounding his. He groaned at the perfection of the moment and gave himself over to the demands of his body. She moved with him, into him, her soft gasps and heavy sighs creating a sort of music that sent his own blood into a dizzying dance.

With every stroke, he claimed her. With every touch, he adored her. With every breath, he hungered for her. He felt her climax shudder through her and before the last of it had died away, he joined her and the two of them fell into a scatter of stars.

Three hours later, Ivy turned her head on the pillow and looked at the man lying next to her. They'd come together again and again as if neither of them could bear the idea of being apart even momentarily. She'd never experienced anything like what Tanner made her feel. Just looking at him turned her heart over in her chest and she realized with a jolt that she was falling in love with him. Ivy bit back a groan and closed her eyes briefly. How had this happened? She hadn't wanted this. Hadn't expected it. Hadn't been looking for it.

And now that she'd found it she wasn't entirely sure how to handle it. The problem here was, when Tanner had been just a neighbor—a potential friend—a small white lie hadn't seemed like such a big deal. Now though, she knew that everything had changed. What she felt for Tanner was so much bigger than what she and David had shared, she almost felt guilty admitting it to herself. But it was true and the other undeniable truth was, when Tanner found out she'd been lying to him, this relationship would be over.

She didn't want it to be over.

Idly, she wondered what might have happened if Tanner hadn't had the foresight to have a condom handy. Lost in the throes of a passion she'd never known before, Ivy had completely disregarded the need for protection. If Tanner had forgotten too, might they have made a baby tonight? And what then? If they had, would she allow a lie to remain between them?

"What're you thinking?" he asked quietly.

She came up out of her thoughts and pushed them all to the back of her mind. Worries for another day. Another time. Right now, she didn't want to risk spoiling what they had.

"Nothing, really."

"You looked pretty somber for nothing." He went up on his elbow and reached out with his free hand to rub her shoulder.

Just that simple touch was enough to stir her up again and she wouldn't have thought that was possible. Would it always be that explosive between them? Would she forever erupt into passion so easily around him?

Would she get the chance to find out?

She took a breath and gave him a small piece of the larger truth.

"I was just thinking I was grateful that you'd had the presence of mind to remember a condom," she said, then admitted, "I wasn't thinking very clearly at the time."

His features tightened. "You should. No kid deserves to be an accident."

The words came so fast and harsh, it stole her breath from her. There was pain glittering in his eyes and the rigidity of his jaw told her that she'd inadvertently struck a nerve. Carefully, she tried to smooth things over. "If I were to get pregnant, I'd never consider my child a mistake, Tanner."

"Maybe not," he allowed, his gaze locked with hers. "But others would. Have."

There was a chill in his voice now, to match the darkness in his eyes.

He pushed one hand through his hair and shook his head as if disgusted with himself for opening this conversation. "All I meant was, I don't make bastards," he said simply. "That's my father's thing."

The casual use of the ugly word jabbed at her. His beautiful eyes were shuttered as if sealing her out. There was old pain there, she caught just a glimpse of it before he disguised it behind a layer of nonchalance. "Tanner…"

"Please," he said on a sharp laugh. "I don't need sympathy. I grew up fine. I've got more half brothers and cousins than anyone should have. I'm only saying that I'm careful."

He brushed aside her concern and she understood the need to cling to your own pride so she wouldn't offer him compassion when he clearly didn't want it. But she also wouldn't let him back away from a subject that obviously needed to be spoken about. "I get that. But there's more, isn't there?"

"What's that supposed to mean?"

It meant that she was beginning to see why Tanner was so closed off from people. He'd had a lonely childhood despite what he was saying and the memories, if not the hurts of it, were still vividly with him.

"Well," she said softly, "How you feel about Christmas for instance."

"I don't need therapy."

"Good. Not a therapist."

He glared at her. "Then drop it."

"What is it about Christmas that you hate, Tanner?"

His jaw worked as if he were biting back a flood of words trying to escape. Lamplight shone on his tanned skin and made him seem golden. And though she could stretch out one hand to touch him, Ivy knew he was farther from her than he'd ever been.

A tense moment or two passed before finally, he shrugged and said, "I never really did Christmas as a kid." He shifted position and sat up, resting against pillows he bunched against the headboard, sheet pooled across his abdomen.

"That's not the only reason," she said.

He gave her a quick look. "Why do you care, Ivy?"

"Call it curiosity," she told him, though it was more. So much more. She wanted to understand him. Wanted to *know* him.

Shaking his head, he said, "Okay, doesn't matter anyway. My holidays were usually spent in an empty hotel room wondering when my mom was going to come back. She was usually off lining up her next lover and didn't have time to do the tree and present thing." He shrugged as if what he was saying meant nothing, though she could see it did. "My nanny usually got me something so it wasn't a complete wash. And whatever my dad sent me always arrived around the twenty-fifth, so it didn't matter really."

A twinge of pity zipped through her. Not for the man

he was now, but for the boy he'd once been. On the outside, looking in and not knowing why. The boy had been alone and miserable. The man was still alone, yet had convinced himself that it was the way he wanted it.

"I can see in your eyes that you're getting all weepy on my account," he said and shook his head with a smile. "You don't have to. I did fine. I *do* fine."

She took a breath and blew it out. "Of course you do. But I don't mind telling you I'd like to step back in time and shake your mother until her teeth rattled."

He laughed a little and she was grateful to see some of the tension leave his features.

"You know," Ivy told him quietly, "you don't have to avoid Christmas forever. Just because you had crappy holidays as a kid doesn't mean you have to continue the tradition. You can make your own choices instead of living with old hurts."

"Here comes the therapy," he muttered, sliding a look at her. "Everybody's got answers. Everybody knows what somebody else should do. What makes you think I'm in pain over something that happened decades ago? What makes you so sure that I'm suffering? I do what I want when I want. I don't need your concern because it's pointless. There is no angry little boy inside me waiting to be soothed, so spare me."

"Wow." She sat up, drawing the sheet with her and clutching it to her chest. All of her earlier warm, fuzzy thoughts were quickly dissipating. Okay yes, she loved him. That didn't mean she was going to sit there and be a target for him. "For a guy who's put it all behind him, you sound a little sensitive on the subject."

"Why shouldn't I be?" he demanded. "Where do you

get off giving me advice, anyway? What do you know about pain, Ivy? Easy enough to sit on the sidelines and tell everybody else how they should *get over it* and move on. Well you don't know jack about what my life is like."

"No, I don't," she said, fisting her hand in the fabric of the sheet and squeezing. She wasn't sure how they'd gone from spectacular sex and cozy afterglow to this raging argument, but she wasn't about to let him talk to her like that. "But I know enough to stop licking old wounds. I know that shutting myself away in a house where I never have to speak to anyone isn't the answer."

"Is that right?" His dark eyes went wide as he feigned astonishment. "And you've come by this magical knowledge how? Watching TV? What great pains do you have to deal with? Hell, you live in a town that might as well be Christmas central!"

A sharp jab of hurt bit into her and Ivy lifted her chin to glare at him. She knew what this was, damn it—why they were having this ridiculous fight. They were both feeling emotionally shaken by what they'd shared and they were both going into defense mode. Oh, wasn't that wonderful, she thought. And just when had she gotten so insightful, anyway?

"Fine," she said, scooting off the bed because she needed to be standing on her own two feet, not sharing the mattress with a man she wanted to kick, "you don't want advice, your choice. But don't bother to assume that you're the only person on the planet who's had trouble."

"Ivy—"

"No," she stopped him, thoroughly disgusted with

him now. "You said you had a mother and father. Are they still alive?"

"Yeah…"

"My dad died when I was a little girl," she told him. "I miss him still."

A flicker of what might have been regret crossed his face briefly. "Look, maybe I was out of line…"

She tipped her head to one side and stared at him. "Have you ever loved anyone, Tanner? I mean *love?*"

His gaze darkened. "No."

"Well, I have."

He blinked but that was the only sign of surprise he showed her. She didn't care. All she wanted to do now was get out of this house and away from him. But she wasn't going anywhere until she'd clued him in on a little something.

"Four years ago, my fiancé David was in a car accident and died."

"Damn it, Ivy…" He came up off the bed and made to go to her, but she scrambled back and away, holding up one hand to keep him at bay.

"Three weeks before our wedding," she said, "I went to David's funeral." Tears blurred her vision, but she blinked them back. Somehow they'd both torn open old wounds and were now taking turns dribbling salt on them. All to avoid talking about the emotional connection they'd made. She didn't know who she was more furious with. Tanner? Or herself?

The only way out now was to keep on going. "I could have curled up in a ball and reveled in the pain," she whispered. "I could have shut myself up in the house and never talked to anyone again. But you know what, Tanner? That's not life. That's just taking up space. So you keep going forward. You don't stay trapped in the past, you move on. You keep breathing because that's what life is."

Her breath was hitching in her chest and she felt the tears clogging her throat now, too. Damn it, she didn't want to cry in front of him. That would just put a capper on this scene, wouldn't it?

"Ivy, I didn't know."

"No, you didn't," she muttered, heading for the open bedroom door. "And I wasn't looking for sympathy either, Tanner, so spare me that."

He grabbed his jeans, tugged them on and followed her when she swept from the room like a queen dragging her sheet cape behind her.

"Damn it, Ivy, don't go."

"There's no reason to stay," she told him, gathering up her clothes and dressing as hurriedly as she possibly could.

He grabbed her arm, but she pulled free. "I don't much like you right now, Tanner, so I'm going home."

"This is my fault?"

She tossed her hair out of her eyes and stepped into her sandals. "It's not about *fault,* Tanner. It's about this going really wrong really fast and now I need to leave."

"Who's hiding now?" he asked.

She stilled, lifted her gaze to his and gave him a sad smile. "Touché, Tanner. Nice shot. Now just…shut up."

Before he could stop her, she threw the front door open and was stalking down the steps. He watched her go and wished he could rewrite time. If he could, he'd have avoided the argument entirely. They'd still be upstairs, in his bed. Instead, he was standing alone in the dark.

When she arrived the next afternoon for work, Tanner was waiting for her in the hallway. He'd done a lot of thinking the night before and it had occurred to him that he knew how to fix what had gone wrong between them. So he'd gotten up early, driven to Lake Tahoe to do some shopping and now he was back, prepared to accept her thanks. Then he'd take her upstairs again and remind her why they were so good together.

"Tanner." Ivy stopped just inside the doorway and looked up at him.

He saw the shadows beneath her eyes and knew she'd spent the night as sleepless as he'd been. Somehow that made him feel better. And he was more sure than ever that he was about to end the stalemate between them.

"Ivy, I did some thinking," he said.

"Yeah, me too," she said and scrubbed both hands across her face. "I really think we should talk, Tanner. I need to—"

"Do me a favor?" he asked, bringing the package he'd been holding behind his back forward. The white box was long and narrow and wrapped with a string of red ribbon. "Open this first."

"What? Why?"

He lifted one shoulder. "Does it matter? Just open it."

She took the box from him, shot him another curious glance and then pulled the ribbon free. When she opened the box, she blew out a breath and whispered, "It's lovely."

"I wanted you to have it," he said, glad that she liked the diamond-encrusted white gold watch.

"Why did you buy it for me?" she asked and her voice was soft, curious.

"I wanted you to have it."

"Because of last night."

"Well," he said, *"yeah."*

She snapped the box closed and handed it back to him. "No, thank you."

"What?"

"I don't want the watch, Tanner," she said and now she sounded tired. "I'm not interested in your money or your presents. If you're sorry for last night, just say so."

He opened his mouth then closed it again. Tanner didn't do apologies. When he had a regret, he gifted his way out of it. He'd learned early and well from his mother that the way to win a woman's forgiveness was with shiny presents. And, he told himself in disgust, it had always worked for him before. *Trust Ivy to be different.*

"You can't do it, can you?" she whispered, shaking her head. "You can't bring yourself to say you're sorry."

His hand fisted around the jewelry box as irritation swept him. This wasn't going at all as he'd planned. Damn it, why did she have to be so difficult? Why couldn't she just accept his gift and let it go?

"It's just a gift, Ivy," he said tightly.

"No, it's not," she argued. "It's a bribe."

"Excuse me?"

"It's saying *accept this and stop being mad.* Well, forget it, Tanner. I'm still angry and a pretty watch isn't going to change that."

"What the hell do you want from me?" he demanded.

"Too much," she said, then brushed past him on her way to the kitchen. "Now, I've got a lot to do, so I'm going to work."

He stared down at his rejected offering and wondered where he'd gone so wrong. Since the moment he met her, Ivy had been like no other woman he'd ever known. What had made him think she'd allow herself to be bought off by trinkets? He looked off down the hall toward the kitchen, and told himself that for the first time in his life, he was completely out of his depths with a woman.

He didn't have a clue what to do next.

Nine

For the next couple of days, Ivy tried to stay as far from Tanner as possible. Not an easy task, considering she spent a few hours each day at his house. Even worse, all she could do was think about their night together. What she'd found in his arms, what he'd made her feel.

She was on a tightrope—trying to keep her balance in a situation that was designed to splinter her equilibrium. She wanted him and couldn't have him. Wanted to tell him the truth and had to keep lying. Wanted to quit but couldn't bear the thought of leaving.

How in the world had her life gotten so complicated?

Oh, she never should have slept with him. She'd known at the time that it was a mistake of giant proportions. But instead of thinking with her head, she'd let her too-hungry body lead her down a road that was going to go nowhere but misery.

What she should have done was quit her job. She knew that.

Or, tell him the truth and let him fire her.

In fact, she had made up her mind to be honest with him and tell him everything, that morning she'd arrived to find he'd bought her a diamond watch of all things. Imagine him thinking that she'd want the stupid watch in the first place—sure, he didn't know she was a farmer, but how many housekeepers did he know who wore diamonds?

"Idiot," she muttered, taking a pot roast out of the oven and setting it on a cooling rack on the counter.

Was *I'm sorry* so far out of his lexicon that he couldn't even imagine saying it? Instead he'd had to drive at least two hours to go shopping only to turn around and come back? Was buying something that much easier than apologizing?

Oh, she supposed he'd meant well enough, remembering now the expectant expression on his face as he had watched her open his gift. He'd no doubt assumed that once she caught sight of the shiny bauble, all would be forgiven and she'd fling herself into his arms.

She didn't know whether to be amused or sorry for him.

Did he really believe all he had to do was toss diamonds at her and she'd be happy as a clam again? How could he think it would be that easy? That she could be bought? Had every woman in his life been so cheaply acquired? Well, if they had, then he was in for a rude awakening when it came to Ivy Angel Holloway.

But even as she thought that, she realized that maybe he didn't care. He'd been avoiding her as strictly as she had him for the last couple of days. She'd heard him typing or muttering from behind the closed door of his office. But he hadn't spoken to her since she'd handed him back the watch.

So where did that leave her?

"You know exactly where," she whispered. "You're in love with a man who doesn't even know who you really are."

A scratching at the back door caught her attention and Ivy gratefully shut down her self-pity party to check it out. She opened the door to a cool night, with a sharp wind racing through the trees and found a bedraggled dog staring up at her through huge, limpid brown eyes. One ear stood straight up, the other flopped over his head. His fur was matted over a well-defined rib cage telling Ivy that he hadn't eaten in quite a while. He wasn't wearing a collar, but he was sitting politely on the porch, watching her hopefully.

In a quiet, soothing tone, she asked, "Well now, who are you?"

The dog's tail whipped back and forth across the porch and he regally lifted one paw as an offering.

Charmed, in spite of the dog's straggly appearance, she reached out carefully to gently hold his paw before stroking the top of his head. He leaned into her touch as if hungry for the connection and Ivy's heart melted.

"Poor baby. How long have you been on your own?"

Even as compassion swelled inside her for the poor little thing, anger blistered the edges of her heart as she realized just what had happened to this dog. She knew all too well that sometimes people from the city drove through the area and abandoned pets they could no longer keep for whatever reasons. It infuriated her that anyone could be so callous as to just drive away from what had been a member of their family. But she'd seen it too often to be surprised by the action.

"Bet you're hungry, as well as lonely, aren't you?"

The dog whined a little and she turned for the kitchen, intending to get him food and water. She stopped abruptly when she ran into Tanner standing just behind her. She shrieked, then clapped one hand to her chest. "Seriously? You need to not do that to people. I'm going to have a heart attack before I'm thirty if you keep that up."

"What is that?" he asked, looking past her to the dog.

"It's a dog."

He grimaced at her. "I know that. What's it doing here?"

"Looking for food," she said, with a glance back at the poor creature now staring up at Tanner. "And some company."

"That's probably the dog that's been leaving his calling card on my lawn," he muttered.

"Probably," she agreed, and moved to stroke the dog's head again, as if to make up to him for Tanner's surly attitude. But the animal wasn't interested in her attentions now. Instead, he stood up and walked straight to Tanner, then sat down again, placing one paw atop Tanner's foot.

Typical of animals, it went directly to the one person who was less than happy to see it. Ivy couldn't help smiling, despite the fact that she didn't think the little dog was going to get much of a welcome reception.

She knew how it felt. There was no shining warmth in Tanner's gaze for her, either. But then, they'd spent the last couple of days studiously avoiding each other, so what did she really expect? Shaking her head to dislodge the wayward thoughts, she focused instead on the dog and the man staring down at it.

"He likes you," she said.

"He's filthy."

"And starving, no doubt," she added, moving past the duo staring at each other with mixed looks of suspicion and curiosity. "His family must have dumped him here at least a week ago. Looks like he hasn't eaten in days."

"Dumped him?" Tanner asked, shooting her a look. "What?"

She dug around in a cupboard for two bowls. One she filled with fresh water and the other she carried to the counter. Shaving off a couple of generous slices of the freshly cooked pot roast, she broke them up in the bowl and then carried both offerings to the dog.

The animal glanced at them, but wouldn't tear his gaze from Tanner to eat, regardless of the fact that he had to be desperate for food.

Ivy shook her head as she watched the little guy. He was no bigger than a medium-sized spaniel, but he looked even smaller thanks to the fact that he'd been scrounging for survival on his own. He must have been terrified, she thought sadly. New sights, new sounds, nothing familiar and no pack to turn to.

"City people," she whispered with a shake of her head. "They drive out to the countryside and dump whatever pet they no longer want along the roadside. Then they take off again, leaving behind a poor animal who has no idea how to survive on its own."

"What the hell kind of people would do that?"

She smiled at him, pleased that he was as outraged by the practice as she was. "You'd be surprised."

"Don't know why I would be," he muttered, going down on one knee to study the dog more closely. "Mostly, people suck."

"On this one point, I'll agree."

He flashed her a smile, then turned back to the dog.

Tentatively, he rubbed the animal's head and smiled as the dog whined a little in appreciation of the affection. Then Tanner scooted the food bowl closer to him and watched as the animal politely ate what he'd been given instead of wolfing it down in huge, starved gulps.

"So, what am I supposed to do with him?" Tanner mused, reaching out to pet the dog again.

"You could call the pound," she suggested, almost as a challenge, to see what his reaction would be. He didn't disappoint her.

"The *pound?*" He looked at her in astonishment. "Won't they just put him down?"

Pleased at his response, Ivy said, "If he's not adopted, then after a week or so, yeah, they would."

"Well screw that."

Ivy smiled to herself. She'd been wondering how the two of them would ever start speaking to each other again after they'd left everything so muddled and confused between them. Then this little dog had appeared and in their shared concern, that last night together was, if not forgotten, then at least set aside. For now.

She'd have to be honest with him eventually, tell him who she was and then she'd have to live with the knowledge that anything they might have had together was ended. But that was for another day.

Tanner King might not be very fond of people, she thought. But, as she watched him with the dog, she knew that he had a full and generous heart, no matter how he might pretend otherwise.

"Okay then," she offered, "if you're going to keep him, then we should take him to the vet and get him checked out. And buy him a leash and a collar."

He shook his head slowly as the dog finished his meal and turned to Tanner, leaning up against him with a heavy sigh of relief at having been found and accepted. Laughing, Tanner said, "And shampoo. Definitely shampoo."

The dog sighed with contentment again and stretched out on the kitchen floor, completely at home.

Tanner waited until just before Ivy was leaving for home to say, "Thanks. For helping with the dog. He probably hasn't slept in a week. He's practically unconscious."

"He likes his new bed then?"

Tanner grimaced. "No. He likes *my* bed. Anyway, thanks."

"You're welcome." She hitched her shoulder bag higher and looked at him.

Weren't they being polite?

He hated that things were so strained between them. He hated that their incredible night together had ended so abruptly. Mostly, though he hated that they hadn't repeated it. Just having her here in the house, Tanner's body was taut and ready all the damn time. Now that he'd had her, the desire he'd felt, rather than being sated had only been enhanced. Now he knew what she felt like, tasted like and he wanted her again and again.

Hell, he could hardly draw a breath without inhaling her scent—real or imagined. His dreams were filled with her and every waking moment was a study in torture. He had to find a way to get her back into his bed.

"About the other night," he said.

"I know," she said softly. "It was a mistake."

He jolted. "A mistake?"

"God, yes," she breathed. "It never should have happened, Tanner. It just makes everything so… complicated."

That's what he'd thought at first, too. That's why he'd bought her the stupid watch. But it wasn't. The mistake, he thought, was not making love to her again. "Doesn't have to be," he said, "it's only complicated if we make it that way. If we just take it for what it is—"

She looked up at him and in the bright kitchen light, her eyes looked impossibly pure and deep. "Which is what?"

Her features were wary, and there was a shadow of regret in those beautiful eyes of hers. He didn't know what she was thinking. How the hell could he? He knew what he wanted though. Now all he had to do was convince her that he was right.

"It's two adults who want each other. Why does it have to be more than that?"

She laughed sadly and shook her head. "Because it's not enough. Not for me."

"It could be."

"I don't want it to be," she countered quickly, then reached out to lay one hand on his forearm.

Heat skittered along his skin and Tanner sucked

in a deep breath to calm the suddenly raging sense of need clawing at his insides. He took her hand in his and stroked his thumb across her knuckles until he saw her shiver in response.

He should have expected this. Ivy Holloway was not his usual kind of woman. She was home and hearth. She was the forever kind of woman, not the pick-her-up-at-a-club-and-forget-her-the-next-day type. Which meant Tanner was out of his element completely. He didn't do forever. Hell, he barely did months.

But he wanted her in a way he'd never wanted anyone else. So who could blame him for trying to convince her to step out of her comfort zone and try something different.

"Why the hell not, Ivy?" He drew her in closer, needing to feel her in the circle of his arms. Her breasts pillowed against his chest and he wanted her more than his next breath. "We were good together. *Great.*"

"Yeah, we really were," she said, swallowing hard as if she, too, were feeling the swamping flood of heat that was roaring through him. "That night was…really fabulous, Tanner. I mean that. But I'm just not the *fling* kind of girl, you know? Besides, there are other reasons why this should not be happening."

He caught her scent and thought nothing in the world had ever smelled better than whatever the hell it was she used to wash her hair. Everything in him was hard and tight and desperate to hold onto her. He didn't know what she was talking about, but as far as he was concerned, there was no good reason for turning your back on what they'd found together.

"I didn't say this was a fling. Who says that anymore?" He gave her a slow smile filled with the promises of what he'd like to be doing to her at the moment instead of talking. When she didn't respond, he said, "Fine. So I'm not talking about forever, but there's no reason you have to label this—whatever we have—as a fling. I'm talking about now, Ivy. What we feel. What we want. What we could be to each other."

"Yeah," she said with a laugh that had no humor in it. "I get that. And that's why I can't. One of the reasons, anyway."

"Give me another." He ran his hands up and down her back and felt her move languorously beneath his touch.

"I work for you?"

"I could fire you."

"You probably should," she whispered.

"What?"

"Nothing," she said and reluctantly stepped back out of his embrace. Turning her face up to his, she said, "I really can't, Tanner. Trust me when I say one day you'll understand."

He didn't know what was going on with her, but damned if Tanner could ever remember a time in his life when he'd had a woman turn him down so neatly. Along with taking a ding out of what some considered his too healthy ego, her rejection slapped at what he was feeling for her. Because if she was trying to pretend she wasn't as turned on as he was, she was a liar.

"That's bull, Ivy. I know what you're feeling. I know you want me just as badly as I want you."

"I really do…"

"Then what's the problem?"

"Tanner…"

"Look, if you've got something to say to me, say it now."

"I should," she said with a short nod. "I really should. But I'm not going to, because apparently, I'm a coward. Good night, Tanner."

She left and he stood alone in the brightly lit kitchen watching her disappear into the darkness.

"You're impossible, you know that, right?" Ivy shook her head as she stepped into the kitchen the following day.

"Can't fault a guy for trying," Tanner told her, watching her reaction as she looked around the room.

The watch hadn't worked. He knew that, though he still wasn't entirely sure why not. An expensive watch would have swayed not only his mother, but every other woman he'd ever known in a heartbeat. Ivy, though, was a whole different story. So he'd tried to keep that in mind when he set up this little surprise.

The dog barked and jumped at her in excitement, as if even he knew something special was going on.

Ivy turned in a slow circle, letting her gaze slide across the kitchen as she did so. Every surface was covered in flowers. He'd bought out Carol Sands' shop, forcing her to close for the rest of the day to make a trip into the city to stock up fresh.

There were vases and bowls filled with roses and daisies and some kind of weird purple flower. There were ivy plants and orchids and even a few tulips. The scent in the room was overwhelming and the brilliant splashes of color were a feast for the eyes.

But all he had eyes for was Ivy.

"You like?"

She smiled and looked at him. "I'd be crazy *not* to like," she pointed out. "But Tanner, you don't have to make a big statement like this."

He shoved both hands into his pockets and shrugged. "I saw your reaction to the watch, believe me, I know. At least, I'm learning."

Ivy winced and walked toward him, trailing her fingertips across a dark peach rose. "I'm sorry, Tanner. But when you gave me that watch as if you expected it to buy your way out of an argument…"

"It always has before," he told her, not ashamed to admit that he'd fallen back on tried-and-true in an attempt to heal the breach with her.

She shook her head again and smiled wryly. "What am I supposed to do with you?"

"I can think of a few things," he said, reaching for her.

But Ivy stepped back, preventing his touch. "It wouldn't solve anything, Tanner. Don't you see that?"

"What's to solve? I want you. You want me. End of story."

"I wish it were that simple."

"It could be. You're making this harder than it has to be."

"And now we're having the same argument all over again."

They were and that hadn't been his intention at all. There was only one thing left to do. To say. "Ivy, I'm… sorry."

She blinked at him, clearly surprised. Well, she wasn't the only one. He couldn't even remember the last time he'd apologized to anyone. But as he'd already acknowledged, Ivy was different.

"Whatever's going on between us, I want to fix it."

Reaching up to cup his jaw briefly in the palm of her hand, she whispered, "Oh, Tanner. I don't know if we can."

Over the next few days, the tension between Ivy and Tanner only escalated. Neither of them broached the subject that seemed to hover over them. Ivy did her job, but there were no more shared moments while Tanner worked on his next project. She steered clear of him and he missed her interference.

Which only went to prove that he'd been right about hiring her in the first place. And the next time he talked to Mitchell, he was going to tell his old friend that in no uncertain terms. If he'd never let Ivy into his life, then Tanner's world would be just as it always had been. Quiet. Controlled. Orderly.

Well, mostly.

After all, Hairy was a part of his world now, too. And the dog had become such a part of Tanner's routine, he could hardly remember life without the little mutt. A bath had lightened the dog's fur color to a honey gold and a couple of good meals had already started filling him out.

Funny, when he was a kid, all Tanner had wanted was his own dog. Of course, moving from palatial hotel to hotel was no way of life for a dog of the kind he had wanted. A boy's dog, not one of those purebred, prissy types older women and young girls carried around in their purses.

Yet, once he'd grown up and had his own place, he'd never once considered getting a dog for himself. It hadn't seemed important anymore. Now, he couldn't imagine why not.

Tanner and Ivy had taken the dog to the vet to get his shots and the news that in spite of being malnourished, Hairy was in surprisingly good condition. The vet guessed his age at about three and told Tanner that with love, good food and exercise, he should be perfectly fine in a week or so.

It took far less time than that.

Hairy had taken command of the glass and wood palace that Tanner called home. He slept on the designer couches, or Tanner's bed, had his own food and water bowls in the kitchen and lay at Tanner's feet while he worked. Ivy took him for a walk most every day when she arrived and sometimes, Tanner accompanied them. Those walks were quiet adventures though, since each of them not only refused to speak about what was between them—they also avoided even brushing up against each other. And the banked lust pulsing inside him was threatening to engulf him completely. But the damn woman was more stubborn than he'd have guessed.

She treated him as she would have an acquaintance. Someone she didn't know very well and intended to keep it that way. There were no more easy smiles, no casual touches of her hand to his and no snooping in his office to see what he was creating next. Which was just as well, Tanner told himself since the game he was working on now starred an avenging angel with the face and figure of Ivy Holloway.

He couldn't seem to tear her from his mind any more than he could train his body to not respond to her.

God, he wanted her.

Every time he saw her, he remembered what they'd

shared on that one amazing night. But whenever he thought about reawakening the passion between them, something held him back. Maybe it was that last conversation. She'd made it clear enough she wasn't interested in another bout of hot, sweaty sex. And damned if he'd coerce a woman into his bed, for God's sake.

Plus, there was something else.

She'd been damned secretive about why she was turning away from him. He had to wonder why. As much as he desired her, admired her, Tanner couldn't get past the fact that she was an unknown variable. He liked order in his life for the simple reason that, as a child, his life had been chaos. With rules, order, there was no room for disarray.

No room for pain or betrayal.

But you got a dog, his mind argued.

Hairy was different, he assured himself. A dog learned the rules and mostly kept them. But a woman like Ivy? Hot then cold? He couldn't count on what she'd say or do from one moment to the next. She didn't even believe in rules. Life with Ivy would be nothing *but* disruptions.

He thought about the feel of her skin, the taste of her mouth, the heady sensation of claiming her body with his and told himself that maybe chaos had its place. Then he'd come back to his senses and realize that sex would only cause problems. Better to maintain an even keel. Keep their relationship as platonic as she seemed to want it.

"Probably best all the way around anyway," he muttered.

He just wished he could stop thinking about her every damn minute.

Reaching down to pat the dog, Tanner then leaned back in his office chair and fired off an e-mail to the programmers at his company. He was almost finished with the preliminary sketches of the characters for the new game and as he thought it, he glanced at the woman he'd drawn only that morning. Ivy's face stared back at him from the page. Her eyes, her nose, her mouth, swollen from his kisses. Her image held a flashing sword in the air and the wings that spread from her back were alive with power.

First, she had become Lady Gwen. Now, he mused, she was Aurelia the Avenger.

He was in bad shape.

"Damn it," he muttered, shaking those thoughts and more from his mind. He was starting a new game. Something he usually thrived on. Building characters, creating scenes, devising the ins and outs of the rules to be followed. Rules. Games, like life, needed rules. But Ivy kept shattering his.

He rubbed the back of his neck with one hand and grumbled under his breath. He'd met Nathan's deadline, his company was about to become the hottest thing in computer gaming and still, he was sitting here like he was in mourning.

What the hell was going on?

Why, Tanner wondered, did he feel as if there was something left undone? Something…wrong.

Ivy put the finishing touches on the chocolate cake she'd made for Tanner and told herself that this just couldn't go on. The last few days had been so hard, she simply couldn't let it continue. She had to tell him the truth. Had to get everything out into the open. She was walking around with what felt like two hundred pounds on her shoulders. On her heart.

She just wasn't built for lying.

Her grandfather had been so right, she thought, suddenly wishing Pop were sitting in his favorite chair at home, so she could go and talk this over with him. But he and her mom were both in Florida, happily building the new Angel Nursery. She'd talked to them both a day or so ago and had managed to hide her own misery in the face of their happiness.

She didn't need to worry her family long-distance. Besides, she'd dug this hole for herself, it was going to be up to her to dig her way out. Ivy only wished she knew if Tanner cared for her. Heaven knew the man was so shuttered and closed off, it would take an act of God for him to admit it, but if she could believe those feelings were there, she could live without the words if she had to.

Maybe.

But even if he did care for her, would it last once he knew the truth? From what little he'd told her about himself and his family, she knew that he didn't trust many people. So when she admitted to tricking him deliberately, she couldn't imagine that he'd take it very well.

Understatement.

She groaned and set down the frosting knife. The last few days had been so hard, being around him and not touching him. Desire flared inside her every time he came anywhere near her. To be so close and yet so far away from him at the same time, tore at her in a way she'd never imagined possible. But it was more than just the wanting, she told herself grimly. It was Tanner himself. Loving him and not being able to tell him so was the hardest thing she'd ever done.

She remembered that last heated conversation and the words she'd said kept haunting her. *I'm a coward.* She hadn't liked the sound of that. Or the way it felt. She'd never run from anything in her life, damn it and she wasn't going to start now.

Ivy had thought this all over for days and she had finally reached a major decision. She was through lying. She was through playing games and keeping secrets. It was no way to live.

She loved Tanner King. After David died, Ivy had never expected to fall in love again, but now that she had, she refused to hide from it. Refused to chance losing it because she was too afraid to admit that she'd made a mistake.

She'd seen from the first day that Tanner had a trust issue. Why else would he shut himself off from everyone and everything? Work in a small room in his house and never get involved with anyone? It was all about trust. And how could she expect Tanner to trust her when she was lying to him every moment she kept quiet about the truth?

"So, no more lies," she said softly, liking the sound of it. No matter what happened to her and Tanner now, she would at least know that she'd been honest with him.

When her cell phone rang, Ivy was grateful for the respite from her own crazed thoughts. She glanced at the caller ID, then flipped the phone open and said, "Hi Dan, what's up?"

Her farm manager said, "Didn't want to bother you

while you were at King's place, but Ivy, there's a problem with the decorative bridge you wanted across the creek in time for the Harrington wedding."

"What?" she asked, barely managing to stifle a groan.

Dan Collins started talking fast and Ivy frowned as his words sunk in. There was a huge wedding scheduled for the coming weekend and everyone at Angel Christmas Tree Farm was working hard to make sure it came off without a hitch. The happy couple was from San Francisco and the bride was the daughter of a very wealthy man.

The wedding was bound to make the society pages of the city's largest newspapers and with that kind of word-of-mouth, Ivy's neophyte wedding business could really take off in a hurry. She couldn't afford to have any mistakes.

"Okay, so you're saying the lumberyard ran out of white cedar?" she repeated. "How is that possible? Having wood available is their job!"

"Well, they're not out, so much as they're behind in their deliveries."

"Great."

"Not too bad," Dan told her. "Most of the bridge is completed. It's only the railing the crew hasn't finished."

"Yes, but we still have to get it painted and let it dry before the wedding." She rubbed her forehead as a headache began to erupt. "So when can they get it to us?"

"Friday," Dan said.

"*Friday?*" Ivy's voice broke on the word. "That's

impossible. We need that bridge completed and ready for photos by Saturday afternoon."

"Yeah, I know, and I think we've got it covered," he said quickly. "If it's okay with you, I'm going to send a couple of the boys out to Tahoe to pick up the load and get it back here today."

"Of course it's okay with me." Ivy slumped against the counter as relief coursed through her in a thick wave. "You scared me to death, Dan."

He laughed. "Sorry, but since you're the boss I've got to run this stuff by you."

"Well, as your boss," she retorted, her voice teasing, "I'm ordering you to stop giving me heart palpitations. Or Angel Christmas Tree Farm is going to have to find a new manager."

"I'm not worried," Dan told her. "You can't fire a man who used to give you piggyback rides."

Ivy laughed at the memories he awakened. "Fine, fine. Get the guys on it right away though, okay? Will the crew be there to finish this up tomorrow?"

"You bet they will and they'll have that bridge built, sanded and painted by Thursday. I guarantee it."

"Thanks, Dan. Don't know what I'd do without you." She hung up, tucked her phone into her pocket and froze when Tanner's voice boomed out into the otherwise still room.

"You own Angel Christmas Tree Farm?"

Ten

She whipped around and her gaze locked with his. He was standing in the doorway, hands braced on the jambs, glaring at her as if he'd never seen her before. This was *not* how she'd planned for him to find out the truth.

"Oh, God. Tanner…"

"You are the owner of the Christmas tree lot."

It wasn't a question this time. It was a statement, said in a cold, hard voice, that sounded nothing like the man she'd come to know. This was going to be much harder than she'd thought it would be.

Hairy trotted past Tanner and went straight to Ivy. He sat down at her feet, looked up at her and whined a little as if in sympathy.

"Answer me."

"Yes," she said. One word and it couldn't possibly convey what she was feeling. Ivy's heart sank. She finally completely understood that old saying, as an icy hole opened up in the pit of her stomach and her heart dropped right into it. The look on Tanner's face chilled her to the bone.

She was so used to seeing a flash of humor in his eyes or even that shuttered look he got when he felt she was getting too close. The expression on his face now was one she'd never seen before. This wasn't hot fury, this was cold rage. His features were taut and his eyes were eerily blank as he gave her a look usually reserved for bugs under a microscope.

"You've been lying to me since the day you walked in here."

Stomach churning, eyes filling with tears she refused to shed, she nodded. "Yes. I have."

"Look at that," he mused in a sneer. "So you are at least *capable* of honesty."

That stung. Until he'd entered her life, she'd always been honest. "Damn it, Tanner. I didn't mean—"

"Please. Of course you did."

"Okay yes," she admitted, feeling a frantic rush inside to get out everything she wanted to say. "I did lie to you deliberately. I wanted to try to make you—"

"Horny? Well, congrats. It worked." He pushed off the doorjamb and folded his arms across his chest in a silent maneuver that told her plainly that he was already shutting her out.

"No," she argued. "That wasn't it."

"And I should believe you?"

This wasn't what she'd wanted, but maybe it was no more than she deserved. She had set out to trick him. To lie to him. To seduce him into not only liking her, but the town, the valley, so that he'd stop making trouble for her farm. She hadn't exactly gone into this with the best of motives. Was it any wonder that she was now getting kicked in the head by her own maneuvering?

"I only wanted to get to know you. To let you get to know me," she told him, words tumbling from her in a wild rush. "You were so determined to make trouble for the farm and you stayed locked up here so no one could talk to you, so—"

"Ah," he said, moving into the kitchen with a panther's deadly grace. Every move was quiet, contained and only defined the fury she felt pumping off of him in thick waves. "So your lies were *my* fault. You were forced to come into my house and lie to my face because I gave you no other choice."

Afternoon sunlight speared through the kitchen windows. The wall on the clock ticked so loudly, it echoed the heavy rhythm of Ivy's own heart. Hairy's whining crept up a notch in volume as if he sensed the tension mounting in the room.

She looked into Tanner's familiar eyes and read only anger churning in those depths. Her heart ached and the cold that had a grip on her insides only deepened. She'd waited too long, Ivy told herself. She should have confessed all to him days ago.

"Tanner, you can at least listen to me," she said, never taking her gaze from his, despite how much it hurt to look at him and see nothing of the man she loved looking back at her.

"Why should I?" he countered, closing in on her. "You have more lies for me?"

"No." She sighed a little, then took a breath and said, "I was going to tell you today. I'd made up my mind that I couldn't pretend anymore."

"Yeah," he said dryly. "The strain must have been hard on you."

Through her misery, through the pain, her own temper started to flicker brightly. Yes, she had been wrong to lie to him. But she was apologizing, wasn't she? Standing here in front of him, letting him take potshots at her without firing back. Didn't that count for anything?

Oh, Ivy had been dreading this confrontation. She'd known it was eventually coming. How could it not? He couldn't live in Cabot Valley and *not* find out the truth about who she was. But somehow, she'd hoped to find a better way of telling him than this.

Why hadn't she confessed all after their night together?

She knew why. Because she loved him. Because she had known even then that when the truth was finally out, she would lose this time with him.

Now she had to pay the price.

She lifted one hand to reach for him, then let it fall to her side, an unfulfilled wish. "It was. I hated lying to you. After that first day, I knew it was a mistake. But I couldn't find a way to tell you the truth, either."

"That's a lie, too, Ivy," he said quietly. "You didn't want to tell me. You were too busy trying to win me over."

"Okay yes," she admitted. "That was part of it. Sure. When Mitchell—"

His eyes went wide and a fast rush of color filled his cheeks. "Mitchell? Damn it, I hadn't thought. Of course Mitchell was in this with you. He's the one who hired you! He *had* to know who you really were."

"Don't blame him," she said quickly, wishing she

could pull her own words back. She hadn't meant to spill the beans on Tanner's friend and lawyer. That part had slipped out. "He called to talk to me about the complaints you'd been making and we started talking and things..." she threw her hands up in the air helplessly, "...just took off from there. I don't even remember whose idea it was originally."

"That's perfect," he muttered. "My best friend is in this with you. Both of you lying to me."

"You didn't give us much choice, Tanner," she snapped, feeling the growing edge of temper beginning to boil within.

He laughed. "So this is my fault?"

"No. I didn't say that," she said. "All I'm saying is that you don't make it easy, Tanner. You won't talk to people. You shut yourself away in this house and—"

"You've been here two weeks, Ivy. Every damn day for two weeks. You've had plenty of chances to talk to me. You just didn't."

"I knew going into this that I shouldn't lie to you, but I didn't know what else to do."

"Talk to me? Tell me the damn truth?"

"Oh, because you were so easy to have a conversation with," she retorted, feeling the sting of his accusation even as she admitted he wasn't that far wrong.

"You're really something," he said and his voice was low and tight. "You had me fooled. I really bought it all—hook, line and sinker. Have a good laugh every night when you went home, did you?"

"It wasn't like that," she insisted, wondering how she could salvage any of this.

"Then how was it?" His eyes narrowed on her as

he chuckled darkly. "Must have panicked you when I showed up over at the farm."

"Yeah," she said. "It did."

"Now that I think back on it, you did look more than surprised to see me. But I've gotta hand it to you. You recover fast."

Temper and misery were warring inside her and they were so tangled up now, she couldn't even separate them. His jaw was tight, his full mouth flattened into a grim line and his eyes were practically throwing off sparks.

"You took me on a tour," he said, with a slow shake of his head. "Introduced me to the owner, or who I thought was the owner..." He stopped, tipped his head to one side and waited for her to fill in the blank.

"My grandfather. Mike Angel."

"Right." He nodded. "So the family that lies together stays together?"

Okay, he could say what he wanted about her, maybe she deserved most of this. But her grandfather was off-limits. Mike had been against this from the beginning and damned if she was going to stand there and let Tanner King insult him.

"Pop had nothing to do with it," she told him. "He tried to stop me."

"But he didn't."

"No." His eyes were so dark now, Ivy couldn't even read the anger there anymore. He was locking himself away even as she stood there and watched him. Shutting her out. Shutting himself down. And there was nothing she could do to prevent it.

Seconds ticked past and the only sound was Hairy's tail thumping against the floor as if he were somehow trying to reach one or both of them.

"What about the sex, Ivy?" Those words were whispered, but the force behind them was clear enough. "All that a lie, too? You turn yourself into a martyr for the cause?"

Insulted now, she straightened up, lifted her chin and looked him dead in the eye. "No, it wasn't a lie. None of it was."

"And I should believe you because you're such an upright, honest person."

"You should believe me," she said, "because that was the most beautiful night of my life."

He tipped his head to one side and looked at her as though he'd never seen her before. "I don't believe you. I think you were closing your eyes and thinking of England."

"*What?*"

"Old joke," he told her grimly. "And not funny."

"And not correct, either." This time, she did reach up to him but he jerked his head back before she could touch his face. "Tanner, I slept with you for one reason and one reason only."

He backed her up against the kitchen counter until she felt the icy edge of the granite against her spine. "What are you going to tell me now, Ivy? Truth? Or another lie?"

"I won't lie to you again, Tanner."

"Right."

He was waiting and he was looming and he was taking up every square inch of breathable air in the room. Her body was humming because of his closeness even while her stomach spun with nerves.

The temper building inside her was frothing, bubbling up through the thick layer of regret coating her stomach.

Did he really believe she could have slept with him just to save her farm? Did he know her so little? Think so little of her? Yes, she'd lied, but that didn't mean she was a horrible person. For God's sake, they'd shared more than his bed. They'd spent time together, talked, laughed.

She'd fallen in love with him and all the while, he hadn't known her at all.

What a joke on her, Ivy thought. She'd lost her first love through an accident and now she'd lost the love of her life through her own damn fault. But maybe, she decided as she watched him watching her, they never would have stood a chance anyway. Because Tanner King didn't want to need anyone. And she needed to be needed.

She looked at him and knew it was over. Whatever they might have had was gone, blown away as completely as autumn leaves in a stiff winter wind.

There was no going back. There was no undoing what had been done. No more than she could unring a bell.

Since it was over, since she had nothing left to lose, she vowed that she would at least, leave on the truth. That much, she owed to herself.

"You know why I slept with you, Tanner?" she asked, keeping her gaze locked with his so he would read the truth of her words in her eyes. "Because I love you."

A long moment passed before he pushed up and away from her. "Oh, please. You expect me to believe that? You *love* me? How convenient."

She laughed now and the sound was harsh and brittle even to her own ears. "Convenient? Not even close." Ivy pushed one hand through her hair. "My God, do you think loving you is something I asked for? I've never met a more difficult man to love."

"Thanks very much."

She shook her head and walked to the kitchen table, where her purse was slung over the back of one of the chairs. Picking it up, she slid it onto her shoulder then turned to look at Tanner again.

"I'm sorry I lied to you Tanner. I really am. But mostly, I'm sorry *for* you."

He just stood there in a wash of golden sunlight, glaring at her as if she were an intruder. "I don't need your sympathy. I don't need anything from you."

"That's the really sad part," she told him. "You need so much. You need someone to love you. Someone to show you how to live outside the closed-in, sealed-off palace you've built here."

"And that's you, I suppose?"

"Could've been," she agreed, heart aching as she walked to the kitchen door. She turned the knob, then looked back at him over her shoulder. "I want you to remember that, Tanner. I would have loved you for the rest of my life." She gave him a tired smile. "But that's not your problem anymore. Oh, and one more thing. You don't have to fire me. I quit."

She walked outside, closed the door quietly and left the man she loved and the future they might have had together behind her.

"You're fired."

Mitchell Tyler laughed into the phone and Tanner gripped the receiver so tightly, he was half surprised it didn't snap in half.

"Not funny, Mitchell," he snarled.

"Oh, please. You can't fire me."

"I just did."

Ivy had been gone for only a half hour and already, the silence in the house was beating at Tanner's brain like a hammer wrapped in silk. Every room echoed with her memory. He could still hear her voice in his mind. See her eyes at the last moment before she left, glistening with banked tears.

He could still feel the sharp stab of betrayal. So what better time to call the friend who'd set him up.

"You rotten, no-good…" Tanner muttered darkly.

"Tanner, what the hell is going on?"

"Ivy Holloway," he said. "Owner of Angel Christmas Tree Farm."

"Oh."

Tanner snatched the phone from his ear, gave it an astonished look, then slapped it back to his head again. "Oh? That's all you've got to say? You lied to me, damn it."

"Yeah, I did," Mitchell admitted freely.

Tanner grumbled under his breath and stalked a fast circle around the kitchen. Hairy was just behind him, his nails skittering on the polished wood floor. The chocolate cake Ivy had made still sat in the middle of the table, its scent wafting to him every time he got close. And even with all that had happened, even with the rush of anger still churning inside him, he couldn't help wishing that instead of chocolate, he could smell that flowery citrus scent of Ivy's.

Which made him the biggest damn fool in the world.

When he thought he could speak without shouting at his longtime friend, Tanner demanded, "Aren't you the guy who said you would always tell me the truth whether I wanted to hear or not?"

"I am."

"Then explain this to me."

Mitchell muttered something Tanner didn't quite catch and then said, "I tried to tell you what I thought before and you didn't want to hear it. You didn't leave me much choice."

He laughed a little at that. Both Ivy and Mitchell had somehow found a way to blame *him* for *their* lies. "How do you figure that?"

"Because you were being an ass, Tanner," Mitchell said flatly. "Calling the damn sheriff, threatening lawsuits every day when you called me incensed over a Christmas tree farm of all things. You were making yourself insane and aggravating the ulcer you already gave me."

True, he admitted silently. But the betrayal was still there. "I trusted you."

"And you still should."

He laughed shortly, without humor. "Why's that?"

"Because I'm your friend, Tanner," Mitchell said on a heavy sigh. "We've known each other forever and I still have your back."

"You mean the one with the knife in it?"

"Jeez, you should have been an actor, not an artist," Mitchell muttered.

"And you should have told me who she was."

"You never would have let her in the house."

"Exactly," Tanner said. Then in the next moment, he realized all that he would have missed by not meeting Ivy Holloway. His mind dredged up dozens of images of her, one more haunting then the next. Ivy laughing.

Ivy reaching for him. Ivy leaning over him, helping him solve the problems in the computer game. Ivy getting soaking wet while they bathed Hairy together.

Ivy.

Always Ivy.

"How'd you find out?" Mitchell asked after a long minute of silence.

Tanner stopped at the bay window in the kitchen and looked out the glass at the deepening twilight beyond. His gaze shifted unerringly to what he could see of the tree farm. The roofline of Ivy's house stood out as a darker shadow in the gloom. He pictured her there, alone, as he was. And he told himself that he shouldn't care where she was or what she did.

He'd trusted her and she'd lied to him.

Simple.

"I overheard her on the phone with her farm manager," he said. "When I confronted her, she told me everything. Threw you under the bus, too, though I don't think she meant to."

Mitchell chuckled. "I can take care of myself."

"Why'd you do it, Mitch?" Anger drained away now, leaving just bafflement. "Why'd you set me up? Why'd you help Ivy against me?"

"It wasn't against you, Tanner. It was *for* you. I love you like a brother, but you're shutting yourself off. Except for me and your brothers and cousins, you never see anyone anymore. You're closing yourself off, Tanner, and I don't like seeing it."

His friend's voice was serious, concerned. Tanner could admit, at least to himself, that maybe Mitch had a point. He *had* been more closed off in the last year or two than he used to be. He wasn't even sure why. It had been a slow-building thing, the pulling away from the world. He'd simply turned his back on...pretty much everything, he realized.

Hell, he hadn't been to visit any of his brothers in a couple of years. Hardly even spoke to them on the phone anymore, now that he thought about it. Working with Nathan on the game had been as close to sociable as Tanner had managed to get in longer than he cared to think about.

But that was his choice, wasn't it?

"And this was your answer?"

"Seemed like a good idea at the time."

Lights came on at the tree farm. Small white twinkling lights, strung between the telephone poles and wound through the branches of the trees separating the farm from his place. Had they always been there, Tanner wondered. Had he just never noticed them?

What else hadn't he noticed?

"Tanner, don't be so hard on Ivy."

He laughed and rubbed his eyes, trying to ease the headache pounding behind them. "Why shouldn't I be?"

"This whole thing was my idea, after all," Mitchell said softly. "Look, see it from Ivy's perspective. You were threatening her home, her livelihood. The King name carries a lot of weight in California. She knew that if you wanted to make real trouble for her or the valley that a judge would listen to you. Her life was on the line."

"Yeah, I guess..." He turned around, pulled out a kitchen chair and dropped into it. Reaching out one hand, he dragged a finger through the frosting on the cake and brought it to his mouth. Perfect. Of course.

"Besides, what did she really do that was so awful?" Mitchell asked. "She woke you up. Introduced you to your neighbors. Showed you how to *live*. So she had to lie to do it. If you'd known what she was up to, you never would have gone along with it, so cut her a break."

She had done all that. And more, Tanner thought, but didn't say. There were some things he wouldn't admit even to his closest friend. Things like what he'd been feeling for Ivy. Like the fact that his dreams were full of her. That his body hungered for hers. That since she walked out, he felt as though his heart had been ripped from his chest.

"Still want to fire me?"

"No," Tanner said and leaned back in his chair, kicking his legs out in front of him. "But if you come anywhere near me in the next couple of weeks, I'll kick your butt for you."

"Understood. And thanks for the warning."

When he hung up, Tanner realized that even though Mitchell had been part of the deception, that relationship was safe. He wouldn't turn from a years-long friendship even though Mitch had been part of the lie.

So why couldn't he forget what Ivy had done?

Because, he told himself, Ivy had betrayed him on a much deeper level.

She'd touched something in him that no one else ever had.

She had said she loved him.

And that lie he couldn't forgive.

Eleven

Ivy missed him.

Three days after she'd left his house, with angry words ringing in her ears, she ran her hand over the orange mesh walls of the bounce house and sighed at the images rushing through her mind. The first time Tanner had touched her. The first time she'd come apart in his arms. And the moment when she knew there would be more to come. How was she expected to forget about him, when his memory was all around her?

There were a couple dozen people wandering around the farm at the moment. Families visiting their Christmas trees, others having lunch or shopping, and then there was her own crew putting the finishing touches on the setup for the wedding that was being held in the morning. There were at least a hundred things she should be doing. Instead, she was lost in her own thoughts.

She'd known it would be hard to be without Tanner. But she hadn't realized just how empty she would feel.

She had spent the last few days like a sleepwalker. She did her job, checked final arrangements for the big wedding that weekend and tried to pretend that everything was normal.

But it wasn't. And never would be again.

God, she thought, turning around to lean back against the inflated rubber castle, when David had died, she'd wanted to curl into a ball and cry for months. She'd thought her life was over and for a time, it had been. But she'd recovered, found her feet again and finally moved on.

Losing Tanner was so much more overwhelming. She hadn't lost him to death, she'd just lost him. He was right next door and might as well be as far from her as David. And this time, the pain was so huge that crying didn't help. Didn't ease the crushing pressure in her chest. She didn't want to cry, she wanted to fall into a hole and drag it in after her.

But once again, she couldn't give in to her own inner turmoil. There was even more at stake now than there had been four years ago. So she would keep walking. Keep working. And keep dreaming of what might have been.

God, she was an idiot. Why had she done it? Why had she started a relationship with a lie?

"Ivy?" From a distance, Carol Sands, the local florist, shouted to her.

"Yeah! Coming!" She dragged herself out of her thoughts and headed off to solve the latest crisis. No time to feel sorry for herself. That would have to wait until night, when she lay alone in her bed trying to sleep.

She joined Carol and fell into step beside her, pitifully grateful for something to focus on besides herself and her own gloom.

"The bride's room is ready," Carol told her, a huge smile on her face. "I brought the flowers for the vase arrangements over now and stored them in the refrigerator. I'll bring the bouquets in the morning."

"That's good. The bride should be here by eleven." Ivy glanced at the people she passed and smiled at those she knew. Hopefully no one would notice that her smile wasn't exactly filled with warmth.

Carol was still talking. "Dan's got the umbrella tables set up in the meadow and the scarlet tablecloths Mrs. Miller stitched are at the gift shop in the back room."

"Right. We'll get everyone on it early tomorrow so it'll be perfect by the time the bride gets here." Bride. Wedding. Happily ever after. Well, she thought, at least *someone* was getting a happy ending. Her heart twisted in her chest, but she swallowed past the knot in her throat to say, "If you can be here by eight-thirty, we can get the centerpieces arranged and the crew will be here to help you out."

"That's great, thanks, Ivy." Carol grinned again and shoved her bright red hair back behind her ears. "This is a real shot for me, doing the flowers for a wedding this size."

"I know." This, she thought, was exactly the reason she had lied to Tanner. Why she had risked so much to try to reach him.

Since Angel Christmas Tree Farm was so far from any major city, the locals had quite a hand in helping with the event weddings. Carol's flower shop was growing by leaps and bounds. Mrs. Miller's alteration and tailoring took care of the tablecloths and any other sewing emergency. Bill Hansen's garden supply shop handled the tables, chairs and even the striped umbrellas that would shade wedding guests at the reception.

These events were helping an entire town to grow and thrive. Was it any wonder Ivy had been worried enough by Tanner's complaints to the sheriff to risk everything? Small consolation now though, she told herself. Had she saved her town only to doom herself?

They walked into the meadow and Ivy stopped to look around. The decorative bridge across the creek was perfect, just as Dan had promised. It gleamed snow white against the lush green background of the meadow grass and surrounding trees. It would be a perfect photo spot, she thought, letting her gaze slide across the hundred round tables that were scattered in a precisely laid out arc around the main table that was for the bridal party. Everything that could be done ahead of time was ready. The rest would wait for tomorrow.

She took a breath and let it slide slowly from her lungs. "I know how much this wedding means to all of us, Carol. So we've got to pull this off flawlessly."

"We will," her friend said.

Ivy hoped so. Because God knew, she'd given up a lot for this farm and a future that didn't look nearly as shiny as it had only two weeks ago.

Ivy was still walking his dog.

For three days he hadn't seen her, but the signs were plain enough. Hairy was exhausted and the leash was never where Tanner had last left it. So what kind of woman, he asked himself, proclaimed her love, walked out the door and then sneaked back in to visit a dog?

He pushed one hand through his hair and then scraped that hand across his face. His eyes felt gritty and he hadn't shaved in days.

He couldn't sleep. Couldn't work. Couldn't stop thinking about Ivy.

He'd told himself to forget about her. That she was a liar. Not to be trusted. That her claim of love was just another part of the game.

"But damn it, if that's true, then where the hell is she?" He glanced down at Hairy who looked up at him, as if trying to give his opinion.

Tanner stroked the dog's head and told himself that Ivy wasn't responding the way he'd expected her to. He'd seen this game played out far too often in his childhood to not know the moves.

She should be coming back to the house, trying to see him. Trying to convince him how much she loved him. She should have been there, trying to sway him, reel him in with tears and pledges of eternal devotion.

Scowling, he pushed out of the chair and walked to the back door. He threw it open and as he was slapped by a vicious wind, Hairy raced outside into the early night.

Moonlight spilled out of a clear, star-studded sky and painted the ground with shadows. The trees in the yard whipped and danced in a gale that had been growing steadily for the last hour.

He listened to Hairy's excited barks as the wind howled around him, but Tanner's thoughts were too busy churning to pay much attention.

"Why is she bothering to come and walk Hairy while

at the same time she's deliberately avoiding running into me?"

He shook his head and tried to make sense of it all. He didn't understand what she was thinking or what she was doing. If she wasn't trying to hook him, then why bother with the dog who loved her? None of this made sense.

He'd been waiting for her return since the moment Ivy had left. And now, he suddenly realized why. Because that's what his mother would have done. What his mother had done again and again in her all consuming quest for a fairy-tale ending she had never found.

His mother wouldn't have dreamed of announcing her love and then walking away. She had always found a way to stick around a man who didn't want her, trying to change his mind.

"Apparently," he mused aloud, "Ivy and my mother are two very different kinds of women."

Hairy's barking became more frantic and Tanner bolted from the porch to see what was wrong. The wind pushed at him, as if trying to shove him back into the house and he wondered where the hell the storm had come from. The sky was clear, but the wind was howling. Then, as quickly as it had kicked up, the wind was gone. As if it had never been.

Tanner finally reached the dog and it was then he heard what Hairy had. Voices. Shouting.

At Ivy's place.

Then he remembered the big wedding that Ivy was counting on to keep her farm safe was tomorrow. The windstorm had probably played havoc with all of her preparations.

Hairy barked again as if asking him what he was waiting for.

Tanner's brain shouted at him that this was the answer to all of his problems. If Ivy couldn't hold the wedding, she couldn't make the loan payment. If she couldn't do that, she'd lose the farm.

If that damn farm was gone, he'd have the peace and quiet that had once been so important to him. This was, in effect, the answer to everything.

Cursing under his breath, he sent Hairy back into the house.

Ivy was running through the meadow, shouting directions to the crew that had stayed late to make the final arrangements for the wedding.

"Good thing they stayed," she muttered under her breath as she looked around at the chaos created by the sudden wind blowing through.

Already, people were racing around under the soft shine of moonlight and the harsh glare of spotlights arranged around the meadow. Tables were turned over, neatly stacked umbrellas had taken flight and were lying every which way across the grass and into the trees. The delicate archway where the ceremony would be held was on its side and the ribbons streaming from it lay limp on the ground.

"Great," she said, reaching for the umbrella at her feet. It was heavy and cumbersome, but she managed and carried it to where the guys were already stacking the others they had gathered. "All that work and it's torn down in half an hour."

"We'll get it back up," Dan assured her. He glanced

at the clear sky spreading overhead and shrugged. "At least it's not raining."

"God, bite your tongue," she said quickly. "Have the guys set the tables back in their spots. With any luck, the wind's gone for good. We should be able to have most of this put back together before morning."

"On it," he answered and stalked off, shouting orders at a few of the men.

After that, Ivy just worked. She kept her head down and her mind blank as she busily set about fixing what Mother Nature had wrecked. As Dan had pointed out, it could have been worse, she consoled herself. If that wind had been accompanied by a summer storm, the meadow would be a sea of mud and they'd have had to come up with an alternate wedding site fast. As it was, this could be fixed and the bride and groom would never know anything had gone wrong.

Running across the meadow to join Carol in reattaching the bows to the arch, Ivy caught movement out of the corner of her eye. When she took a better look, she recognized Tanner, striding up the lane connecting the farm to the meadow. He stopped dead, met her gaze for a heart-stopping moment, then moved off without a word to join the men gathering up the fallen tables and chairs.

She took a deep breath as she watched him pitch in and help. She wondered what he was doing there, but couldn't afford the time to stop and ask him. A part of her wanted to believe that Tanner's being there might mean more than just a neighborly act. After all, when had he ever been neighborly? But at the same time, she remembered the distant expression on his face as they'd stared at each other, and she realized that whatever his reasons for being there—nothing between them had changed.

"What is it?" Carol asked, handing Ivy a length of white satin ribbon.

Her gaze fixed on Tanner until he was lost in the crowd of men working under the moonlight. Then she turned to her friend and forced a smile. "Nothing. It's nothing. Let's get this done, Carol."

Two hours later, Ivy was exhausted, but the crisis had been averted. Under the pale moon, the meadow lay lovely and perfect, as if it had never been disturbed. All was ready for the big event in the morning.

The dozen or so people who had worked so hard stood in a circle congratulating each other on a job well-done. They lifted cans of cold soda provided by Ivy in a toast to their efforts and laughed together over the night's activities. Tanner was on the periphery of the group and his gaze was locked on her.

His expression still unreadable to her, she watched as he took a long drink of the soda and then laughed at something one of the men said to him. If things were different, she thought sadly, she would walk up to Tanner and give him a big kiss as a thank you for all of his work tonight.

Instead, she was forced to remain quiet and still, uncomfortable under his steady regard. When Dan spoke up, she was pathetically grateful for the interruption.

"Did you guys see King there, climbing that tree to get the umbrella down?"

"Hell yes," someone else said with a hoot of laughter. "Don't know how the damn thing got that high, but King scrambled up that old oak like a monkey."

Tanner smiled at the men and said, "Couldn't have

been as funny as Tony falling off the bridge into the creek."

"Too true," Dan agreed.

Tony D'Amico grinned, despite his soaking wet clothes. "I thought I could lean far enough over the bridge to snag that damned thing. Turns out I couldn't."

"You were all great," Ivy said, speaking to them all, though her gaze fixed on Tanner alone. "I really appreciate everything you did, so I'd like to propose a toast."

Everyone lifted their cans of soda and waited. Tanner's gaze burned into hers and Ivy felt a rush of something hot and wicked pouring through her. Still, her voice was even and steady as she said, "To Angel Christmas Tree Farm and Cabot Valley. May this wedding be the boon we all need. And may we all remember tonight and what we accomplished…together."

"Together," everyone repeated and took a sip.

Tanner waited until the rest of them had drunk their toast before he lifted the canned drink in his hand toward her. *Together,* he thought solemnly. Tonight, he'd been a part of something. He'd belonged in a way he never had before. He'd worked with a group of people he never would have met if it hadn't been for Ivy and he'd helped them accomplish a task important to all of them.

It was an odd feeling for him.

And now it was over.

With his gaze locked on Ivy's, Tanner took a slow sip of the too sweet soda, then deliberately turned away. He couldn't look at her, awash in moonlight, without wanting to hold her, lose himself in her. But that time had passed. Now that the situation was resolved, there was no place for him here.

Still holding the can of soda, he walked down the dirt path that led to the front of the farm and the road to home.

The wedding was a huge success.

Not only for Angel Christmas Tree Farm, but for the town. The catering, flowers and decorations had all been wonderful. The guests who had driven out from San Francisco for the wedding had enjoyed themselves immensely and the bride and groom couldn't have been happier.

Still reeling from the number of people who had asked for her business cards at the event, Ivy sighed. Business would soon be booming, she knew. As soon as the article about the wedding hit the city newspapers, she knew Cabot Valley would experience the kind of success they'd all been dreaming of.

So why wasn't she happier?

She'd done it. Made a name for herself as an event destination. Salvaged disaster and created perfection. She'd seen to it that her hometown succeeded as well as she had and her plans for the future were brighter than ever before.

She should be blissful.

But then, how could she be really happy without the man she loved?

Without even the hope that they might one day straighten everything out? Yes, he'd come to her rescue and worked alongside her and her friends the night before the wedding, but since that night, she hadn't seen him. Not even a peek. Oh, she didn't expect to run into him in the early morning when she went to his house to take Hairy for a walk. After all, she went in the morning because she knew he'd be sleeping. But couldn't he have come by the farm again? Couldn't he have said something to her before he left that night?

"But then, what's left to say?" she asked herself glumly as she walked into the Cabot Valley bank. Her steps echoed on the polished linoleum and she sighed a little as she noted at least five people in line for one open teller. No quick trip for her this time.

She pushed thoughts of Tanner to the back of her mind to torture herself with later. For now, she had the final payment for the wedding in hand, and she wanted to pay off a big chunk of the loan she'd taken out to make all of this possible.

Ivy nearly groaned aloud when she spotted Eugenia Sparks in line. The woman was the biggest gossip in town and never had a kind word to say about anyone. The fact that Eugenia was even now talking to Rose Doherty in a voice that carried clear across the bank only irritated Ivy more because of the subject of Eugenia's venom.

"That Tanner King is a snob, if you ask me," Eugenia was saying, her voice carrying through the room to bounce off the high ceiling. "Too rich by half. Thinks he's too good for us is what," she continued with a sharp jerk of her head. "Imagine, the man's lived here in Cabot Valley for *months* and he never so much as shows his face at one town gathering. Thinks he's too good for us small-town folks. Not natural, if you ask me, a man staying to himself that way. Who knows what he's up to in that big fancy house of his."

Rose's eyes were glazed and Ivy thought she looked like a rabbit hypnotized by a snake, unable to look away.

Ivy, though, wasn't.

Spurred on by the emotions swirling inside her, Ivy forgot all about making her loan payment. Instead, she walked right up to Eugenia and looked her dead in the beady little eyes.

"Don't you talk about Tanner King that way," she said and had the pleasure of seeing the older woman's eyes widen and her mouth drop open in shock. But Ivy wasn't through. In her peripheral vision, she caught Rose's smile and encouraging nod, but Ivy would have continued anyway. "He's not a snob, either. Did you ever think that maybe he's lonely? That he doesn't know anyone in town?"

"Well…" Eugenia puffed up her chest and tried to speak, but Ivy was on a roll and not to be denied.

"You say he's never been to one town function in the months he's lived here? Did anyone *invite* him? No." Furious and hurt on Tanner's behalf, Ivy defended him hotly and didn't have to ask herself why. She just kept talking. "Maybe it's not easy for someone to just show up unannounced when he doesn't know a soul. Maybe if someone had gone out of their way to invite him, he might have attended."

Eugenia huffed an outraged breath and narrowed her eyes as if for battle. Ivy met the woman glare for glare and refused to back down until her opponent did. Finally, Eugenia marched off to the teller when it was her turn and Ivy was left standing in line, practically vibrating with insult.

In the stunned silence of the bank, Ivy suddenly realized that she might as well have painted a sign over her head that read *Foolish Woman in Love*. Now, the town wouldn't be talking about Tanner, they'd be talking about her.

Fine, she thought as she turned and stalked out of the building. Better her than a man who couldn't defend himself against small town cats.

"I'm, er, sorry you had to hear that," the bank manager said in a low undertone. "But you shouldn't pay attention to what Eugenia Sparks has to say. No one does."

The man needn't have worried. Tanner hadn't given a good goddamn what the old woman with the sharp tongue had had to say. He'd been too busy watching Ivy and listening to her outraged voice as she defended him to her friends and neighbors.

He stood in the glass-walled office and looked out at the lobby without really seeing it. Ivy's words echoed over and over in his mind. He saw her eyes, glistening with tears she refused to let fall and he heard her voice, furious and hurt. And as he relived every moment of that little scene, the hard, icy shell around his heart cracked painfully.

He drew a deep breath and let it out again as his mind raced and his heart began to heal. He'd spent years hiding himself away, cutting himself off from anything that might connect him to another living soul. He'd been determined to protect himself from betrayal and yet, that was the biggest lie of all.

Living an insular existence wasn't really living. So what was the point?

The only question was, was it too late for him to change his life?

"Mr. King," the manager said softly, "is everything all right?"

He turned to look at the man in the crisp business suit. "Not yet. But if I have anything to say about it, it will be."

Ivy was still furious the following morning when she sneaked across Tanner's yard to collect Hairy for their walk. She never had gone back to the bank to make her loan payment, so she'd have to do that as soon as she was finished here. But she couldn't ignore Hairy. She knew darn well that Tanner would get involved in his work and forget all about the little dog that needed some exercise.

She walked up the porch steps and turned the knob. The man never remembered to lock his doors, so it was no problem to let herself in. She quietly stepped inside and shrieked when she saw Tanner standing in the kitchen, clearly waiting for her.

She slapped one hand to the doorjamb to brace herself and took a deep breath to ease the pounding of her heart. Hairy barked a greeting and she leaned down to pet him even as she glared up at Tanner. "Why do you keep scaring me? Is it personal?"

He smiled. A gorgeous, make-his-eyes-sparkle grin that made her knees wobble and did some truly amazing things to the pit of her stomach.

"I've been waiting for you," he said.

"Yeah, I can see that," she told him and realized that he'd known all along that she was coming here every morning to walk Hairy. "Why?"

"I have something for you." He pulled an envelope from the back pocket of his jeans and handed it over.

It was thick and white and had the logo of the local bank in the upper left hand corner. "What is this?"

"Open it and see."

She did and when she unfolded the sheaf of papers inside, her heart nearly stopped. It was the deed. To Angel Christmas Tree Farm. And across the top, in bright red ink was stamped Paid In Full.

Ivy swayed in place and instinctively shot out one hand to the jamb again, to help her maintain her balance. Stunned beyond words, she only stared up at Tanner in complete shock.

He was still smiling.

"Surprise," he said with a shrug. "The tree farm is yours, free and clear."

He looked so pleased with himself. Ivy shook her head, staring wide-eyed at him. It was the diamond watch all over again, she thought. He was still trying to buy her. To use his money to make an impact. And now he bought her *home?*

"You son of a bitch." Her voice was low and filled with the tears clogging her throat. "How could you do that?"

"What?" Confusion settled on his features but his eyes looked suddenly worried.

More furious than she'd ever been, Ivy couldn't believe that only yesterday she'd been defending him to the town. "I told you before, Tanner. I don't give a damn about your money. You can't buy me. Not with a watch. And not with a paid off loan."

"I'm not trying to—"

"Who gave you the right to stick your nose into my business?" she demanded and threw the loan papers at him. They hit him square in the chest, bounced off and landed unnoticed on the floor. "You don't own me. You never will."

She turned and sprinted down the steps and across the yard. Ivy heard Hairy behind her, yipping excitedly as he chased her.

Tanner was just a step or two behind the dog. Damn it, he'd been up all night, waiting for her and trying to find the words he wanted to say to Ivy. But he hadn't come up with a thing. Instead, he'd just handed her the loan papers, hoping she'd understand.

Clearly, that was a mistake.

"Ivy, wait!"

She didn't even slow down, but his legs were longer than hers and desperation fueled his every step. He caught up with her at the base of an ancient oak tree. Hairy raced in delighted circles around them while Tanner grabbed her arm and spun her to face him.

"Let me go," she demanded as one tear tracked down her cheek.

That silent slide of sorrow punched Tanner dead in the chest. He'd brought this strong woman to tears and he wanted to kick himself for it. Which he would find a way to do. Later.

"Just listen, all right?" He blew out a frustrated breath and stared down into pale blue eyes that haunted him every moment. "I've screwed this all up royally," he muttered. "I'm not trying to buy you, I'm trying to tell you I *love* you."

She went perfectly still in his arms and Tanner took a relieved breath. At least he had her attention.

Meeting his gaze with her tear-filled eyes, she asked quietly, "And do you always say *love* with your checkbook?"

He winced, then shook his head. "I've never said *love*

at all," he admitted. "Maybe that's why I'm so bad at it. But I do love you, Ivy."

A brief smile curved her mouth and was gone again an instant later. Hope awakened and then died inside him just as quickly.

Irritated with himself, he released her and stalked off a few paces. "I don't even know how to say all of this. I've been awake all night trying to figure it out."

"You have?"

He glanced at her. "This is all your fault, you know."

"Really?"

"I heard the sarcasm there, but yeah, it is. You're the one who challenged me. Made me put my past behind me to look to the present and maybe even a future. You're the one who convinced me that Christmas isn't about misery, but about family."

She smiled again, but Tanner was too wound up to react to it. He felt as though he'd been waiting his whole life to get these words out and by damn, she was going to listen to him.

His gaze locked with hers across a distance of four or five feet. "You walked out on me, but you kept walking my dog."

"Yes," she said, voice soft and eyes shining.

He took a step toward her. "You're the one who wouldn't speak to me, but defended me in public."

"That's me," she agreed, her delectable mouth curving into a knowing smile.

He moved closer and his voice dropped, becoming a low throb of want and need. "You're the one who made me believe in happy endings, Ivy. You. It was always you."

"Tanner…" she sighed as he closed the last of the distance separating them.

"So now, you're just going to have to love me back," he said, "because I'm not going to let you go."

She lifted one hand to cover her mouth and made no attempt to stop the rush of tears coursing down her cheeks. Tanner pulled her into his arms and held her tightly, finally feeling his life slide into place. He kissed the top of her head and held on to her for both their sakes.

"Don't cry, Ivy," he whispered. "It kills me to see you cry. If you don't stop, I swear I'm going to go shopping for you again and then we'll have a big fight and—"

She lifted her head and stared up into his eyes. Laughing, she shook her head and said, "What could you possibly buy me, Tanner? You already gave me my *home*."

He used his thumbs to tenderly brush her tears from her cheeks as love settled into his heart and his soul, warming him thoroughly for the first time in his life. "The only thing I want to buy you is a ring, Ivy. One you'll wear forever."

"Oh, Tanner. Is that a proposal?"

"No, this is. Marry me, Ivy," he said, smiling. "Make me crazy for the rest of our lives."

She grinned up at him and threw her arms around his neck. Snuggling tightly to him, she said, "I love you so much, Tanner. Of course I'll marry you." She pulled her head back to look into his eyes as she gave him a stern warning. "But, you'll have to get used to working with noise because I want at least six kids and they'll all want to play in the Christmas tree fields."

"That sounds just right to me," he told her, resting his

forehead on hers. "In the last few days, I discovered I can't work in the quiet anymore. An empty house is no way for a man to live."

"I guarantee you'll never be alone again, Tanner," she said, going up on her toes to meet his kiss.

In the early morning light, in the shade of an oak, with a dog leaping against them excitedly, Tanner held his future securely in his arms.

And it was a deep summer Christmas.

Epilogue

It was the best wedding ever to be held at Angel Christmas Tree Farm.

The entire town of Cabot Valley had turned out to celebrate with one of their own.

Tanner stood to one side, with Hairy beside him, decked out in a brand-new collar with flowers threaded through it. The dog was humiliated, of course, but he—just like Tanner, would do anything for Ivy.

Watching his bride dance with the four-year-old son of the town florist, Carol, Tanner smiled. The little boy laughed with delight as Ivy spun in circles, moving to the rhythm of the music piped out on the overhead speakers.

"No Christmas carols," he mused, surprised to find he almost missed them.

"You look like a happy man," Nathan King said as he walked up to join him.

"I really am," Tanner said and felt the truth of those simple words slide into his heart. He'd never expected to find this kind of love and acceptance. He'd never hoped to be able to look into a woman's eyes and read her love for him written there. And he'd never known just how much love could change everything.

"She's a beauty," Nathan told him, lifting his bottle of beer in a toast.

"That she is," Travis King said, coming up on his cousin's other side.

All of the King cousins had attended the party and Tanner was grateful. Family was the constant of his life. And now he and Ivy would build their own branch of the King family dynasty.

"Rico's giving the bartender tips," Jesse said as he joined the others.

"Garrett's talking plants with Ivy's grandfather," Tanner told them. "Apparently, our cousin is thinking of expanding King Organics into public nurseries."

"With this family, there's always time for business," Travis said on a laugh.

"Not today, though," Mitchell said as he walked up and slapped Tanner on the back. "Today's the day my best friend gets to listen to me say *I told you so* for the first but certainly not the last time."

Tanner laughed and it felt good. Hell, if he had to listen to Mitchell gloat for the rest of his life, having Ivy would be worth it.

The music stopped then segued into another, slower song. On the improvised dance floor, Ivy set Carol's son down and turned to stare across the distance at her husband.

A slice of sunlight speared down from between thick

white clouds to lay across Ivy like a blessing. She wore a strapless white dress that belled into a wide skirt. Her long hair was hanging loose in tumbled curls and a wreath of yellow roses encircled her head while lemon-colored ribbons trailed down her back.

He left his cousins behind as he walked to the only woman he would ever love. "Hello, Mrs. King."

"Dance with me?"

"Always," she said, moving into him and locking her gaze on his.

Taking her in his arms, he swept her into a dance that had everyone else clearing the floor to watch. But there were oblivious to their guests. It was as if the two of them were alone in a private, romantic world of promises and new beginnings.

"You are the most beautiful woman I've ever seen," he whispered.

"Don't look now, Mr. King, but you're talking like a man in love," she said softly.

"I am indeed," he said and lowered his head to hers. As they kissed, a cheer rose up from the surrounding crowd and Hairy barked his approval.

* * * * *

A sneaky peek at next month...

Desire™

PASSIONATE AND DRAMATIC LOVE STORIES

2 stories in each book - only £5.30!

My wish list for next month's titles...

In stores from 19th August 2011:

❏ What a Westmoreland Wants – Brenda Jackson
& Stand-In Bride's Seduction – Yvonne Lindsay

❏ Claiming Her Billion-Dollar Birthright – Maureen Child
& Falling For His Proper Mistress – Tessa Radley

❏ Sweet Surrender, Baby Surprise – Kate Carlisle
& The Secretary's Bossman Bargain – Red Garnier

❏ The Billionaire's Bedside Manner – Robyn Grady
& Her Innocence, His Conquest – Jules Bennett

Available at WHSmith, Tesco, Asda, Eason, Amazon and Apple

Just can't wait?

MILLS & BOON Book Club

2 Free Books!

Get your free books now at
www.millsandboon.co.uk/freebookoffer

Or fill in the form below and post it back to us

THE MILLS & BOON® BOOK CLUB™—HERE'S HOW IT WORKS: Accepting your free books places you under no obligation to buy anything. You may keep the books and return the despatch note marked 'Cancel'. If we do not hear from you, about a month later we'll send you 4 brand-new stories from the Desire™ 2-in-1 series priced at £5.30* each. There is no extra charge for post and packaging. You may cancel at any time, otherwise we will send you 4 stories a month which you may purchase or return to us—the choice is yours. *Terms and prices subject to change without notice. Offer valid in UK only. Applicants must be 18 or over. Offer expires 28th February 2012. **For full terms and conditions, please go to www.millsandboon.co.uk/termsandconditions**

Mrs/Miss/Ms/Mr (please circle)
_____

First Name
_____

Surname
_____

Address
_____

_____

Postcode
_____

E-mail
_____

Send this completed page to: Mills & Boon Book Club, Free Book Offer, FREEPOST NAT 10298, Richmond, Surrey, TW9 1BR

Find out more at
www.millsandboon.co.uk/freebookoffer

Visit us Online

0611/D1ZEE